# OUT OF HER MIND

## SALLY HART

BLOODHOUND
— BOOKS —

# PROLOGUE
## TEN YEARS AGO

Tick tock. Time was up. He couldn't move. Couldn't leave her. He belonged with her, and it crushed him that he had to go. The heat from her body long gone, his happiness had generated enough warmth to envelop them both. He rested his head tenderly against her chest and caressed the hard scars running down the inside of her forearm.

Her closeness brought to the surface the good childhood memories he hadn't thought of in years. Like the times she came home after a modelling job. She would be at her happiest, and she'd scoop him up and hug him tight. Her little prince.

Eyes wet, he blinked furiously. He mustn't spoil these last moments.

'Thank you,' he whispered. His gratitude was so profound, her long estrangement from him was forgiven. All her trespasses no longer mattered.

He pushed up from the bed, cursing when the old mattress springs dug into his palms.

'I'm sorry I've got to go.' His voice was hoarse from talking. While brushing the tangles from her hair, he'd chatted about everything she had missed. He wasn't one for lengthy speeches and afterwards his soul felt cleansed.

God, the irony. It was probably a long time since someone had felt cleansed in her flat.

He bent over and kissed her forehead. Alongside the fruity scent of the cheap shower gel he'd used to wash her, was the cloying smell of death.

She was at peace. It was his gift to her: release from the shitty existence she had chosen instead of him. He envied her. His nightmares would never be free of the addictive hunger.

Over the last few hours, the knot in his stomach had loosened. The connection they'd shared – her recognition, then acceptance – was an intimacy he hadn't experienced since his previous life. But how long before loneliness fuelled more urges?

In his strange confession, he'd spoken about the person whose existence he had denied. His guardian angel. If he could find acceptance here, then maybe his happiness depended on finding her. A familiar spark glimmered deep inside. He beat it down. No. Not yet. He wasn't ready.

Picking a route through the beer cans and drug paraphernalia, he headed towards the door. An empty syringe crunched under foot; his shoes sticking on the ingrained layer of grime and neglect beneath all the detritus. He looked into her sightless eyes one final time before he stepped over the threshold. Other sounds became real again: shouts from an upstairs flat and the undulating hum of the last fragments of evening traffic intruded into the hall.

Six hours had passed since he'd followed his mum, put his hands around her neck and ended her life. No one would understand why he'd done that, but it still disappointed him the rest of the world hadn't taken the trouble to notice.

# CHAPTER ONE

I t was quiet. Sarah didn't dare say it out loud, in case she jinxed the rest of the shift, but she loved the unit like this. When a fragile peace replaced the hustle and bustle of the day. The glaring lights, responsible for several nagging headaches, were dimmed to a gentle glow. Loud, urgent footsteps became soft creaking of shoes, and the staff lowered their voices, as if in awe of the hospital at night.

In the eight-bedded intensive care unit, the regular whoosh of the ventilators accompanied the alarms that erratically punctuated the struggling silence. Unnoticed during the day, at night the unsynchronised sighs sounded like a chorus of soft snores: the last puff of air before the next grating inspiration.

Her nursing colleagues were doing their hourly observations, checking monitors and, if necessary, making minute adjustments. Satisfied no one needed her assistance, Sarah leaned forward at the computer, planning to update their online patient handovers, when she was startled by the sound of the nearby phone.

'Hello, ward twelve. Staff Nurse Knowles. Can I help you?'

'Well, hello there, Nurse Knowles, and how are we today, or

should I say this evening?' The gentle Irish lilt mellowed what would have otherwise been a deep and guttural voice.

'It's this morning,' laughed Sarah, 'and I'm fine, thanks, Bryan. Only one more to go, then I'm looking forward to a whole week of relaxation. How about you? How's it going in the madhouse?'

'Considering it's the wrong side of freezing, and a weekend, it's not as hectic as it can be in A & E. As for relaxing next week, I find that very hard to believe. You'll either be tackling a DIY job I'd be quite willing to do for you, or you'll be in a gardening frenzy, not stopping until you're exhausted.'

'I happen to like pottering about or being in a frenzy,' she protested. 'It's what I do best. So, did you just phone to check on me, or was there another reason?'

'What other reason do I need...? Okay, you've got me. We've an overdose patient in and out of consciousness. A place has been found in the medical assessment unit and the on-call doctor in her wisdom is playing a let's-wait-and-see game, but it wouldn't be a bad idea to get an ICU bed ready for him. If you have one.'

'We do at the moment.' She felt the usual flutter of anticipation. So much for her quiet night. 'Do you know anything about this poor guy yet, like a name?' She glanced up as a nearby stool scraped on the floor.

'No name. Only that this "poor guy" took more than a handful of pills, downed with a bottle of whisky.'

Bryan's sarcasm was not lost on Sarah. He'd made it quite clear on a number of occasions that he thought nursing these suicide attempts was futile. But this was a view Sarah couldn't accept. She pushed away a stray strand of hair that was threatening to get under her surgical mask. *If only you knew, Bryan, how close I had once come to being one of your lost causes.*

The unfolding drama at bed three prevented Sarah from thinking about that dark period of her life. 'Sorry, Bryan, got to go. Keep me posted on whether you need the bed.'

She slammed down the phone and went to rescue Anne, who

was struggling to stop her patient disengaging from the ventilator. Tubes and infusion lines were swinging alarmingly as he writhed around; panic had undoubtedly gripped his mind as the sedation hold had weakened. He was in danger of hurting himself or anyone who tried to break through his delirium, so they had to re-sedate him. Ducking under a swinging arm, Sarah grabbed the flailing limb.

'It's all right, we're here to help you.' She bent over until her mouth was next to his ear. 'You're in hospital. You were in an accident.' Sarah continued to speak slowly, hoping her voice was reaching a part of him that could process what she was saying. 'Let the ventilator breathe for you. Don't fight it.'

Gradually his muscles relaxed, and his vital signs stabilised.

'God, he was strong,' exclaimed Anne, as she rubbed her upper arm. 'I wouldn't like to pick a fight with him when he doesn't have a bloodstream full of morphine and propofol.'

'Are you okay?' Sarah could already see a red mark forming, vivid against Anne's fair skin.

'Yeah, I'll live, and thanks for coming to my rescue. I guess he's not ready to reintegrate into the real world – whoever he is.'

John Doe gazed upwards, his blue eyes vacant: devoid of the confusion and fear that must have haunted him moments before.

Sarah hated the thought that a person could remain anonymous for more than a few days. Someone must be looking for him. Family? Friends? Incessantly checking their phone, waiting for news.

---

Sarah's cheeks burned. 'How many times do I have to tell you? There's nothing going on between us.'

'Oh yeah?' Anne glanced across at her friend in the passenger seat and giggled.

Sarah crossed her arms, narrowing her eyes. Not this again.

Only last month it was about her possible future with one of the new doctors. Now it was her and Bryan.

'All I'm saying is, he likes you. He's a nice guy, so what's the problem?'

'If you think he's such a nice guy, why don't you go out with him? Or isn't he rich enough?'

'Ouch!' Keeping one hand on the steering wheel, Anne grasped her chest. 'That cut deep. You know I'm saving myself for Colin Firth. I'm Bridget Jones to his Darcy.'

'Just focus on the road, Miss Jones. I know what you're like when you get distracted.'

Sarah knew Anne meant well, but it wasn't as though she needed a man in her life. Nearly two years since Mike's death, and the realisation of how permanent their separation was would still unbalance her when she least expected it. A discarded orange on the supermarket floor had upset her the other day. Without warning, a memory of Mike juggling the contents of the fruit bowl in their kitchen one Sunday afternoon had popped into her head. Oblivious to the curious shoppers, tears had run down her face as his ghost chased the offending orange.

It had got better though. Numerous jobs in her house kept her occupied on her days off; and she had friends, like Anne, who she could talk to. But she missed the closeness she'd had with Mike. The easiness of their love. Particularly now.

Biting her lip, Sarah looked out of the window. They were passing Ledforth Abbey, their journey nearly over. At the edge of the frost-covered field, lingering mist shrouded the twelfth-century Norman abbey, adding to its mystique. Since moving to West Yorkshire, Sarah had enjoyed many walks around the walls of the ruin and along the neighbouring river. She'd watched Shakespeare plays within its grounds, bewitched more by the evocative surroundings than the productions themselves. This January morning, however, the starkness of the icy landscape only added to her anxiety.

One more night shift, then she had decisions to make. She hadn't told anyone about her worries, scared that it would make them more real. But she couldn't go on like this, even if it was all in her head. If left, these things would only get worse. And she couldn't let herself get like that again. She couldn't.

The jolt of the car, as it halted outside her house, interrupted her muddled thoughts.

Anne swivelled in her seat to face her. 'You went quiet on me, then. Are you all right?'

'Yeah, I'm fine.' Sarah forced a smile. 'It's after doing nights, you know how it is. I zoned out. I was thinking about the patient Bryan brought up just before our shift ended.' Sarah prayed Anne wouldn't push it any further.

'The guy who'd overdosed. Is he going to be okay?'

'I think so. He was lucky he was found quickly.' Sarah felt the stiffness in her jaw throb as Anne scrutinised her face.

'Well, I'll let you off, just this once.'

'You're so generous,' replied Sarah, grateful to Anne for letting it slide. 'Of course, the real reason was you're boring, and I was falling asleep. But being a good mate, I wasn't going to say that,' she joked, escaping out the passenger door before Anne could answer back.

---

Through his windscreen, he watched as she climbed the steps to her front door. It was an unnecessary risk, but he couldn't get enough of her. She was his drug.

'I've waited so long; soon you'll be willing for me to come to you,' he whispered. 'Sarah, my angel.' He loved the way her name could hide in a sigh, for only him to hear. 'Sar-rah, Sar-rah.'

He owed her everything. Did he occupy her thoughts as much as she dominated his?

She had tied her hair in a ponytail, and he ached to release it, and run his fingers through the freed expanse of rich, soft brown hair. The morning sun played on the hint of red highlights. Just like the radiance of the first drop of blood...

The heel of his hand slammed on the van's dashboard. No. No. He hit the unforgiving surface again and again until the pain pushed away the craving. Stifling a sob as he cradled his throbbing hand, he wiped his nose on his sleeve. The resulting mess on his dark jacket ignited another flash of anger. He was fucking disgusting. But he was back in control.

Damn his stupid hysterics. Sarah had gone. A car engine started up, and he stared as Anne drove away. A flicker of annoyance prickled within. Why the hell did she need a friend like her? He didn't like criticising Sarah's choices, but he was sure she could do much better. He had got to know the little bitch for the information he could glean from her, and every second he had to put up with her boisterous laugh was excruciating. At least when Sarah joined him she wouldn't need any friends. She'd have him.

He sighed and flexed his fingers to relieve the stiffness in his hand. The blue Golf disappeared around the corner, and he reached for his keys. It was time to do more digging.

# CHAPTER TWO

I n life, Pamela Harrison had been beautiful. Even after the unflattering throes of death, there was something very graceful and serene about her, as if she were posing for the camera, and the last flash would release her from her stillness.

'They'd everything in front of them and he snatched it all away,' muttered Detective Chief Inspector Peter Graham.

'We'll get the bastard.'

The DCI tore his gaze away from the photo board. 'What?' he snapped.

'Sorry. I thought you were talking to me.' At the other end of the incident room, their scene-of-crime officer shifted uneasily, causing the rectangular table he was sitting on to wobble.

'Oh God. No, I'm the one who should be sorry, Jack.' Offering a tired smile as a truce, Peter straightened; arching his back to try to get rid of all the tension. 'This whole mess is getting to me.'

The younger man dismissed his apology as unnecessary. 'We've all been under a great deal of strain the last few months. You more than anyone. You've been after this guy from day one.'

'And three bodies later we've got damn-all evidence. Until now, if those latent prints you lifted from her shoe give us anything.' Peter frowned at the photographs. 'He's been careful to clean up and hasn't previously left so much as an extra crease on their bedding. Is it possible we've got lucky?'

Not waiting for an answer, he picked up a mug from his desk and paced around the room. He raised the drink to his mouth and cringed when the cold black coffee hit the back of his throat. Shit, it tasted bad. But anything to clear his head.

They had spent most of the last twenty-four hours at the crime scene. Nerves were frayed. When the call had come through that a woman's body had been found, the modus operandi was sickeningly familiar. And there was no escaping the facts. Pamela Harrison, a radiographer at the local hospital, was the fourth victim of The Beautician.

Peter wasn't a fan of the press giving out nicknames, but he had to admit this one was apt: describing how the killer dressed and beautified the women post mortem. As the senior investigating officer, he would soon address his team of investigators from the homicide and major enquiry team, and over the past three months he'd wished this moment would never arrive. At least if they had finally found some evidence then he could begin to hope that this nightmare might end without any more women dying.

'Maybe his sudden carelessness is a sign he's becoming desperate, or he wants to be caught,' said Jack. 'You're worried he's changing his MO, aren't you?'

'Something is wrong, but I can't put my finger on it.' Despite searching Pamela's house they hadn't found a matching shoe to the one that had been placed on her foot. And that bothered him. 'If he is collecting souvenirs from the women, then have we overlooked items missing from previous crime scenes?'

The phone ringing stopped any further discussion, and Jack reached across a mountain of papers to pick up the receiver. 'Hello?'

Peter dropped in the nearest chair and stifled a yawn. He'd

grabbed three hours' sleep in the early hours of this morning, and saying he was tired didn't even come close. Rubbing his chin, he grimaced at the stubble prickling his hands. Right now all he wanted was a shower and shave, but perhaps next month he'd take time off, disappear to the Dales for a few days. And pigs might fly. Bloody hell, he couldn't remember when he'd gone on a proper holiday. Well, that wasn't strictly true, last year he had gone with Liz to Scotland. They'd spent the first two days arguing, and then she had left him to wallow in self-pity, their six-year marriage over.

'And you're sure?' Jack's voice was getting louder, and Peter sat forward. Who was he talking to?

'That's great news. Yes, he's here with me. Send the file along to the incident room, we'll look at it here.' As Jack grinned, he looked across at Peter. 'Yeah, I'll tell him, and Jen, thanks.'

After disconnecting the call, the scientist gave a loud, jubilant cry of 'Yes!' and thumped the table. 'Jenny came up trumps. She's found a match for the latent fingerprint, and you'll never guess whose name popped out of the database.'

'Holy shit. Someone we know?'

'Does the name Carl Cooper ring any bells?' Jack laughed at his astonishment. 'Oh, and Jenny says you owe her a drink.'

The Saturday traffic was unrelenting, and exasperated horns blared. Peter hit his brakes as a car pulled out in front of him.

'Asshole.' Although he wasn't sure whether he should direct this to himself or the disappearing driver. It was because of his own bloody stubbornness he was here at all. He didn't need to attend the scene of the accident, if it turned out to be an accident, but there was no way he was missing this.

Could Carl Cooper be their man? Under their noses this entire time. His first meeting with the law student had been nine months ago, at the start of their investigation, when there was hope the murder was a one-off – a lovers' tiff or a sex game gone bad. Upon hearing of his sister's death, Carl had wept uncontrollably. Later he would describe his relationship with his younger sister as a close one, having to constantly band together against an overbearing father. Peter had believed his grief to be genuine.

There was no love lost between Carl's remaining family but, dynamics aside, no evidence had pointed to a budding serial killer in their midst. It had appeared as if Juliet Cooper had been in the wrong place at the wrong time, attracting the deadly interests of a sick individual. That theory had driven the investigation away from what now looked like the truth.

No. It didn't feel right. Peter gripped the steering wheel. What he did acknowledge was that his job had been made all the harder. As more women fell victim to The Beautician, his team's work was under increased scrutiny, and this latest revelation could make matters worse. Although he had kept his senior investigator status, Superintendent Crosby's presence at this morning's briefing was a stark reminder that their lack of progress would be seen as his failure.

Of course, if he were wrong, this could be the beginning of the end. Peter indicated to turn into a small lay-by where two parked patrol cars and a familiar black BMW confirmed he had arrived at the right place. Blue-and-white police tape zigzagged down the woody slope, its loose ends waving in the breeze, beckoning him to follow their seductive trails. The snow that had been forecast for the north of England began to fall.

Peter remained seated in his car as DS Doug Marsden hurried up the overgrown bank towards him. The word 'hurried', when applied to Doug Marsden, demanded a change in definition. His mismatched body often fought for control. His long legs strode over the ground, as if he had all the time in the world; whereas his shorter, bulky top half led the race, his red and often exasperated face passing over the finishing line a few seconds before the rest of him.

As he watched the ungainly approach, Peter could tell a rare mood had descended upon his friend. Doug was angry. The pumping of his arms, fists clenched, seemed to power him up the last incline.

The car's suspension groaned as he clambered into the passenger seat. Breathless, he accepted a cigarette. 'Thanks. Thought you'd quit?'

'I had,' Peter replied, bending forward slightly to light his. He inhaled, then glared at the cigarette in disgust. 'I don't even like the bloody things anymore.' He glanced at Doug through the growing haze. 'Bad?'

Doug snorted. 'The ground couldn't have been more trampled if a herd of elephants had got together for their annual ball. Anything useful to us has long gone, thanks to those incompetent fools.'

Peter wondered who the poor sod was who'd had to deflect Doug's wrath. They couldn't really blame the local police for reopening the scene of what they'd assumed to be an alcohol-related incident. But, still...

He cursed under his breath as the initial flurries of snow intensified. 'The final elephant being Mother Nature. I guess we're lucky the car wasn't towed away. What have they got so far?' Peter had read the report before leaving HQ, but he preferred the facts fresh in his mind before he walked around a site.

'The stolen car was discovered early Thursday morning, just after 2am by a couple driving home from a party in Wakefield.' Doug reached into his inside coat pocket, producing a well-thumbed notebook. 'A Mr and Mrs Warrington,' he added, after checking his notes. 'It was the faint glare of the headlights that first alerted them. The husband scrambled down to see if the car had been abandoned and, finding the driver unconscious, called for an ambulance.'

*Brave man.* Peter wouldn't have fancied making his way there during the night, and certainly not on his own. He climbed out of the car and walked to the edge of the lay-by. The gradient in front of him offered many treacherous places to trip the wariest of feet. It was interesting that the site of the accident, at the edge of a clearing, was only now visible to him.

'I don't remember reading a second interview with our passers-by?' He raised his voice to compete with the flow of traffic.

'That's because there wasn't one,' said Doug, joining him. 'They were treated as brave, honest members of the public. It wasn't till this morning that it was noticed the incline prevents anyone from seeing the headlights from the road. We're bringing them in for questioning.'

Peter waited for Doug to continue. His enthusiasm fading. The blizzard that rushed up the bank to greet them stung his face, and he pulled together the edges of his tweed jacket, envious of his colleague's winter coat. In his hurry he'd left his grab-bag, containing his outdoor gear, in his locker.

'The male driver was admitted to intensive care with injuries to his head and chest. Interestingly, his blood-alcohol content was low, so not a factor in the accident, despite his breath smelling of beer at the scene.'

The absence of another set of skid marks in the forensic report, implied no second vehicle was involved. 'Do you think it was deliberate?'

'Guilty conscience, perhaps.'

'Perhaps,' echoed Peter. 'Has he regained consciousness?'

'No, not yet. I sent two of our men to the hospital as soon as they had identified him. When Carl wakes up, we'll be among the first to know.'

As he clambered down the embankment, Peter thought about

the timeline. Pamela's body had been found yesterday, Friday morning, but preliminary findings suggested she had been killed forty-eight hours earlier. So it was feasible that Carl could have strangled her sometime between Tuesday night and Wednesday morning and then ended up here the next day. The police had found nothing suspicious in the car, but to be fair to them they hadn't expected to.

He slowed as he neared the canvas tent now protecting the wreck from the elements. From the photos, he'd seen that the jagged opening carved out by the hydraulic cutters had left the interior of the car exposed to the previous days' wet conditions. Anything useful would have been obliterated, but he was leaving nothing to chance. Careful not to disturb anything, he entered the tent.

His pulse raced as he crouched next to the crumpled shell. The passenger side of the car had crashed into a tree. Both rear windows had imploded, and fragments of glass littered the back seats.

As Peter stared at the twisted framework, memories battled to the surface. He had no defence against their ferocity. Metal screeched: crunching and contorting. Screams pierced the air. The smell of petrol overpowered him.

Peter recoiled. His lungs burning. He had to get out.

In his haste to put as much distance as possible between himself and the tent, his feet slipped on the lethal mixture of grass, mud and snow. Later, when he reflected on his escape, he would put it down to pure luck, rather than any sure-footedness on his part, that he hadn't fallen flat on his face.

He approached the edge of the clearing and slowed. His legs shaking, he clutched at the nearest tree. The callous edges of the damp bark dug into his hands as he hauled his thoughts back into the present.

Someone coughed behind him. *Good old Doug, here to rescue me from myself. Right on cue.* Swallowing the unexpected bitterness,

Peter turned to face him. He was, however, spared the need for talk, as they were both distracted by a shout.

A scene-of-crime officer had emerged from the tent holding aloft a transparent evidence bag with a lone black stiletto shoe inside.

# CHAPTER THREE

Sarah plunges her feet into the soft, untouched snow on the edge of their driveway, laughing as her bright yellow wellies disappear from sight. After waving goodbye to her friends, she leaves the blanket of clean snow that sparkles in the falling afternoon sun. She dances over the cleared areas, not caring about the treacherous ice.

The snowman greets her in the hallway: its bottle-top grin glinting wickedly. She jerks to a stop. But the ice that failed to slow her outside is now beneath her feet. Sarah clutches at the surrounding air, unable to halt her glide towards the waiting embrace. In the warm hall, the snowman's features twist and melt; its coal-black eyes scowl as its cavernous smile grows wider...

She's upstairs. Running. Its rasping breath caresses the back of her neck. The clink of gnashing bottle tops echo along the endless landing. No choice. Nowhere else to go. Sobbing, Sarah grasps the doorknob. Her hand slips on the sticky wetness. She stares at her bloodstained fingers as the knob turns...

Sarah snapped into consciousness. Exhausted by the struggle to wake, she lay still. Her breathing loud. Surrounding her.

As the panic subsided, shouts and cries of laughter forced their way in. Light slunk in from around her blackout blind, confusing her. Who was awake at this hour?

Oh, of course, it wasn't their night-time. She eased her aching body away from her wet sheet and moaned at the illuminated dial of her clock. Two hours' sleep. Was that all?

She was having the same recurring nightmare. It would start out innocently enough: arriving back from school, pleased to be home. Sometimes she was an adult, but always she started out with a sense of belonging, of being in a place where she had been most happy. The dreams ended with that door, and the memory of the horror before waking.

In her sleep yesterday, Mike had appeared on the landing. Shaking his head and mouthing frantically at her as the flames raged. She couldn't understand what he was trying to tell her and had watched powerless as the fire that had killed him, consumed him again. Behind him was the door, and even Mike couldn't stop her from opening it. She had woken up crying.

At least she hadn't dreamt that today. And even though her imagination had created a snowman Stephen King would be proud of, she could blame the weather, the neighbours' children outside, and working nights for the nightmarish appearance of the evil Frosty.

She sighed and sat on the edge of the bed. The perspiration on her hair and back rejoiced in the cold air and she shivered. Should she forget about sleep? Go downstairs and make lunch? It wouldn't be the first time she had gone to work after having a tiny amount of kip. But it was only half past eleven: six hours before her alarm was due to go off.

Plumping her pillows and pulling the duvet around her, she lifted her legs back onto the bed. Sarah tried to relax and not think about her dream, or the reason for its recurrence. Earlier, she'd made the decision not to ignore possible signs that her depression was once again rearing its ugly head. But couldn't there be a simpler explanation? She'd worked lots of overtime recently to cover staff shortages. She was exhausted.

As Sarah sank further down the bed, her gaze fell on her cluttered table and the growing pile of books waiting to be read. Next week she'd devote a whole day to reading. Quality Sarah time, to wallow in her own company.

While planning her week off work and listening to the noisy children playing in the snow outside, Sarah dozed. Fitfully at first, then deep and dreamless.

A few hours later, after a hot shower, Sarah was almost ready to meet work head-on. She looked at her reflection in the mirror. Not too bad. Although the more she studied the dark rings below her eyes, the more obvious they became. Nothing a thick concealer and loads of make-up wouldn't fix. But time had once again got the better of her, and she would leave the safety of her home without a smidgen of make-up.

Oh well, maybe Aidan Turner will be busy tonight, sparing her the embarrassment of having to elope without her proper face on. Thinking of the good-looking *Poldark* actor reminded her of Anne's Darcy comment. She smiled as she ran down the stairs. *We could go out as a foursome.*

Sarah stepped into her kitchen and froze. What the…? She grabbed at nearby furniture as her legs gave way. Her thigh crashed against her sideboard, but she barely noticed, eyes riveted on the roses.

The vase of pink roses on her table. Where the hell had they come from? Who had put them there?

Sarah clamped a hand to her mouth, trying to stifle her gasps. Her throat closed, denying her panicked lungs air. Above her pounding heart, was there an alien noise? A footfall? A whisper of movement or a breath not her own?

Nothing. Familiar idiosyncrasies of the house, like the creaking of the radiators as they heated up, triggered palpitations. But nothing that sounded wrong.

Light-headed, Sarah breathed in deep. Still... someone had left those flowers.

How had anyone got in? She could see the inside latch on the back door was locked. And she'd been so careful. It had become her routine, especially over the last few weeks, to check the doors and windows.

*Got to move. Get help.* Hand shaking, she retrieved her mobile from her jeans pocket; swearing when it slipped from her clammy fingers. 'Fuck.'

She cringed. Not because her sob may have alerted someone to her whereabouts, as the clatter of the phone hitting the floor and sliding under the sideboard would have already done that, but at how scared her voice sounded. How defeated.

Sarah bit her tongue. She was stronger than this. Had been through far worse and had made it. *Come on. Pull yourself together.*

'You're not scaring me.' Her mouth was dry. The words no more than a raspy whisper. But this small show of defiance spurred her into action. She dashed round the table and grabbed a breadknife she'd left on the worksurface, before twisting to face the empty room.

On rubbery legs, she edged to the back door. 'I've called the police. They're on their way.' Anyone hiding close by would know she was lying, but it might make them hesitate, giving her a chance to get away.

She fumbled for the handle, pushing and finding resistance. It was locked. Sarah leaned against the door and brandished the knife in front of her. What now? Should she make a run for it? Grab her keys from her coat in the hall and escape out the front?

As she considered her next move, a dash of red caught her

eye: red peppered with small silver dots. Stuck out of the pedal bin, almost within her reach, was a piece of cellophane. Its familiar pattern kick-started a memory: head down, coat held closed against the bitter weather, jogging towards the automatic doors. Oh God. She'd popped in to get some petrol before starting her night shifts and remembered admiring the flowers. Especially the roses, wrapped in red cellophane peppered with small silver dots.

Could she possibly have bought a bouquet and then forgotten she'd done so?

Sarah lowered the knife. When was that? No, it wasn't her. It couldn't have been. It was two nights ago. And she definitely would have seen them in the middle of her fucking kitchen since then.

Wouldn't she?

A few weeks before, Sarah wouldn't have contemplated such a thought. Now, after everything else, the familiar fear took hold. Not of an unknown intruder, but of herself.

Her conviction that someone else was in her house faltered but she checked everywhere, knife held tight, until she was satisfied she was alone. Teary and feeling very foolish, she returned to the kitchen and slumped at the table.

What an idiot. She brushed away tears. *For fuck's sake, Sarah. Get a grip. A knife!*

Jesus. Talk about an overreaction.

Reaching for the roses, she took a leaf between her fingers, hoping that touching it would spark a memory. The vase, which had been a wedding present from work, was placed on top of her 'ICU nurse by day, zombie slayer by night' coaster.

There was nothing sinister about any of it. She would have used that very same vase and that identical coaster. She simply couldn't remember. Sarah pressed her fingernails into her temples in frustration. Why couldn't she remember?

Was it such a big deal forgetting that she'd bought something?

Last week, Anne had been complaining how she'd gone out of her way to buy washing liquid only to discover she'd already picked some up between shifts a few days before. A weary smile tugged at her lips as she recalled how people at work had teased Anne, saying she was growing old.

Anne! Shit, she'd be pulling up in front of her house. Sarah checked the time and frowned. Was it only fifteen minutes since she'd seen the flowers? It seemed so much longer.

Although there was still opportunity to make something, Sarah felt nauseous at the thought of food. She'd go into the sitting room and watch through the window for Anne's car instead. However, as she entered the hall, the quietness of the house was stifling. Her hand shook as she gathered the front of her cardigan closer to herself. Edgy, she grabbed her coat and bag. She hoped fresh air would help to clear her head.

Outside, the cold sneaked through her layers, and Sarah shuffled from one foot to another to keep warm. The faint glow cast by her hall light was enough to see by, and she peered at her watch. It was seven o'clock; leaving half an hour to drive to work and find a place to park.

Where was Anne?

Sarah left the limited shelter offered by the small porch and inched her way down the white steps. By the time she'd woken up it had stopped snowing, and although it had settled that morning, there was only about an inch now on the ground. Beyond her gate the crispiness had turned to sludge. If it was fairly clear here then the main roads shouldn't be too bad.

Having bought the Toyota recently, Sarah had no worries about it not starting in the freezing weather. She sat in the driver's seat, cupping her hands in front of the heater, enjoying the growing warmth on her skin.

Of course... the receipt. She dived into the storage tray next to her. When she got in the car it was a habit of hers to dump anything in there that she happened to have in her hand. Usually full of loose change, sweet wrappers and receipts, it was relatively empty due to a sudden clean-up a couple of weeks ago when Bryan had teased her about the messiness.

Whilst keeping an eye out for approaching headlights, Sarah searched through the small number of receipts. The one from the petrol station wasn't there.

Sarah sighed and massaged the back of her neck. It had been a long shot. She'd probably thrown the receipt in the bin outside the garage.

However, she did find one for the latest Disney compilation CD she'd bought for Ben but had yet to give him. She grimaced; it had been ages since she had seen him. Next week, she would visit him and take him out for the day. She'd had years of practice in gauging his mood within a few minutes. If going out was out of the question, they would sit in his room and listen to music or watch his favourite Disney films.

As the windscreen demisted, Sarah's view expanded. And apart from her neighbour's West Highland terrier snuffling around in his usual window spot, there were no other signs of life.

She dialled Anne's mobile, followed by her home number, and received no reply from either. On her way then. Sarah phoned work next to say that they'd be late.

'Well, that's weird,' said their ward clerk, as Sarah explained she was waiting for Anne to pick her up. 'Anne's brother phoned this afternoon to say she wasn't feeling well, and wouldn't be coming in. He thought it was the flu. I guess she went straight to bed and forgot to tell him to let you know.'

Anne's brother, Richard, had recently moved back into the area and was staying down the road from his sister, so it made sense that if Anne had fallen ill she'd have contacted him. Strange how it had come on so fast though. She'd pop over to Anne's tomorrow, find out how she was. Right now, she had something worse to worry about – where on earth was she going to find a parking spot at this time?

———————

Deciding in favour of the lift rather than the stairs, Sarah raced to the door, only to see it close before she could get there.

'Oh shit!' She hit the call button repeatedly in a vain attempt to call the lift back.

'My sentiments exactly.'

Sarah spun round. She hadn't realised there was anyone behind her.

'Sorry. I didn't mean to scare you. It's just that you said what I was thinking so beautifully.'

Sarah blushed and returned the man's smile. 'I'm embarrassed now. That wasn't very professional of me.'

'Don't worry, I won't say anything, unless threatened by torture.' The man's voice was soft, his speech punctuated by a faint North Yorkshire accent.

Sarah laughed. 'Oh, I don't think there's much danger of that. Except maybe for me,' she added, 'as I'm already late for my shift.'

A bell indicated the arrival of the second lift, and as they walked in, side by side, they fell silent. She sneaked a glance at her companion: dark collar-length curly hair framed an angular face. Grey flourished in the mass of curls and deep crow's feet marked the way to a pair of magnificent blue eyes. Sarah hadn't seen him in the hospital before. Was he a doctor? No, she didn't think so. The mud-splattered black trousers and trainers he wore, together with a blue shirt and brown jacket, suggested he was a visitor. The ensemble was stylish, except for the general unkemptness suggesting a change of clothes hadn't been on his agenda for a while.

As if aware of her scrutiny he turned towards her, and Sarah looked away quickly. Although less agitated since leaving the house, she wasn't in the mood for any further conversation.

The one person Sarah did want to talk to wasn't with her. But that could be for the best. Anne would want to help, but how could Sarah explain that she thought she was going mad?

Oh God, something else occurred to her. What if she'd left the petrol station without paying for the flowers? It was possible, wasn't it? She couldn't remember picking the roses up and making that crucial decision to buy so maybe she'd simply walked out with them, her mind elsewhere. Sarah's chest tightened as she visualised herself doing just that. She cringed, squeezing her hands together, anticipating the next time she would go there.

'Excuse me. I think this was your floor.'

Startled, Sarah saw the lift had stopped, and the man was holding his arm up to prevent the doors from closing.

'Oh... sorry. Miles away.' Sarah gave him an embarrassed smile as she walked past him. How crazy had she looked? Probably very, judging how he was staring at her.

'Are you okay?'

She swallowed hard. The stranger's concern threatened to unravel any fragile strength she had left. 'Fine. I'm fine.' Aware her voice sounded unnaturally loud, she hurried towards the sanctuary of the ICU, her cheeks burning.

After entering the unit, Sarah used a paper towel to dab cold water onto her face before she donned a mask. Was she fine? Less than an hour before, she'd been brandishing a breadknife at thin air. No, she was far from fine.

She hurried round the corner and nearly collided with her colleague, Tilly, who was precariously carrying ventilator tubing under one arm and a small box under the other.

'Hey, careful! I've already dropped this lot once. Of course, they simply watch me struggle, no offers of help,' Tilly grumbled, nodding in the direction of the desk, where the other nurses looked on in amusement.

Without waiting for a reply, Tilly off-loaded the tubing into her arms. 'You might as well help me seeing he's going to be your patient tonight. And, as some people are too busy chatting,' she added loudly, 'I can hand him over to you while we settle him in. He was Anne's patient last night, but as she's deserted us he's all yours. We've moved him and his two police guards into a separate side room.'

Sarah followed, having yet to mutter a word. Thank God for Tilly. This is what she needed – a bit of normality.


As they turned him onto his left side, Sarah digested what Tilly had told her minutes before. John Doe was Carl Cooper, and he was a suspect in a police investigation. She glanced over at the silent police duo in the corner: her cellmates for the night. It wasn't exactly the happy ending for John Doe she had envisioned.

They had finished repositioning him when she saw the two policemen push themselves away from the wall, their bored postures broken. Sarah instinctively checked the monitors before she realised they were not looking in their direction. Her heartbeat quickened as she saw a figure standing in the doorway.

'Hello, again.' His blue eyes left her for a moment as he fumbled underneath his jacket, before producing a flat black wallet.

'I'm Detective Graham, from the Criminal Investigations Department.' He offered Sarah his ID, and she peered at the faded photograph. His hair had been shorter then, but it was definitely him. She read the name alongside: Detective Chief Inspector Peter Graham.

'I wanted a quick word with those two over there,' he explained, gesturing towards the two policemen. 'If that's okay?'

'Yeah, of course,' Sarah hesitated, 'but could you please do it outside so we can finish our handover.'

The detective hesitated, then after staring for a moment at the inert form on the bed, nodded his agreement.

'God, if you hadn't said anything he would have carried on as if we weren't here,' whined Tilly as soon as the police had shut the door behind them. 'Some of us have homes to go to.'

*The police included,* thought Sarah, sick of Tilly's moaning. As Tilly continued to tell her about Carl, Sarah studied her patient. His dark, lank hair was plastered to his pale face and his carotid pulse fluttered quickly in his neck. The rhythmic rise and fall of his chest was a sign of life beyond his control. She didn't need her years of nursing experience to know his condition had deteriorated.

Scanning the ICU chart, Sarah frowned. She was looking at a classic case of hypovolaemia; he was losing blood.

Tilly agreed. 'They think his injuries are more extensive than they first realised. He's had an echo and there are no signs of a tamponade. So, it could be abdominal. Dan is on call and he's speaking to the registrar about the plan of action.'

'Could you run that past me again?' The DCI's frown was growing deeper at each medical term she threw at him, and Sarah was enjoying seeing him out of his depth. In the small room, his six-foot-plus frame had towered over her but now, as he placed his elbows on the chart-laden tilted table, his head was close to hers.

She took pity on him. 'The doctors think Carl is bleeding from somewhere. We can't get his blood pressure to rise despite giving him intravenous fluids and blood products.'

'Will he need surgery?'

'Possibly. We've scanned his heart and there doesn't appear to be any trauma there. It could be that there was damage to his bowel, or his spleen, which went undetected. A blunt injury caused by a seat belt, as in this case, can cause this sort of problem.'

The detective sighed and pressed his fingertips to his eyes. Not wanting to intrude, Sarah backed away. After a few moments, he walked around the end of the bed and stood over Carl. Stooped, his manner was like that of a grieving relative. Then he straightened, and a briskness returned.

'If he does regain consciousness and says anything – doesn't matter how insignificant – I want to know about it,' he said to the officers. And, after exchanging a few hushed words with them, he turned to go. 'Er, Nurse Knowles?'

Sarah tore her gaze from the syringe driver she had been trying to concentrate on.

Above his mask, his eyes smiled. 'I'm sorry for the inconvenience but let me assure you that all these precautions are necessary. Our presence here is for his protection too.' He paused. 'Have we met somewhere before today?'

*What, apart from when I was acting neurotic in the lift?* she wanted to ask. Instead, she shook her head, avoiding meeting those intense eyes.

'No, I don't think so.' She didn't look back up from the syringe driver until he had gone.

# CHAPTER FOUR

A nne didn't know what scared her most: the realisation she wasn't lying safe in her bed or the trickle of memory that slowly filtered past her pain and confusion. As the trickle cascaded into a torrent, it flooded her synapses, saturating all rational thought.

He was going to hurt her. Kill her. Oh God. She jumped up and ran.

No, something was wrong. She hadn't moved. She had to get away, but why wasn't she moving?

*What's he done to me?* She felt strange: disembodied. She tried to lift her head, and the resulting nausea and dizziness was swiftly followed by blackness. But not before she heard a low animal-like screech, distorted with fear.

When Anne came to, all was silent. She was facing downwards, her forehead resting on something soft. Certain she had raised her head before blacking out, she braced herself and tried again. Stabbing pains hit the back of her skull and spine. She retched. And her whole body was alive with agony. The terrible screeching returned.

He stood motionless on the balcony. Listening to her screams. He had no pity for the bitch, but he was glad the fall down the cellar steps hadn't killed her. She was more useful to him alive.

Closing his eyes, he sniffed in sharply. He felt taller. Stronger. The doubt was gone.

He hadn't intended for this to happen. Anne had seen him following her and had slowed down, giving him no choice but to gesture for her to stop. Her look of recognition had rapidly changed to pleasure. She'd flirted as he led her to the rear of her car to see a fictitious dodgy light, angering him. Did she actually think he was interested in her?

After he had struck her and pushed her into the van, he had panicked. Worried he had lost his way again. But it was okay. He did have a plan. So right, it was instinctive. Her disappearance was the next move in the game.

Oh, thank God. She wasn't paralysed. The soft, cold object her head was resting on was her right arm. No feeling, but movement. Painful, wonderful movement.

The first few attempts to push up ended with her collapsing on her front, and she was overwhelmed with the desire to give in. Prostrate. Broken. Waiting for whatever would kill her first: her injuries, the cold, dehydration, or her kidnapper. Thinking of him sent shockwaves through her. She remembered the anger in his eyes as he'd smacked her across the face.

No. She had to move. Gritting her teeth against the intense throbbing in her head, back and legs, Anne sat up. She hung onto the floor until the wooziness subsided and then peered at her surroundings: a small room, where stone slabs ran into stone walls. A cellar, perhaps. She massaged life back into her freezing arms. A single light bulb hung overhead, its dim glow failing to reach the dark corners.

How long had she been unconscious? There were dried splashes of blood on the floor. She tentatively touched her forehead, wincing as she fingered the congealed scab. Not daring to move quickly in case everything spun again, Anne straightened her legs in front of her.

Agghh. Shit. Pain exploded in her right ankle. Even in the poor light she could see it was twice the size of the other one.

The fact that the waning bulb was not the only light source present hadn't escaped her. She had filed it away for later when her brain could cope with it. Time was not on her side. As she reached towards her damaged ankle, there was a footfall from somewhere behind her.

Scrambling around, she succeeded only in landing on her front again. She looked up to see a dark figure silhouetted on the top step before the light clicked off and a door closed.

'Noooo,' she cried hoarsely. 'Don't leave me. Please... don't.' Anne froze. The darkness was so thick she was immediately lost in it. Too scared to move, she stayed where she had fallen. The cold floor: her anchor.

She couldn't see anything. Panic loomed, see-sawing between the fear of what he would do to her on his return and being left on her own. Her jagged breathing echoed around her but was too soon swallowed up in the void.

What was that? A scraping sound. Was someone else here with her? Anne strained to hear. She had only caught a glimpse of him before the door shut. What if he hadn't left and was watching her from the darkness?

Her heart pounded so hard it hurt. Paranoia gained a hold, as she imagined his face close to hers. Her hand shook as she raised it in front of her. What if her fingers touched him?

No. Stop it. She mustn't lose it. That way was madness.

Anne sucked in a deep lungful of stale air. Focus. Not on him. But on getting out. She hauled herself sideways, hissing through clenched teeth every time her ankle bounced on the rough stone. When she reached the wall, she sagged against the bricks. Her vision tunnelled. Tears hot on her moist skin.

# CHAPTER FIVE

'Anne?'

No reply. Sarah dropped Anne's spare keys back into her handbag, and glanced round the chaos that was her friend's flat. Her own house was in need of tender loving care, but Anne's was bordering on needing special measures. The joys of working nights. Unwashed breakfast dishes were stacked on the coffee table, and piles of clothes smothered the entire sofa. Anne's leather coat was strewn over the top of the nearest pile.

She's here. 'Oh, thank God,' Sarah whispered, briefly closing her eyes. Of course she was here, sleeping off whatever bug she'd picked up.

Sarah was crossing through into the kitchen when she shivered. Not sure why, her apprehension grew as she turned to look over at the bedrooms. *This is silly.* Scolding her fears, she marched across the flat. She reached out for the handle to Anne's room, then hesitated...

The handle morphs into a wooden doorknob before her eyes. It's wet, and she pulls back, puzzled. A cold sweat creeps over her. Her heart thumps. It beats with the music that fills her head. The whole world is stained red; she is staring at her sticky hand as the knob turns.

Sarah cranes her neck, focusing through the tinted mist. What is that on the bed? As the music reaches its peak, she sees the blood. Blood everywhere: on the sheets, on the body, darkening the long hair. A silver locket is pulled to one side – the chain broken.

Sarah screams as the person standing in front of her smiles a snowman's bottle-top grin.

———

The room lurched, and she fell against the door. It clicked open. Struggling with what she had seen, she didn't focus on the bed straight away. It was empty. She slid down the door jamb and, crouching low, hugged her knees. Her breaths came in painful wheezes. The air tasted foul.

Sarah opened her eyes and found a disgruntled cat staring back. Why was she…? How long had she been on the floor? Shit. The bed. Her heart raced as she scrutinised the unmade bed. She stared at the white duvet lying haphazardly over Anne's clean sheet. What was happening?

Sarah crawled over and patted the mattress, not trusting what her eyes were telling her. She was so sure… Of what exactly?

Samson, Anne's cat, gave her one more disdainful look and then stalked out of the room. She pushed up from the carpet and stumbled after him into the hall, reaching out to the sideboard to steady herself as the landline rang.

'Hello?'

'Anne?' the male voice asked.

'Er, no.' Her puzzlement equalled that of the other speaker. 'Is that Bryan? It's Sarah.'

'Sarah!' Bryan boomed down the phone. 'I'm sorry, I didn't recognise your voice.' He paused, 'Er, is everything all right? You sound upset.'

'Anne's missing. She was off sick last night, and there's no sign of her here...' She broke off, aware of how lame it all sounded. 'I guess I'm overreacting.'

'I'll be right over,' Bryan said, ignoring any protests.

Sarah was feeding Samson when it occurred to her to wonder why Bryan would be phoning Anne.

While she was waiting, Sarah cleaned the kitchen, feeling like an intruder yet wanting to keep busy. After speaking to Bryan she had struggled to come up with an explanation for what she thought she had seen outside the bedroom. Maybe she'd caught Anne's mysterious illness and had a temperature. She didn't feel hot, but a fever would certainly explain an hallucination. Her head was throbbing and the harder she tried to remember what she had seen, the less sure she was that she'd seen anything. The kitchen, and a raid on Anne's stock of paracetamol, had been her best bet. She was finishing the washing up when the doorbell rang.

Sarah glanced at the clock as she let Bryan into the flat. Four o'clock. She was glad she didn't have to think about work. Her headache was getting worse, and she wasn't sure she could have coped with it tonight.

Her night shift had been bad enough – her self-confidence taking a knock after forgetting about buying the roses. And although she had performed well on autopilot she'd felt compelled to ask her colleagues to check her calculations and decisions, blaming tiredness for her sudden lack of confidence. She briefly wondered about Carl, and whether he had needed surgery.

Sarah realised Bryan was talking to her. 'I'm sorry, what did you say?'

'You look tired. Have you had any sleep?'

'No, not much,' she admitted. 'I was up at midday phoning Anne's mobile and landline, then when I couldn't get through to her brother, I called her sister. She wasn't expecting to hear from Anne till next week.' Sarah sighed. 'And I think she was puzzled as to why I was so worried. Anne has a habit of disappearing off the radar, especially if there's a new man in her life. But, she was surprised when I told her about Richard, as he was supposed to be away with work.'

Seeing Bryan's bewildered expression, Sarah explained about the phone call to the ward apparently from Anne's brother.

'Do you really think something has happened to her? Maybe she woke still feeling rough and went to see her GP,' Bryan reasoned, as he arranged his long legs over one of the wooden stools.

'Why hasn't she texted or called me back? Oh, I don't know...' Sarah broke off and covered her face with her hands. Was it really that strange she hadn't heard from her friend? Days could sometimes go by without them contacting each other, and Anne was always forgetting to charge up her phone.

What Bryan said did make a lot of sense. Although if Anne had felt crap then surely she would have stayed indoors in case it was Covid or the flu. Sarah couldn't get rid of the overall feeling that she was right to worry. 'Her winter coat is here,' she continued. 'At first I thought it meant she was here too, but then I remembered Anne had been moaning on Friday night because she hadn't brought it with her. And her car's gone.'

'Which suggests she may be at her doctor's, or shopping if she's feeling better. Have you contacted the hospital in case she was admitted last night?'

Sarah wanted to scream at the baffled look on Bryan's face, but she merely nodded.

'Then I expect she'll turn up, right as rain. And wondering what all the fuss was about.' Bryan eased himself from the stool and moved to her side. He placed his arm across her shoulders. It felt strangely heavy, as if its weight plus her tiredness would drag her down.

Gently he pulled her towards him and hugged her. 'Everything will be fine,' he whispered.

Sarah relaxed against him, needing the contact. He held her to his chest, but his jumper tickled her face and a faint smell of stale sweat added to her growing discomfort. She tried to step out of his grasp. His arms tightened. He caressed her forehead with his lips. His hot breath quickened on her skin, and his hands trembled as he eased them down her back.

No, she didn't want this. The edge of her blouse was pulled up. Oh God.

'Bryan, stop this, please,' she cried, hitting her hands against his chest.

For a moment he kept her pinned there; he did then step backwards, only to grip her upper arms.

'You're hurting me!'

Her words filtered through, and his hands relaxed. His eyes full of hard desire, then they too softened.

'I-I'm sorry, Sarah. I thought...' He tailed off. He withdrew, horror on his face. Abruptly he turned and, walking to the counter, snatched his coat.

'Don't worry about Anne.' He spoke fast. His cheeks were fiery red, and the violent colour was seeping into the pale skin of his neck. 'I honestly think she'll turn up.' He reached the door of the flat and paused. 'If you need anything let me know.'

Sarah assured him she would, and he left without glancing back.

As soon as the door closed behind him, Sarah exhaled loudly. She walked over to the window and peered at the top of his bowed head as he went to his car. *Bryan? What the hell were you doing?* For a few seconds back there… She shuddered, refusing to dwell on what might have happened.


Despite her worry about Anne, exhaustion won, and Sarah nodded through an episode of *Pointless* on the Challenge channel; she usually enjoyed the quiz programme, but even when the two finalists won the money it barely registered in her tired brain. She rubbed her eyes and sat forward, trying to avoid falling into an undignified sleep on Anne's sofa.

What should she do? Her headache was almost gone, but the thought of venturing outside to go home wasn't a pleasant one. She tried Anne's mobile, but it went straight to voicemail again, as did Richard's. What was going on? There'd been no one at Richard's house when she'd popped over earlier in the afternoon, but she'd posted a note through his door telling him to contact her. If he really was working away, Sarah had no idea when he would be back.

Well, being here would feel like she was doing something, and it wouldn't be the first time she had crashed at Anne's. During the initial few months after losing Mike it had become a common occurrence for her to drop in uninvited for a night or two.

When Anne walked through the door, she would be there for her. To help her through… what? If she walked in with Richard, she'd feel like such an idiot. Relieved, but an idiot.

Sarah's stomach rumbled. Having eaten hardly anything since she had got out of bed, she was starving. Right, she'd phone for a takeaway, and if Anne hadn't arrived back after that then she'd stay the night.

One deep-pan special, and one garlic bread later, there was no sign of Anne. Sarah licked her greasy fingers. 'Well, Samson. It looks like you've got company tonight whether you want it or not,' she told the sleeping cat, who was half hidden between discarded clothes on the other end of the sofa. The tabby's ear twitched. If he hadn't the temperament of Atilla the Hun, Sarah would've reached out and stroked the soft fur. But she left him alone knowing all too well that a sleeping Samson was the most agreeable Samson.

# CHAPTER SIX

P eter stuck his head through the open doorway and glanced around the incident room. It was depressingly quiet. Other than a few phone operators, and the hunched figure of their office manager, the room was empty. He didn't doubt his team were as committed as ever to finding their man, but he was edgy knowing the investigation had changed direction since identifying Carl as the prime suspect.

The usual flurry of activity: the house-to-house inquiries, interviewing family and friends, and following potential leads had kept the team busy over the weekend, but the overall feeling in the Monday briefing was that the end was finally in sight. He disagreed. It was all too easy.

Peter slid behind his makeshift desk. What they did know was that the wrecked car belonged to Carl's housemate, Nihar. He had reported it stolen last Thursday morning when it had gone missing from outside their home.

It wasn't until a few days later that Nihar had found a note from Carl, hidden under a pile of post, telling him he'd borrowed his car.

Even though two of his investigators had already interviewed

Carl's housemates, Peter was planning to visit them at their house later that day. He grabbed a pen to scribble the questions he had flying around, but after a few minutes of doodling his mind strayed.

Resting his chin on his hands, Peter studied their whiteboard. The case against Carl was looking solid, and he winced as he recalled the psychologist's conclusion. She had been satisfied that Carl fitted the physical and psychological profile. A son of a retired judge; predicted to fail his law studies this year. Estranged from his remaining family – a loner, who'd had no long-term relationships, in spite of his good looks. But was it enough to lead to such a high level of violence?

Carl's prints had been lifted from Pamela's shoe, and the matching stiletto found underneath the driver's seat in the wrecked car. All circumstantial, yet when added to the fact that Carl was directly linked to the first victim, the chain of evidence was compelling. But there were many unanswered questions. For instance, why take only one shoe with him, and leave the other at the scene of the crime? And Pamela's foot had been crammed into the black high-heeled shoe that was a full size smaller than the others found in her wardrobe.

Peter flexed his arm to get rid of pins and needles, stood and wandered over to the window. Although he had escaped back to his flat last night for a shower and rest, the overactive heating in the offices had squeezed dry any precious reserves of energy.

Peter leaned against the cool glass and closed his eyes, willing his body to relax. When he opened them, he was rewarded by a slightly misted-up view of Ledforth. Their building was in the centre of town, but they were high enough to see the river meandering through fields and past the abbey in the distance. This time the impressive view did nothing to lift his spirits.

He had spent the majority of the morning with Carl's parents, struggling with his need for diplomacy, an unwavering dislike for the couple, and his guilt at his failure to find their daughter's killer. Carl's father had dismissed the ridiculous allegations against his son as police incompetence. Well, actually, he'd narrowed it down to Peter's incompetence.

He needed a break, and as if on cue his stomach growled its approval. Peter looked at his watch. God, was it one thirty already?

Grabbing his jacket, he resisted the temptation to head over to see what snippets of information had come in and strode to the door, winking at a young phone operator as he passed. She ignored him, sending his spirits even lower.

To combat his despondency, he opted for the stairs. After sprinting down the five flights two stairs at a time, Peter ran back to the top. On his way he passed DI Khenan Bacchas, a fellow police inmate.

'Care to join me?' he panted. 'It does wonders for beating back old age.'

Peter grinned as he left Khenan shouting after him, 'I'm younger than you, yah cheeky git. And it doesn't work, yah look bloody awful.'

Khenan was waiting for him on his second descent. 'I don't want to disturb your beauty regime right now, but can you pop in later to see me? I need to pick your brains.'

'You must be desperate,' Peter replied, his legs grateful for the excuse to stop.

'Scraping the barrel, mate. Everyone else is busy on that case of yours,' Khenan added with a smile, ducking out of the stairwell before Peter could respond.

Peter laughed. He had become friends with Khenan during a fighting crime seminar, when a mutual love of soul music lightened an otherwise dull weekend. A catch-up was long overdue. Judging by the familiar weariness etched on Khenan's face however, he doubted a relaxed chat over a beer or two would be on the cards. Khenan was involved in a difficult investigation. Someone was killing prostitutes in the town, and since the available manpower had reduced due to his own murder case, Peter was happy to help any way he could. The strain of dealing with two ongoing major cases had repercussions throughout their force.

When he reached the ground floor again, he rested on the wall, pretending to be engrossed in the public noticeboard while getting his breath back. He had always prided himself on his level of fitness, so he was dismayed how breathless his exertion had left him. Nothing a few good gym sessions and a smoke-free year wouldn't put right.

'Detective Graham?'

She was sitting on one of the benches behind him, and there was an embarrassing moment of blankness as he tried to remember where he knew her from.

'We met at the hospital the other night.' She glanced away; her cheeks turning bright red as she gathered up her bag.

'Of course, Nurse Knowles.' An image of her in the lift, hands clasped, came to him. He was suddenly very intrigued as to why she was here. 'What can I do for you?'

'Well actually, I was loitering. I've already spoken to the officer at the desk and filled in the paperwork,' she explained, standing and nodding towards the reception. 'He helped me as much as he could.' The tone of her voice suggested she was disappointed. Her smile wavered. 'I was trying to decide what to do next.'

'Is there anything I can do?'

She stared at him, undecided, her hazel eyes searching his, then she shook her head. 'No. I don't want to bother you.' Arms folded, she moved towards the exit.

'You wouldn't be.' Perhaps it was because he'd met her for a second time, but his interest was piqued. Could her uneasiness be anything to do with their suspect on ICU? He couldn't imagine how, but he hated coincidences. 'I've an appointment later today, but you caught me nipping off for a break. There's a café nearby, we could talk there.'

---

Sarah pushed her empty plate out of the way and leaned forward, placing her elbows on the red Formica table. It wobbled precariously.

'We've been friends for over ten years; Anne wouldn't disappear like this. I know something has happened to her. I finally managed to speak to her brother's flatmate, who told me that Richard's been on a training course in Dumfries for the last few days – which makes no sense. I mean, it couldn't be him who had phoned work. There's no sign of her on Facebook. I've tried the hospital and everyone I can think of who knows her. I don't know what else to do.'

Sarah's face was pinched with worry, her complexion was pale against her dark jumper. Her fingers worried at her earring as she stared at the steamed-up window, her mind in another place. Something else was bothering this woman. Something bad. Peter trusted his instincts, but he was unsure how to proceed. Would she even welcome his intrusion? 'Sarah, is there anything you aren't telling me?'

His voice retrieved her from wherever she had slipped. 'No. I just have this strong feeling that Anne needs help. That's the problem, there's nothing concrete I can offer.'

Eye contact had returned, although she was first to break the silence. 'I've taken up far too much of your time; I better let you go.' Sarah slid her chair back and then paused, smiling ruefully. 'Maybe the police constable was right: she's got a secret boyfriend and is, at this moment, having great sex, while I'm here fussing as she's had the audacity not to text me for two days.'

'I hope he didn't say that,' Peter exclaimed, planning to tear strips off him if he had.

'Oh no, well, not in those words anyway – I added the "great sex" bit,' Sarah laughed, blushing, 'and it's probably true. I've been a bit preoccupied lately, and in all honesty, Anne might have met someone special and not told me about him. Taking a sickie is hardly an offence, is it?'

Not waiting for a reply, Sarah stood to go. 'Thanks for the lunch. It's time I went home and stopped being neurotic.'

Peter hurried to open the door for her, while she struggled to put her gloves on. A fast brush-off was not what he had hoped for. But what had he expected?

'Listen, take my number. If you need any advice or anything...' He tailed off, observing her reaction carefully as she took his card. Whatever was troubling her, it couldn't have anything to do with Carl, but he found himself wanting to help.

He followed her outside. The wind, although tainted with car fumes, was a welcome freshness after the cocktail of cooking fat and sweat abundant in the small café.

Sarah turned towards him and smiled. Small droplets of sleet appeared between them, bouncing along the currents of cold air. She opened her mouth as if she were going to say something, then maybe thinking better of it she simply lifted her gloved hand in a wave before she backed away.

When Peter couldn't see her anymore he looked towards the failing afternoon light. The threatening sky was beating a short winter day into submission.

# CHAPTER SEVEN

He pressed his face along the thin crack of light, yearning for a glimpse of movement. Barely noticing the wood beneath him digging into his cheek. Longing to connect. Did Sarah sense him too? Was she walking around the empty rooms and feeling his presence?

He was pleased how much discipline he had. Her closeness was torture. That was why he had hated her; hated her as much as he now loved her. At the beginning he hadn't recognised how her power over him was a good thing. He had fought against it, wanting to destroy her. It wasn't until he realised his self-control was being tested that he understood.

He remembered the first time they had properly met. It was at the beginning of his growth when his new sense of power was frightening. A lot had happened to him since then. He wasn't the same person.

***

Sarah's eyes filled with tears, and she shook her head angrily. This was crazy. It was her house. Her safe haven. So why did it feel so wrong? A cold sweat tightened her skin. Familiar shapes were different: tainted. The silence, usually comforting and welcoming, had a sinister edge.

She stopped in front of the black wrought-iron lamp, half expecting its knotted feet to command a life of their own and scuttle with crab-like steps back onto the mantelpiece. It looked at her blankly from her small coffee table, the white shade shining with light and innocence.

Sarah pressed her knuckles to her lips as she sank to her knees. Over the last few weeks, she'd found objects moved around her house. But nothing that couldn't be explained by tiredness or a disorganisation that came with working shifts. So what if she couldn't remember taking a book off her shelf and leaving it on the table. And who didn't sometimes lose things around the home? Not to mention those sodding roses.

But this? There was no bloody way she'd moved that lamp. She wouldn't. It had been on the mantelpiece since she'd bought it, for Christ's sake.

Was someone getting into her house? That was madness. Who would do something like that, and how? There were no signs of forced entry: all windows were shut, and her door was locked when she arrived. Her search had revealed no hiding places, nor any shadow that didn't have a right to be there.

Should she phone the police? And say what? Nothing appeared to be missing. They'd laugh at her.

Sarah turned the lamp off and lifted it back into its original space. As she did so, she glanced over her shoulder. She couldn't spend tonight here on her own. Another impromptu stay at Anne's would hopefully give her time to plan her next steps.

Whilst she was upstairs packing a bag, her conviction that she hadn't moved the lamp weakened. Because she couldn't remember doing it, didn't mean...

Oh God. Was she ill? Really ill?

It was the most likely explanation. Especially if she chucked the nightmares and the peculiar hallucination into the mix.

Worried about the recurring dreams, she had already booked an appointment to see Matt tomorrow evening and she'd tell him everything. Her first visit to Dr Matt Grainger had been a few years ago, and she considered him a friend as well as a doctor. He would be surprised to see her. It had been a long time since she had needed Matt in a professional capacity, even though he'd insisted on checking up on her. Once she had joked he'd be sending her a bill for their chats, after another one had finished with him asking about her mental health.

Now she wondered whether the psychiatrist had known all along something like this would happen.

Sarah hovered in the hallway, toying with her phone. She didn't normally mind her own company, but tonight was different. Although she had no doubt Bryan would want to help her, it wasn't his face she conjured up in her mind.

# CHAPTER EIGHT

The inevitable news coverage about their unconscious suspect had created the usual eruptions and incriminations: the reporters being called irresponsible, and in turn the police labelled as tight-lipped and obstructive. Peter had let them get on with it. There had been more important matters to deal with, and they would've struggled to keep a lid on the developments much longer anyway.

Their new piece of information was, in fact, a direct result of the newspapers. Not that any member of the station was freely going to admit that, unless over several pints of good beer. A barman, upon seeing the publicised photograph of Carl Cooper, remembered him sitting in his pub Wednesday evening. The Black Bull was within walking distance of the victim's house and according to the witness, Carl left with another man not long before closing time.

Peter had planned to accompany Doug on an 'over the bar' interrogation. However, after receiving Sarah's phone call, he was now on his way to the address she had given him.

She didn't say what was wrong, but the conversation had left him with no doubt that she needed help. With what, he had no idea. Apart from establishing over lunch there was no longer any Mr Knowles, he knew little else about her. Yes, he was very curious about Sarah. In truth, he'd found it hard to focus on anything else since their lunch.

Slowing for the next bend, he peered ahead. The weather had deteriorated, and he was unable to see more than a few metres. He shifted uncomfortably in his seat. His earlier euphoria – caused by Sarah choosing to call him rather than someone else – disappeared.

*Come on, Peter. You can do this.* He glanced anxiously in his mirror. Headlights behind him. His clammy palms slipped on the steering wheel. The swish of the windscreen wipers was loud in his head, obscuring any coherent thoughts.

Not now. His breath caught in his throat; his chest constricted. Aware he was on the edge of a panic attack, he pulled over. Struggling to remain calm he opened his door, banging his head on the window as he did so. The fresh, wet air tasted no sweeter, gave no relief. Breathe in. One. Two. Three. Four. Five. Soaked in a cold sweat, he reached for the glove compartment, the catch difficult for his numb, contorted fingers. Breathe out. Six. Seven. Eight. Nine. Ten. Even as the pain in his chest increased, and his rasping gasps were loud in his ears, he despised himself. Breathe in... As he lifted the brown paper bag to his face, the tendrils of shame teased his mind. Breathe out...

They had told him the accident hadn't been his fault. He knew differently. Gradually, breathing into the bag eased his physical pain. The constriction in his chest disappeared and his hands, though tingling, took on a more normal shape. Not a full-blown assault this time, nevertheless it left him drained. Closing his eyes, he sat for a while, listening to the rain bouncing off the car's roof.

It was nearly a year since the last panic attack, and he could at least attribute a solid reason for this one. Seeing the mangled wreck the other morning had sparked too many memories. He was only surprised it had taken more than forty-eight hours.

The previous attack had been completely out of the blue. One moment he was having a quiet drink in the corner of a Scottish pub, and the next he was fighting for a lungful of air. His beer went cascading across the table. He had staggered out, pushing past disapproving faces and leaving a vocal landlord in his wake.

The next day he had driven back from Scotland alone. The crash, three years ago, had not only ended their daughter's short life, but also their marriage. A shared loss, even one so great, had in the end been no match for self-blame and guilt. He had dived straight back into work. And, although fighting crime was a strange form of therapy, it had saved him. His dedication had turned into an obsession – and not necessarily a healthy one – but, at the time, it had been either that or a quick decline into alcoholism. Mind abuse had been the better option.

A gust of wind, laced with handfuls of rain, burst through the open car door, bringing him quickly back to the present. Shit. He didn't want to add pneumonia to his list of problems. As he climbed out of the car, he decided that he shouldn't be so hard on himself. He wasn't ready to give up on life just yet.

---

'Didn't you drive here?' asked Sarah, puzzled at the bedraggled figure standing in the doorway.

His soaked raincoat hung limply over one arm, and with his other hand he was trying to straighten out his tousled hair. 'I had car trouble. Had to leave the wretched thing about a mile down the road.'

'Oh no.' This only added to Sarah's misery. She was guilty of bringing him out here in awful weather. He'd driven from the other side of town, and for what? Her previous paranoia now felt ridiculous. Not used to succumbing to such fear, she was ashamed of her panicky behaviour.

Peter had moved into the centre of the room and was looking around with interest. 'This is a nice flat you've got here,' he said, staring at the colourful abstract art that adorned the walls.

'It's Anne's place. She always loved garish colours, said it matched her personality. Let me take your coat.'

He winced at the damp patch he was making on the carpet. As he mumbled an apology, Sarah could see he was processing the fact she had asked him to Anne's flat.

When she returned from the bathroom with a towel for him, he was examining a framed photograph on top of Anne's sideboard. It was a photo of her and Anne, arms around each other, laughing into the camera.

'That was taken a few years ago,' she said, pointing at the picture. It was one of those awkward selfies, angled so Anne's big floppy sun hat took centre stage. They were both peering out from under its brim: brunette, tanned Sarah, and ginger, freckled and burnt Anne. 'We had a weekend away in Newquay; celebrating her thirtieth.'

'Have you heard any news?'

'No, nothing. I've a spare key to this place and I was twiddling my thumbs at home. Besides, someone has to feed Samson,' Sarah finished in a rush, grateful to the cat for supplying her with another excuse.

If Peter had been in a quandary about the identity of the mysterious Samson, the timely appearance of the fluffy feline would have dispelled any doubts. He meandered in from the kitchen and, ignoring the two of them, headed straight for the sofa.

Sarah had to admit that he was a beautiful cat. His thick black fur was tinged with amber and, as he claimed his favourite vantage point between two large cushions, he swished his elegant tail with that air of aloofness Sarah associated with cats. She was a dog person, and Samson had done nothing to redress the balance. He was a nasty cat, with a foul temper. The way he peered out from beneath those black tufts, as if he were permanently scowling, betrayed his true temperament.

'I wouldn't do that if I were you,' she warned, as Peter went to pet Samson. 'He's not very friendly. Anne was– is the only person he lets anywhere near him. I have to leave his food and run.'

'A real character then,' Peter replied, making a dignified retreat. 'Was there any food left out for him when you arrived?'

'No, nothing but a hungry and bad-tempered Samson.' Sarah gasped as the significance hit her, hammering home with dreadful certainty. 'Anne would never have willingly left Samson to starve. Something or someone prevented her from returning here Saturday,' she exclaimed. Staring at Peter she prayed for him to share her conviction.

'Unless she knew you would look after things for her while she was gone? I'm not saying nothing has happened to her,' he continued, hastily, 'we just need to cover every possibility.' He perched on the edge of the sofa, oblivious to any danger posed by the recent sole occupier. Samson glared at him. 'Have you spoken to any of her neighbours in case she left instructions with them?'

Sarah nodded. 'Anne only sees the elderly man across the hall on a regular basis. I spoke to him yesterday, and he had no idea where she could have gone. The couple next door have gone away for a month, and they aren't due back till next week, and that only leaves the boy downstairs. And she would never have told him anything. He gives her the creeps.'

'Have you met him?'

'Yes, and he's harmless enough. Works nights as a security guard.' *Please let him take this seriously. She wouldn't disappear. Unless...?* 'You don't think he's got her, do you?' Sarah blurted out.

'Who?' asked Peter, looking confused. 'The boy downstairs?'

'No, the one they call The Beautician.' Her voice shook, and she wrapped her arms round her waist to hold herself together.

She swallowed back the bitter taste of the greasy lunch she'd eaten earlier. *Don't let it be true.*

'There was another murder not far from here,' Sarah continued doggedly. 'A few days ago. She worked at the hospital. I didn't know her, but I think Anne had spoken to her a couple of times, and–'

'Sarah.'

She stopped. Thoughts, now checked, tumbled over each other.

'You haven't seen the evening news?'

'Not yet. Why?'

'I've been working on The Beautician case,' he confessed. 'We've got a suspect, and if we're right then he couldn't possibly have taken Anne.' Peter paused before saying softly, 'It's Carl Cooper.'

Astonished, Sarah covered her mouth. 'No,' she mumbled through her fingers, as she struggled to connect the image of her patient lying helpless on his bed to the horrors he was accused of committing. His hand she had held…

She barely made it to the bathroom in time before the bacon and eggs she'd eaten at lunch finally had the last say and she was sick in the toilet.


'I'm okay. Honestly, I feel a lot better now,' Sarah said, for what felt like the tenth time.

Looking far from convinced, Peter joined her on the sofa. Samson was nowhere to be seen. And Sarah was suddenly grateful she'd had the foresight to move Anne's piles of clothes into her spare bedroom. 'It'd been coming on all afternoon, all it needed was a little encouragement.'

'Expertly given by yours truly,' Peter exclaimed woefully.

Sarah laughed. 'I'll try not to hold it against you.'

'Would a nice hot coffee help my case?'

'Hmmm, maybe.'

Heading towards the kitchen area, Peter paused. 'And then you might tell me the real reason why you asked me over here.'

Not sure how to reply, Sarah trailed behind him. She leaned on the breakfast bar as he searched for the coffee. He found it next to numerous tins of cat food, and as he reached for the sugar, his shirt became taut over his broad shoulders. Sarah couldn't help but admire his physique, wondering how it would feel to be held in those strong arms.

The wet patches on his clothes had almost vanished, but as he flicked his hair away from his face, drips fell onto his shirt. The white material darkened. A red mist descended...

Not taking his coal-black eyes off her – trapping her in his stare – he wipes his gloved hands over his shirt. The bright red stripes mingle with the splatters of blood. The white cries out in contrast. As he steps towards her, he smiles sweetly, raising his hand as if to offer friendship...

Her scream shattered Peter's nerves, demolishing the endings with one hard swoop. If this were a cartoon he'd be hanging onto the ceiling for dear life. Instead, looking at her wide eyes, he felt as though they had been mysteriously spirited into a low-budget horror movie. And judging by her terrified expression, the guy in the rubber monster suit was standing directly behind him.

He spun around, his heart in his mouth. And confronted nothing. What the hell? He turned back as she screamed again, but still saw no one. Sarah ran across the room in a state of blind panic and Peter followed, at a complete loss as to what to do.

'Sarah! What is it?' he yelled, hoping to stop her flight. He caught up with her as she fumbled with the lock, thumping the door in her rush to leave. As he placed his hand on her shoulder, she screamed, and he was holding onto a wildcat. She squirmed around to face him, pelting his chest with blows. He retreated, but too slow to avoid a hard knee in his groin. Falling to the floor, the radiating pain gripped him, and he was momentarily blind.

From a foetal position, he squinted through a wash of tears. He raised his arm to defend any further attacks, but Sarah had withdrawn. Gritting his teeth against the pain he pushed up onto his knees. 'And I thought we were getting on well,' he groaned. As the agony lessened, he gingerly probed his injured bits. Perhaps his wouldn't be a future of forced celibacy, after all.

Badly shaken, but worried about Sarah, Peter crawled unsteadily to her side. She had retreated into the corner, curled up tight with her knees pulled to her chin. Her face hidden, she didn't look as he approached.

'Sarah? Are you okay?'

There was no answer.

'Sarah?' Cautiously, so not to alarm her, Peter parted the tangled curtain of hair. *Oh, shit.* Sarah stared straight ahead – her face blank.

# CHAPTER NINE

Spirals of colour tumbled garishly over one another. Intricate patterns defied logic, and the illusion of impossible depth tricked her aching eyes. Primary colours merged, the resulting whirlpool offering what? Oblivion?

'Sarah.'

Slowly she shifted her focus away from the picture. Oblivion shunned, Sarah turned her head towards the voice, grimacing at the stiffness in her neck. Feeling like she was waking from a bizarre dream, she stared uncomprehendingly at the face in front of her.

'I think she's coming round.'

Sarah frowned. 'Matt, what on earth are you doing here?'

Relief crossed the doctor's face. 'Your detective friend here called me,' he explained, gesturing towards Peter, who was hovering over his shoulder.

Peter lifted a hand as if to acknowledge his guilt.

'It sounds like you gave him quite a scare.'

'What happened?' *And why are you both looking at me like that?* she thought wildly. Trying to ignore her throbbing head, she struggled to her feet. 'Did I faint?'

'Don't you remember?' blurted out Peter incredulously.

Matt silenced him with a quick shake of the head. 'Help me get Sarah to the sofa. Examination first, then questions,' he said firmly.

Their voices became distant as Sarah drifted away. Events of the evening replayed in her mind – the memory as dissociated as one of Anne's abstract paintings. She saw herself running from the kitchen, pure terror stamped across her face. Flashes of Peter's shocked expression intermingled with hers. Trembling, she watched the drama unfold; her mind distancing her from the players.

'I remember,' she said, flatly. Her voice hardly recognisable. 'In the kitchen... oh my God!' Her head pounded. Stopping her thinking. Please... let... me... see. But the more she tried, the further away it all went.

Sarah was dimly aware that strong arms were guiding her to the sofa. She was sure a revelation was just beyond her reach, and she groaned in frustration.

'Are you okay?' asked Peter, sitting next to her.

She nodded, smiling weakly at him. 'I'm trying to make sense of what I saw. But I can't quite...' Sarah broke off, exasperated. She felt stupid. What must he think of her? The image of him writhing on the floor, clutching his groin, came to her and she cringed.

'It's all right, Sarah,' he was saying. 'When you're ready tell us what you do remember.'


Sarah was worn out. They had talked for seemingly hours. First she had told them everything, then they had bombarded her with questions: like when had it all started, and how had she felt about it? Matt asked the latter one a lot. She guessed he had come to the conclusion that she was having a breakdown. Couldn't blame him. Hadn't she had the same thought?

She could deal with scepticism from Matt about her mental stability, but she looked over at Peter with trepidation. It was impossible to gauge what he was thinking. His face had remained unreadable throughout, his eyes had softened and shown concern at appropriate moments, but he had given nothing else away. She was glad she wasn't on the other side of an interrogation desk from him. He would be a formidable adversary.

'I wish you'd come to see me weeks ago, Sarah, rather than trying to face this alone,' said Matt. He removed his glasses and wearily rubbed his eyes. 'I think we've put you through enough tonight. You need to rest.'

---

'What do you think, doc? It's serious, isn't it?'

Closing the door behind him, Peter faced Matt in the small hallway. Conscious he might be intimidating the poor man, he settled back on the door frame.

'It could be, yes.' Matt looked up shrewdly at Peter. 'May I ask what your relationship is with Sarah?'

Peter thought hard before replying. Studying the doctor's face he didn't see any hostility, but he could tell Matt was trying to make his mind up about him.

'We've only just met, but although I don't know her very well, I hope she would consider me a friend. And I want to help her any way I can,' he added. Damn it, that was as near to the truth as anything.

Matt nodded, satisfied. 'She's been through a lot these past few years,' he said sadly. 'Maybe it's all too much for her. But, if it is depression then we can do something about it.'

'And if it's not?'

'Let's tackle that if we come to it. Okay?' Taking Peter's silence as a cue to leave, Matt turned to go.

'Wait. What do I do if… well, if she sees something again? Or goes into another fugue state?' The wildcat he could cope with, it was the time he couldn't reach her that had freaked him out. Waiting for help to arrive. No idea whether she could be brought back.

'Call me and I'll come straight over.' Matt sighed. 'She doesn't want to go into hospital, but it may be unavoidable.'

Peter re-entered the flat and found Sarah standing in the kitchen. She was wringing a tea-towel through her hands and looking at him nervously.

'Well, what's the verdict? Am I to expect the men in white overalls to come and drag me off kicking and screaming?'

Her smile was fleeting and far from carefree, but her pale face and his heart were both transformed by it. Unexpectedly tongue-tied, he swallowed hard. Then, with a start, he realised she had interpreted all the wrong messages from his silence.

'The jury's still out. But, hey, there's always the bribe left,' he quipped lamely.

'Your timing's lousy, detective. You think I'm crazy, don't you?'

'No. I don't,' he said, silently cursing his unexpected ardour, 'I think something is happening to you that we don't understand. And I'd like to help if you'd let me.'

She remained quiet for a short time, before confessing she had planned to reveal everything to him when she had phoned earlier that evening. 'I never counted on a practical demonstration. And, I'm sorry I hurt you,' she said, blushing.

'Well, you certainly know how to cripple a guy,' he joked. Seeing her flinch, he tried again. 'Look, I've had worse, so don't worry about it. I'm fine. Really.' He stepped forward and placed a hand lightly on her shoulder. 'I bet I could even dance the can-can, if you begged me.' This time she smiled.

Aware they were standing close, he backed off slightly, not

wanting to crowd her. Besides, he needed to keep a clear head, and that was difficult when she was near.

While Sarah made a hot drink, they kept the conversation light-hearted. She appeared happier listening, and so Peter chatted about his childhood in the small North Yorkshire town of Thirsk, and how he'd wanted to follow his dad into the police force.

'Why did you come to Ledforth?'

'It was my ex-wife's idea. Liz hated living in the country. She wanted our children to grow up away from stifling village life.' The thought of Jess made his heart ache. He pictured her happy face, framed by an expanse of blonde curls. *I miss you, bunny.*

He shook the image away, closing his eyes to the grief. Aware that Sarah was staring at him curiously, he forced a tired smile. 'It's a long story, and best told over a few drinks. Preferably stronger than chocolate.'

'Well, when you're ready, I'll supply the time and you can bring the drink. Agreed?'

'It's a date. But I'm warning you, my story lurks in the depths of depravity.'

Both armed with a steaming mug, they wandered back to the settee.

'The man you saw in the kitchen, are you sure you didn't recognise him?'

If Sarah was troubled at the sudden change of topic she didn't show it. 'I don't think so. If he doesn't look like the snowman from hell, then his face is in shadow. I realise how it sounds, but all I remember is how he made me feel when he stared at me.'

'Could he be someone from your past?'

Sarah tensed. 'No, I wondered that, and there's no one.'

She was staring down at her lap, and Peter's gut feeling was that Sarah was lying. But why? And did she know she was doing so? He recalled the look on Matt's face when she had described her nightmares; were they both hiding something from him?

He wanted to push her further. Certain the answers were there if only she'd let him in. But seeing how exhausted she was, his resolve wavered. 'It's late. Matt was right, you need to rest. We can talk tomorrow.'

Sarah looked relieved. She sipped her hot chocolate, before saying, 'I am tired. Feel like I've not slept in days. I'll go and fetch you a duvet and pillow for the sofa.' She moved to get up, then hesitated. 'Thanks for this, Peter. I hope I'm not keeping you from your work?'

They had decided earlier that someone should stay with Sarah. Happy for an excuse not to drive, he had volunteered. 'The curse of a chief inspector is that work is never far away,' he replied, unclipping the small black pager from his belt, and retrieving his mobile from his pocket. 'If they needed me, both would go off in quick succession.'

In his panic Matt pressed the call button without first considering the time. The sleepy, confused voice made him reconsider the wisdom of having this conversation during the night.

'I'm sorry, I shouldn't have phoned this late.' He hurried to allay fears, 'No, don't worry, she's okay. But we do have a problem: she's beginning to remember. And she's not stupid, it won't take her long to start putting two and two together. She'll realise she's been lied to.'

As he listened to the predictable 'Oh my God,' and 'What shall we do?' he stared through his windscreen at the block of flats. Most of the windows in the small complex were in darkness, leaving the lit lamp-posts scattered around the hedged entrances and the communal grounds as the main sources of light: their beams filled with white glistening raindrops. Out of those windows still showing signs of life, he wasn't sure which flat Sarah and Peter were in. He was glad she wasn't alone.

Thinking of Sarah filled him with self-loathing: she had trusted him, and he had betrayed her. It was fitting he was sat here in the shadows. He didn't deserve to be there in the light: comforting her and pretending he was as confused about everything as she was.

The voice at the other end of the line had fallen silent. Matt sighed. 'Look, if I'd thought this through I'd never have called you at this hour.'

His co-conspirator was so understanding it was annoying. A tiny part of him was glad he wouldn't be the only one getting little or no sleep. 'Well, we have to do something soon,' he pushed. 'A detective friend of Sarah's is now involved. I think he's already suspicious.'

After finishing the call, he made no move to start the car. When he'd left Anne's flat he had grabbed his briefcase from the boot and wrote down all that had happened: Peter's account of Sarah's erratic behaviour, followed by her own description of what she saw. His barely legible scribbles were squeezed onto the last pages of his workbook.

He closed a fist around its edges. What if he threw it all in the nearest puddle? Months of consultation notes with different clients destroyed. Would he care? Let's face it, there was a real possibility that he'd already thrown his career away.

# CHAPTER TEN

Pressing her ear against the door, Anne listened. Longing to hear anything. A voice. Thud. Scuffle. Anything so she didn't feel unbearably alone. Her breath, harsh and rapid: the only sound in the vacuum. Why had he left her like this? If he was planning some awful end for her then why didn't he bloody get on with it?

*Come on, you bastard. I'm here.* Having used all her remaining energy clambering up the cellar steps, her hand barely made a noise as she clawed at the timber. What was he waiting for?

After grabbing her, maybe he didn't know what to do. She knew who he was. He couldn't simply let her go, saying *Oh I'm dreadfully sorry. It's all been a horrid mistake! You won't tell anyone, will you?* But if it had been a savage impulse, brought on by reasons she could only wonder at, then perhaps he was regretting his actions. Anne clung on to that hope, her sanity depending on it.

It made sense. He hadn't killed her because he couldn't bring himself to complete his sick fantasy. She could have a chance after all. If only she could talk to him, plead with him to spare her life.

And she would plead. Anything to survive. In another time, outside the darkness, Anne may have squirmed at the thought of pleading for her life, but not now. The pain in her ankle was excruciating. The first time she'd had to struggle to push her trousers and pants down to wee, her cheeks burning with shame, she'd promised herself she would do anything to get out of there.

She wasn't ready to die. There were so many things she had to do. Travel. Be a wife. A mum. Oh God, her family. What would they think? Her friends. Sarah.

Sarah had been through so much. She couldn't leave her.

There it was again. Every time Anne thought of her best friend she got an urgent sense she was missing something. Something big. What was it? And why did she have the feeling it was connected to why she was here?

She had to get out. But to do that she had to talk to him. See him. Anyone. Please.

# CHAPTER ELEVEN

A raucous yell from a drunken male echoed across the street. Tight miniskirts and shirtsleeves in the cold wind accompanied another Monday night on the town's social calendar. Groups of smartly dressed young men and women, defiant against the wintery weather, were moving from the pubs towards the nightclubs.

A girl ogled him greedily. Her eager eyes registered disappointment as he ignored her smile. It wasn't that he couldn't join in their social games (he had found it increasingly easy); but tonight was special. Being close to Sarah had thrown him off balance, and he craved a quick fix.

Picking up speed, he strode towards the seedier parts of Ledforth. Darkness inhabited the doorways and alleyways. As he headed towards Mill Street, he touched the knife – caressing the cold steel with shaking fingers. He focused his mind on the thrill ahead. The predatory hunger excited him. Filled him.

He spotted a huddled figure standing next to a lamp-post. As he approached, she straightened with a flick of her hair and a forward thrust of her hips. The orange glow from the light above danced across her barely concealed cleavage. He waited as she mechanically quoted her rate to him; her cheap perfume assaulting his nose. The thud of her knee-high boots accompanied the creak of PVC as she led him around the side of a building, into a private courtyard. Music blared out from a nearby club.

Probably puzzled by his lack of movement, she pressed against him and, unzipping her top, placed his hand over a breast. Her cold flesh shuddered at his touch. He squeezed hard and was rewarded by a squeal.

'So, you like to be rough, do you?' If the sudden pain had surprised or frightened her, she hid it well. Her breathing quickened as he shrugged off his large black coat, revealing his bare chest. Ignoring her protests and lewd talk, he turned away to place the coat on a pile of empty beer crates. Not in the line of fire.

She stepped close again, offering her fingers for him to suck. He resisted the impulse to bite on the red painted nails. As she ran her other hand down his body, along the outline of his tattoo, she didn't see him palm the knife. Easing his penis out of his trousers, she didn't see him grip the handle and hold the knife aloft.

He grabbed a handful of hair and traced her hairline with his lips. 'Kneel. Put your hands behind your back,' he whispered, his voice thick and slurred. He couldn't wait any longer. Thrusting the blade downwards, he plunged it into her body. *Yes. And again. Yes. Yes.*


He had been alive; invigorated by the rush of sensations. But, as the intensity died, so did his elation. All these quick, meaningless killings were powerful, but the images soon diminished.

Angling the rear-view mirror, he stared at his reflection. Except for small splashes of blood, he was flawless. Not even a thin sheen of sweat betrayed him.

His van was the only vehicle left in the small car park. But he checked the dark expanse of tarmac before reaching below his seat and retrieving her bag. After discarding the other contents into a black bin liner, he used one of her wet wipes to clean away the blood on his face. His coat and gloves would hide the large splashes until he got home, and if he did get stopped he was confident he'd wiped clean his shoes sufficiently to fool any passing glance.

Happy he had left nothing to incriminate himself, he drove out of the parking lot. He wished he could see the horror on the face of whoever found her. Maybe it would be a young couple, sneaking out of the club planning to discover each other, who tumbled over the thing now only fit for nightmares.

He was frustrated he wouldn't see his handiwork uncovered, but that was one luxury he couldn't afford. At least the whore had served her purpose. With his feelings for Sarah in tight rein, he was able to think clearly again.

Naked in front of the full-length mirror, he studied his body. Despite the poor light offered by the antique standard lamp there was no denying his fine physique. The shadows emphasised the hardness of his muscles. The dark contours rippled as he flexed his broad chest.

The blood had dried, merging with his tattoos. Raising his hand to his mouth he licked his fingers, one by one, before slowly running his hand across his chest. Preening after the kill. It amused him that he was behaving like a predator in the wild, and he smiled at his reflection.

His hand froze on the way to his mouth, and his breath stopped. Transfixed, he stared in horror at the subtle changes happening in front of him. He whimpered, as his father's eyes glowered back. The rest of his reflection unchanged, there was no mistaking that hateful glare. They pierced his own, rooting him to the spot. A warm wetness splashed against his leg, heightening his humiliation.

'Noooo!'

His shout rang in his ears, as his immobilised legs broke free. He was too late. In the few seconds it took to reach the mirror he could hear his father's voice. It echoed all around him, crushing his mind. Dragging him into the past.

---

'You stupid little bastard! Can't you do anything right?'

The large, burly hands clamped down on him. 'No, Daddy. Please.'

'I'll teach you to forget your scales, you little good-for-nothing. Do you think I enjoy this? Standing here every day listening to your pathetic attempts?'

Coarse fingertips dug into his scrawny shoulders, making him cry out in agony. 'Daddy, stop. You're hurting me.'

The grip tightened, pressing him mercilessly on the unforgiving surface of the wooden piano stool. The top of his bare legs, not protected by the flimsy grey material of his school shorts, scraped along the rough splintered surface. Hot tears spilled. And when he thought his spine would break, the pressure was released.

'We're paying for these fucking lessons… no, wait, I'm sorry… I should say your granddad and mum are paying.'

The slurred voice was climbing the octaves his shaking fingers had messed up.

'I'm indebted to my whole bloody family,' a hand banged on the top of the piano, 'and I can't create anything to sell because I've got to listen to your crap every day.'

The alcohol-laden breath surrounded him, and he flinched as the unshaven face was thrust next to his. 'The least you can do is get it right,' his father growled into his ear.

He blinked, struggling desperately to focus on the keys. Snot dripped from his nose. The first note. The second. The third note, harsh and dissonant, caused a sharp intake of breath from behind him.

———

Slumped on his bedroom floor, he relived the tortured memories of his past. His fingers throbbed with the rebirth of suffering. The slamming of the piano lid had broken two fingers on his left hand and three on his right. But, the lessons had continued.

He had clear memories of his mother sitting by the large bay window during his music lessons, her long dark hair capturing the light beautifully. But the softness had always been mockingly out of reach. As if her real presence had inhabited somewhere far away, out of that house.

When he was punished, there was his mother with a sad, distant expression. Why hadn't she loved him? If only she had looked at him he would have known she had loved him, or even cared enough to pity him. The only time their eyes would lock was when it was her turn. When it was her who wanted punishing.

On his twelfth birthday, she had left them both. And ten years ago, he had gone to find her. It was with a sense of wonder that he had shared her final moments of life. Her beautiful eyes had never left his, and he had seen first recognition, then acceptance. The intimacy had overwhelmed him. Those few hours he had spent with his mother were happy ones. He remembered brushing her hair and talking to her, as she lay beside him on the bed. Her limp, cold hand in his. At the end she had embraced his existence. A single tear pooled at the corner of his eye. It was all he had wanted.

· · ·

It was careless of him to crack the mirror. Feeling the small cuts on his hand, it was strange he couldn't now remember how it had happened. He dismissed the mystery quickly. It wasn't important.

Having showered, he needed food and sleep. It was always the same after his hunting trips. Ravenous hunger, then exhaustion.

As soon as he and Sarah were together there'd be no reason for him to kill. She'd show him other things he could be good at. He grinned at this. Toying with his dressing-gown cord, he fantasised being with her. He could see her in this kitchen, cooking a meal for them both. She would be preparing vegetables, and he would be sitting at the table, reading his evening paper. Happy to be together in silence. He imagined her slim curves, accentuated by a clean white apron tied around her small waist, and the way she swayed slightly at each chop of the knife. The taste of her perfume as he crept up behind her and grabbed her. How she would pretend to be cross. Scolding him, before melting into his arms, fierce longing on her face.

He gasped as the excitement grew, the need for food forgotten. Twisted over both his hands, the cord became taut. His knuckles whitened. Closing his eyes, he saw her full lips part and heard her moan his name, as he kissed her neck. He savoured the slightly salty taste of her soft skin, flicking his tongue in and out of her ear. He gently cupped her firm breasts.

Not wanting to spoil the fantasy he kept his eyes closed as he shrugged loose his dressing gown. His hand moved faster as images aroused him. The terrified face of the blonde prostitute. The elite group of special ladies. And, as he climaxed – Sarah. Sar-rah. His angel.

# CHAPTER TWELVE

Peter grimaced as he tried for the umpteenth time to get comfortable. He was too tall, and too damn old, for sofas. Knowing it was unlikely he would manage even one more wink of sleep, he levered his legs out of retirement. A whiff of cat rose with him.

He hadn't heard anything from Sarah since she'd retired to Anne's spare bedroom. Hopefully, she'd managed to drift off okay, and the nightmares had stayed away.

They'd left a light on low in the kitchen in case Anne came home, and as Peter glanced around, he spotted the photo of Sarah and Anne. Not completely severed from his own bad dreams, he involuntarily compared the cheerful image to those women who adorned their gruesome wall of fame.

*Christ.* Peter padded over to take a closer look, praying his tired brain was playing tricks. He covered the rest of the picture with his hands, leaving Sarah's eyes staring out at him.

Of course, he'd already realised Sarah, like many others, fitted the killer's type: brunette with hazel eyes. The likeness was not glaringly obvious: all the women had different face and body profiles.

But those eyes. Here. Now. Those eyes looked exactly like all the ones that had haunted him over the past nine months.

*Careful, Peter. You're getting obsessed. Seeing things that aren't there.*

He'd thought he had known Sarah from somewhere. Could this be why? Feeling ridiculous, Peter used his phone to take a close-up of the holiday snap. When he compared her image to the ones at work, he would probably see that, apart from a vague likeness, there was nothing else there. Let's face it, he wouldn't be the first detective to get so embroiled in a case that his obsessiveness ripped into his personal life.

It had to be his imagination working overtime. Nudging him. In case he lost the urgency.

He sighed. Time to admit the truth. He didn't think Carl was the killer. No, it was stronger than that: he'd bet his life The Beautician was still at large.

Not wishing to wake Sarah prematurely, Peter took his phone into the bathroom and pulled the door to. Despite the early hour Doug answered on the second ring. 'This better be important,' he growled. 'Don't you ever sleep?'

'It's on my list of things to try on my next day off.'

'And until then we both have to suffer,' replied Doug ungraciously. 'Give us a sec.'

While he waited, Peter sat on the toilet lid and rubbed his tight leg muscles. They'd been sore since his stair run the previous day. Damn, thinking about his sudden exercise brought to mind the hurried conversation he'd had with Khenan. He'd forgotten that he'd promised to go and see him. Fine friend he was. He'd pop in for a chat as soon as he could.

'Right. Now I've had a piss, I'm all yours. Tell Dougie what the matter is. Your damsel in distress proved too much for you to handle?'

Peter had spoken to Doug last night and had only told him he was visiting a friend who needed a little help with something. Was he always so transparent?

'It was interesting,' he replied carefully, not wanting to go into any details until events were clearer in his own head. 'But that's not why I've phoned. Did you learn any more info from the barman last night?'

'Nothing concrete. He saw a man he claims was Carl arrive at around ten o'clock Wednesday night. Apparently he'd been in a few times in the past. Always sat alone, not speaking to anyone. But, this night in question, another man joined him. They'd had a busy period and the barman can't be certain when the second man had entered the pub.'

'And they definitely left together?'

'So he says. I left DC Adams to look through the CCTV,' replied Doug yawning. 'Sorry, but some idiot woke me up.'

Peter ignored the dig. 'Did they look like they were friends?'

'This is the curious part. The barman said that our pal in intensive care was acting nervous. Fidgety. I quote "I never once saw 'im smile, but that night he looked as though he was t'meet the devil 'imself".'

'And did he describe this devil?'

'No horns and a tail, I'm afraid. Very ordinary: tall, grey hair, beard. He thinks he was in his late sixties, but he didn't take much notice. Have you got something?'

'Only a bad taste in my mouth. Are you in the mood to annoy our super?'

'Am I ever?' said Doug. 'Do I take it then you don't think Carl's our man?'

He should've known Doug would have come to the same conclusion. 'Let's just say I'm not going to sit around waiting for him to confess, if he ever can.'

Distracted by a noise, Peter left the bathroom and saw Sarah standing next to the sofa. He gestured to his phone, mouthing 'sorry'. The last thing he'd wanted to do was to wake her up.

'It's okay,' she mouthed back. 'Coffee?'

He nodded. 'I've got to go now, Doug, but I'll see you at the station in about... two hours.' It was six o'clock now, and that would give him time to go home, shower and change.

'Oh whoopee, a late morning,' muttered Doug sarcastically. 'Don't even start to tell me the virtues of seeing a new day begin, or I promise it'll be your last.'

And then Doug hung up, leaving Peter grinning at the phone. 'I love you too, you big shitbag.'

'Thanks. You certainly have a way with words. Or is it me who's bringing out the best in you?'

Laughing to cover his embarrassment, he joined Sarah in the kitchen area. 'Would it hurt if I admitted that my love had been directed elsewhere?'

'Someone else is your precious shitbag? Oh, how could you?' moaned Sarah, feigning anger, yet not succeeding in keeping a smile off her face. 'And I thought you were a nice guy.'

'Don't be deceived by my Yorkshire charms. I'm a scoundrel.' Peter continued to joke around, even as pictures of Sarah's panicked face from the night before came to him. His heartbeat quickened as he watched her make breakfast. Would she have another vision, or hallucination, or whatever the hell they were?

Sarah, however, appeared relaxed. And, she was even interested in hearing, over toast, about Doug and the past scrapes they'd had the misfortune of sharing. 'He sounds quite a character,' she said finally.

'We're the real Dalziel and Pascoe of the district.'

'I won't ask which one is which.'

'Hey. I wasn't going to mention your Winnie The Pooh pyjamas, but...'

'Are you disrespecting The Pooh?' Sarah frowned, pointing a finger at him.

'Never! I promise that would never happen.'

It was great to see Sarah laughing, and he found himself

enjoying her company immensely, but all too soon it was time for him to leave. And it was with a sense of sadness that he returned to his world where a happy-go-lucky bear had no place. Sarah also seemed sorry he had to go. Or maybe that was wishful thinking.

---

Peter scanned the room. Most of the team had been on board from the first murder, but there were a few new faces belonging to detectives rustled in from other areas to help. The fresh anticipation he'd seen on Friday had dwindled, replaced by a dogged determination.

'The toxicology report is clear,' he continued. 'Pamela wasn't drugged before strangulation. The assailant broke into her house via the back door and, more than likely, attacked her when she was asleep. He knelt on her arms, preventing her from fighting back. And, like the previous murders, the patterns of bruises around the neck suggest he applied pressure then released and then squeezed again, continuing until she finally died. He prolonged her death deliberately.'

On the front table, a young DC breathed in sharply. Their new researcher was clearly struggling with the reality of the last few hours of Pamela's life.

'There were no signs of sexual assault,' Peter added, his gaze met briefly with that belonging to the young officer, 'and after he killed her, he applied her own make-up to her face and dressed her in clothes and a scarf from her wardrobe. This all follows his MO.

'What is slightly incongruous is the stiletto shoe jammed on her right foot. There's no doubt it is a pair to the one found underneath Carl's car seat, but it's too small and Pamela's friends have told us she didn't wear high heels due to a bad back. They look new, so one of the jobs to be allocated will be to track where they were purchased from, and by whom. The only fingerprints on them are from our suspect, but we need to be thorough on this.

'Now, according to the coroner's report, she died sometime between Tuesday night and Wednesday morning, and we know Carl Cooper was definitely in the area Wednesday evening. He was seen in The Black Bull, a public house on London Road, a short walk from Pamela's house. He arrived alone, ordered a beer, and sometime after ten was joined by an unknown white male, whose description can be found on page five.' He paused while there was a rustle of pages.

'The CCTV images from the pub have given us something interesting.' Peter gestured at the large screen to his right. 'We can see Carl leaving the pub at five past eleven and walking towards his car. He's alone but before he gets in the Astra... see... he turns round and waves to someone on the other side of the car park.'

'Someone who isn't in the camera's field of vision,' Doug grumbled.

'No, but if you look here,' Peter pointed to the bottom left of the screen, 'now!' he cried, stopping the footage. A fuzzy form had appeared. While the camera had swiped left it had caught a figure running out of the car park. 'Could you enhance that at all?' he asked their computer technician.

'I'll give it my best shot, sir.'

'There's something else. Moving the images on two minutes you can see the top of a silver car as it passes the pub, travelling fast.'

'Going in the same direction as Carl,' said Doug. 'We'll run through the area's automatic number plate recognition system footage for that night, if we're lucky their CCTV cameras may have picked up our mysterious silver car.'

Peter nodded. 'Even if the driver turns out to be an innocent in all this, they may be able to shed light on how Carl ended up in the bottom of a ditch after skidding off the road. Where he was found by our good citizen Mr Warrington, who parked in a lay-by planning to conduct close liaisons with not Mrs Warrington but his secretary, Miss Webster. A fact he unwillingly divulged in a second interview.'

'Lucky bugger,' someone muttered, causing a round of laughs.

Peter waited until everyone had quietened down. 'So far, enquiries into Carl's recent activities have revealed nothing useful. He was at lectures during the day and his housemates have no idea why he later decided to borrow his friend's car. We know his was at a local garage having a new clutch fitted, but we don't know who he was planning to meet. And, incidentally, his housemates haven't had a bad word to say about him.

'IT haven't found anything on Carl's computer to link him with the other victims, however it's obvious he's spent a lot of time lately looking through folders of photos of his sister at various social functions. It may prove to be nothing, but I would like someone to keep searching through them in case something or someone pops out.'

'I hope the bastard never wakes up.'

'I would agree wholeheartedly,' replied Peter, unsure where the heckle came from, 'when I'm one hundred per cent sure he's our man.'

He raised his hand to the murmurs around the group. 'I know, I want to believe we have him too, but I'll be honest, I have misgivings about it. If he isn't guilty then maybe he knows who is. Someone will have to go back to the pub tonight. We need to ID the man he was seen with.'

Peter had to give the superintendent credit: up until now he had sat silent, not offering any contribution to the briefing. But a progression from sitting back in his chair to leaning forward, and the increase in fidgeting, suggested he wouldn't stay quiet for long.

Indeed, a few minutes later Superintendent Crosby stood up. 'Can I have a word, please, DCI Graham?'

Exchanging a glance with Doug, Peter briefly contemplated the wisdom of staying where he was, forcing the super into a public showdown rather than a private interrogation.

Crosby didn't give him a chance. As he reached the door, he spoke without looking behind. 'In my office.' And although he was speaking softly, there was no mistaking that this was a command.

Peter sighed. 'DS Marsden will finish up and allocate today's jobs. I won't be long.' At least, he hoped not. The last thing he wanted was to be taken off the case.

As he walked out it took all his control not to throw something hard at Doug: the humming of Chopin's *Funeral March* wasn't funny.

———

The other incident room, housing the team working on the prostitute killings, was a hive of activity. With Crosby's warnings ringing in his ears, Peter searched the room for Khenan. He spotted the Jamaican detective leaning over a table, engrossed in conversation with a female colleague. They were huddled together, studying a large map.

He looked up and waved Peter across. 'Hey, thought you'd forgotten about me.' Not waiting for an apology, Khenan was quick to do the introductions. 'I don't believe you've met DS Louise Clark before. She's transferred to us from York. Lou, this is DCI Peter Graham.'

Peter smiled at the blonde-haired sergeant. 'Welcome to the station. I hope he's not teaching you any bad habits.'

'Well, not yet. But there's plenty of time.' Louise turned towards Khenan. 'I'll wait for you downstairs. Nice to meet you, sir,' she added, nodding at Peter.

Khenan watched her go and picked his bag up from the table. 'I'm afraid duty calls. I don't know if you've heard, but our prostitute killer has struck again – a girl on Mill Street. She was found in the last hour, so we're off to the scene now.'

'He's accelerating then.' Peter did a quick calculation in his head. 'It's, what, ten days since the last one? Look, I'm sorry I didn't get back to you. Is there anything I can do now?'

'It's okay, it was nothing specific. I wanted to discuss some aspects of these murders with you, make sure we weren't missing anything.' Khenan paused, before sounding more upbeat. 'But maybe we'll get more answers today. There's all the signs he's beginning to lose control and getting sloppy: he left us quite a collection of prints ten days ago.'

Khenan sighed. 'All bloody useless so far, though. At least, it doesn't sound like your man is going anywhere fast.' He slapped Peter on the back. 'You're doing all right, mate. Or maybe not,' he added, seeing his face. 'Listen, I better go. When we're free of all this crap, why don't you come round for a meal? Kaleisha is looking forward to one of your dodgy bedtime stories. Her words not mine.'

'Your daughter is a tough critic,' Peter answered with a smile.

Rather than following Khenan, Peter sat on a nearby table and stared at the whiteboards that dominated one wall of the room. Although technology played a large part in modern policing it still came down to timelines and flow charts. The first mark on a board at the beginning of an investigation was like a starter firing his gun to announce the onset of a race: a marathon between predator and prey. Every single question mark and dead-end symbolised a whole heap of shit that wasn't known.

One team needed a breakthrough soon. He had to agree with the superintendent, however reluctantly, that the public was losing faith in them. They had two killers and no significant leads.

Crosby had agreed to give him time to follow up on other

avenues, but not before grimly reminding him the clock was ticking.

Whilst studying the other team's boards, not for the first time Peter toyed with the idea the killers knew each other. After the first call girl had been found, there was speculation as to whether The Beautician was the culprit. No one wanted to believe they had another serial killer on their hands, and yet the ferocity of the attack dictated this wasn't going to be a one-time offender. It was the viciousness that had convinced Peter there were two separate murderers. The MOs were completely different: the prostitute killings motivated by anger and sexual gratification, whereas The Beautician appeared in complete control of his emotions.

It was The Beautician's control that had given him nightmares. There was no sense of increased urgency. What did the three-month gap between each murder mean? Was he a frequent traveller and leading a normal life in between? Could it be his twisted need was satisfied so he didn't feel any desire to deviate from his macabre timetable? It would make him highly unusual.

In contrast, the prostitute killer's pattern was escalating. Peter remembered the first girl had been stabbed to death last September, two months after they had discovered the second victim of The Beautician. The next one had been attacked in December.

A game of 'you do one' then 'I'll do one' between the two had gripped the town and surrounding areas. Now the prostitute killer was breaking the pattern: murdering two in quick succession.

What if he was wrong, and it wasn't a case of them playing one off against the other?

Peter was so engrossed that he didn't see Doug enter the room. He jumped at the sound of his voice. 'I thought you might be here. The doctors have woken Carl up. He's not making any sense, but fingers crossed he'll be able to talk to us soon.'

Peter was silent for a moment, prompting Doug to ask, 'Are you okay?'

'Yeah. Sorry, I was thinking.'

'Anything interesting?'

'No. Just going over old ground.' Peter sighed. 'I hope you're right about Carl. We're in dire need of fresh earth.'

# CHAPTER THIRTEEN

O h God. Something was wrong. Sarah's pale face wore a sad, distant look as if what she had seen was beyond her comprehension. Barely glancing at him, she leaned heavily on the door, waiting for him to pass into the house.

'What is it, Sarah? What's happened?'

She had been okay this morning when they agreed to meet up at her home later. Maybe coming into the empty house on her own had sparked off another episode.

Wordlessly, she gestured for him to lead the way through the door on his right. Nerves jangling, Peter entered the room. And, at first, everything appeared ordinary. A large bay window made the rather messy lounge bright and airy.

Being a fan of Victorian architecture, with its high ceilings and cornices, he immediately liked this room. He liked how the large, dark bookcases that covered one wall, rather than domineering the décor, blended into the homely feel. His town flat was convenient, and, yes, the view from his balcony was nice (if you didn't mind rooftops), but it was too modern and characterless for him. He was processing this as his gaze fell upon the cluttered coffee table. What he had initially taken for piles of magazines he could now see were, in fact, photographs.

There were group shots – he presumed they were family – and those taken at various holiday locations. A dark-haired, clean-shaven man featured smiling in many. But they all had the one thing in common: a figure had been cut out.

Sickened, Peter stepped over the discarded albums, and walked over to the window, where Sarah stood, silently watching his reaction.

'Our wedding photos were also...' Her bottom lip quivered, and he reached for her. He held her tight, feeling the distress sweep through her.

Over her shoulder, he could see the framed pictures on the mantelpiece were all violated in the same way. Sarah had gone from all her photographs. Who on earth would do that?

Sarah stirred in his arms, and as he loosened his grip she pulled away. He sensed her reluctance to let him in too close.

'Do you know who did this, Sarah? Have you called the police?'

She shook her head. 'Before you arrived I was sitting here trying to understand.' Using the flats of her hands, she wiped her eyes angrily. 'Why would anyone do this?'

'When did you arrive home?' he asked, wondering if she'd disturbed the intruder.

'About an hour ago. I spent the rest of the morning at Anne's. Her brother, Richard, had arrived back from Dumfries. He's really worried about Anne too. We both met with the police at her flat, then I drove here. All the doors were locked, and the house was empty.'

'Do you have a spare set of keys?'

'I had a copy cut of my front door key, but it's in the kitchen drawer. I've already checked and it's still there. Mrs Wilson, the elderly woman who lives next door, used to have it, but I took the spare back when I accidently left mine at work last year. I keep forgetting to give it back.'

Peter searched her house and checked the doors and windows. Not finding anything amiss he was about to return downstairs when he saw the loft hatch above her hall landing. He couldn't see any easy way of accessing the small door, so he shouted to Sarah, 'How do you get into your attic?'

Receiving no immediate reply, he was heading downstairs when Sarah appeared from the sitting room and pointed at the understairs cupboard. 'There's a small stepladder in there. The plan is to eventually fit a proper pull-down ladder but I– Do you think someone's in the attic?' she finished in alarm.

'I wouldn't think so,' he answered calmly, so not to panic her, 'but as it's a mystery how anyone got in, it would be silly if I didn't check.'

'Oh my God, I didn't even think about the attic. Apart from a couple of old cases, and a few boxes of clutter, it's empty.'

Following him back up the stairs, Sarah watched as he climbed the ladder and pushed open the hatch door. 'The last time anyone went up was a few months ago when I asked Bryan, a friend of mine from work, to take up a box of Mike's things.'

Peter could see why she would need help: he was over six foot and had to stand on the top of the ladder to poke his head and chest into the loft space.

'There should be a torch near you,' Sarah called up. 'Bryan left one for me in case I needed it.'

Silently thanking his lucky stars that no one had yet lunged out of the darkness at him (perched precariously as he was, any assailant would definitely have the upper hand), Peter felt to his left. At first his hand encountered nothing and, as the light from the hall didn't reach far beyond the hatch, he had to pat blindly. Finding the torch, he shone the beam all around the attic, lighting up the exposed rafters of the pitched roof. The floor was a patchwork of insulation criss-crossed with wooden joists, but a few boards had been laid to provide a platform for storage. Sarah was right: apart from a few boxes near the hatch, some suitcases and larger boxes pushed to the far end, and scraps of wood and rope close to him, the space was empty.

Should he heave himself up and have a closer look at the far brick wall? He'd heard stories about intruders gaining access to properties through holes in shared attic walls, especially in old, terraced houses like this one. Although, as Sarah lived in an end terrace her only next-door neighbour was Mrs Wilson, and she hardly sounded like burglar material.

'Everything okay?'

Peter hesitated, then after another sweep of the torch he turned off the beam. 'Yeah, it's all fine up here.' He couldn't imagine anyone using this as a quick escape route. By the time he'd moved the hatch door back in place and climbed down the ladder, Sarah had disappeared.

Returning to the sitting room, he found her crouched by the wooden coffee table.

'I guess I should be grateful they're all backed up on the computer.'

'Where did you keep the albums?'

Seeing Sarah apparently mesmerised by the photos he tried again. 'Sarah, where would he have got the albums from?'

'Oh, sorry. Over there, in the bookcase. Bottom shelf. Mike would tease me because I still insisted on printing all our photos out: a practice from the Dark Ages, according to him.'

Peter moved towards the bookshelves. He saw the space the albums had originally occupied; the rest of the shelves crammed with books. Taking his mobile out of his pocket, he scanned the rest of the room. 'Anything else missing, or disturbed?'

'No, I don't think so.'

'I'll have a forensic sent here, see if we can get something.'

.   .   .

'Did you say 12 Blakeley Road, sir?'

'Yes, that's right. Is there anything wrong?' asked Peter, impatiently. He had moved into the hallway to phone the station, and he didn't want to leave Sarah any longer than necessary.

'Well, we have a car heading over to that address already, sir.'

'What?' He must be needed somewhere else. Wondering whether Sarah had any family she could stay with, he almost missed what the handler said next.

'The occupant – a Mrs Sarah Knowles – is connected to a missing person report.'

Damn. If they were chasing it up then there's been a development to do with Anne. He had to know whether it was one Sarah could cope with hearing right now.

In his hurry to check on Sarah before rushing out to intercept the officers, he brushed too close to the hall table, sending a large handbag flying to the floor.

'Oh hell,' he muttered, squatting to retrieve the bag and its spilled contents. As he shovelled make-up, tissues and loose change his hand touched something cold and metallic. Curious, he delved further, and found a big pair of scissors jammed down, its point snagged against the black lining. And next to the scissors was a photograph, screwed up and pushed to the bottom of the bag.

He was digesting this unexpected find as Sarah appeared in the doorway. Seeing her opened bag in his hand she stared at him unsmiling. Something in her expression sent a shiver down his spine, but in a second it was gone, and he wasn't sure that he hadn't imagined it.

Realising the interior of the bag was facing away from her he proceeded to scoop the rest of her belongings inside. He smiled, hoping she had missed the guilt that must have crossed his face. 'Sorry, I knocked it off as I was walking by.' He handed the black leather bag to her. 'More haste, less speed.'

Now she smiled back, increasing his confusion. 'Are they sending someone?' she asked.

He nodded, moving towards the front door as he heard car doors slam. 'I need to pop out for a few moments. I'll explain when I get back. Will you be okay?'

It was her turn to nod, her puzzlement clear.

———

He bunched his fists in anger. What was he doing there? Why him? *He shot the detective. The first bullet caught him in the back, its impact sending him flying forwards down the steps. The second entered above his hairline and shattered his skull.*

A scuffling at his feet destroyed the image, and he kicked out in frustration. A satisfying yelp rewarded him.

'Stupid mutt.' One of these days he would enjoy punishing the sniffling little runt.

Looking out through the gap in the net curtains, he saw the man he had recognised as Chief Inspector Graham, who had reached the police car and was talking to two officers. Graham turned and gestured towards the house, and for one awful moment he thought he was pointing at him.

Why had she called him, of all people? Why not...? Well, it was too fucking late now. Panic gripped. What the hell was going on? He was sure they couldn't know about him, but why DCI bloody Graham?

He let the lace curtain fall back as he heard a movement behind him.

'I think Barrie wants a walk, Auntie,' he said loudly, scooping up the struggling dog. 'He's making an awful fuss. I won't be long, then we can have a nice cup of tea before you have one of your naps.'

———

Sarah turned to face them as they followed her into the kitchen.

'Have you found her?' she asked the young blond officer. 'You said you had news.'

He stared at her curiously. Self-conscious, she ran her hand through her hair and motioned them to be seated. She must look a sight. Finding all her photo albums ruined had been a horrible shock.

No one spoke until everyone was sitting around the dining table: Peter took the seat beside her and the two constables (she couldn't remember their names) sat opposite them. What had Peter told them about why he was here?

The older officer said, 'DCI Graham has informed us of your break-in, and we understand this is a difficult time for you, so I'll come straight to the reason why we're here. Your friend's car has been found. It was reported abandoned on Abbeyfield Road. Can you think of any reason why she would park on that road? Does she know anybody who lives there?'

'I don't think so. But it was on her way back home. She dropped me off after work on Saturday morning,' Sarah explained. 'And then she could have driven up Abbeyfield Road to bypass the traffic.'

'There's something else.' Reaching into his pocket, he pulled out a small clear plastic bag containing a piece of jewellery. Sarah leaned forward, heart pounding. 'We found this broken silver locket on the driver's seat. Anne Baxter's family didn't recognise it, and we wondered if you would be able to confirm it belongs to her.'

The officer held out the bag. She didn't move to take it from him, and he placed it gently on the wooden table and slid it closer to her.

Her mouth dry, she reached for the necklace. The locket was exquisite, engraved with tiny rosebuds. She understood why her mum had loved it. The rush of blood roared in her ears. Her hand shaking, she picked it up and turned it over, half expecting to see the smudges left by her mum's fingers.

Broken. Her mum would've been so upset.

Peter was talking from far away. Asking her what the matter was. She couldn't reply. This was her mother's locket. But that was impossible. Broken. Why was it broken?

'Sarah?'

She squeezed her eyes shut. Someone was screaming. Clamping her hands over her ears, she willed them to stop. Shut up! Why didn't they shut up?

# CHAPTER FOURTEEN

'How is she?'

Matt was scared. The unspoken fears he'd kept hidden last night now mocked him. When he did finally meet Peter's worried eyes he took a moment to weigh up his options. At the flat he had formed a favourable opinion of the policeman; Sarah obviously trusted him. But how much of her background had she told Peter?

'I've given her something to help her sleep. She's suffered a big shock.' Matt hesitated, before asking, 'How much do you know about Sarah and her family?'

'Hardly anything at all,' admitted Peter. 'We met three days ago at the hospital, and then at the police station when she reported the disappearance of her friend.' He looked apologetic, as if his brief acquaintance with Sarah fell short of what was required. 'She's told me her husband was a fireman, and that he died in a warehouse fire, but that's it.'

'She's a special person. I don't want to see her get hurt.' Matt saw his message was being understood. If Peter were passing through, then now would be the time to leave.

Sitting on the edge of one of the big armchairs, Peter didn't flinch under Matt's scrutiny. 'Neither do I,' he said quietly.

'Okay then. I think Sarah is suffering from repressed memory.' Matt paced up to the bay window; his statement lay uneasily between the two men.

'Repressed memory of what?'

Matt hesitated, unsure of where to start. Viewed through the vertical slats of Sarah's blind the dull afternoon offered him no rays of inspiration. A man, with his dog, walked briskly by. Its lead taut, the little dog was being dragged along. Matt imagined he could hear the scraping of nails as the poor dog's paws scrambled for hold on the wet pavement. He understood exactly how the dog felt.

The pedestrian glanced up from under his hood, and for a fraction of a second their eyes met. Embarrassed, Matt turned away, moving back to the centre of the room.

'She was born Sarah Campbell, daughter of Chief Constable Oliver Campbell. When Sarah was eleven years old, her mother was killed, murdered in their home, and her brother left for dead.'

'Bloody hell,' Peter exclaimed shakily, 'I remember that case. It happened before I joined the force, but we talked about it in training.'

'Then you'll know they were found by Sarah's father, when he returned from work. Shortly before he arrived home, Sarah had been dropped off by friends after going swimming and, finding the front door locked, waited for him in the back garden, oblivious to what had happened in the house.'

Waiting for Peter to process what he had learnt, Matt allowed his mind to remember back seven years when Sarah was sitting opposite him in his surgery. Fingers entwined, watching him read this distressing period of her life, readily admitting that this current, bleak bout of depression was likely related to losing her mother in such a cruel way. And yet, had there been any other signs that it was more than depression she was fighting? Signs he had missed. Even when he had reason to look for them.

'They never found the killer and wasn't the brother brain damaged?'

Matt nodded, sadly. 'He was left with a severe head injury.'

'Let me get this straight,' said Peter, 'you're saying these recurring dreams and flashbacks she's having are of real events. Finding the body and coming face to face with her mother's killer?'

'I think so. You must understand Sarah believed she was telling the truth all those years ago. It isn't going to be easy for her to come to terms with the fact that she wasn't.'

Peter seemed sceptical. 'How do we know it isn't these new memories which are false? How realistic is it that these are more reliable than her old ones? What did the police counsellor say at the time?'

'She never saw one. Her father refused to subject her to anything that would distress her more. She appeared happier not talking about it, and so she was left to grieve with her father.'

Seeing Peter's shocked expression, Matt felt obliged to stick up for the late Mr Campbell. 'Don't judge him too harshly. His children were all he had left. To his way of thinking, running away and making a fresh start down south was salvation for them all. Sarah told me from that time, until he died from pancreatic cancer twelve years later, he managed to provide a comfortable and happy existence. And I believed her.'

Unable to give Peter all the answers he wanted Matt sighed, frustrated at his own lack of experience in dealing with this sort of thing. 'This type of memory dissociation is complex, but not impossible. Especially if someone has suffered an overwhelming harrowing experience. A few of my colleagues have worked with similar cases where repressed memories have resurfaced, turning their clients' lives upside down.'

Removing his glasses, he searched his pockets for a tissue to clean them. So automatic was the ritual he barely registered he was doing it.

'Sarah first began struggling with depression seven years ago, a short time before she met Mike. Nothing serious. Insomnia and uncharacteristic mood swings prompted her to see me. Our counselling sessions, and a brief rest from work, soon helped her to bounce back. Of course, Mike probably played a greater part in her recovery.'

'And you didn't see any of this coming, not even in your counselling sessions?'

'I don't lead my patients. Sarah showed an unwillingness to allow me to probe too deeply. I didn't push her,' retorted Matt, flinching indignantly.

The truth hurt. How long before the extent of his guilt was revealed?

Peter's face softened. 'I'm sorry, Matt. I'm finding this difficult to understand, let alone accept. What will happen now?'

'I would prefer it if we persuaded her to go into hospital for observation. She won't like it but with her mind in the state it is there's no telling what she might see, or do, next.'

Peter stared at him thoughtfully. 'You think it was her who cut up those photographs?'

'From what you told me I think it's likely. Her paranoia, and periods of disorientation, could be her running from the truth.'

'But why now, and not seven years ago when she first came to see you? Don't these things need some sort of trigger?'

'I've been wondering that myself,' replied Matt, surprised at Peter's astuteness. 'Maybe the trauma of losing Mike was enough.

'You probably don't know, but they met in my waiting room. Mike had been suffering from work-related stress, and the fire service's occupational health sent him to me. I said afterwards that I should have billed them both for the twenty minutes they waited together, as it turned out to be the therapy they needed.' He smiled at the memory.

'She continued seeing me on and off for a while and even when she refused my professional help after Mike died, I've checked up on her. I thought she was doing okay.'

Putting his glasses back on, he squirmed as Peter moved from the chair arm and sat on the edge of the cushion with his elbows on knees; steely eyes fixed firmly on him.

'Bullshit!'

'What?' Matt spluttered. Peter had spoken quietly, and he wondered whether he had misheard him.

'I said bullshit. All you've told me is meaningless. Now, I want to hear what you haven't told me: the real reason you think Sarah has these repressed memories.'

Matt was thinking of how to reply when there was a sound of breaking glass. Exchanging shocked looks, they raced into the hallway. If anything happened to Sarah he would never forgive himself.

---

Peter reached the bottom of the stairs first and bounded up them three at a time. The door to Sarah's bedroom was open.

'Sarah, are you okay?' he shouted, lunging into the room. It was empty.

'I'm in the bathroom.' Her voice came from behind him. Turning, he saw Matt disappearing through a doorway.

Peter hesitated, not sure if he should follow in case she needed privacy. However, a few seconds later, Matt herded a sheepish Sarah out onto the landing.

'Come on, let's get you back to bed. You didn't cut yourself, did you?' Matt asked her anxiously.

Sarah shook her head. 'I wanted a drink of water. The glass slipped. That's all. Please, Matt, don't fuss.' She smiled weakly at Peter as she shuffled past. 'My heroes.'

'Now, Sarah, I've given you a sedative; what did I tell you about staying in bed?'

'It won't happen again, doctor.'

Her attempts at lightening the mood didn't fool either of the two men. As she allowed Matt to help her back on her bed, Peter saw a single tear betray her true fragility.

'Sorry I scared you two. I'll behave myself from now on. Matt, can I have a word with Peter? Is that okay?'

Matt studied her, then nodded. 'As long as it's quick: you must rest. Keep it brief,' he warned Peter, as he turned to leave. 'Don't push her,' he added, under his breath.

The door closed, leaving them alone. Her eyes were shut, and she was so still Peter thought she had already fallen asleep. Thinking he should let her rest, Peter took a step backwards.

Sarah opened her eyes and reached out for him. 'Peter?'

'Yes, Sarah. I'm here.' He sat on the edge of the bed.

'Tell Matt he could get a fortune selling this stuff on the street.' Her speech was a little slurred.

'Well, that's an expensive suit he's wearing today... I wonder...?'

Sarah managed the briefest of smiles. 'I need you to do something for me. Contact my Aunt Carolyn. Tell her about the locket, about everything. She'll want to help.' She licked her lips, struggling to continue. 'Her number is on my phone. Show her the locket. She'll recognise it and tell you I'm not crazy.'

After what Matt had told him about Sarah's family, the fuss about the locket made sense. It obviously wasn't her mum's, but in Sarah's confused, messed-up mind...

Taking a deep shaky breath, Sarah pushed up on her elbow. 'I know Matt thinks I cut up those photos. I don't blame him. But I didn't, Peter. I know I didn't. You believe me, don't you?'

Peter told her what she wanted to hear. Hiding his doubts. Betraying her.

Looking relieved, she sank back down. Her eyes closed as

soon as her head touched her pillow. He began to stand up, but Sarah grabbed his arm. 'I'm sorry you've met me when I'm such a fruitcake,' she said.

'You're not–' She stopped him by placing her fingers over his lips. 'Please, let me finish, Peter. I know you've got a lot on your plate right now, and I'll understand if…' her eyes began to droop, 'if you want to walk out of here and not come back.'

Peter took her hand in his. 'You don't get rid of me so easily. You see, if it's all right by you, I'd like to get to know you better – fruitcake or not.'

She snored gently, her breaths long and steady.

# CHAPTER FIFTEEN

After quietly closing Sarah's door so he wouldn't wake her, Peter walked into the bathroom. There was no sign of broken glass, and he guessed that Matt must have already cleared it up. Dousing his face with cold water, he thought about the doctor. The look on Matt's face when he had used Doug's 'bullshit' method of questioning on him was enough for him to know he was right: he was deliberately not telling him something. But what?

The doorbell rang. He grabbed a towel and dried his face vigorously, trying to eliminate any lingering patches of tiredness, and then hurried down the stairs in time to see Matt open the door to a hooded figure.

'Jack!' called Peter, 'Thanks for coming quickly. I owe you one.'

'Normally I'd say no problem, anytime, but we're rushed off our feet.' Shrugging off his wet raincoat, Jack gazed around the hallway curiously. 'There are proper procedures for this sort of thing, you know.'

'Yes, and I really appreciate this.' Peter patted Jack on the shoulder. Seeing Matt standing awkwardly by the door, Peter made the introductions. 'Sorry, Matt. This is Jack, our very own CSI. I wanted him to cast his professional eye around the place, see if there's anything to corroborate Sarah's story.' The men shook hands. 'And, this is Matt, a... friend of the lady of the house.'

Matt blushed at what had been a deliberate hesitation on Peter's part. Until he knew what Matt was hiding, Peter wasn't certain of anything and gaining a small psychological advantage couldn't hurt.

Leaving Matt to squirm, he led Jack into the sitting room. 'To tell you the truth, apart from these photos you can see, there's no evidence of a break-in. There's no obvious points of entry or exit, but this isn't the first time Sarah has thought an intruder may have entered her house.'

Jack set his bag down carefully next to the coffee table. 'This is important to you, isn't it? I feel I should meet this lady who has stolen your affections.'

'Who are you, my mother?' grumbled Peter, trying not to laugh. 'Work now, and talk later.'

'Yes, sir.'

Leaving Jack grinning like a Cheshire cat, Peter lingered in the no-man's land of the hall. Through the kitchen doorway, he saw Matt slumped at the table. How hard should he go in? Time wasn't on his side, and he wanted to find out what Matt was hiding before his police work pulled him away; but then he didn't want to risk alienating the doctor.

Unsure what path to follow, Peter nevertheless joined Matt in the kitchen. He had barely stepped inside the room when Matt spoke. 'I'm sorry. You're right to question whether I'm Sarah's friend. I've let her down, and I'm not sure she'll ever forgive me.'

Peter remained silent. Not wanting to inhibit any chance of honesty, he chose to lean back against the kitchen units rather than sitting down with Matt.

'What I've told you about Sarah is true, but what I didn't tell you is she wasn't alone when she visited me for the first time. For moral support, I guess, she brought along her aunt.'

'Her Aunt Carolyn?' Peter saw Matt's surprise. 'When I was upstairs Sarah asked me to contact her.'

Matt nodded. 'She lives in Devon. Her support was the main reason the family moved there after the murder.

'When we were introduced I had a feeling straight away that she wasn't happy Sarah had come to see me. At the time, I assumed it was the usual mistrust I face in my everyday working life as an interfering busybody.' Looking up at Peter, Matt allowed himself a small smile. 'Most people want to attempt to face their problems alone rather than accept a psychiatrist's help.'

Having had similar misgivings about counselling in the past, Peter shifted uncomfortably. Had Matt sensed something? He felt a short burst of anger towards the doctor at the intrusion; however, when Matt appeared unaware of his discomfort he decided he was being paranoid.

'After I returned her niece to her intact, I thought nothing else about it,' continued Matt, 'so, I was surprised to see Carolyn waiting for me outside my office the next day.

'At first I refused to see her – client confidentiality and all that – but she was adamant she needed to see me. I was intrigued. The woman who had appeared stand-offish in my waiting room was now begging me to see her. Saying she didn't know what else to do. I finally caved in.'

'What did she tell you?'

'Her aunt didn't only tell me, she showed me. She gave me the folder of evidence her brother had entrusted with her before his death. He had made her promise not to tell anybody about any of the contents, especially Sarah, unless his daughter started to show signs of remembering.'

'Remembering what?' Then Peter gasped, horrified. 'Oh my God, the murder. He knew.'

'There was evidence that placed Sarah in their house at the

time of the killing. Somehow Oliver convinced the investigating officers to strike the findings out of the official case file.'

Peter didn't know what to say. How and why had Sarah's father done the unthinkable? Actually withholding evidence about his own wife's murder. 'Fuck.' Breathing out slowly, he tried to stay calm. 'But why?'

'There was a video showing an interview with eleven-year-old Sarah. After watching it I think I understood. Although obviously upset, and clinging onto her father's arm the whole time, she was clear on her story. Their front door was locked so she waited in the summerhouse for her dad, and she wasn't there long when she heard his car in the drive. She describes running around the side of the house to greet him.'

'But it wasn't true,' deduced Peter sadly.

'No. She was in the summerhouse, but she was found by a policewoman, huddled in a corner – cold and uncommunicative. They think she'd been there for over an hour. You can imagine her father's joy, after thinking he'd lost her too.'

'She was allowed to lie?'

'No,' replied Matt firmly. 'You must understand it's not as simple as that. It was as if her brain had given her a story she could cope with. During the interview, when it was suggested to her it hadn't happened the way she was remembering it, she became very distressed. And she then went blank: one moment she was in the room, the next she wasn't. It was like her mind had switched off.'

Peter recalled how Sarah had zoned out at Anne's. He had panicked at seeing her vacant face and not being able to reach her. It would have been torture for a father of a traumatised girl and he must have worried that the next time they might not get her back at all.

Still, Peter found it hard accepting Sarah's father had withheld evidence from the actual crime scene. 'What did they hide?'

'It'll be better if you see it yourself. I phoned Carolyn last night after I left you both. She's on her way here; due sometime this evening.'

He should press Matt into telling him now. Emphasise the deep shit he'd gotten into by not releasing this information to the police. Instead, looking at the doctor sitting at the table, head in his hands, Peter took pity on him. He had an awful suspicion that Matt wanted him to see what was in the evidence folder, so he didn't have to put it into words.

He had to know one thing. 'Were you ever planning to tell Sarah?' he asked, softly. 'Or was this a "wait and see if she explodes" scenario? I expect you'd be able to write a few good papers on such a fascinating case.'

Matt flinched as if he'd struck him. He opened his mouth to maybe protest before changing his mind and closing it without uttering a word.

Having not seen an ashtray earlier Peter had put an unlit cigarette back into his shirt pocket, now he pulled out two and offered one to Matt.

'Er, no, thanks,' Matt appeared surprised, 'I don't smoke. Although it could be a good time to start,' he joked feebly, not looking at Peter. The thin smile disappeared quickly.

'Well, I'll tell you something, it sure isn't a great time to try and quit.' Peter sighed, hesitating before putting the cigarettes back in his pocket. The gesture had been made to mend bridges, but the truth was he was dying for a cigarette right now. In a bid to divert his cravings he straightened up and headed for the kettle.

'Do you want a coffee?' Peter asked. He turned round in time to see Matt raise his head and stare across the kitchen at him.

'Please... black.' Clearing his throat, Matt started again. 'You're right. I should have told Sarah or, at least, suggested she saw someone with more experience with childhood trauma.'

'All these years I've pretended to myself I had Sarah's best interests at heart, and at any sign she was beginning to remember

I would leap in. Do the right thing. The truth is, I was excited by the opportunity to document a real-life case of repressed memories. And, yes, I did write a paper,' he admitted. 'Leaving out the details, of course.'

'Of course,' said Peter acidly.

'But I didn't show it to anyone.' Taking off his glasses, Matt massaged his eyes. 'She and Mike became my friends.'

He sighed, raising his fist as if to punch the table. At the last second he stopped, perhaps realising he had hold of his glasses, and his hand hovered unsteadily as he let them fall unharmed. The lenses made a dull ping as they hit the wood. Thrusting both his hands onto his lap, Matt became silent, his stare fixed on the spectacles.

With one hand on the handle of the kettle, and feeling it reach its boiling point, Peter absurdly wondered whether he would feel the same pent-up energy in Matt if he placed his other hand on his shoulder. As the kettle's switch clicked off, signalling an end to the ferocious bubbling, Peter had the idea that if humans were fitted with a similar automatic off button he'd be out of a job.

He placed the steaming mug of coffee in front of Matt. 'There you go. Look, over the next few days, weeks, Sarah will be mad at you. I'll be mad at you. But I do believe you when you say you did what you thought was right at the time. Sarah will realise that.'

Matt glanced up at Peter gratefully, his thin face naked without his glasses on. The red marks on the bridge of his nose almost matched the redness of his bloodshot eyes. He reached for his drink as Jack entered the kitchen.

'Anything promising?' Peter asked, not hopeful.

'Well, I've finished down here.' Placing his case onto the worktop, Jack began to put the rest of his kit away. 'As well as the photographs and albums, I've powdered the door locks and windows, but because we don't know the points of entry or exit I'm working blind. I'll need everyone's prints for elimination if I do get anything useful.'

'Thanks, Jack. I owe you.'

With the extra distractions Peter had completely forgotten about the things he had glimpsed in Sarah's bag. 'Wait a minute. I have something else for you.'

The bag was nowhere to be seen in the hallway and Peter began to worry that he'd messed up giving it back to Sarah. She would have had plenty of time to hide any incriminating evidence while he was outside talking to the officers.

Incriminating evidence? Was he blaming Sarah then? Matt had told him he was worried she was becoming unstable, but would she destroy all her photos? And cut up her own wedding album?

If he were to make any sense of this, he had to step away. Be more detached. He was already too close.

In her lounge, he walked towards the window and almost tripped over the black bag lying behind the sofa. Sarah must've come here to see where he'd gone. Peter breathed a sigh of relief when he saw the scissors and photo were still there.

Back in the kitchen, Jack deftly placed them into plastic evidence bags. 'I'm afraid I can't promise to rush these through, Peter. What with everything else we've got going.'

'It's okay, I'm grateful you came over, Jack. You've been a great help already.'

As he left the house, Peter cast an uneasy look back. Had he missed anything? Something was bugging him; he just didn't have a clue what it was. But, until they had proof Sarah wasn't imagining an intruder, there was sod-all he could do, and he was needed at the station. Matt was going to stay and had promised to let him know when the aunt arrived. Peter glanced up at Sarah's bedroom window and then, thrusting his hands deep into his pockets, continued down the steps.

# CHAPTER SIXTEEN

P eter was surprised when Sarah opened the door. He had expected her to be in bed sleeping off the drug that Matt had given her a few hours earlier.

'You must be a sucker for punishment,' she said, as she beckoned him in. 'Well, I promise this time there won't be any drama.'

She was wearing a pretty Japanese floral print dress, and her hair was wet and her skin glowing from a recent shower.

As he slipped by her, a scent of flowers wafted towards him, and he was suddenly conscious of how he must look to her. A day's worth of frustration and sweat clung to his suit, and he had, at the very least, a ten o'clock shadow on his face. He reached up to straighten his tie before remembering he had already taken it off in his car. 'How are you feeling? I thought you'd still be asleep.'

'Matt certainly hoped I would be, but once I awoke to the smell of cooking, there was no way I was missing out.'

And there was indeed a lovely aroma in the air. Food had been low on his list of priorities, and he hadn't realised until then how hungry he was. Any sustenance he'd gained from the two slices of bread with a smattering of egg mayonnaise, supposedly their canteen's healthy option sandwich, had vanished long ago.

'I'm a bit shaky,' Sarah admitted, 'but I'm okay. The sleep helped, and so did finding my favourite aunt busy in my kitchen. She arrived this evening. At first I thought you had worked miracles and whisked her up north, and then she tells me Matt phoned her last night.'

Sarah didn't seem angry at this, and Peter guessed they hadn't told her the real reason her aunt had rushed up to see her.

'So long as I'm not expected to drive, or operate heavy machinery, I'll be fine. Although, I now know how our patients feel when we sedate them. To be honest, I feel a bit pissed,' she added, with a grin.

Peter grinned back as she took his arm. 'Mmm, I should have a word with Matt. Here I was thinking a bottle of wine was how to win over a woman's affections.'

'Watch it, Detective Graham,' she warned, hitting him playfully. 'It takes at least a bottle and some cake to win over this girl.'

'I'll bear that in mind.'

Walking into the kitchen, Peter looked uncomfortably at the dining table. Someone had gone to a lot of trouble to set it beautifully, with a red tablecloth and in the centre there was a collection of flickering tea lights. He hoped it wasn't for his benefit as he couldn't stay for long.

The most colourful addition to the room was, however, the woman standing at the oven peering through its glass door anxiously. Her grey hair was tied back with a yellow scarf, and she wore a red apron over a long flowing tie-dyed dress. Numerous bracelets adorned her thin arms and, as she stood up ramrod straight and appraised Peter, she pushed them away from her hands as if they were annoying her.

'I hope you're hungry, Sarah. I wasn't sure about your oven, so

I popped in extra Yorkshire puddings in case they didn't turn out right. I've got enough to feed an army.'

'Well, I may have found another willing volunteer. This is Peter; he's the detective I've been telling you about.'

A smile lingered on the aunt's painted pink lips for a moment then disappeared without reaching her eyes. Peter had a feeling she wasn't pleased to see him.

'How about it, Peter? No one can cook a roast dinner like my Aunt Carolyn.'

'It smells great, and I would love to, but I'm afraid I can't,' he said reluctantly. 'There's a few things I need to chase up at work.'

This was true, but he had also picked up on the slight stiffening of Carolyn's shoulders when Sarah had invited him to stay. In fact, now the prospect of having to share a dinner table with him had vanished, the aunt visibly relaxed.

'Why don't you take some away with you, detective? I'm sure my niece will have Tupperware I can use.' A strong Devonshire accent warmed her speech up despite the coolness in her attitude towards him.

'That would be lovely, thank you.' Peter sat at the table with Sarah. 'Where's Matt?'

'I sent him home,' said Sarah. 'He was driving me mad, fussing around me like a mother hen.'

'There's good reason for that. He's worried about you.' He was annoyed at Matt. He had, after all, assured Peter he would stay to keep an eye on Sarah.

'He's popping back later on, and I promised to call him if I needed anything.' She yawned, then smiled an apology. 'It's the lorazepam. I don't think I'm going to have any trouble sleeping tonight.' She leaned forward and whispered, 'I'm sorry about the candles; my aunt brings her own etiquette with her.'

He was imagining Carolyn having a collection of tea lights and a bright tablecloth stored away in a Mary Poppins tapestry bag for emergencies, when a large Tupperware container was placed in front of him.

'Please dish up for me, Sarah dear. I'll see the detective out.'

'Okay, Auntie.' Sarah grinned at Peter, and when Carolyn was out of earshot said, 'Don't worry, her bark is far worse than her bite. And please tell her I'm all right. She keeps looking at me like she's afraid I'm going to break.'

Rising from the table he followed Carolyn out of the kitchen. But rather than ushering him outside, she pulled him into the living room. She peered furtively over his shoulder while biting the edges of her thumbnail. 'I have to thank you for not telling Sarah about what her father did.'

Peter suddenly understood the subdued welcome.

She stopped attacking her nail and held up her hand to prevent him from interrupting her. 'Matt's told me what you think. And you're right, I've got to tell her. And I will... just not tonight. Tomorrow, I promise.'

She stared anxiously at him, most likely wondering how much pressure he was going to pile on her. When he nodded, the relief softened her features.

'I realise it must have been incredibly hard for you to keep your brother's secret, but Sarah has to know. She has to be able to deal with this.' *Whatever is revealed,* he thought grimly.

'And I'll help her through it.' Carolyn studied him hard. 'What about the photos? Should we be worried about an intruder? Sarah is convinced someone has also been rearranging her stuff.'

He sighed. 'I know. Matt thinks it's these memories messing with her head. But I'll send a couple of uniformed officers here tomorrow so she can file a report.'

She moved to go around him, signalling the clandestine meeting was at an end, but he remained where he was as something else occurred to him. 'Did Sarah tell you about the locket?'

'Yes, she did, and I don't know what to think. I promised I

would go to the station in the morning and have a look. But, I mean, it can't be Molly's, can it? It's been missing since that awful night.'

'I honestly can't see how. I expect it belongs to Anne, and when she sees it again I'm sure Sarah will realise that too.'

# CHAPTER SEVENTEEN

Having sneaked in early Wednesday morning to tackle the mounting paperwork in his in-tray, Peter's resolve had soon evaporated. It always angered him that when there was a major crime and all their lives were supposed to be on hold, someone saw the need to pile departmental audits and budget targets on his desk.

Suppressing the desire to push all the offending faxes and outstanding work straight into the bin, he had turned on his computer instead, and was researching the murder of Molly Campbell.

Although the person responsible had never been identified, the finger of blame was quickly pointed towards a man in prison for life who had previously sent death threats to Oliver. He'd readily admitted to orchestrating the whole thing, said he had hired a professional killer on the outside to kill the chief constable and his family.

Peter wondered if he had wanted his money back. Leaving the son battered but alive, and fleeing the house before Oliver, presumably the main target, arrived home hardly smacked of a professional hit. Now factor in the real possibility that Sarah had encountered the killer… Why hadn't he killed her too?

He glanced at his notepad where he had doodled around the name of the senior investigating officer. Convinced this particular case would still be in the forefront of the detective's mind, he wanted to speak to him.

He was considering his best course of action when there was a timid knock at his door. He usually had an open-door policy, partly so he had one ear on what was happening outside his small office, but not wanting to be disturbed he'd closed the door that morning. 'Come in,' he commanded. Shutting his pad, he looked up as their researcher hovered in the doorway.

'Sorry to disturb you, sir. DS Marsden has finished and wanted to know whether you had anything to add before he concluded the meeting.'

'I doubt he put it quite as eloquently as that.'

The young DC blushed.

'It's okay, tell him I trust him completely, and I'll join him in five minutes so he can fill me in.'

She was about to leave when Peter was struck by a thought. 'Hold on, you may be able to help me with something.'

Looking puzzled, no doubt wondering what on earth she could offer advice on, the DC slid awkwardly into the seat in front of his desk.

'You were involved in a case a few years back before I transferred from Thirsk. The one in which a woman had sudden memories of being kidnapped and raped when she was younger. Ended up with convictions, didn't it?'

'You mean the Bonner case? Yeah, it was awful, sir. I was in uniform at the time. The poor woman had her life turned upside down in an instant. One moment she was taking her children to school, like she did every morning, the next she was screaming, and no one could calm her.'

'Did you believe her? I mean to not know something in your past so huge and then for it to suddenly be there.'

'Has something happened, sir? She hasn't retracted her story, has she?'

'No,' he reassured her, 'it's the idea of the repressed memories I'm interested in. And please, in here all the sirs aren't necessary, okay?'

'Okay. I was sceptical at first, we all were. It would have been wrong for us not to be. But when we met and talked to her, there was no doubt she was traumatised.' She hesitated, before adding, 'Some still thought she was being hysterical, making it all up to get back at the accused for some reason.'

'There was no obvious connection between them?'

'No, none that we could find. And whether you believed her or not, it turned out she was right about him. Thanks to her we were able to link him to three previously unsolved rape cases, and he was finally put behind bars. I researched it at the time, and the more I read up on the subject the more I realised how little we know about the brain. If you're asking me if I believe it's possible for our memories to lie to us, then yes I do.'

Peter was about to question her further when his mobile rang. The caller ID flashed up as Sarah's home number.

'I'm sorry, I need to take this.' He waited until he was certain the researcher had got the message and was on her way out of his office before he answered. 'Hi.'

'Oh, hello, detective.'

Expecting to be talking to Sarah, Peter was disappointed. He recognised the strong West Country lilt, and as she hesitated he brought to mind an image of the caller worrying at her thumbnail. 'It's Carolyn Wright. I'm sorry to disturb you, detective, but Matt said you wanted to help, and I'm not sure what to do.' She was speaking quietly, as if she were worried she'd be overheard.

'What is it? Is Sarah okay?'

'Yes, it's me that isn't. I've not long come back from the police station, and I don't know what to think of it all. The locket Sarah wanted me to look at. It's Molly's.'

'Are you sure? It's almost thirty years since you've–'

'It's Molly's. I recognised it straight away, detective. She wore it every day after Oliver gave it to her for her fortieth. It has their initials engraved inside. But how? That's what I don't understand. Who's had it all these years? And the chain... the chain was broken,' she cried, her voice rising sharply.

'Carolyn, you have to calm down. Where's Sarah? Does she know?'

'Yes. She stayed here to speak to the officers you sent round but demanded to know what I thought as soon as I walked in the house. She upstairs now, sorting through old photos of Molly: looking for extra proof that it was her locket. She's all riled up, wanting to contact the Lincolnshire Police to tell them it's been found. What shall I do?'

'Don't let her do that. The police heading Anne's case will already be thinking along the same lines. I have to look at what's in the folder first. I need to know what her dad was hiding. There's a good chance Sarah took the locket.'

'No, she wouldn't,' protested Carolyn. Her voice had dropped to a whisper, and Peter heard an element of doubt creep in.

'When they re-examine this case, that's one of the first conclusions they'll come to, unless we can prove otherwise or come up with another plausible alternative. How does a locket, missing since her mother's murder, turn up in Sarah's friend's car? A friend who, incidentally, is also missing.'

The worry over Anne's disappearance had become official this morning. Listening to the local radio on his way into work he had heard the first tentative requests to the public for any information regarding the whereabouts of missing nurse, Anne Baxter.

'Look, I'm not saying it's what I believe,' he added, 'but there

113

are many things that don't make sense here; and coupled with the fact her father deliberately kept her from the investigation, we–'

'I knew my brother well, detective. And if he thought he had aided the killer to escape justice in any way it would have destroyed him. He couldn't do it. He did what he did to protect Sarah. Surely you can see... Oh!'

'What? What is it, Carolyn?' Peter spoke urgently into the sudden silence. He thought the connection had been broken, that Carolyn had put the phone down on him, but then he could hear her breathing. He stood up, his ear clamped to the phone. He was about to fling more questions at her when he heard a different voice – faint, but unmistakably hers.

The older woman sounded shaken. 'Sarah, I'm sorry! I didn't see you there.'

Sarah must have come closer because Peter now heard her clearly. 'You have to tell me, Carolyn. What did he do?' In comparison to her aunt, her voice was low and calm.

Oh God. This was bad. Hoping the receiver was still at her ear, Peter said, 'Let me speak to her, Carolyn. Please.' But his plea went unheard.

---

Rush hour over, the journey took just under ten minutes. On normal days, Peter would have rejoiced, but now, shifting impatiently in the driver's seat, he swore at every red light.

Before leaving the station he had spoken hurriedly to Doug. Ignoring his friend's obvious curiosity and offer of help, he had kept the conversation firmly about their case.

Sarah's peculiar complaints were definitely in the forefront of his mind, though, as he left instructions to re-examine any possibilities the victims had complained about items going missing or being rearranged around their houses in the weeks before their deaths.

Her problems were extremely unlikely to be connected, but he wanted to make sure they hadn't overlooked anything. His tiredness the other night had exaggerated their similarity, but still the physical likeness between Sarah and The Beautician's victims troubled him.

His experienced colleagues would cope fine, but he took his position of command seriously, and part of him baulked at leaving his team. As he drummed his fingers on the steering wheel waiting for another light to change, he wondered when his growing absence would be seen as detrimental to the investigation. After his meeting with Superintendent Crosby yesterday, it was already thin ice he was skating on.

The clock in the car showed it was nearly ten. Again. Every time he had glanced at the digital display it had hardly moved. Maybe it was broken.

Deep down he didn't think Sarah was capable of hurting Carolyn; nevertheless, the way Matt had described her as possibly unstable kept nagging at him. How would she react to the knowledge that her dad had lied for her? And, more crucially, how does sudden disclosure affect someone's repressed memories? Would everything simply pop into place, like in the Bonner case, or would her mind reject the truth?

He was out of his depth. What he should do professionally was to contact the Lincolnshire Police, tell them about the new evidence, and let them reopen the case. But what would that achieve? Expose Sarah to probing and damaging questions that would lead where? Possibly nowhere. He needed to see what her father had risked his reputation, career and, even worse, maybe a killer's conviction for.

Sarah's road was thankfully free of parked cars, and he pulled up in front of her neighbour's house. As he sprinted up the steps, he heard raised voices. The door was locked, and it shuddered under his hands as someone pounded on it from inside. What if she hurt Carolyn? She couldn't. Wouldn't.

He bent down to the waist-high letterbox and peered through. 'Sarah, what's happening?'

The shouting continued. 'Let me out! I mean it, Carolyn, I can't stay here.' The door rattled. 'Give me the key.'

'Not like this, Sarah, please.' Carolyn sounded like she was close to giving in. 'Where will you go?'

'Anywhere away from you,' yelled Sarah.

'We need to talk about this.'

'Oh, like Dad did? He pretended to be strong, and all he did was to run away.' With one more thud on the door, Sarah moved.

Peter tried to see where Carolyn was standing but could only see Sarah pacing up and down. 'Let me in!' He shifted slightly as the wetness from the ground seeped through his suit trousers.

'This is typical of him. Did you know when he eventually told me he was dying of cancer he had been in pain for months; he had brushed it under the carpet and didn't tell anyone until it was too late. And then it was, oh okay, I'm going to die, but don't worry, we've had a good time. Well, fuck that. It wasn't okay – it never is. Everyone I love leaves me, and I'm supposed be all right with that? Good old Sarah, she always bounces back.'

Peter grimaced at the bitterness in her voice. Out of the corner of his eye he saw the curtain twitch in Mrs Wilson's window and hoped she wouldn't call the police at the commotion. That was an explanation he could do without.

'And do you want to know why?' Sarah continued to rant, 'It's because I didn't want to let my dad down; he was tough. But he wasn't, was he? It was a lie.'

'No,' Carolyn shouted back. 'He was the strongest man I've ever known, and he loved you so much.'

'Then why didn't he help me to remember? Why didn't he trust me enough to tell me?' Her voice faltered as her legs gave way, and she slid slowly down the wall. Her fight, for the moment, exhausted. 'My God, Carolyn, he had twelve years.'

Sarah's white face was now visible to Peter, and her whole

body was shaking. Hating his voyeuristic position at the letterbox, he banged on the door again, demanding to be let in. He let out a huge breath when Carolyn did so, and she sagged against him, her relief shuddering off her in waves.

'Are you all right?' he whispered to Carolyn, reluctant to push her away but needing to reach Sarah as quickly as possible. She sniffed, then nodded. In contrast to Sarah's, her face was red and blotchy, her wrinkles deeper, as if the tears had etched permanent lines into her skin. She stiffened as Sarah spoke.

'Sometimes I would catch him looking at me so seriously, and I thought it was because I reminded him of Mum, but what if it were something else. What if it was doubt in his eyes?' Now she wasn't shouting, a childlike quality had crept into her voice. 'What if I find out I'm not the person I think I am?'

'Sarah, you must stop this,' cried Carolyn. 'You were only eleven when your mum died, there was nothing you could have done.'

'You don't know that.'

Sarah struggled to her feet. Perhaps Carolyn sensed a chink in her anger because she stepped over to her and embraced her, saying over and over how sorry she was.

Peter hung back, watching Sarah's face closely. She was staring wordlessly over her aunt's shoulder at the open door and hadn't yet acknowledged he was there.

Their eyes met. 'Don't follow me,' she mouthed silently, and before Peter was able to react she pushed Carolyn into him and raced out of the house.

# CHAPTER EIGHTEEN

Quick. She had to run. Had to get away. Peter was shouting after her, but Sarah lowered her head and ran. Not looking where she was going, running purely on instinct, she rejoiced in the freedom. The air her lungs sucked in hungrily was icy cold, and her body woke up: in pain. Alive.

To clear her mind she focused on the symphony of sounds: her footfalls; her breaths; the soft rubbing of her jumper against her skin; even the swish of her ponytail.

At the end of her street she turned left and continued to run uphill. It was a route she had jogged numerous times, but she was running hard. A dull ache in her right side was growing into a sharp, stabbing pain. Her leg muscles were cramping and, as she reached the top of the hill, her legs almost buckled from under her. If she didn't slow soon she'd collapse. Finding a morsel of self-control, Sarah decreased speed and by the time she ran through the park gates she had slowed to a jog.

Peter was torn between chasing after Sarah and helping Carolyn. As he stood on the pavement, he recalled the determination in Sarah's face when she bolted for the door. There was no madness there, only a desire to get away. Although deeply worried about her, his instinct was she was dealing with the revelations in her own way. She was nearing the top of her road; soon she'll have disappeared altogether, and he'd be left staring up an empty street.

Muffled wails from indoors interrupted his indecision and he went back inside. Carolyn was sitting on the bottom step in the hallway, her head touching the wooden banister, her face crumpled with regret. One of her hands clutched her chest, and Peter was concerned that her wails were more than distress about Sarah.

He rushed to her side and crouching down, studied her. A thin layer of sweat glistened on her forehead. 'Are you okay, Carolyn? Are you in pain?'

Taking in a juddering breath, Carolyn shook her head. One of her hair grips had dislodged and hung precariously from a few stray grey strands. It wobbled as she continued to move her head slowly from side to side.

'What have we done? That poor, poor girl.' The hand that had been clutching her chest flew across to grasp his arm. Her bangles clashed together. 'Go and find her.'

When Peter didn't instantly leap up, Carolyn begged him again to go. 'I'm fine,' she maintained, pushing him away. 'I need a bit of time to gather myself, but I'm all right. Please, Peter, she's all on her own.'

He didn't need any more persuasion; however, he insisted on first helping her into the sitting room. Carolyn leaned heavily on his arm, and once he had lowered her gently onto the sofa, Peter hesitated. He couldn't abandon her like this.

Someone crashed into the hall, and for a split second his heart leapt as he thought it was Sarah. Disappointment as Matt rushed in was quickly replaced by relief. At least he didn't have to leave Carolyn on her own.

'What's happened? Where's Sarah? Door is open and...' Matt stopped when he saw Carolyn. 'Oh my God, you look awful.'

'I'll be okay once everyone stops fussing,' protested Carolyn, throwing a defiant glance Peter's way. 'We have to help Sarah.'

'Carolyn told her the truth.' Eager to find Sarah, he ignored the mortified look on her aunt's face. 'Sarah ran off, and–' Peter held up his hand before Matt could interrupt, no doubt with a thousand questions. 'I need you to stay with Carolyn, make sure she's okay.'

Shit. He had no idea where Sarah would go. 'Is there anywhere she would head for?'

'I don't know,' replied Matt. He combed his hands through his hair, and Peter saw he was struggling to comprehend what had taken place. 'She goes running in Hillside Park. So she might go there. At the far side there's a children's playground and from the nearby benches you get a view over Ledforth. After she lost Mike, Sarah often went there to sit.'

'I know the place,' Peter told them grimly. He had once led an investigation into a series of rapes in the park and knew its layout well. It wasn't far, and he prayed Matt was right.

Addressing Carolyn, he asked, 'How much does she know? Did she see anything from the folder?'

'No. She snatched it from me, but I think seeing her dad's writing on the front stopped her. Until then I'm not sure she believed me. There was an envelope attached: a letter for her. She took that.'

Matt groaned. 'This is what I was afraid of. Her mind could unravel. I'd better come too.'

'No, I need you to stay here in case she comes back.' Trying to convey his concern about Carolyn he tilted his head towards her.

It looked like Matt would argue, but after glancing over at the sofa he nodded. 'I'll ring you if we get any more ideas of where she might be,' he called as Peter left.

———

Jogging had always been great therapy for Sarah. When she had left home to study nursing she had joined a student running club and found it a good way to make friends. If she were a bit low then a run would lift her spirits. She had never lost control though. Not like this. Back at the house, a madness had taken over; telling her to get out.

Sarah remembered Carolyn's shocked expression as she pushed her into Peter. With a half gasp and half sob, she slumped onto the nearest bench. She pressed her fist hard up against her mouth. No tears. Staying angry would give her the strength for what she had to do.

Once her breathing was steadier, and the pain in her side had eased, Sarah reached into the front pocket of her jeans. With a shaking hand she brought out a crumpled white envelope and smoothed out its creases. Her handwritten name was on the front.

The writing was unmistakably her father's. A vivid picture popped into her head of him sat in his study, ballpoint pen in hand, shoulders slouched, as he studied a trainee's work. His serious face, lined with concentration, always lit up when he saw her watching him.

After he had left his job as chief constable he had grown a beard and, in a young Sarah's eyes, this had completed his metamorphosis from a policeman into a college professor. Sarah had liked the new look, but she had suspected her dad had missed his old life more than he had been willing to say. She was beginning to realise how he had sacrificed everything for her. Now she needed the why.

Why had her dad lied to her?

Sarah was sliding her thumb under the flap when someone spoke.

'Hello, I knew it was you.' The voice, although friendly, was too loud.

Startled, Sarah looked up. The sun was shining brightly, blinding her. She shielded her eyes with her other hand in an attempt to see the face; barely able to make out a dark figure looming over her. 'The sun's in my eyes. I can't see who you are!'

The man stepped back, apologising profusely, 'Oh, I'm sorry, I didn't mean to frighten you, Sarah. I was walking by and saw you up here, and thought I'd come and say hi.' He appeared horrified he had scared her.

Now she recognised him, her heart rate settled below 200 beats per minute. Sarah stuffed the envelope back into her pocket and smiled hesitantly at the hospital porter. 'It's okay, don't worry. I was miles away, and you made me jump, that's all.

'Hi, Rob,' she said, as his name came to her. She was hoping a quick hello would send him away. The last thing she wanted was a long conversation right now, but to her dismay he didn't seem in any hurry to leave.

'Robbie, please. Everyone calls me Robbie.' He gave her a big grin. A section of limp grey hair fell across his forehead, and he smoothed it back as he waited expectantly for her reply, looking disappointed when one was not forthcoming.

Sarah wasn't sure whether it was the drop in adrenaline or the shock at what Carolyn had told her, but she began to shiver. Folding her arms around her waist she tried to control her shudders. *Of course, next time I lose it and flee I could remember to bring my coat with me,* she thought. *It's a freezing winter day and here I am wondering why I am bloody cold.*

'You're shivering; are you all right?'

Oh God. She'd almost forgotten he was there.

'I'm fine, thanks.' Under his scrutiny, Sarah felt uneasy again. 'But I do need to get going. I was in a hurry when I left the house

– forgot my coat,' she added, in way of an explanation. She stood up quickly, hoping he wouldn't try to lend her his jacket and was relieved when no such offer came. 'Nice to see you, er, Robbie. I'll, no doubt, see you at work.'

As Sarah backed away, he seemed to want to go with her. He stepped towards her, but then simply held out his hand. Not wishing to offend him she reached forwards and was taken by surprise when Robbie grasped her fingers and pulled them up to his face.

'You need to take care of yourself,' he said quietly, before kissing the back of her hand. He tightened his grip, perhaps on the verge of saying something else.

Alarmed, Sarah pulled back. 'I... I will. Don't worry.' Not giving him the opportunity to continue, she moved away. 'Bye, Robbie.'

'Goodbye then.' His loud, clipped way of speech added formality to the whole affair, and Sarah had to fight a sudden urge to giggle.

As she headed down the hill towards the playground she didn't dare turn round. What if he followed her? He was harmless, but she hadn't been acting rationally, and he was the sort of guy who'd hang around to make sure she was okay.

Was she? Sarah didn't have a clue. She'd gone through such a myriad of emotions in the last hour: from denial and anger to being scared and now bordering on mania, she was exhausted thinking about it.

When she did pluck up the courage to look behind her, he was walking the opposite way towards the tennis courts. As she watched his retreating back she felt bad for him. He had only wanted to help, and she couldn't get away fast enough. The next time she saw the porter at work she'd make an extra effort to be friendly. He was a bit of a joke amongst the ward staff, especially as he had a tendency to hang around the nurses' station after dropping patients off. She'd got the impression he was a loner.

Oh God. Work. That was something else she would have to deal with. How could she go back in a week's time? She couldn't. Not until she'd made sense of everything that was happening. What if she was never able to remember properly? Would she become a loner like Robbie? Would her colleagues talk about her behind her back?

'Sarah.'

Shaking violently, Sarah turned and saw Peter walking cautiously towards her. Unable to stop shivering she had no choice but to wait while he approached. He acted apprehensive, as if unsure what sort of cornered animal he was facing. Having taken off his coat, he was holding it out to her. A peace offering.

Her teeth were chattering hard. 'Your lip-reading skills suck,' she managed. 'I told you not to follow me. At least you're not carrying a white flag, or I'd... I'd have had to hit you.'

'I've got one in my pocket just in case my wit and charm didn't work.'

Suddenly grateful to Peter for coming to find her, Sarah gave him a weary smile. 'You still want to waste your charms on me?'

'Definitely,' replied Peter, enveloping her in the lovely, warm folds of his coat. 'Are they working?'

'Well, I've not run away again. Yet.'

She let Peter guide her towards a bench. Although there was a bright blue sky overhead, not many people had been fooled out into the open. In the playground, only a few hardy parents were shuffling around, huddled in their winter coats, whilst their children played on the slide and swings. Their strange exchange had attracted curious glances though, and there were muted encouragements to leave the play apparatus. *Before the mad-looking lady in the red jumper does something crazy,* thought Sarah.

Peter's mobile rang, making her jump. Smiling sheepishly, he answered it while pulling her close. And she sank into him, thankful for the extra heat, listening as he reassured the person on the other end of the phone that she was okay.

She wasn't sure.

After agreeing to keep the caller informed, Peter disconnected. Sarah looked at him expectantly.

After a slight hesitation he said, 'It was Matt. It was his idea to look for you here.'

Sarah smiled. 'I remember once when I invited him to join me on a run. He accused me of nearly killing him.'

'Do you always run as fast as today? If so, then you're wasted as a nurse.'

'You should see me on a ward round. Zoom and I'm... I'm...' Sarah tried unsuccessfully to control her quivering lip. She covered her face with her hands as all her pent-up anger and confusion caught up with her.

# CHAPTER NINETEEN

His rage hurt. It had started in the pit of his stomach and now his whole body was on fire. It burnt his insides with intensity.

Standing behind the dense branches, he watched as the policeman covered her shoulders with his coat. Two small figures moving closer together. And here he was, on the outside, observing. He was the controller, and yet she was beyond his reach.

His hand shaking, he positioned his finger and thumb either side of Detective Graham's head. From his high vantage point on the hill they were both like tiny dolls, and he imagined squeezing his skull until it burst. God, the pleasure it would give him to hear the bones crack and shatter.

He should be with her. Not that interfering bastard. It wasn't fair. When he had seen her run from the house, he'd been overjoyed. He had laughed at the anguish on the detective's face. Following her in his car, he'd planned to swoop in when the opportunity presented itself. Be her knight in shining armour.

And now? Agghh. Clenching his teeth, he felt the familiar hot surge as every one of his muscles tensed up. They cuddled on a bench; he blinked away tears. Staggering backwards into the hidden copse, his wrath and frustration boiled over. He let out a cry: a long, loud bellow that scoured the back of his throat. Taking a deep breath, he yelled again, his wide-open mouth not uttering a sound. The noise of his fury was only for him to hear, to drive the rage away. There was no stamping of feet, or flailing fists. He kept his body as still as possible as he strained against his own power.

He couldn't lose control, it was too soon after the prostitute. It was only a matter of time before he started to make mistakes, and he had to finish this with Sarah. He had to know why she had tormented him for all these years. Sinking to his knees, he replayed the killings in his head; not the times he spent with his special girls, but his quick fixes. He wasn't proud of those, but it was the violent and brutal ones he needed. The images would soothe him. And although the relief would be short-lived, it was better than letting the alternative happen.

Concentrating on the stabs of the knife, remembering how satisfying it had felt slicing the soft flesh, he didn't immediately register he wasn't alone.

The appearance of the young boy in the small copse was so unexpected he wondered whether he was really there. When the boy spoke, a small pulse quickened inside him.

'Have you seen my ball? I've lost it,' the boy demanded in a high-pitched voice. Not getting an answer, he tried again, 'My ball – I kicked it through the trees. Have you lost something too?' Chewing the scraggy end of one of his yellow gloved fingers, the boy stayed on the far side of the den, his light blue eyes darting left and right over the carpet of pine needles.

His age was about four or five, and bundled up in a dark blue coat, yellow wool hat with matching gloves, he reminded the man of another child long ago. One whom he had bullied mercilessly.

He hadn't thought about his younger cousin for a long time,

and for an instant he was back on the deserted beach, pushing Tom towards the incoming tide. Shouting and laughing at his terrified expression.

'My name is Seth.'

'What?' he croaked, looking at the boy in confusion. The memory broken.

'You called me Tom. I'm Seth.'

'Of course you are. Silly me. What colour is your ball, maybe I can find it for you?'

Smiling, the boy started forward.

'Seth! Where are you?' a female voice called from the other side of the undergrowth.

Before he could stop him, the boy had answered her, and with a rustle of leaves a tousled head pushed into his hiding place. The blonde curls so closely matched the ones peeking out from beneath the boy's hat there was no mistaking this was his mum.

'Boo! I thought you were looking for your ball, not playing hide and seek.'

She hadn't yet seen him. He struggled to keep calm, still pumped up from the images that had not long been racing through his mind. Time slowed down. Small puffs of cold air escaped her mouth after each breath and lingered as if reluctant to leave her red lips. The upper part of her body, thrust through the bushes, was covered by a thick, padded coat but he imagined what was hiding underneath.

The blood pounding through his arteries was so loud he was stunned she hadn't realised he was there.

Raising her arm she pushed branches away as she moved further into the little clearing. 'This is a great den you've found here, Seth.'

Seth didn't turn towards her but tugged at her scarf and pointed. She finally looked in his direction. Her face registered shock, and then fear.

'Mummy?' The boy must have picked up on her anxiety because he was now eager to leave.

'It's okay, I won't hurt you.' He forced a smile as he reached towards the retreating pair. His fingers touched the arm of the child's jacket, and he felt the cool smoothness of the fabric.

---

As Peter pushed open the door of the café, he was pleased to see that it was empty of other customers. Steering Sarah in front of him, he headed for the corner table, furthest from the food counter.

He said hi to the young woman who was leaning against the worktop. Her boredom broken; the promise of work, however brief, animated her and she gave him a welcoming smile.

Sarah kept her head down, and he wondered whether she felt the girl staring at her. She was wearing his large black coat: her slight five foot five frame ridiculous in it.

Perhaps recognising that they needed space and wouldn't be people who would want to engage with idle chatter, their hostess took their orders quickly and retreated behind the counter.

They waited for their food in silence, Sarah gazing out the window, lost in thought, her eyes dry. Constantly moving fingers, intertwining with each other, betrayed her anguish.

Peter surveyed the café, remembering how it had provided them with a lifeline of coffee and hot butties during their rape investigation. It had changed hands and undergone a makeover since, losing its greasy look for a more modern, clean one. Surrounded by mass-produced art prints, all related to different types of coffee, part of him hankered for the straightforward butty-and-pie place it used to be. As far as he was concerned, being offered several kinds of beverage to go with your healthy paninis, wraps and various bean salads only complicated your lunch hour.

He was, however, grateful when a steaming cup (albeit a small one) of double espresso landed in front of him. His thin suit jacket had been no protection outside, and it was only now he was realising how cold he'd got. Warming his hands, Peter sipped the hot liquid as Sarah began to talk.

'I know my dad did what he thought was right.' She looked directly at Peter. 'I do understand that. I only wish he'd have told me before he died.'

'He wanted to protect you.'

Sarah nodded sadly. 'And I guess I needed that. It wasn't until after he'd gone I realised how much I owed him for my life. He kept everything together after Mum was killed.

'In the beginning it was horrible, we were all so sad. I missed my mum, and I had lost the brother I'd always known. It could have finished us, but it didn't. Dad wouldn't let it, he kept saying that Mum was watching us, and she would be cross if we didn't keep going and come out the other side smiling. It was his way of making it better.

'A lot of my memories are good ones. Our family was such a happy one before that night, and I know Dad sacrificed a lot to make sure I was okay afterwards. And I was okay.' She appeared to mull this statement over for a few moments. 'Aunt Carolyn was great. My cousins, who I'd only ever seen at Christmas times, suddenly became my new adoptive brothers and sisters.

'Poor Carolyn,' she hissed between her teeth, 'I pushed her.' Sarah's eyes widened at the memory. 'Oh, God, Peter. I was so angry. I didn't mean to...'

'She'll understand. It was a huge shock.'

'It wasn't her I was angry at,' she admitted. 'It's me. I'm the one who's been lying all these years. How can I not remember what happened? If I was there, then why don't I remember?'

'I'm no expert, but it may be similar to what can happen to a witness of a crime. I've seen eyewitnesses completely draw a blank when it comes to describing events. In times of intense stress our minds can play tricks.'

'Well, mine has played one hell of a trick on me,' she grumbled. 'At least I now know why I'm going mad. Who knows, maybe I couldn't have coped if I'd remembered it all straight away. It's bad now, but back then, when I was young, I would have been a mess.'

Theatrically raising his eyebrows, Peter was relieved when Sarah reacted as he had hoped she would.

'Yes, even more than I am now,' she retorted, smacking Peter on the arm. 'At least I understand why Carolyn reacted as she did when I first told her I was going to see a therapist. I said my GP had suggested it because I was struggling to sleep and feeling low. It was like I'd told her I was giving everything up to become a hermit on a secluded island somewhere.'

'That sounds tempting.'

Sarah gave him a tired smile. 'Mmm, you're right. Maybe that's the answer.' She stabbed her untouched salad with her fork. 'There's a place off the coast of Ireland, called Skellig Island. Mike and I visited there on our honeymoon. There are actually two islands, the larger one is called Skellig Michael – much to the amusement of Mike, at the time – and apart from a few stone huts, there is nothing except jagged rocks surrounded by sea and sky.' Giving the salad up as a bad job, she laid her fork down and sat back in her chair. 'I could be happy there.'

'I was imagining more of a Hawaiian beach, surrounded by women in grass skirts. No, not the arm again,' Peter said, laughing, as he dodged another blow.

'You're missing the whole "hermit" bit,' she protested, a little too loudly.

The café was beginning to fill up, and an elderly couple sitting at a nearby table glanced over. Leaning forward, Sarah lowered her voice. 'Seriously though, getting away sounds good.'

Carefully, he placed his hand on hers. 'No one would blame

you if you did. Put away the folder, decide what to do when you return. Or, give the folder to me; maybe you don't need to know.'

'No, I have to deal with this now,' she replied firmly.

Peter was momentarily distracted as a police car went past outside, its siren blaring. He was wired to react to the sound. An occupational hazard.

Pulling her hand away from his, Sarah sat up straight. 'When did Carolyn tell you about all this? You knew before this morning… did she call you last night?'

Peter shifted uneasily, causing his metal chair to scrape on the floor. He cringed at the noise. 'I think you better ask her?'

'Peter, I'm asking you. Don't lie to me. Please.'

He sighed. 'It wasn't Carolyn who told me. It was Matt. Yesterday afternoon, while you were sleeping.'

'Matt, but how…' She was obviously struggling to digest what this meant. 'How long has he known?'

'You need to talk to him,' he began, but seeing her expression he relented again. She didn't need any more lies or half-truths. 'Carolyn went to see him after your first session at his clinic.'

'But that was years ago,' Sarah declared, astonished. 'All this time, and he never once thought I should know.' She pursed her lips.

'You said yourself maybe it was better you didn't. Now he knows the torment you've been going through the last few weeks, he feels bad,' he finished lamely.

'Bad!'

'More than bad. He's worried what emotional backlash you'll have.'

'You mean how crazy I'll become?'

Sarah buried her head in her hands. 'It was me who destroyed those photos, wasn't it? I know what everyone's thinking. I cut myself out so I wouldn't be reminded of mum.' Sarah continued quickly, cutting off Peter's automatic denial, 'It's all right, it's all beginning to make sense now. But that's why I can't hide from it anymore. Everyone lied to me, including myself, and I have to know what really happened.'

He was realising the futility of fighting her on this. As he met her stare, he saw determination and anger; any sign of vulnerability was gone.

'And despite anything Matt might say, I am strong enough. I certainly can't carry on like I have been.'

Sarah paused as another police siren sounded outside. 'And, anyway, it's not that simple, is it? It's not just me remembering my past. There's Anne... I need to stay at home in case... well, in case she contacts me.'

'Well, there's the offer of my place if you ever want a change of scenery. My sofa has the added bonus it doesn't smell of cat,' he added, not wanting to make her feel uncomfortable.

He didn't have to worry though, as Sarah smiled shyly. 'I would love that. Thank you.'

This time it was Sarah who took his hand in hers, and he hardly dared to breathe as their fingers interlocked. He reached across and stroked her cheek with his other hand, and for one fleeting moment she nestled against it, before pulling away. 'I have to go home. There's a letter I've got to read.'

Peter stood up to pay their bill. As he passed the window, he saw two panda cars in front of the park gates.

After taking Sarah to his car and telling her he wouldn't be long, Peter went over to see what was going on. He approached one of the attending uniformed officers and showed him his ID. 'Do you need any help?'

'It's all right, sir. I think we've got this one covered. A man, reportedly hiding in bushes, gave a mum and her son quite a scare.'

'Are they okay?'

'The mother is a bit freaked out, but they're fine,' he replied, gesturing back along the pavement.

Looking over the policeman's shoulder, Peter saw a tall,

SALLY HART

blonde woman talking earnestly to a female officer. At least, she was trying to, but was getting constantly interrupted by the small boy tugging on her hand. Any excitement he'd initially felt at seeing the police and hearing the sirens had clearly died because he was determined his mum was going to leave at once.

'It sounds like the man was high on drugs. The woman says he was sweating and breathing heavily. Apparently he grabbed hold of her son's coat, but she was able to pull him away. He didn't chase them. If you ask me, he wanted money to buy his next fix.'

Unfortunately, it wouldn't be the first time they'd had a problem with drug usage in the park, and Peter agreed it was the likely scenario. He couldn't help wondering if the constable would sound so uncaring if the man was found unconscious in those bushes.

As though he'd read his mind, the PC continued, 'The park security did a quick search of the area where they saw him, but he was long gone. We're going to have a look around now, just to be on the safe side.'

# CHAPTER TWENTY

How long had he kept her here? Days? Weeks? In her darkest moments, Anne wondered whether this was where she had spent all her life, and her memories of an outside world were false.

*Come here, puss.* She smiled at Samson. He was sat at the edge of the darkness, licking his fur. *Here, puss.* He glanced at her disinterestedly as she tried to reach him.

Memories coming and going. When she was lucid, Anne hung on tightly to those images. But the ghostly presence of reality came more briefly as time passed.

Her mouth had no saliva, making it hard to swallow. She attempted to lick her chapped lips, but her swollen tongue refused to work. She was dying. Anne knew that. Just didn't know how long it would take.

Where was that stupid cat? She needed to get up and find him. He'd be hungry. Maybe she would lie in for a little while longer and then look. The silly thing had probably fallen asleep next to the boiler.

*Here, puss.*

# CHAPTER TWENTY-ONE

## FEBRUARY 1994

The party was how he had feared it would be: full of happy noise he wasn't a part of. Maybe he wasn't capable of fun. He had wowed at the magician's tricks with the other children. Had even tried to laugh loudest to prove he was there. It didn't help.

The boys his own age, who had been friendly when he'd first arrived, had soon grown tired of him. His social failings had alienated them, and they'd gone upstairs. He wasn't invited.

Hands shoved in his pockets, he tried to look at ease. Smiling at the games being played in the centre of the room but cringing inside as he pressed hard against the wall. Back straight, he imagined melting into the bricks; disappearing, surrounded by unseeing eyes. His piece of magic more magnificent than any performed by a cheap entertainer.

The only reason he was invited to the birthday party was because they'd felt sorry for him. It was always the same after they had moved to a new house. Neighbours would fall over themselves to meet them, befriend them, saying things like: 'Oh, it must be so hard for your son to join a strange school mid-term'; 'He must miss his mum and his old friends'; 'Of course, he can come round here for tea.' It didn't take long for the offers to dry up. Here would be no different.

He couldn't even blame his dad; their relationship had faded into nothingness. Once he had reached his teens the bullying and beatings had stopped. Not that his dad had shown any remorse over them. He guessed he wasn't worth the effort. Hitting a tall, lanky kid who might eventually have the balls to fight back wasn't as satisfying as hurting a little boy who couldn't defend himself. Most days they hardly acknowledged each other.

If his dad chose to stay in his studio pretending to paint canvases whilst drinking his life away, then good for him. He couldn't give a fuck. A few times he had considered leaving home; he doubted his dad would've even noticed he'd left. But where could he go? He had no close family, and no idea where his mum had gone.

One day, he had wandered round their house looking at the luxury furniture and latest high-end gadgets – mostly bought by his dad's inheritance money, as any salary earned from his early success as an artist had probably long gone – and decided he would be stupid to turn his back on it all. The stuff meant nothing, but he'd miss the large amounts of pocket money. If nothing else, his dad was generous. Guilt?

As he thought of his dad he squeezed his hands together. His broken fingers hadn't been realigned properly, although his mother had tried her best, and the misshapen knuckles were stiff. Massaging them hard helped keep the hate alive.

'Hi there.'

He flinched at the closeness of the female voice.

She smiled at him as she picked up a discarded paper plate from near his feet.

'It… it wasn't me.' His cheeks were hot with embarrassment.

'Sorry?'

'The plate. It wasn't me who dropped it.' Horrified, and

wishing he really could disappear into thin air, he didn't know what to think when she started laughing.

'I'm sure it wasn't you. Anyway, there'll be plenty more thrown on the floor by the end of the day,' she said, showing him the bin bag she'd already half filled with rubbish.

Despite being only fifteen, he was a good inch taller than her, and he couldn't help but smile back shyly as she peered up through his curtain of black hair. He liked her face: she was very pretty. Expecting her to turn away, he recoiled in surprise when she dropped the bag and grasped his hand.

'Come with me. The disco's starting soon, and I need a partner. Let's show everyone how it's done.'

'No, I can't,' he protested feebly.

'Oh, come on. I bet you're an Oasis man. My daughter, Sarah, loves Take That. I think she secretly thinks her old mum is past it, but I've got a few good moves left.'

---

Imagine it. Him. Enjoying a party? It was crazy how an eleven-year-old girl's birthday party had changed everything. As he trudged through the snow, he tried to remember the last time he'd felt happier.

Molly was genuinely concerned about him. And she liked him. She wasn't stuck-up like their other neighbours. Rich people in their big five- or six-bedroomed houses, surrounded by large gardens and long drives, usually couldn't give a shit about anyone else. Not that he cared about that sort of thing. Having no one to chat to over a picket fence didn't bother him. He preferred it.

After his mum had left them, his dad had sold the old place and moved in with one of his young worshippers. It hadn't taken the stupid doe-eyed woman long to realise that the poor, sad, divorced artist was in fact a drunken monster. They had moved twice since. This picturesque Lincoln suburb offered nothing that he hadn't seen, and rejected, before.

At least, he'd believed he needed nobody. Now he was confused. For a few hours she had made him feel wanted and a part of something.

Knowing he was going to see her again filled him with such happiness, he was scared in case he messed up. He had spent all day at school daydreaming: imagining his life if she'd been his mum. The two of them against the world.

She couldn't be more different than his real mother. He'd never been a source of joy for her. Not really. More an inconvenience.

He often wished he had known his mum before years of drink and drugs had ruined her. It was three years since she'd ran out on them, and eventually he would go and find her. He didn't bear her any ill will. Yes, she'd let him down, but it wasn't entirely her fault. He wanted her to be happy, and, who knows, maybe she would be glad to see him.

Head down, deep in thought, he almost lumbered past their driveway. The gates were open, and unlike the majority of the neighbouring properties, no attempt had been made to clear the snow from outside the house. Turning the corner, he stared with surprise at the large snowman in the middle of the drive.

Another time he might have trampled the snowman to the ground, but not today. Instead, he stepped over a maze of frozen footprints and picked up a bottle top, pressing it into the gap in the snowman's smile. He then touched the brightly coloured scarf tied around the bulky neck. Did it belong to the mother or daughter? He sniffed it, however, any lingering smell had been destroyed by the damp.

His nerves jangled as he approached the front of the house. Pushing back his hood, he ran his hands through his black hair; he didn't need to look in a mirror to know that it would be sticking out at all angles.

Over the last few months he had let his hair grow, mainly to annoy his dad, but also in a half-arsed attempt to look like Eric Draven from his new favourite film, *The Crow*. Both goals had failed miserably, and he had to pile on lots of gel, so he didn't look like the scarecrow from *The Wizard of Oz*.

His good mood started to slip. He'd had a detention after school, and not wanting to be late for her, he'd come straight over. Would she think it weird he hadn't changed out of his uniform? His armpits felt sticky under his shirt; and after fiddling with his tie that refused to lie straight, he stuffed it in his coat pocket.

Shit. The sharp blade scraped his fingers. He'd forgotten it was there. It'd been a stupid experiment: to see what he felt like with a knife. What an idiot he was. What was he going to do with it now? He could throw it under a hedge and collect it later. But what if a child found it? He licked his dry lips. No, he'd just have to keep it.

Upon reaching the porch steps, he hesitated. The butterflies in his stomach were making him feel sick. The invite was to spend the afternoon with her son, Ben, but secretly he hoped it would be the two of them.

Ben was one year higher than him at school, and they'd barely exchanged more than a few words. They had nothing in common. It was his group of friends at the party that had judged him lacking, leaving him in a room full of giggling girls.

The sixteen-year-old would be taking his GCSEs this year, and would probably ace them all. He doubted he would stay for his. His teachers at his old school had predicted good grades if he concentrated hard on his work. They had asked his dad to try and motivate him at home to study. That was a laugh. Luckily, his dad was too self-absorbed to worry about his progress in anything, which suited him fine; his sort of encouragement was the sort he could do without.

At lunchtime, he had seen her son with his groupies, tucking into his food and laughing inanely. He'd wished Ben was eating poison. Not a fatal dose, but enough so he would be ill in bed, leaving him alone with Molly.

Realising the reality of the afternoon would fall short of his fantasy, he was on the verge of fleeing when he heard voices. Not ready to meet anyone, he panicked and hurried backwards. His feet missed their footing in the snow and down he went, landing flat on his back.

Fuck! He scrambled up, covering his trousers in more snow in his haste to escape the humiliation of being found sitting on his backside, legs in the air.

Why did everything always go wrong? Sniffing back tears, he waited miserably for the inevitable, but no one came. When the owners of the voices didn't appear from round the corner, he plucked up the courage to take a peek. The path was empty.

He was about to turn away when he heard her. His heart beating fast, he stepped across to the open window. Although his legs were shaking, either from the cold or excitement, he wasn't sure which, he was able to peer easily over the outside sill without having to go on tiptoe.

The inside of the window was steamed up, so he only had the small horizontal opening to look through. She had her back to him, taking something out of the oven. As she turned her head slightly, his breath caught. He'd be in big trouble if he was seen, but he couldn't move. It wasn't until the son spoke from somewhere to his left that he realised he was there.

'Do I have to, Mum? He's weird. He gives me the creeps.'

He pressed his fingers hard against the rough stone of the window ledge.

'Please give him a chance, Ben. You hardly know him.'

Warmth flooded through his body. She was sticking up for him. Of course she was. His view of her was obstructed as Ben moved across the kitchen and put an arm around her shoulders.

He wasn't quite as tall as his mum, so the gesture looked awkward.

She sighed. 'Look, I know he's...'

'Weird,' interrupted Ben, reaching round her and plucking a biscuit from the oven tray.

'Stop it,' she grumbled, slapping at his hand playfully. 'I was going to say I know he's strange. But he seems lonely, and I feel sorry for him. So, I expect you to make him feel welcome.'

'Okay,' Ben surrendered, mouth full of biscuit, 'but next time you find another lost cause it's Sarah's turn to suffer.'

A small sound escaped as he stifled a moan, and he ducked as Ben turned towards him. Although why should he care if he saw him? No one cared about him. She didn't. The phrases 'I know he's strange' and 'I feel sorry for him' spun around in his head, and he squeezed his eyes shut against the pain. He had mistaken pity for friendship and love.

Ben's voice rang out above him. 'I'll shut this before we freeze to death. And Mum, don't you think we're a little old for having friends around for homemade biscuits? Next thing, you'll be making us lemonade to go with them.'

The window banged shut, saving him from her reply.

He sank into the snow and taking the snowman's scarf from his pocket, buried his face into it. Unbidden, his dad's voice mocked him, joining her in shredding his pathetic hopes. And his hope had been pathetic. Why should she have liked him? He was strange.

*Isn't that what I've always told you, son? You're a nasty little freak, who's not going to have any friends. You're going to be alone forever.*

'No, it's not true. Shut up,' he pleaded, gripping his head in his hands.

*He's strange.*

*He's more than strange, he's a fucking weirdo. A psycho!*

'No, I'm not.' Anger building, he pushed up and lashed out at the surrounding snow. Kicking wildly. 'Don't say that. Stop it!'

142

He ran along the driveway and ploughed into the large snowman. His body juddered as he launched into the impacted snow. Roaring with rage, and fists flying, he pounded the head; imagining he was hitting real flesh, he then pelted its body with blow after blow. When the pain in his exposed hands became too much to bear he changed to kicking and stamping on what remained. Then, with one last cry of frustration, he stopped.

The mist lifted. Panting, he glared at the mound of snow. Ha. He'd killed their snowman. Smashed it. Ha. Fucking obliterated it.

Wiping his mouth, he took one last swipe with his foot before staggering back towards the house. Retrieving the scarf, he moved away, planning to leave quickly. The front door opened.

# CHAPTER TWENTY-TWO

## FEBRUARY 1994

'Hi. Sorry, I should have told you our doorbell is temperamental. Have you been here long?'

He considered making a run for it, but then he stuffed the scarf into his pocket and turned slowly towards her. He shook his head.

'Good. Come on in, get out of the cold. Ben's waiting for you.'

*Yeah, I bet he is.* His legs heavy, he shuffled nearer to her, and she waited in silence as he climbed the steps. Keeping his eyes firmly fixed downwards, he mumbled his thanks. It wouldn't do to forget his manners now, would it? Swallowing his resentment, he managed a small smile for her. 'I fell in the snow. I'm all wet.'

'Oh, sweetheart, so you are.' She stepped closer to him. 'Did you hurt yourself?'

'No, I'm fine.' He wanted to reassure her, make his excuses and get away as soon as possible. 'I'll go home, and–'

'Don't be silly, I can dry your clothes here,' she interrupted, ignoring his protests as she pulled him further into the large hallway. 'You can wear Ben's clothes. Ben,' she called up the stairs, 'he's here.'

As they listened to the approaching footfalls, he didn't need a crystal ball to know how this next bit was going to pan out. And, he wasn't disappointed.

'Why are you all wet?' Ben laughed, staring at his trousers. 'Couldn't you wait?'

His face burned, and there was a pounding in his head.

'Ben,' his mum warned, 'don't tease him. The number of times you've come home covered in snow this last week. Between you and Sarah, my washing load has doubled.'

'That's true. I'm sorry, mate. You should see me after having a snow fight with my sister. She wins every time.'

He didn't want to accept Ben's apology. They must think he's stupid; did they believe he couldn't see through their charade of being nice to him? It made him want to puke.

When he reappeared in the kitchen after changing clothes, he pretended he didn't notice Ben trying not to laugh again. He knew he looked ridiculous: the three-quarter-length sleeves, the scarcely concealed midriff and the jeans hanging a couple of inches too short.

Humiliated, he handed her his wet bundle of clothes.

'That's great. I'll drape them over the radiator in the hall and they'll be dry in no time.' She offered him a smile: false and lacking in warmth. 'I'll take that as well,' she added, reaching for his coat he held tightly in his left hand.

'No!'

Startled, Molly backed away and stared uncertainly at him.

'Sorry. I'd like to keep hold of it. It's… well…' *Think of something,* he screamed inside his head. 'My mum gave me this coat before she left us, and I don't like to leave it somewhere I might lose it,' he finished lamely. God, he sounded so pitiful.

His lie worked as she was instantly gushing over him. Saying how hard it must be, and if he ever needed someone to talk to. Blah, blah, blah. He was glad when she let him follow Ben upstairs. The last thing he wanted was to spend any time with him, but it was better than having to listen to all the shit she was dishing out.

'Welcome to my domain,' declared Ben, gesturing for him to sit on the bed. 'It's my sanctuary against the world, and completely Sarah-free. You don't have any siblings, do you?'

He shook his head wordlessly.

'Well, you're not missing much, I can tell you. You've not lived through anything until you've lived through one of her moods. Always wanting something.'

Did Ben's sister realise how he talked about her behind her back?

He sat stiffly on the edge of the bed. The layout of the room was similar to his own – they were both good-sized, with large windows – but where his was plain and ordered, Ben's was cluttered.

There were numerous posters on the walls, and already he was beginning to feel like they were closing in on him. They showed random people skiing down mountains; urban landscapes with skateboarders doing their flying jumps and other stupid things. He recognised Kurt Cobain, from Nirvana, stuck next to a Green Day poster, but there were others he didn't know. Why did people want pictures of pop stars staring at them? Silent strangers in silly poses.

Framed family photos stood on every shelf, and the sudden jealousy hurt. Realising Ben was quietly studying him he blushed. Not knowing what to say he stared at his bare knees peeking out from the pair of ripped jeans he had borrowed. His fingers played with the edges of the frayed material.

After a few seconds of uncomfortable silence, Ben spoke. 'I'll put some music on. Who do you like to listen to?' he asked, as he walked towards a shelf full of cassettes and CDs.

Taking Ben's posters as inspiration, 'Er, Green Day are cool,' he said. Was relieved when Ben nodded his approval.

'Cool,' Ben echoed back, reaching for the nearest group of

CDs before heading over to his bookcase, where his stereo and speakers filled up the top shelf.

Thinking the older boy was taking the mickey, he scowled behind his back. He watched sulkily as Ben cleared the space around the bottom CD deck, throwing a hat and a pair of gloves over to what was probably supposed to be his work desk.

How the fuck did he get good grades in his exams?

He moaned as the bass intro thumped into the room; the loud music syncing with his banging head. All he wanted was to go home.

Maybe sensing his discomfort, Ben turned the music down. 'Look, I'm sorry I laughed at you earlier. Why don't we... wait, what's that?' Ben was pointing beside him. 'Oh my God, is that Mum's scarf?' He glared accusingly. 'Why the hell have you got my mum's scarf in your pocket?'

'I... I found it outside. It was on the ground, I didn't know who it belonged to.'

'Liar.' Ben stood up, and planted his face a few inches away from him. 'It was around our snowman, and you took it. Wait until I tell Mum.'

'No, please. You can't. I was going to give it back.'

'Like hell you were. No wonder you didn't want her to take your coat. All that stuff about not wanting to lose it. It was all bull.'

As Ben pushed closer, he recoiled and stiffened his body against an attack. But the other boy snatched the bundle of wool peeking out from his coat pocket. The red-and-pink scarf snaked out, at first freely, and then it snagged on something. Pulling on it hard, Ben gasped as the knife dropped on the floor.

'Is this yours, or have you nicked it as well?' The contempt in his voice was palpable, and he sneered as he bent towards the unsheathed blade.

Taking his eyes off him, Ben never saw the blow coming. It was with an almost comical flop that he fell against his desk.

Standing over him, as pens and paper rained on Ben, he felt a small spark inside. He was wondering what it was when Ben turned his face towards him. My God, was that fear he saw? He wanted to snigger. It was funny that this boy who had clearly despised him was now scared of him. The spark grew.

Stooping to pick up his knife, he grinned as Ben scrambled to get to his feet. He let out a small giggle when a chair was knocked down as Ben backed unsteadily away. He hadn't hit him hard, nevertheless a red mark had appeared. With a look of disbelief, Ben rubbed his cheek.

The blade was pointing towards the injured teenager as Ben lunged to his left towards the door. Without thinking about what he was doing he thrust the weapon forward, and Ben yelled as the knife caught his hand.

The spark flourished, and he finally knew what it was as it raced through his body: it was power.

They both stood there watching the blood drip from the small cut. The tip of the blade had sliced across Ben's palm, and what had started as a thin, red horizontal mark was now oozing into the creases, tracing the intricate pattern of his palm lines.

'Now you've done it.' Making small keening noises, Ben tried to stem the blood by closing his fist and pressing his hands together.

'That must hurt,' he told Ben. His voice was steady and didn't betray the way his heart was racing. As if there were two of him: one shit scared, and one in complete control.

In comparison, Ben's reply was shrill. 'Of course it bloody hurts.' His eyes flickered between the moving knife blade and the door. 'I need my mum. Please let me go downstairs. I'll tell her it was an accident. I swear I will.'

'I don't think so. What if she doesn't believe you?' He saw Ben turn ashen as he picked up the gloves that had previously been discarded on the desk. 'You don't mind if I borrow these, do you?' he asked pleasantly.

Not sure what would happen next, but beginning to enjoy himself, he reached over to the stereo and turned the volume up further. An electric guitar riff blasted from the speakers.

He wouldn't really hurt Ben, only frighten him. Maybe he could make him wet his trousers; show him how it felt to be laughed at.

# CHAPTER TWENTY-THREE

## PRESENT DAY

W as that it? Sarah checked inside the envelope again. There had to be more than two pages. Surely what her dad had to say to her couldn't fit in such a short letter?

Hands shaking, she placed the letter on the table in front of her. Tears welled up as she recognised the familiar scrawl. Biting down on her lip, she leaned forward to read. The overhead light cast her shadow over the paper, and her world darkened.

> 10th May 2006
>
> My dearest Sarah,
>
> This is the hardest letter I've ever had to write, and one I hope you will never have to read. If my instructions have been carried out like I asked them to be, then the only reason you are holding this letter is because you are remembering what happened the night your mum was killed. And I am so sorry.
>
> Please don't hate me for lying to you. For years I watched you, waiting for any sign something wasn't

*right, waiting for your real memories to surface. That*
*time never came. You seemed happy, despite the blow*
*fate had dealt us, and I wasn't willing to spoil that. It*
*was what your mum would have wanted.*

   *Enough of my excuses. I know you will be pissed at*
*me now, and you have every right to be so. Use that*
*anger, Sarah. Use it to help you find out the truth.*

Her vision too blurred to continue, Sarah wiped her eyes and
tried to refocus on her dad's writing. Peter squeezed her
shoulder.

   *The evidence told us you had been in the house. I*
*just thanked God you were safe. I honestly don't know*
*what I would have done if I'd lost you too. What I'm*
*trying to say is, please don't blame yourself for anything.*
*You were only eleven. There was nothing you could have*
*done.*

   *After the interview (the one on the video) we did try*
*again. A few days later we sat you down and suggested*
*you might be trying to forget what really happened. It*
*was awful, you became so upset, throwing things and*
*hitting people. And then nothing – you collapsed and*
*didn't talk or eat and drink for twenty-four hours. When*
*you did come round you couldn't remember being angry,*
*or even us taking you back to the station. I wasn't going*
*to risk it happening again. Although there were a few*
*sceptics on the team, believing you were faking it, I*
*KNEW you weren't, and I had enough clout back in those*
*days to protect you from any more questioning.*

*The folder is now yours to do with as you wish. You've always had considerable strength, Sarah, but if it is all too much then burn it with my blessing. You can't change what happened; all that matters is your happiness.*

*One last thing, please don't hurt the messenger. I hadn't confided in my sister until now – last night in fact – and wow, you think you're mad at me. You know what she's like when she's left out of the loop – and this is one big loop. If I weren't already dying, I think she would have killed me.*

*God, I have no idea how to finish this letter. Sarah, I'd give anything to be with you, to help you through this, but I made my choices – rightly or wrongly. Just remember you made me so happy and proud.*

*Give Ben lots of hugs. I love you both so much,*
*Dad*

Sarah forced the table forwards. Her chair fell to the floor with a bang as she shoved past Peter, struggling against his outstretched arms. She made it as far as the hallway before falling to her knees. Torn between giving her space and comforting her, Peter hesitated, putting the letter into his pocket and then crouched down beside her.

'I knew this was going to be too much for her. I'm calling Matt back,' declared Carolyn.

'No. Don't.' After a couple of deep shuddering breaths, Sarah hoisted herself onto the bottom stair. 'I'm okay.'

Sarah smiled gratefully at Peter as he gave her a tissue. 'At least I stocked up on tissues last week. I must have known I was going to need them.' She sniffed loudly.

'And we've got plenty of shoulders for you to cry on. Isn't that right, Carolyn?'

Peter received only silence back. Carolyn had been in Matt's corner when he had unsuccessfully tried to persuade Sarah to agree to hospitalisation, or 'in-house therapy' as he called it. His suggestions had fallen largely unheard by Sarah as she had refused to even look at him upon her return. Despite saying she understood why she'd been kept in the dark, it was clearly proving hard for her to forgive.

Not knowing whether he was doing the right thing by letting her read the letter, Peter had hoped to have Carolyn's support. But judging by the aunt's expression, if it backfired, the blame would sit squarely with him.

When Sarah disappeared upstairs, wanting to be alone, the atmosphere in the kitchen didn't improve. Carolyn had barely spoken since Matt had left. She was standing rigidly at the worktop, leafing through a recipe book and glancing at the ceiling every few minutes as if wishing she could see what her niece was up to. He doubted she was taking in much of what she was reading. Peter watched her for a while until she tutted loudly and stared across at his drumming fingers. Realising he'd been tapping them on the wood he sat back. 'Sorry, bad habit.'

Unable to bear the tension and inactivity any longer, Peter armed himself with two mugs of coffee and ventured up to the landing in front of Sarah's room.

'Sarah? I hoped it may be a good time for caffeine.' Peter held his breath, hoping he was doing the right thing.

'And a good time to check up on me?'

'Is that okay? I can leave yours here and drink mine in the kitchen if you'd rather I left.'

Relieved when Sarah told him to come in, Peter pushed open the door. The mugs wobbled precariously in his hands, and Sarah hurried over to help. 'Thanks, Peter. I was going through old photos,' she explained, leading him to the pile of albums on her bed. 'I'd retrieved them from the spare room this morning after Carolyn returned from the station. There's one here of the four of us on holiday in Italy.' She pointed to the group shot. 'I was about nine or ten, I think.'

He craned his neck to see, as she cleared a space for them both to sit down. The pictures he had seen online of the parents didn't do them justice. They had been a very handsome couple. Standing together in front of a stone fountain, her father looked happy and relaxed with his arm around his son, while her mother was hugging a young Sarah in front of her.

'It's a lovely picture.'

'One of my favourites. Mum had always wanted to take us to Italy, having fallen in love with the place during her childhood holidays. She would have loved us to have lived out there.'

Aware Sarah was watching him closely, he kept his face impassive as he studied the locket plainly visible in the picture.

'You look so much like her,' he said finally.

Sarah smiled. 'Thank you. Dad was always telling me the same. It was almost like he had to keep telling me so I wouldn't forget her.' She gasped, 'Oh God, I guess that's something I should be grateful for.'

'What?'

'All the best memories are with me. I wasn't so messed up that I lost all those.'

'Maybe that's what your father thought. He didn't want to risk you forgetting everything.' He continued warily, 'Some memories are best forgotten. Your brain managed something we all sometimes wish for – the bad stuff to be filtered out. Perhaps you shouldn't fight it.'

'I wish it were that simple. And believe me, there are a lot of days I would want to forget but can't.' Sarah straightened her back and, folding her arms, glowered defensively.

'Sorry, I didn't mean to be flippant. I can see how hard this is for you.'

His face must have clouded over because Sarah's expression softened. 'What bad stuff did you want to forget?'

'I had a daughter.' He hadn't planned to say anything about Jess, but she'd caught him off-guard. Sarah took a sharp breath, and he didn't need to glance up to see the pity in her eyes.

'Jess was two and a half, and we were taking her on her first proper holiday to Scotland. We were supposed to set off early, but because of my work it was evening time when we finally left home. And so we met a young, inexperienced driver travelling too fast for the road conditions. He lost control and...'

'Oh, Peter.'

'I would never want to forget her... of course I wouldn't, but sometimes...' He sighed. 'The night I came to Anne's flat, I'd had a panic attack. I lied when I said the car had broken down.'

'I wish you'd told me.'

'I was kind of hoping to come across as your knight in shining armour, rather than a tired middle-aged man with his own shit.'

'You're middle-aged?' she quipped. 'Sorry. I have an awful habit of trying to crack a joke when the last thing I feel like doing is laughing. It used to drive Mike crazy.' Sarah put her coffee mug down and placed a hand on his knee. 'Seriously though, Peter, since we met, it's all been about me.'

'It's fine.'

'No.' Sarah shook her head violently. 'No, it's not.'

'Yes, it is. Right now, you need help, Sarah. And I'm here for you. If it makes you feel any better, you can care for me when it's my turn to have a breakdown.'

'Promise?'

Peter gazed into her eyes. 'I promise.' God, he ached to pull her close. Clearing his throat, he looked away hurriedly. Not the right time.

'The other reason I came up was to show you this.' He

retrieved her father's letter from his inside pocket. 'Your dad also wrote on the back. I thought you should see it.'

'I missed it,' she whispered, taking the letter. She gave him a nervous glance before reading the few lines scrawled on the last page:

*I don't know if you remember my old work colleague and best friend Geoffrey Beaton, but he was the officer in charge on our case. Find him. If he's still alive, I know he'd be willing to help any way he can.*

'Do you remember him?' Peter asked. He had recognised the name straight away from his search earlier in the morning.

'I don't know. There was someone Carolyn used to talk about, a friend of theirs before she moved to Devon. But I'm not sure whether he was called Geoffrey.'

'Wait a minute.' She reached behind them on the bed, and after moving a few large albums to one side she picked up a smaller one. 'He might be in here. These are ones taken at my eleventh birthday party. There'll be lots of snaps of family and friends in here. I've not seen these for a long time.'

Peter waited for Sarah to open the book up, but she sat there, her hand not moving from the cover.

'Shall we take a look then?' Not receiving a response, Peter began to panic. Was she going into another fugue state? Alarmed, he called her name, and Sarah jumped slightly.

'Oh, sorry. I'm not sure I want to look at these photos.'

As she struggled to explain, Peter leaned forward. 'What do you mean? Is there something about this album in particular?'

'No, not really. And I know what you're thinking, but there's no flashes of hidden memory or any reason other than I don't feel comfortable looking at them. I never have. It was so close to when it happened. My party was at the weekend, and a few days later everything changed.'

They met Carolyn on the landing. She was breathless as if she had climbed the stairs a little too quickly.

'You have a visitor, Sarah. Bryan from work.' She glanced down into the hall before adding quietly, 'I've told him to call back, however he's quite insistent. Refuses to go until he's spoken to you. I virtually had to push him into the living room.'

Damn. Sarah planned to patch things up with Bryan, he was a good friend, but she wanted more time to think.

'It's okay, he's probably worried about Anne. Could you show Carolyn these?' she asked Peter, giving him the letter and album. 'I won't be long.'

She hadn't reached the bottom step when Bryan appeared in the hall, carrying a bunch of flowers. 'A peace offering,' he said, thrusting the bouquet towards her awkwardly, 'to say sorry for, you know... being an idiot.'

Sarah stared at the flowers. Not pink roses, but a winter assortment wrapped in red cellophane peppered with silver dots. Her hand shook as she took them. 'Er, thank you, they're lovely.' None of this was Bryan's fault, but she needed him to leave. The thought of the roses only reminded her of what a mess she was in. 'Listen, Bryan, this isn't a good time. There's a lot of things going on.'

'If this is about the other day, Sarah,' began Bryan, 'then–'

'It isn't, I promise. Anyway, that was my fault, I should have told you I wasn't interested.'

'No, I crossed the line,' he said firmly. 'I'd still like to be friends, but if you don't then I'll understand. I was well out of order.'

Remembering his brutal strength, and how he had glared at

her when she'd pushed him away, like he had hated her, she nodded.

'Yes, you were.' Seeing shame shadow his face she realised she was unconsciously rubbing her upper arm where he had grabbed her. Part of her was pleased. He'd hurt her. He should suffer.

The uncomfortable silence was broken when Peter and Carolyn came down the stairs. Sarah saw Bryan's eyes narrow. 'Is everything all right? Your aunt said you were resting.'

'Yes, I did,' piped up Carolyn. 'Not that you took any notice,' she added huffily, before disappearing into the kitchen.

'If you'll excuse me, I have to go back to the station.' Peter gave a brisk nod to Bryan, who visibly relaxed.

'Is it Anne?' Bryan asked. 'I saw her brother on *Look North* this morning. Has there been any news?'

'No, I'm afraid not,' said Sarah. She guessed Peter was deliberately being stand-offish, not wanting to make anything difficult for her. How much of their conversation had he heard?

'Is there anything else I can do for you?' Peter asked, glancing meaningfully at Bryan.

'No, I'm fine. I'll give you a ring tonight, okay?' She reached out and brushed his arm as he passed.

Bryan stepped back, scowling; the action clearly hadn't escaped his attention. 'Well, I guess I had better be off too,' he said, as soon as the front door had closed.

Sarah hoped her relief wasn't too obvious. 'As I said, Bryan, this isn't a good time. But I do want to be friends. I'll explain what's going on when I've got my own head around it all.'

He nodded slowly. 'Just as long as you know you can come to me if you need anything. I would hate myself if I'd ruined that.'

# CHAPTER TWENTY-FOUR

## FEBRUARY 1994

He stumbled in the deep snow and fell against the brick wall that lined the small path. Unable to run anymore, the revulsion of what he had done gripped him without mercy. Bending over, he vomited hard. Would the powerful contractions expel all that he used to be? Before…

Fuck! Why had he…?

He squeezed his eyes shut and wished it would all disappear: the past hour bundled up in the blizzard blowing around him and carried off. He would wake to find it was only a dream: a stimulating, but disturbing, nightmare. The wind tugged at his coat, threatening to unbalance him, and he hunched low.

Oh God. Surely he wasn't capable of…? He pressed his knuckles to his mouth. The violence. The blood.

Their shocked faces flashed into his mind, and he cried out in physical pain as he struggled to block the images. They would paralyse him. He could feel them trying to surface on a wave of nausea.

Why had they pushed him so far? It wasn't his fault. If Molly had left them alone then he wouldn't have had to chase her. None of it was his fault. The unfairness of it – that his life was over and there was no turning back – hit him and he started to cry.

Dropping forward onto his knees, cradling his clothes and trainers he had snatched from their hallway, he cried tears of self-pity. He had nowhere to hide. Lifting his wet face up to meet the raging snow, he heard sirens in the distance.

They couldn't find him like this: sniffling and cowering like a frightened animal. He rose unsteadily and peered over the wall. The back of his house was in darkness.

Where was his dad? Maybe he was in his studio, but it was irrelevant anyway, asking him for help was out of the question. There was no way he would stand by his son. He wouldn't spit on him if he were on fire. No, he was alone.

Thankful for the cover provided by the snowstorm, he heaved himself into their garden. Expecting the light of a police helicopter to shine down, he was stunned when a few minutes later he had made it safely to his bedroom.

The heating was on and the difference in temperature made his head spin. There was no time to waste, yet he desperately needed to think. He sat on his bed.

---

The bedroom was bright. The daylight pouring in from the window was painful it was so intense. He heard laughter outside. It must be Ben and his sister playing in the snow. They had been building a snowman, he was fairly sure of that. Shaking his sluggish head, he approached the glass, shielding his eyes against the glare. They sounded happy. Maybe if he concentrated he would wake up from his nightmare of a different reality.

For a moment, he was back in his own room – his empty sanctuary, stark compared to Ben's. Screwing his eyes up, he tried to rewrite past events. Claw back his life. Their lives.

No. His mind was slipping. Ben's room was no longer all

bathed in sunlight. A dark corner was growing, slowly consuming the light. He struggled to look away as an awful gurgling sound came from the shadows. A hand reached towards him.

———

'What the hell happened? Are you hurt?'

The voice was far away. Urgent. Tugging him back. Hands grasped his shoulders, shaking him.

'Are you all right? Oh God, is this your blood?'

He focused on his father's face. Why was he so upset? Was he actually worried about him? 'Dad. I didn't mean to do it,' he whispered. 'I swear I didn't.'

'Shit.' Seeing his dad flinch angered him. How dare this bastard judge. 'Why do you care?' He pushed his dad to one side and stood up. Fuck, he was stiff. Had the enormity of what he had done aged him physically? This morning he was eternally angry yet young, now he was a spent old man. How long had he been sat on his bed?

Turning to his dad, he asked, 'Are you going to help me then?' He braced himself for a fight, for ridicule. What he didn't expect to see was compassion. 'Dad?' His voice choked. 'What have I done?' He moved to hug him and moaned when his father backed away. 'Don't leave me.'

'The blood… on your clothes. You can't touch me.'

Trembling, he kept his arms out straight, waiting for that one embrace to make things better. 'It wasn't my fault–'

'Shut up! Let me think.' His dad paced up and down. 'Did anyone see you?'

His arms fell. Had anyone seen him? The question ricocheted around in his head. He had frantically stamped on any memories straining to resurface – instinctively knowing now was not the time to start unravelling the details – but the vision of her was strong. The one memory: an oasis in the chaos. How she had comforted him, even after what he had done.

'I said, did anyone see you?'

If he hadn't imagined her, then once her shock wore off she would tell the police. The thought filled him with dread and yet he hesitated. Wasn't that what he deserved?

'I... I don't think so. I came round the back.'

His father strode to the window and pulled the curtain to one side. The dark sky was still full of tumbling snowflakes. He found it hard to process time; it must be a few hours since he was out in the snow, but it seemed what was falling now were the very same flakes which had fallen on him. Each one soft and cold on his upturned face. The memory was so vivid he shuddered.

'You need to strip. We have to get you cleaned up.'

He glanced down and was surprised to see he was wearing Ben's clothes.

'You have to get a grip,' his father commanded. 'They'll be here soon.'

As he unfastened the unfamiliar jeans, his fingers struggling with the buttons, something occurred to him. 'You haven't asked me what I did. Who I hurt.'

His dad was tugging clean clothes out of the wardrobe, and he answered without looking at him. 'I drove past their street on my way home, saw all the police. They were cordoning off everywhere. I don't want to know anything else.'

The son was shocked to feel a sense of loss in amongst all the shame.

# CHAPTER TWENTY-FIVE

W hat was she doing to him?
*Thwack.*

She kept messing with his head. His increased agitation was because of her.

*Thwack. Thump.*

The force of the blows juddered up his arms; the punch bag shuddered with the onslaught.

It was always her. Back in the early days when he was fighting urges he didn't understand, and now, when he had come to realise how much she meant to him.

*Thwack. Thump.*

He had once hated Sarah. Many of the details of the days following the Campbell killing were unclear, but he remembered that all he had thought about at the time was her. Wondering why she didn't tell them it was him. The waiting intolerable, he'd nearly died of suspense.

The police did come knocking but, to his surprise, accepted his dad's assurances he had stayed at home all evening – ill and unable to go round to his friend's for tea.

He had later heard someone from inside prison had boasted

about orchestrating the murders. Nevertheless, even when his dad had finally let him out of the house and the police and press had left the street, he'd obsessed about her.

He had worried incessantly about what plans she had in store for him, and if she had something other than justice on her mind. She never came back to school, but he became convinced she was behind every wary look and every whispered comment.

It had got so bad he'd planned to run away. Maybe he wouldn't have become so angry with everyone if he had. The idea of suicide had also played on his mind. In the end, it was his dad's fault he had chosen to stay.

The night he had got close to leaving was the first time Ben's broken body had almost reached him in his nightmare. His shocked voice crying 'of course it bloody hurts' reverberated around him, even after he had woken up shaking. Pressing his face into his pillow, he had decided to end it all.

He had also dreamt about Molly. He'd squashed the slivers of thought that were daring to speculate on what words she would haunt him with. The fact he was curious had filled him with dread.

He was only a few steps from the front door when he'd heard clinking glass from the kitchen. Standing unseen in the dark, he had quietly watched as his father stood at the window. Silhouetted in the moonlight, the familiar frame that had once instilled fear in him, looked bent and beaten. His arms straddled the sink, and his head hung low as his shoulders jerked uncontrollably.

It was inconceivable that his dad was crying, and even when he heard the sobs, part of him had wondered whether it was a trick to keep him from leaving. He had stayed there while his father poured the contents of his drinks cabinet down the drain. He'd then returned to his bedroom.

It was the following morning that his dad had told him he was selling the house. He had spoken to his sister in the Republic of

Ireland, and, once she had heard they were struggling, she had offered to have them stay on her farm indefinitely.

Struggling? Is that all they were doing back then? Would his aunt have welcomed them with open arms if she had known the truth?

He had no idea whether he would have killed himself but staying with the family had been a mistake. Okay, the constant threat of Sarah had gone. But the old man's sideways glances and awkwardness had driven him mad.

At first, he had enjoyed the manual farm work, and each day he had pushed his body to its limits. However, as his physique grew there was something in him that was slowly dying.

Looking back over his time in Ireland he did remember being normal for a while. Well, as normal as any hormone-driven teen with a dark secret. A secret he would occasionally visit in his mind. He'd had to be careful though, as the more he revisited the images the more the little itch to tell someone grew. To start with he thought it may be guilt that was driving the desire to confess, but then he realised he simply wanted people to know what he had done. What he had achieved. Why he was different from everyone else.

His dad hadn't wanted to discuss anything to do with the murder. The one person who knew the truth couldn't meet his eyes most days. This had infuriated him. He wasn't a stranger to violence. Had this sober version of his father honestly forgotten the torment he used to inflict on his family?

Sweat stung his eyes. He clamped his gloves hard on either side of the quivering bag and his ears missed the hard thumps of leather on leather.

As he refocused on the present, he buried his face in the towel draped over his wet shoulders. He usually received a buzz from a workout, thriving on the burn from his muscles, but today he struggled to feel anything other than aggravation and a headache he'd had since the park.

It never did him any good to reflect on his past but seeing the scared look in the little boy's face had reminded him of his cousin.

When the physical demands of farm work weren't enough, it was frustration that had led to the bullying. First it was an occasional unkind word, then a push or a pinch when no one was looking. Childish, yet satisfying.

It had escalated, and at the seaside he had gone too far. And even though he'd helped his dad pull the boy out of the water, thanks to his cousin's snivelling blabbing, their life on the farm was over.

His aunt had driven them to the airport; the normally chatty woman unnervingly quiet and refusing to look at him. He was sorry about that because she'd been good to him.

The fact he hadn't offered any explanation for his behaviour had not gone down well. And when she caught him smirking at his dad's obvious discomfort, she had concluded he didn't feel any remorse over what he had done. She was wrong.

He didn't hate those he hurt. It was a way for him to feel in control. To feel his existence had meaning.

When he had found his mum, she had understood. Not at the beginning when her poor abused body fought back, but when she was able to look at him from a place untouched by the substances her weak mind had been dependent on.

He hadn't intended to kill her. Not at first. It was curiosity that had driven him to search for her online and, once he had typed in her maiden name, she was easy to find. His rush of emotions as his mum had stared out from his laptop surprised him. She appeared a lot older, and life had stripped her of her good looks, but her eyes were the same. She was laughing in the pictures; he saw, however, the sadness in those deep pools of blue. And by the time he had travelled to the small seaside town, he'd been convinced there was going to be a tearful, but joyous, reunion.

Standing outside her flat, he didn't have long to wait. He had stood shaking as his mum had walked towards him, her arm entwined with another.

It was the middle of the afternoon, and her companion had looked as inebriated as she had. As they had staggered past, the word 'mum' got stuck in his throat, and he had stood there like a gormless idiot. For a full five seconds she had stared into his face with no sign of any recognition. So wasted she didn't recognise her own son.

It had been over twenty years since she'd seen him, but he couldn't let it go. She'd squandered her second chance in life and sacrificed their relationship for nothing.

But he'd changed that. They had reconnected and, at the end, both their lives had meant something. It was after this first special experience that his thoughts had turned to Sarah.

He needed to punish his body further and headed towards the weights section. A movement off to his far left caught his attention. He'd chosen a quiet time of the afternoon, when a lot of the gym's clientele were back slouching in front of computers or working through their dreary lives, and so he had hoped to have sole use of the equipment. It didn't look like he was going to have his wish.

The slimy 'I know it all, so you have to kiss my arse' manager was leaning against the reception counter talking – or rather flirting – with two women dressed in shorts and T-shirts. One of them laughed, and he was imagining the insufferable idiot had asked them what they thought of his oversized dick, when they both turned round and stared in his direction.

Oh shit. Pretending he hadn't noticed them, he continued to the dumb-bell rack. Choosing two 50kg weights, he was swinging a leg over the bench when he heard them approach.

'If we can interrupt… It's time to do what I actually pay you for and show these lovely ladies around our fine facilities.'

He squeezed his fingers round the dumb-bells. The sarcastic

bastard. Smile in place, he turned. 'No problem, in fact it'll be my pleasure,' he said, looking the women up and down, making them blush.

Thirty minutes later, and two more gym subscriptions in the bag, he leaned against the cold tiles of the shower cubicle, gasping under the spray of freezing water. The powerful jet soon warmed up, but his skin tingled with the memory of the initial shock.

His jaw muscles ached in unison with the rest of his body from half an hour of inane smiling. He was planning to ride out the rest of the month before handing in his notice, but he wasn't sure how much more he could take. Perhaps it was time to quit, as he'd only applied for this second job in order to befriend Anne. It certainly wouldn't come as any big surprise to the management. Although even 'dickhead' would have to admit he had gone well above his quota for recruiting new members.

The temptations were also hard to bear. One of his special ladies had joined for a few sessions before he had followed her home and spent the night with her. Apart from Anne, she was the only client he had seen outside the gym. Innocent flirting was fine, but he couldn't let the other thing happen again. Not so close to his own life.

Towelling off, he walked towards his locker, and then stopped to appraise his reflection in one of the mirrors above the sinks. He was skittish and was contemplating another raid on supplies after his shift tonight; something to calm his nerves. The man in the mirror looked tired and a little jaded around the edges, but that was all. Okay, so maybe no medication. He'd almost got caught last time, so it wouldn't be a bad thing to try without.

He was putting his leather jacket on when one of the other employees poked his head around the changing-room door.

'Sorry, mate. I know you're off, but the police are here. They want to have a word about that nurse who's gone missing.

They've spoken to us out on the shop floor and James told them you knew her better than most.'

He didn't reply.

'Er, shall I tell them you've already gone?'

'No, it's okay. I'll see them now, but I'm not sure how much help I'll be.'

# CHAPTER TWENTY-SIX

A floorboard creaked. Sarah froze, halfway out the door, only breathing when her aunt's soft snores continued undisturbed. She had left the hall light on to minimise the risk of her stumbling on her way to the chest of drawers, and she could see Carolyn's faint outline on the bed.

Her resolve wavered. After they had moved in with her uncle and aunt, she had often crept into their room in the middle of the night, needing comfort and always finding it. Maybe she didn't have to do this on her own.

But then that's what she had been doing. Facing the fear she was going mad. On her own.

With a heavy heart, she headed back to her room. Unfastening her dressing gown, she let the brown manilla envelope fall onto the duvet. Now she had it, the defiance she'd felt taking it while her aunt slept evaporated. Pushing the guilt away, Sarah stared at the plain, unassuming packet.

Yesterday, after Peter had tracked Geoffrey down and she'd spoken to him, she'd agreed to wait until he'd arrived, and they could then all help her through it. And she hadn't woken up with the intent of going against that, but after struggling awake she didn't want her mind to gnaw at the remaining pieces of her nightmare. Scared to go back to sleep, her thoughts had turned to the envelope. The temptation was too much.

*Well, come on then,* she goaded herself. *You've got it. Open the damn thing.*

Sarah didn't move. It was one thing to want to take charge, but now she had possible answers in front of her, she hesitated. Only two days ago, the faceless man in her dreams was a figment of her imagination. A product of stress and tiredness. And now? The possibility he was real, terrified her.

And what if her condition, or whatever it was, turned out to be permanent? It could all be for nothing, and she was going to be screwed up forever.

Looking away from the bed, her gaze flitted round the bedroom before settling on a picture of Mike. Sarah picked it up. 'Oh, Mike. I'm lost.'

She heard his voice, telling her that he had faith in her, knowing she would never give up. Would he be disappointed in her?

'I miss you.' She brought the frame up to her lips before placing it back down.

Clear what she had to do, Sarah reached for the envelope.

Downstairs, she rejected the cosiness of the dark living room for the open-plan kitchen. It was too early for any twilight glow from outside, but she didn't turn on the overhead light, letting her eyes adjust to the darkness. Her bare feet hit the cold tiles, and she shivered as the stone leached her body heat rapidly away.

Wrapping her hands round a hot coffee did nothing to banish the cold or lift her mood. It had felt the right thing to do to return her dad's evidence to Carolyn's room. Unopened. But, having no distraction meant she had no defence against the nightmare that was now seeping into her consciousness. The most disturbing aspect that had haunted her since she had woken up covered in sweat involved her brother. Not young Ben, with his hopes and dreams ahead of him, but older Ben, whose life was tragically mapped out.

Through his open bedroom door she had seen him sitting on the edge of his bed. He was hunched over, his hands cradling his head; the areas where his grey mop of hair thinned drastically over his healed wounds clearly visible.

This Ben didn't belong. Even in the messed-up world of the sleeping. He'd looked up at her, and where she had expected to see the dimpled scar that ran down the left side of his forehead there was a fresh gash. Blood, like dark red tears, dripped onto his lap.

'Why did you leave me, Sarah? I was waiting for you, and you didn't come.' The stammer that had inflicted his speech since his brain injury had gone. And the acute awareness in his sad eyes had affected her more than the blood.

This part of her nightmare was so vivid, merely thinking about it distressed her and she had to take deep breaths to push away the encroaching panic. She was sat trembling at the table when her aunt walked in. Shit. Had she woken her up putting the envelope back in the drawer?

'What's wrong, Sarah? What's happened?' Carolyn moved towards her in a flurry of silk and cotton, but then paused in the middle of the kitchen. Gasping softly, she asked, 'Have you remembered something?'

Relieved Carolyn wasn't angry, Sarah unintentionally let out a deep sigh making her aunt jump. 'No. I didn't sleep well, that's all,' she lied, looking down at the table. Growing up in Carolyn's care Sarah had quickly learnt that her aunt had an uncanny knack of detecting any lies or half-truths and could probably boast a hundred per cent success rate when it came to getting to the bottom of all her children's mischiefs.

Sarah raised her mug to her lips and her unsteady hands caused the rim to knock against her front teeth. She cursed as droplets splashed the front of her dressing gown.

She needn't have worried about facing any third degree though as, rather than the probing concern she was expecting, Sarah was surprised when Carolyn tutted and turned away.

'Well… I don't suppose you've had any breakfast yet. I could cook us the bacon I bought if you'd like?'

Was that relief in her voice? Sarah felt a sudden surge of resentment towards her aunt: it was her fault she was in this mess. If Carolyn had told her all those years ago, rather than choosing to confide in Matt, then she wouldn't feel quite so alone.

'No,' Sarah replied irritably. 'I'm going to have a shower, then I'll make myself some toast.' Her legs buckled when she stood, and Carolyn moved to help. 'I'm all right,' she said, a little more forcefully than she meant to, and although the outstretched hand was abruptly withdrawn, Sarah didn't miss the hurt on her aunt's face.

As she headed towards the hall, the silence between them was made almost deafening by the clashing of pans. Glancing back, Sarah winced at a particularly loud bang as a cupboard door was slammed shut. If they didn't clear the air soon, she wouldn't have any units left standing.

When she had returned from the park with Peter, neither of them had wanted to make things worse, so their strained apologies had hardly touched the surface. An exercise in papering over the cracks. But by moving quickly on and both pretending what had happened yesterday was okay, they had left the covered cracks structurally unsound.

If she were to rescue her relationship with her aunt, she had to offer an olive branch – but it was too soon to forgive.

---

'I think something happened during the night,' Carolyn confided to Peter as she ushered him into the house. 'Sarah was very pale and shaken this morning, but she wouldn't tell me anything.' Steering him towards the sitting room, she added in low voice, 'Maybe you'll have more luck.'

An orange glow from the gas fire welcomed him in, its heat a lovely contrast to outside. On the far end of the three-seater sofa, facing the flickering flames, was Sarah, her legs covered by a large red-and-blue knitted throw. He was about to speak when her head jerked forward. A soft purring sound made him smile and moving around the sofa he saw her eyes were closed.

A laptop was balanced precariously on her knees. Not wanting to wake her, but worried her computer was close to slipping onto the floor, Peter lifted it to safety. His face was too close to hers when her eyelids fluttered open. Sarah flinched, squealing loudly.

'It's okay, Sarah. It's only me,' he cried, trying to calm her. 'I'm so sorry, your computer was about to fall.'

'Oh, God,' she gasped, pressing a hand against her chest. 'I must have nodded off. Was I snoring?'

'Nooo,' he answered, deliberately letting the no carry on too long. 'But there was a little bit of drool...' he sat next to her, and raised his fingers to her face, 'just there,' he said. Smiling as he pointed to one side of her mouth.

'Thank you, Sherlock,' she complained, laughing now. Rather than batting his hand away, Sarah grasped hold of it. 'It's good to laugh – it's been a horrible morning. I don't expect anything else at the moment, but some light relief helps.'

'Did you have another nightmare?'

Pleased when Sarah answered without hesitation, Peter listened as she told him about her dream. Her face clouding over when she described the part with her brother.

Was it possible she had seen Ben that night? Ignoring Matt's warning voice in his head, Peter asked her outright.

'I don't think so. The bit with Ben is new and yes it upset me, but it didn't feel anything more than a horrid dream.'

Some doubt must have crept into his expression because Sarah said defensively, 'I know what you're thinking, how can someone with no memories of an event distinguish between what's real and what's not. Well, the truth is I feel awful about not visiting Ben over the last few weeks. He found it so difficult during the lockdowns when we could only communicate using his computer. And now I'm putting him through it again. It's played on my mind, more so since reading my dad's letter. The guilt is why I dreamt about him.'

It sounded like she was also trying to convince herself.

'Recently I've made excuses, ones I even believed: I was too tired after work; had too much to do around the house; anything that prevented me going to see my brother.'

'Do you know why?'

'I guess I didn't want to be reminded of my mum, and how we lost her. I wasn't ready to join the dots.' She came to a decision. 'I need to see Ben today. Carolyn was wanting to visit him this afternoon, but I don't think she was keen on leaving me on my own. We'll both go.'

'Does he ever talk about what happened?'

Sarah shook her head, and Peter tried to recall what little snippets he had gleaned about the family. 'He was in a coma for some time after the attack, wasn't he?'

'Five months. The doctors were suggesting we should prepare for the worst when he started to open his eyes to sounds. It was another three or four months before he woke up properly and grabbed Dad's hand.

'I think he's progressed a lot further than any of us thought he would. Sometimes, when you're with him, he acts like the old Ben – laughing and joking – but then it's like someone flips a switch and he forgets what he was talking about a few minutes before. That's when he gets agitated. He knows his brain isn't right.'

'Do you think he remembers?'

'No, I'm sure he doesn't. He loves talking about our mum and he sometimes forgets she isn't here. I see the pain on his face when he realises she's dead.'

'He lived with us a short time after we moved to Devon, then he made things, erm, too difficult, especially with Carolyn's children. Their noise and play aggravated him, and he lost his temper with them. I remember we thought we had let him down moving him into a home, but it was the best thing we did. He thrived there.'

'Did he find it hard moving up here?'

'I was dreading it. I thought it would be awful for him. But he coped well. We've been lucky that this home is as good as the one in Devon. The staff are wonderful to him; most of them have worked there a long time and can read his moods better than I can,' she admitted, with a sad smile. 'Did Carolyn tell you the policemen investigating Anne's disappearance came to see me before lunch?'

Damn. He had meant to check in with the constables last night. He knew the supervising officer had followed standard procedure and had put in a request with his team to cross-reference information in case of any possible connections. 'Did they have any more news?'

'No. They were asking where Anne liked to shop, go out, any hobbies outside work she might have, like the gym she went to. There was nothing new I could think of that I hadn't already told them. After they left, I spoke to Richard on the phone. He's out of his mind with worry for his sister.' She gave a wry smile. 'Prior to falling asleep, I was checking Facebook again in case Anne had posted anything. Although like me, she wasn't on social media a lot.'

Sarah sighed. 'I keep referring to Anne in the past tense.' She let go of his hand and, shrugging off the colourful throw, stood up. Sarah adjusted her grey jumper, so it hung straight over her black leggings, before walking to the window. The misty morning had turned into another lovely winter's day – cold but bright. As she stood squinting into the light, she crossed her arms. 'They suspect I've something to do with her disappearance.'

'Did they say that?' Peter asked, shocked.

'Not in so many words but it was obvious it had occurred to them. They kept looking at me, as if waiting for me to break down. And considering what happened the last time they were here, I can't blame them.'

She didn't look round as he moved to join her. 'I mentioned the locket and then wished I hadn't. They said all lines of enquiry were being investigated and then asked me if I was sure I hadn't had the necklace all these years. Had it fallen out of my pocket whilst I was in Anne's car, or had the chain broken whilst I was wearing it?' She inhaled sharply. 'Oh God, Peter. That's it, isn't it? I've had the locket – I must have. And if I've forgotten that, then what else? What if I did hurt Anne?'

He placed his hands on her shoulders. 'Sarah, listen to me. I won't lie, it's plain to anyone that you've a lot going on, but they only have to look around this house, at the family and friends who love you, and know you, and I promise you if their little antennas are twitching, it's not because they suspect you of any wrongdoing.'

Or so he hoped.

'Family and friends?' she scoffed. 'Carolyn and Matt – we're scarcely on speaking terms; Bryan can't tolerate being anywhere near me since he made a stupid pass at me at the weekend. And you, Peter, I'm sorry but you've only known me for six days. It's hardly a glowing recommendation.'

'You're wrong. Your aunt is, no doubt, at this very moment polishing your banister again in the hope to hear what we're talking about. Matt is constantly ringing up asking me if he could see you.'

He turned her to face him and gently lifted her chin, so she had to look at him. 'And please don't say it's because they feel guilty – you know that's not true. They care for you. And so do I. If you had a bad mojo we wouldn't all be stupid enough to hang around.'

Sarah studied his face for what felt like an eternity, then she reached up and hugged him. 'Thank you, I needed to hear that,' she whispered in his ear, before pulling away. 'Bad mojo?' she asked, wrinkling her nose in confusion.

'It was either that or psychopathic tendencies.'

'I definitely prefer bad mojo.'

# CHAPTER TWENTY-SEVEN

'Don't be surprised if he ignores you. He can get very stressed with people he doesn't know,' Sarah explained to Peter, before knocking on Ben's door.

The sound echoed in the empty corridor, and her stomach flipped as her brother grunted a reply. The image of the bleeding Ben from her dream materialised in her mind. And she had the irrational fear that when she opened the door he would be sitting on the bed, blood gushing freely from his head.

Sarah peered into his bedroom and was almost immediately pulled into a bear hug.

'Sarah! You're here.'

She buried her face into the crook of his neck and felt a rush of emotions: love and guilt fighting for top spot. Surrounded by the familiar smell of his favourite aftershave, she laughed with him. His excitement infectious.

As he rocked her from side to side, his muscles quivered through his T-shirt. 'Ben, not so tight,' she gasped. 'You're squishing me.'

He let go, with a breathy giggle. 'Sorry, sis.'

His grin was already as wide as his face would allow when he saw Carolyn, and Sarah looked on with amusement as his eyes bulged with the added thrill.

'Auntie,' he cried, subjecting Carolyn to one of his huge hugs.

Sarah thought her aunt might complain at his rough welcome, but she was as happy as he was. Releasing Carolyn, Ben glanced eagerly behind her; his disappointment visible as he saw Peter standing in the doorway. His childlike expressions were easy to read, and Sarah sadly acknowledged that her brother had been hoping to spot one or both of their parents waiting there.

In the sudden lull, she introduced Peter as a new friend and Ben stared at him, momentarily sulky before breaking into another grin. He grabbed her arm and dragged Sarah to his table where he had been painting, and then changing his mind, he pulled her towards the window. As he raved about a bird he had spied earlier, not caring that spittle was forming on his lower lip, Sarah noticed the tell-tale signs of erratic behaviour. She sighed. He was going to be very easily distracted throughout their visit. Not even his favourite music would calm him.

Sarah saw the possible answer on his bedside table: a collection of discarded chocolate and sweet wrappers.

Following his sister's gaze, Ben said, 'Will g-gave them to me.' And then, seeing Sarah's disapproving look, added, 'He's my friend, and he knows I like ch-chocolate.' His eyes glinted mischievously, excited as a child on a promise of something sugary.

He chuckled when Peter said, 'I wish I had a friend like that.'

Sarah wasn't amused. Surely the health worker, Will, should have known chocolate and sugar overstimulate Ben. It would certainly explain why he was acting so wired.

A little while later, Sarah was standing outside his room with Peter, leaving Carolyn to spend some alone time with Ben, when she spied Will walking towards them. He was engaged in a conversation with another member of staff but waved at her. Smiling as he dismissed the man talking earnestly at him.

'If it's worrying you, then please talk to management about it,' he said loudly. 'It's got nothing to do with me.' And he turned away from his younger colleague, who looked like he was about to protest but after glancing quickly at Sarah and Peter retraced his steps back along the hallway.

'Trouble?' asked Peter.

'No, he's worried about the next residents' trip into town and wanted to bend my ear about it. No idea why. Anyway, Sarah, it's nice to see you again. Ben was looking forward to your next visit.'

When neither Sarah nor Peter moved towards Ben's room, Will smiled at them quizzically. 'Is anything wrong? It's usually customary for visitors to go in the rooms.'

'My aunt has come up for a visit. We're giving them a bit of catch-up time.'

'Oh, okay.' He combed his hand slowly through his dark hair. 'I'm heading to the lounge for my coffee break. If you need anything then come and find me.'

'Actually, there was something I wanted to discuss.'

As Will lifted an eyebrow and waited for Sarah to continue, she couldn't help but think his fixed smile, with his perfect white teeth, was a touch patronising. At previous care meetings she had got the impression he felt he was better than everyone else, but Ben liked him – and that was the most important thing.

Although Ben was one of the most able-bodied of the residents, his anxieties made him a challenge and when Linda, his old carer, had left due to family problems, Ben had been distraught. So the fact that Will had managed to gain his trust over a relatively short time was a blessing.

Feeling ungrateful, Sarah's face heated up as she chastised him over the chocolate.

'Can I be honest?' asked Will, seemingly unperturbed by her little rant. 'Ben has been depressed lately. I think he's missing you, and I only wanted to cheer him up, but you're right. Seeing how he is this morning it was a mistake, and I'm sorry. It won't happen again.'

He put his hands in his pockets. 'Will you be staying till this evening? We're having a pool tournament in our games room and Ben will be one of the favourites to win.'

'Er, no, I'm afraid we can't.' Sarah's face was red hot. She wasn't sure why, but the care worker was getting under her skin. Maybe it was because he had accused her of neglecting Ben. Okay, not directly, but his insinuation was clear.

'We already have plans for tonight,' she added. Although this was true, and the evening promised to be a busy one with Geoffrey arriving, it sounded lame even to her ears.

'Oh, well, never mind. I'm sure Ben will be happier now he's seen you.'

Resisting the urge to defend herself further, she was glad to get back in Ben's room. And when the time came to leave she gave her brother another big hug.

'I'm sorry, Ben, for not visiting in a while. I promise I'll make it up to you.'

'Will told me you've been busy.'

She pulled back. 'Did he now?'

'Yes, but he told me you still love me, and not to worry, that we'll be together again soon. And here you are.'

Even if the joy in his eyes was confectionary-related, Sarah couldn't help grinning back. 'Here I am, and I do love you, Ben.'

She squeezed her brother hard, and the last line from her dad's letter popped into her head. *Give Ben lots of hugs. I love you both so much, Dad.* She then hesitated before adding softly, 'Mum and Dad loved you too.'

Now it was Ben's turn to push away, and a small frown appeared. 'Of c-course they did.'

'I was wanting to ask you…' she took a deep breath as Ben's hands started to shake slightly in her own, '…do you ever think about that day, Ben? When Mum died.'

He shook his head frantically. His scared open-mouthed look should have stopped her from pressing him further, but she needed to know. 'What happened to you?' she urged, tightening her grip. Hating herself but compelled to ask what she hadn't been able to ask before. 'You have to try, Ben.'

'N-no. I d-d-don't remember.' Breaking away, he raised his hands to scratch his scalp.

It was a sign of extreme agitation, and as his fingernails dug deeper, Sarah tried to back down. 'It's all right, Ben. It doesn't matter.'

It was too late. His distress soared. He screamed and yelled at her to leave him alone. She turned helplessly towards a shocked Peter and Carolyn.

Oh God. What had she done?

The door flew open, and Will rushed in. He gestured for her to move away. 'I'll deal with this.'

With calm words from his friend, Ben eventually relaxed enough to allow Will to steer him to his chair. The repetitive rubbing of his head eased. His right hand dropped away and he began massaging his left forearm. Where he worried at his arm, his skin was dimpled with old scratches.

The carer looked up at Sarah from his crouched position in front of Ben. 'You'd better go.'

As she hesitated, torn between wanting to be there for Ben and yet knowing she was the cause of his anguish, Peter took hold of her arm. 'I think Will's right,' he whispered. 'It'd be easier for Ben if we go. Give him some space.'

Reluctantly Sarah agreed, although she was adamant she wasn't going to leave until she knew Ben was okay. After persuading Carolyn to take Peter's offer of a lift, pointing out that someone had to be at her home in case Geoffrey arrived early, she waited until Will joined her in the visitors' lounge.

His report was good. Ben had quietened down and was

talking about the pool match – a sure sign he was forgetting his earlier upset.

Not wanting to risk Ben getting distraught again, Sarah decided it was best to go without saying goodbye. She was gathering up her coat when Will asked the question she had been dreading.

'What did you say to make him go so crazy?'

'We were talking about our mum and…' Although there was nothing but compassion on Will's face, Sarah recoiled from divulging how she had tried to interrogate her brother. 'Ben sometimes forgets how she died. I should have steered the conversation away from her, but I didn't.'

She couldn't read Will and had no idea whether he believed there was more to it than she was telling him, but she was relieved when he nodded sympathetically.

'It's bad enough losing a parent but when the passing has no meaning and you can't make any sense of it, then it must be hard.'

Ben shouted from his room. 'Will, Will. I need you.'

'I'd better go back to him. You take care, Sarah, and don't beat yourself up about this afternoon – it wasn't your fault.'

She smiled gratefully at the carer, and not for the first time regretted her ill feelings. 'Thanks, Will. Ben's lucky to have you looking after him.'

# CHAPTER TWENTY-EIGHT

U nsuccessfully trying to hide her disapproval, Carolyn waved from the doorway. Sarah felt guilty knowing her aunt would worry all the time she was out, but after seeing Ben so upset she needed to escape for a while. She set off up the hill at her usual steady pace, trying not to think about her madcap run the day before. Her route around the large park, if she turned back when she reached the higher path through the woods, would take less than an hour. Little daylight was left, but the run would be sufficient to clear her head before meeting Geoffrey Beaton.

Sarah was nervous at the prospect of meeting the retired policeman. In his letter her dad had referred to him as his best friend, and she'd trawled through her early memories to summon up a picture. There was nothing. She was beginning to realise how much of that time in her childhood she'd blocked out.

During their phone conversation, Geoffrey had admitted to keeping tabs on her while she was growing up. Whether this was because he'd had genuine concern for her well-being or he'd been suspicious of her amnesia, she wasn't sure. He had, however, sounded friendly and happy to hear from her.

After speaking to him, Sarah had felt optimistic. And Peter was right about her being surrounded by people wanting to help. If she were going to be strong enough to meet her demons head-on then she needed to get rid of the growing fear that her friends would leave.

As she settled into the familiar rhythm of her run, the pressure to think lessened. Autopilot took over, and she only noticed her surroundings again when she was approaching the woody trail.

The tiniest increase in temperature had brought out a handful of joggers, and she wondered if she would bump into Bryan. She looked around but couldn't see the familiar red running shorts. Even when they hadn't arranged to train together, his regular runs often coincided with hers, and she'd had a nagging suspicion that it was deliberate planning on his part.

She should have put a stop to it sooner. Poor Bryan. If she hadn't become so distracted and taken their friendship for granted, then both of them may have been saved the embarrassment of what had happened. She hoped, deep down, he realised they were completely incompatible as a couple. You only had to take a look at his place – immaculate and minimalist – and her place – full of mementos of holidays and her life with Mike – to get an idea of their differences.

She and Bryan would drive each other mad within a week. Of course, Anne's well-meaning matchmaking attempts hadn't helped.

As she thought about how Bryan had behaved at Anne's, it struck her as strange how laid-back he'd been at their friend's disappearance. It was almost as if he had known something about her whereabouts. Was that possible?

Ridiculous. She was being bloody paranoid. Nevertheless she sighed with relief when she exited the park without bumping into him.

It took a moment for Peter to connect the figure on the doorstep to the old news clips he'd studied. Twenty-nine years was time for significant change in most people and retired Superintendent Beaton was no exception. With his curly grey hair sprouting out from under a blue wool beanie hat, and a bushy beard hiding his lower jaw, he was like someone you would find on a seafaring trawler.

'Geoffrey Beaton,' the man exclaimed loudly. 'I hope I have the right house for Sarah Knowles. She's expecting me tonight.'

'Of course, good evening, sir.' The hand that shook his did so with a confident, firm grip. 'Please, come in. Sarah will be down shortly. I'm Peter, a friend of hers.'

'I lost the *sir* as soon as I left the force; Geoffrey will do fine.' He paused and studied Peter with unabashed curiosity. 'You're the chief inspector Sarah told me about.'

'I'm here purely as a friend – I can assure you.'

Before Geoffrey could comment, they heard footsteps descending the stairs, and both turned round as Sarah joined them. The retired detective stiffened. His eyes widened, and he took a swift breath, struggling to regain his composure. Peter wondered what the older man had seen.

Geoffrey stepped forward. He whipped off his hat and attempted to smooth his hair with his other hand. After a short awkward silence, he flung his arms wide. 'Sarah,' he boomed. 'Oh, my dear child; let me have a look at you.'

If Sarah was at all flustered by the enthusiastic greeting she didn't show it. She smiled shyly as she was held at arm's-length while she was 'looked at'.

Perhaps realising her welcome was more subdued he backed off slightly, frowning. 'I guess you don't remember me. It's been a long time. I've gained extra baggage since then,' he said, patting his stomach. 'That's what retirement does for you.'

Carolyn smiled as laughter came from the living room. Trust Geoffrey to lift the mood. He was always the life and soul of any party. She was glad he hadn't altered much over the years, although the big beard would take some getting used to. Would she have found him so attractive back in the old days if he had sported one then?

She was chewing this over when she realised she wasn't alone. Seeing Geoffrey leaning on the door frame, grinning at her, Carolyn felt herself blush. 'Is that what retired policemen do these days – spy on people?'

'Only on the beautiful ones. And before you act all cross, I just want to say you've not changed a bit, Carolyn.'

'Oh, don't be so stupid,' she scolded, even though she was secretly pleased. 'I'm twenty-nine years older, of course I've changed. And as for you, what's going on with the Grizzly Adams look? I'm surprised Madge puts up with it.'

'Grizzly Adams.' Geoffrey laughed heartily. 'I'll take that as a compliment. This took a lot of time and effort to nurture,' he said, stroking his beard. 'Unfortunately, Madge doesn't say much about it these days,' he continued as a more sombre look touched his eyes. 'She was diagnosed with Alzheimer's five years ago. Most of the time she doesn't recognise me, so if she did complain about my facial hair then it would be a very good day for the both of us.'

'Oh, I'm so sorry,' cried Carolyn, walking towards her old friend. 'I didn't know.' The thought of the Madge in her head, vibrant and with a larger-than-life personality – a female equivalent of Geoffrey – being struck with that evil disease made her want to cry out with the unfairness of it all.

'Of course you didn't. These things happen.' The inadequacies of that phrase hung between them until Carolyn broke the silence.

'Do you receive any help?'

'I put Madge in a home last year.'

The defiance in his voice wasn't lost on Carolyn.

'Our son, Adam, lives in Spain. When things got bad with his mum he offered to come back, live at the house for a while. I couldn't let him do that. It wasn't fair on anyone, Madge included, when I couldn't cope with her. But I'll tell you something, it's damn lonely on your own.' He coughed. 'Anyway, how about you? How's what's-his-name, the man who stole you away from Lincolnshire?'

'You know what his name is, and Ron is fine, thank you,' Carolyn answered curtly. She was pleased to see his face crinkle into a grin. 'Look, why don't you make yourself useful and lay the table. Dinner will be ready in about ten minutes.'

As their banter flowed again, she struggled to remove the new image of Madge from her mind. It was at times like this she appreciated her own family and realised how lucky they all were.

She thought of Sarah as one of her own, and nothing short of an emergency at home would have stopped her from coming up, but it was with a sense of longing she now thought of her husband and children.

As she listened to Geoffrey reminisce about the good old days she found her attention wandering. The kitchen clock showed it was nearly seven; Ron would be making a cup of tea before settling down to watch *The One Show,* while across the street her daughter would be trying to steer little Sophie to her bed. Living so close to her granddaughter was a real delight, and if she weren't currently over 200 miles away then she'd be over at her daughter's being conned into telling two or more bedtime stories by the four-year-old.

When she had phoned Ron last night and he heard what had happened with Sarah, he had wanted to travel straight up and join her. Tearfully, she had managed to persuade him not to. She had then lied to him. For the second time since she had received the call from Matt, she had bent the truth to spare her husband's feelings; pretending to be as stunned as he was at the suggestion of repressed memories.

Although shocked and angry at her brother's dying confession she had respected Oliver's wishes. Until she had enlisted Matt's help she hadn't told anyone, and it was the hardest thing she had ever done. The initial fury was in part due to the fact she had been put in such an awful position. During their forty years of marriage, she had always told Ron everything, and as far as she knew they had never had any secrets from each other. And, knowing her husband as well as she did was the reason she didn't confide in him all those years ago. Even if she had convinced him not to say anything, he would have always acted differently towards Sarah. There wasn't a deceitful bone in his body. She dreaded the moment when she would have to own up to him.

In the last few days, her childhood habit of biting her fingernails to the quick had re-established itself, and she was nibbling an already raw piece of skin when Geoffrey's voice cut through her thoughts.

'You don't have to hide in here, you know.'

'I'm hardly hiding,' she snapped. 'It's down to me that people are actually going to eat a decent meal tonight. If it was left to others then...' Carolyn stopped with a sigh. Geoffrey wasn't a fool. 'Sarah says she's forgiven me but... well, maybe it's me who can't forgive myself. I should have told her sooner.'

'When did Oliver tell you?'

'A few weeks before he died. I was so mad at him. At all of you.'

Geoffrey nodded sadly. 'I thought as much when we spoke on the phone back then. I didn't dare ask.'

'Was that the real reason you never came to his funeral? We missed you.'

'I wasn't sure I'd be welcome. And it'd been so long.'

With the remaining cutlery in his fist, Geoffrey sat on the

nearest dining chair. 'It wasn't my choice, Carolyn. He wanted to cut all ties with the past. If he had asked for my help with anything I would have given it.'

She could see her own doubts and fears reflected in his deep-set eyes. 'Tell me honestly, Geoffrey, do you think my brother did the right thing?'

He glanced away before replying, 'I don't know. It could have ruined a lot of careers, mine included. But if you'd seen her in that interview room – her blank face.' The big man shivered at the memory. 'The decision was ultimately his, but I was...' he paused, struggling for the right word, '...relieved when Oliver put a stop to it. Whether he was right with all the other stuff – the getting rid of the evidence – I'm not sure. You saw Sarah grow up; what do you think?'

It was a well-trodden place in her memories, and as she joined Geoffrey at the table the familiar sadness descended. Since Oliver's confession she had spent many sleepless nights picturing the eleven-year-old girl whose life had been turned upside down; trying to imagine the possible secrets hidden in that pale, withdrawn child.

'I remember feeling so grateful she was spared any physical trauma. Yes, she had lost her mum, but thank God she hadn't been at home when the killer had struck. Or so I thought. I was delighted when Oliver asked if they could stay with us.'

It had seemed perfectly reasonable for her brother to want to hide his daughter away from it all. And for the first few weeks after her mother's death, Sarah had stayed with them on her own, while her dad had gone through the motions of finishing their lives in the north.

'When it was front-page news we tried to keep the gruesome details away from her. It was bad enough she had to suffer unbearable loss at such a young age without having to confront how it had happened every day.'

She smiled wistfully. 'The first time we heard her laugh again was music to our ears. I can't tell you if Oliver had regrets over what he did. I can only imagine it must have eaten him up inside to know his actions may have allowed Molly's killer to escape justice, but I do know he was fiercely proud of who Sarah grew up to be.'

With a newly found conviction Carolyn told him, 'And I think it was thanks to her father that Sarah has become the wonderful person she is now.' Her smile faltered. 'But she deserved to know a long time ago, and that burden is on my shoulders.'

'Rubbish. Sarah owes you a lot: you did a splendid job of bringing her up. From what she's told me about her nightmares and flashbacks, it sounds like her mind has decided it's time she dealt with her past. The fact you're here to help her through will mean the world to her. Am I right, Sarah?'

Carolyn swivelled round to see her niece looking suitably embarrassed.

Sarah stepped towards her aunt. 'I seem to be making a habit of listening to private conversations. You'd think I'd have learned my lesson by now. I don't blame you, Carolyn. You were only trying to protect me. I know that.'

Before Carolyn pulled her into a hug, Sarah looked across at Geoffrey. 'I can see why you were a friend of Dad's; you even sounded like him then.'

The two women embraced. Close to tears, Carolyn was the first one to pull away. 'Please speak to Matt. I don't have the right to ask you to forgive him, but I begged him not to tell you.'

Seeing Sarah's lips tighten she was then surprised when her niece slowly nodded. 'I'd already decided to call him tonight. Although I can't promise not to make him suffer.'

# CHAPTER TWENTY-NINE

O ver dinner, Geoffrey had entertained them with stories from his detecting days, and Carolyn's food had revitalised everyone. It was the first proper sit-down meal Peter had eaten in nearly a week, and he had been pleased when Sarah had also tucked in enthusiastically.

When they'd gravitated to the living room for drinks afterwards, the only ones to opt for something stronger than coffee were Geoffrey and Sarah. And now, as they all sat back around the dining table, Peter saw it hadn't done anything to calm their nerves.

'I feel I should say let's bring this meeting to order, or something equally grand,' Sarah said hesitantly, as all heads turned towards her.

Peter squeezed her hand that was clasped tightly on her lap. It was cold and clammy. 'How do you want to do this?' he asked her gently. She frowned with indecision, and he suggested he should take a look in the envelope first.

'No.' Sarah pulled her fingers away from his. 'I want to hear from Geoffrey.' She leaned forward and addressed the retired detective eagerly. 'You said on the phone you remembered what my father had omitted from his final statement.'

Geoffrey took a quick swig from his pint of beer, and his fingers trembled as he wiped the froth from his moustache. He nodded slowly and glanced across at Matt, obviously uncertain how to proceed. The psychiatrist gestured for him to go ahead.

As Matt was the only person remotely knowledgeable about repressed memories, Peter was very glad he had been let back into the fold. Sarah had invited him over, and Peter had remained out of the way when he'd arrived, figuring they needed time to themselves. Although both stony-faced, they had emerged from the kitchen hand in hand. He hoped it meant Sarah would listen to the doctor's advice.

Peter shifted in his seat and refocused on what Geoffrey was saying.

'Delayed at work, your father was late arriving home. The weather was atrocious with strong winds and blizzards, and he described running from the car straight to the front door. Only then did he notice that the door was open.'

Peter wondered how often he had gone through his friend's statement.

'He wasn't immediately worried and shouted out. Your wellies were left near the mat, and he assumed you had forgotten to shut the door behind you. Not receiving a reply he said he called out again, and it was then that he saw your coat lying on the hall floor.' Geoffrey coughed awkwardly. 'I'm not sure how much detail you want at this stage. If we look at the photographs inside and you'll see…'

He reached across for the envelope, but Sarah stopped his hand. 'Please, carry on.'

Geoffrey took a deep breath. 'He saw your coat… and it wasn't until your dad went to pick it up that he realised it was covered in blood.'

'Her blood?'

'Sarah, I...'

'Was it my mummy's blood?'

Peter tensed. Hearing Sarah refer to her mum like that sent a shiver down his back. God, what was going to happen?

Matt cursed and stood up. Everyone else was transfixed. Carolyn's hand flew to her mouth.

'Yes,' Geoffrey eventually said.

Sarah recovered her composure but remained silent as she scattered the contents of the envelope out on the table.

When he saw the large crime-scene photographs, Peter wanted to snatch them all up, protecting Sarah from the horror. Instead, he moved his chair nearer to her, hating his feeling of helplessness.

The focus of the pictures – a child's duffel coat: the cream-coloured wool violated by dark red smears.

Peter's heart ached. The panic Oliver Campbell must have felt when he had found his daughter's coat like that. For the first time he perhaps understood why Oliver had taken the steps he had.

Hearing Sarah mutter, 'Oh my God,' he bent over and placed his face close to hers. 'It's all right, you're safe,' he whispered. He felt her shudder.

'I'm okay.' She nodded repeatedly as her eyes, dilated with fear, stared at the evidence in front of her.

'Do you want a break?' Peter asked, as he gently steered her face towards him.

She parted her lips as if to answer but Matt blurted out, 'I think that's a good idea. Sarah should have time to process all this.'

Putting his glasses on, he reached past Peter's shoulder to gather up the photographs.

'No, Matt. Wait.' Sarah stared at Geoffrey. 'What else did they find?'

'Your fingerprints were found on the bloodied bedroom doorknob.'

After Geoffrey's revelations, everyone had needed a break. Carolyn had gone upstairs for a lie-down; Matt was talking with Sarah in the kitchen. And so Peter found himself alone with Geoffrey.

He glanced over at the closed living-room door. 'Was Sarah ever a suspect?' Peter felt his face flush as he voiced the unthinkable: the question the professional part of his internal wiring insisted was a possible scenario.

Oliver's old friend and colleague shook his head emphatically.

'There was no other evidence to link her directly to the crimes. Her mum must have disturbed the killer in Ben's room and was then chased across the landing into her bedroom. Sarah's fingerprints were found on the bloodstained doorknob, left there when she opened the door and saw what had happened to Molly. To poor, adorable Molly.' Geoffrey wiped a tear away. 'The first time I set eyes on Sarah, after all those years, I thought... well, I thought I was seeing Molly. She looks so much like her.'

Peter shifted awkwardly on the sofa. 'It must have been hard to be so close to the family and yet be in charge of the investigation.'

A flicker of anger crossed Geoffrey's face. 'A conflict of interests, you mean. Yes, well, it was different back then,' he acknowledged gruffly. 'Please do not doubt for one second that we didn't want justice for Molly and Ben. Of course we did. What you have to understand is Sarah meant the world to Oliver; she was all he had left of their former life.

'A con from inside boasted he had orchestrated the whole thing. If Oliver had thought the evidence would have helped find the killer then...' He looked up at Peter, perhaps hoping to see more than he could offer himself.

However, his was an expression that mirrored Geoffrey's own

doubts. Peter didn't have any reservations about Oliver's motives. Carolyn had voiced the exact same sentiment, and he'd seen it countless times: how a parent's love can persuade the most rational of people to commit perjury, crimes or even murder. But to hide evidence?

He felt desperately sorry for the late superintendent, but he wouldn't have done the same in Oliver's shoes. Christ. What could have forensics found in the bloody smears on that coat? Jack would have bloody kittens, for God's sake, if a major piece of evidence like that was removed from one of his scenes.

'Was the coat processed at all?'

Geoffrey sighed. 'Oliver had it pulled twenty-four to forty-eight hours into the investigation. He persuaded people it wasn't important, that he'd taken it into the bedroom without thinking and dropped it in the blood.

'I didn't even know he had kept the original crime-scene photos and reports. When the prisoner's confession was retracted a few years later I contacted Oliver and asked him if he still had the evidence we'd made disappear. He told me he had destroyed it all.'

'Why?'

'He didn't want to risk any future investigations raking it all up and questioning Sarah about things she had no recollection of. The case was re-examined, but no further leads were found. For a group of honest cops we did a damn good job of pulling evidence,' Geoffrey admitted unhappily.

'It's done,' said Peter. 'But what I don't understand is if what Sarah has seen are flashbacks of what really happened, then why was she allowed to escape? Why didn't the perpetrator silence her then, or later? He wasn't to know she didn't remember him.'

'I haven't been able to make any sense of that either. At the time, we didn't think she had encountered the killer. We'd thought it was likely that she'd got blood on herself and wiped her hands on her coat.'

The two men exchanged worried looks. 'Is Sarah's memory still playing games with her?' Peter asked finally. 'Is it possible her mind is filling in the gaps with events that never actually happened?'

'Yes, I think that's entirely possible,' said Matt, as he walked in from the hall. 'I've spent the last half an hour trying to persuade her to let me refer her to our inpatient facilities. I honestly believe time away from here, with qualified staff to help her, would be in her best interests.' He flopped on the sofa. 'She's not having any of it. She is currently sitting in her back garden drinking the wine Geoffrey brought.' He sighed, looking like a man who had already lost an argument. 'She has promised to reconsider in the morning.'

'I can stay as long as this takes,' offered Geoffrey grimly. 'Any sign of problems and I'll take her to the hospital myself – kicking and screaming, if I have to.'

Hearing the determination in his voice, Peter was very grateful they had him in their corner.

Peter grabbed a beer and joined Sarah in the garden. She was sitting on the doorstep, her arms wrapped around her knees, an empty glass in her hand and a bottle of wine at her feet. As she moved over to give him space, she pulled a face. 'It was lovely of Geoffrey to bring a bottle, but I shouldn't have drunk it all. I'm getting a stinking headache.'

Before Peter could reply she asked him what he thought might happen now. 'Do I simply wait for the memories to come?'

'What did Matt say?'

Sarah glanced at him suspiciously. No doubt she'd guessed Matt would have tried to recruit Peter into siding with him.

'He wants me to go to hospital.'

He opened his mouth to speak but Sarah held her hand up. 'No, Peter, please. I know what you're going to say, and maybe he is right, but not tonight. Regardless of what Matt might think, I'm completely rational – if a bit drunk – when I say I'm better staying here. Carolyn will be in the next room and Geoffrey has agreed to sleep on the sofa, for one night at least.'

'It's okay, I know better than to try to persuade a rational woman to do anything she doesn't want to do. It usually ends in pain. My pain.'

She relaxed into a grateful smile. 'Thanks, Peter.' She paused. 'I wouldn't have hurt you too badly.'

'I appreciate that.'

The ensuing silence was a comfortable one, and under different circumstances Peter would have enjoyed the closeness he was sure they both felt.

A movement off to his left caught his attention and he was quick enough to catch a flash of tortoiseshell in the arc of the outdoor lights before the feline intruder dropped over to the other side of the wooden fence. He wondered what secrets that cat saw during his nightly patrols.

Peter looked round Sarah's small garden. Although the grey wet slabs of the small patio had nothing but moss and early weeds to offer, either side of the paved space were beacons of colour: several terracotta pots full of winter pansies and other flowers he didn't recognise.

'It's a lovely space out here.'

'I do my best with it, but I'm not what you would call a natural gardener. Every year I plod to the garden centre and hope for the best that what I pick actually grows. Bryan said he would deck it all out for me. I think he was a bit put out when I said no.'

'Is everything okay between you two?'

Sarah nodded, but he noted a slight hesitation. 'I feel so awful about what happened.'

Peter had questioned her about it last night when their awkward interaction in the hall had piqued his interest. She had assured him it was nothing. A stupid misunderstanding. A quick fumble unreciprocated. But he was certain there was more to it.

Peter pulled a weed from the edge of the patio and crushed it, yanking the leaves apart. Keeping his voice neutral, he asked her how long she'd known Bryan.

'About a year and a half. We met on a mentorship course. He hadn't been in the area long, so didn't know many people in the trust.'

The strength of the wind increased, and Sarah grasped her cardigan tightly. She shuddered and screwed her face up at Peter. 'You must be freezing.'

'I lost feeling in my right buttock a while ago,' he admitted, grimacing as he stretched his legs out in front of him. 'How well do you know Bryan?'

'Please don't get the wrong idea about him. He's been a good friend. Oh, I hate this,' she blurted out.

'It wasn't your fault.'

'I know but, Peter, I've even been wondering whether he's behind these things that have been happening. And that's ridiculous... and so messed up. He would be devastated if he knew.'

'Have you told him what's going on with you?'

'No, he would only want to help and, well, it wouldn't be a good idea, not now.'

Sarah lifted her head, and Peter could see the anguish in her eyes as she explained how Anne had tried to set her and Bryan up. 'Drove me mad with her matchmaking.' She was hugging herself to keep warm and now she doubled over as if in great pain. 'Where is she? Why hasn't she come home?'

# CHAPTER THIRTY

'I can't believe she's toying with me. Not even one tiny sign that she knows who I am.'

The sound of his torch smashing against stone elicited a whimper from the darkness.

'You would've thought she'd be grateful when I left the locket.' His words were slurred and fuzzy to his ears. He exhaled noisily: the breath changing into a humourless laugh that echoed around the cellar. 'Maybe she knows what I've been up to, Anne. Do you think she's jealous?'

He could understand her giving him flak for the prostitute killings. They were messy. But, surely she wasn't cross about his more refined activities. His special ladies. Sarah must realise it was because he adored her.

He spent time with those women, so he was clear-headed when she was near. The eyes that looked up at him while he was ending their lives, mirrored the eyes of the little girl who had told him everything was going to be all right.

Wiping beads of sweat from his face, he examined the base of his thumb with the flickering torchlight. Shit. It hurt. Small spots of blood speckled the bandage. He'd have to be careful the bite didn't get infected.

The memory of holding the small struggling body was fresh: the waiting and not giving in to the temptation to squeeze; letting the drugs do their work. He hadn't intended to kill, however he was so fidgety and on edge despite medicating, he'd welcomed the release.

The only regret he had was he wouldn't be able to use the old lady's house anymore. Never mind. In truth, he was getting tired of all the nagging: can you fetch this for me, can you do that for me?

'Well, Anne,' he said into the inky gloom, 'our game is coming to an end.'

He wasn't surprised when he didn't receive a response. He shifted forward but backed away when a nasty smell hit his nostrils.

'My God, you stink. Phew-ee. If I didn't have this door open I'd be high on your stench.'

This made him giggle. He pushed up from the damp floor and staggered out of the cellar, calling, 'And don't be offended if this is my last visit. These one-sided conversations are getting a little tiresome. And pongy.'

Now there was a cry, but his chuckle all but drowned it out before he slammed the door, silencing the plea for help.

# CHAPTER THIRTY-ONE

'Hey, watch where you're going.'

Not concentrating, the hospital porter had almost pushed the wheelchair into the wall. 'Sorry mate, I've got dodgy wheels here.'

'Yeah? Well, if you ask me a lot of things in here are dodgy,' cried the cross patient. 'It's amazing any of us get out of here alive. And I am not your mate.'

'No, no you are not,' he replied as contritely as possible, catching the amused eye of the policewoman as they passed.

As he smiled at the officer, his mind was glumly reviewing his options. He had none. It would be nigh-on impossible to get into that room. He'd be bloody crazy to try it. Even if he did manage to get through the door, he would have to deal with the bloody guards.

If he had time he could try and plan a way in, but that was the problem, he didn't know if he did have any time. Carl's transfer from ICU had come as a shock. If he was well enough for a general ward, then he was well enough to blab. And he couldn't let that happen.

He should have left it all alone. Looked the other way. Prayed that Carl would simply give up on his self-imposed quest. Well, it was too fucking late now. He had to finish what he'd started. The boy had to die.

The sad thing was his idea had been a good one. Considering he had made it up as he went along, it had initially worked out okay. Carl had been more than willing to meet him at The Black Bull, after swallowing all the garbage about him being a private detective. The way he was all fired up, Carl had probably thought he'd found an ally in his search for his sister's killer. Stupid, trusting fool.

Not having the foggiest how many bisoprolol tablets to crush or what was going happen after he'd added the medication to Carl's beer, he'd hoped for the best.

After they had left the pub, he'd watched Carl stride to his car and had begun to doubt it would work at all. Fearing the effects would be a mild hangover in the morning, and not wanting to miss his opportunity, he had followed Carl in his own car. He remembered how he had been glancing nervously over to the shoes laid on the passenger seat, wondering how on earth he was going to proceed with that part of his plan, when Carl's car swerved across the road. He had cheered.

Luck was on his side, although he had also thanked God numerous times for his success. He was trembling so much as he made his way down the embankment he was sure it had taken divine intervention for him not to slip to his death. As for the ascent, every time he'd stopped to get his breath back, he thought he'd be challenged by someone in the surrounding darkness.

The only time God abandoned him was when he had gone into her house. He couldn't look at the poor woman. He planted his evidence and then got out of there quickly, but he had still felt dirty the next day. The smell of evil had stuck to him.

But he had accomplished what he'd set out to do, and this had made him feel worthwhile again.

He'd arrived at his home and seen the van in the driveway,

and his first thought had been to wake him up. Tell him what he had done. However, even after his success, he had recoiled at the prospect of confronting him.

And now, he was glad he hadn't told him. He'd fucked up. Carl hadn't died after the crash. He'd be angry with him. Very angry.

Leaving the grumpy patient at his bed, the porter hurried past the small group of people gathered outside Carl's room. He shouldn't be here. His grip tight on the chair, he kept his eyes to the front.

'Excuse me.'

*Keep walking. Don't look back.*

'Excuse me, please wait.' A nurse caught up with him. 'The patient's notes are still slotted in the back of the chair.'

He turned round. 'Sorry, love. Here you are,' he said, handing her the pile of paperwork. Shit. His hands were shaking. She would know something was wrong. But she moved off quickly, tutting under her breath.

He glanced over to the side room and saw a tall man in a tweed jacket staring at him. His heart thumped loudly in his chest as he recognised the man from the press conferences. For once, the porter was glad that his face was obscured by a surgical mask. Their eyes met for a second before the detective looked away, more interested in what the doctor was telling him.

The porter pushed the door open and backed swiftly out of the ward. A familiar pain was rising in his chest, and he suspected the sweat sticking his shirt down was not only due to panic.

# CHAPTER THIRTY-TWO

His throat dry and scratchy, Peter gulped down a few lukewarm mouthfuls of the tasteless machine coffee he had grabbed on his way up to the incident room.

There was little progress in the last twenty-four hours to report. The visit to the hospital earlier had been a waste of time. Yes, Carl was out of intensive care, but he was talking rubbish. The only person he'd speak with was his dead sister, and they'd gleaned nothing from his one-sided ramblings. The doctors were unsure whether his confusion would be short-term or whether he had permanent brain damage due to the very low blood pressure he'd had on admission. Either way he couldn't contribute anything to the investigation.

The lack of new developments meant Peter didn't have much to say in this Friday morning briefing and, for once, he was grateful. He hadn't drunk too much yesterday evening, but his thoughts were foggy. It had proved impossible to switch his mind off after leaving Sarah's, and sleep had eluded him.

He was about to speak when the incident room's door was flung open. The resulting bang as the handle hit the wall made everyone shudder – their concentration shattered.

'DI Bacchas, are you trying to give us all heart attacks?' Peter demanded, irritated at the loud interruption. 'I'm in the middle…' His protest faltered as he saw Khenan's face. 'What is it? What's happened?'

Jack appeared behind the inspector, and Peter's uneasiness grew.

'I'm sorry, Peter. We need to talk to you now.' The young CSI looked serious. 'Something has come up…'

'Something?' spluttered Khenan, shaking off Jack's hand that had settled on his arm. 'It's certainly that.'

His impatience was infectious, and in contrast Peter found Jack's reluctance to speak in front of the assembled team frustrating.

'Okay. Everyone except Doug take a break.'

Even the curious got the message, and the grabbing of coats and bags got more urgent as the DI's scowl deepened.

When the four of them were alone, Khenan blurted out, 'A match has come up on one of the finger marks lifted from the prostitute killing three weeks ago.'

'You've found him? That's great news.' Peter was puzzled at the vibes emanating from the other two men.

'This morning I ran the prints I found at Sarah's. They matched our killer.'

'Oh my God. Are you sure?' It was ridiculous of him to ask. Jack was fastidious in his work, and he would have triple- and quadruple-checked this one before lighting the touch paper. But…

Jack didn't look offended. 'Our database – IDENT1 – identified the matches based on its minimum accuracy threshold, and my initial analysis would back that up. Although the different surfaces our marks were deposited on makes comparison harder, it was…' He glanced over at Khenan who was glaring back impatiently. 'I'm sorry, Peter, it's close enough.'

'So, my question is why have our suspect's prints turned up at your new girlfriend's house?' In his agitation, Khenan's Jamaican accent was strong. 'Jack says she's a nurse. Are you sure there's not sumen she hasn't told yah?'

Peter moved fast, but Doug moved faster, stopping him from reaching Khenan. Afterwards Peter wouldn't be sure whether it was Doug's strong restraining arms that saved him from crossing the line or the regret on his friend's face.

Khenan raised his hands. 'Sorry, Peter. I shouldn't have said that.'

'Damn right!' He shook off Doug's arms. 'I need to think...' He pictured Sarah sitting in her garden the night before. Was she lying to him? Why? How was she connected to Khenan's case?

Their office manager poked her head bravely around the door. 'Is everything okay in here?'

Peter beckoned her in. He grabbed a pencil and tore a corner off the nearest notepad. 'I don't have time to explain, but I need you to send a patrol car to this address. Tell them to stay with Sarah Knowles until we get there.'

'Hold on,' cautioned Khenan, 'I'm not sure that's the way to go.'

The sergeant leaned over to read what Peter was scribbling. 'Is this to do with our case? I don't remember her name popping up.'

'No, but it's very important. She may be in danger.'

The urgency in his voice was enough to spur the sergeant on. And as soon as she had bustled from the room, Khenan was out of the starting blocks.

'Are you sure about this, Peter? I understand she's your friend, but if she knows my guy... I'm not saying she's involved, for Christ's sake, but what if he's with her now? Those cops could scare him off.'

Peter was about to argue when Khenan pushed up from the table he was perched on. 'Let's go. We'll talk on the way.'

As the group moved towards the door, Peter stopped Doug.

'I'm sorry, I need you to stay here. Hold the fort.' And this was Khenan's case. It was him going along for the ride, not the other way around.

Khenan strode out in front, not stopping to hold the door open for him or Jack. He whipped his mobile phone out of his jacket pocket and after pressing a couple of buttons muttered under his breath as he waited for a response.

'Louise, meet me at the car. Jack's got us a match. No, not a suspect, which is why we can't go all gung-ho. They match prints from another case... sort of.' Khenan glared at Peter when he said that, as if to say you can explain that one, you bloody idiot.

Peter couldn't blame Khenan for being angry. His elation when he had heard of the match would have been followed by frustration when Jack admitted he'd been working off the record, as a favour. From now on, this had to be done by the book.

As they sped down the stairs they passed the place where he had overtaken Khenan the other day. Was that only Monday lunchtime: four days ago? So much had happened.

As they headed out the back entrance towards the waiting cars, DS Louise Clark caught up. The blonde-haired sergeant glanced at Peter, clearly wondering what he was doing following up a lead on their case.

Before leaping into the back of Khenan's grey BMW, Peter ran to his own car and took out his grab-bag from the boot. He hoped he wouldn't need any of his protective kit, but as they had no idea how this was going to pan out he didn't want to take any chances. Jogging over to the two waiting detectives, he waved as Jack went past. They would see him at Sarah's.

As Louise drove, Khenan filled her in on the latest development. Peter slid down in his seat and tried to zone out their conversation. The same questions kept coming back to him. What did Sarah have to do with Khenan's killer? Why were his fingerprints in her house?

The scissors and screwed-up photo in her bag were troubling

him. If they hadn't been put there by Sarah then why would someone dump them in the bag? Come on. Think. What if the intruder had been standing there when he'd heard Sarah's key in the door, and panicked; had only a few seconds to hide what he had in his hands and then hide himself? But why not take the scissors with him? Unless the means of escape made that difficult in the time he had.

'Oh, shit.' How could he have been so stupid? 'He didn't use the bloody door,' he blurted out, causing the two in front to jump.

'What?' asked Khenan, alarmed.

Still processing the idea that had slapped him moments before, he ignored Khenan. In his rush to reassure her, he'd missed what had been staring him in the face. Casting his mind back three days ago, when he was balancing on her ladder, his attention fixed on the far side of the roof space, he had barely registered the rope and wood near his head. Anyone gym fit could haul themselves through the hatch.

Khenan twisted around in his seat and gave Peter a hard stare. 'We're almost at her house, so anything that will shed light on what we're dealing with would be appreciated.'

'I think he got in and out through her attic – it's the only logical way left, and I missed it. There isn't a pull-down ladder,' he explained, 'but there was a coil of rope near the hatch. I can't believe I didn't see it. And then, well, it looked like Sarah hadn't had an intruder after all.'

Khenan said, 'It's a long shot. But if it's true, then the obvious suspects would be her neighbours.'

'Her house is an end terrace, her neighbour a Mrs Wilson, in her late eighties. We need to look in her attic. God, if I'm right it's possible there's a way through the whole damn street.'

Until now Louise had kept quiet, but as she turned into Sarah's road she said, 'I'm sorry, but why did you say that it looked like there hadn't been an intruder?'

'It's complicated,' he replied, carefully. 'There's a lot going on with Sarah. And yes, don't worry, you'll get to know everything. Just not now. Not until I know she's safe.'

A patrol car was outside Sarah's house. Shit. A policeman was staring out of her bay window. Having no idea why they had been called over there, the concept of discretion evidently hadn't entered the officer's head.

Accosted by doubts, Peter grimly held the top of the passenger seat and waited for the car to stop. Had he jeopardised Khenan's case by acting like he had? His usual analytical mind had been rewired by his overriding fear for Sarah. Well, there was no way he was staying in the car, but he wouldn't have blamed Khenan for demanding it. He didn't, and after a brief discussion outside, Peter ran into the house.

A female PC and Geoffrey were standing guard at the open door to the living room. 'Ah, now we'll get answers and finally find out what's going on,' exclaimed Geoffrey. 'Everyone is gathered in here, detective chief inspector.'

Peter gave him a brief smile, grateful for his presence. 'Thank you. Who else is in the house?' Hearing there was only Sarah and Carolyn, he relaxed slightly.

'We're in here, Peter,' cried Sarah's anxious voice, and he had to fight the impulse to run straight to her.

Geoffrey's eyes narrowed as they were joined by the other two plain-clothes and Jack, hauling his CSI garb into the hall. 'Should I expect trouble?'

'I hope not,' Peter replied, patting his arm. 'DI Bacchas and DS Clark, this is retired Superintendent Beaton.'

As they shook hands, Peter saw Louise taking in the larger-than-life persona of Geoffrey – who, dressed in a red plaid quilted flannel shirt, looked even more like a fisherman.

'Geoffrey, I told my colleagues you were helping us with an old case, and I could vouch for you one hundred per cent.'

'I'm glad for the vote of confidence, although I'm damned if I know why I should need it,' Geoffrey growled. He studied their serious faces. 'Is someone going to fill me in on what we've got here?'

'I'm sorry, sir,' said Khenan, 'we don't have the time to explain now, except to say it's part of an ongoing investigation. Peter?'

'The loft hatch is up these stairs, on the landing. As I said in the car it's not easily accessible; you'll have to use Sarah's ladder that she keeps in there,' he explained, pointing to the cupboard under the stairs.

Peter entered the living room, where the two women were huddled on the sofa. Sarah, visibly shaken, rose to her feet. 'Peter, what on earth is going on? These officers turned up on the doorstep and we were herded into here. They're not telling us anything.'

He gave her what he hoped was a comforting smile. 'It's going to be okay.' Peter addressed the police officer he had seen through the window. 'Did you see anyone loitering near the house?'

'No, sir, the street was quiet. When we arrived, there were these two ladies and…' he hesitated and glanced over Peter's shoulder, 'is he really a superintendent, sir?'

Peter kept his face straight as he guessed Geoffrey had deliberately failed to mention his retirement. 'You'd better believe it, constable.'

Sarah said, 'Bryan popped round this morning to see if I'd heard anything about Anne. He left only a few minutes before the police showed up.'

The PC shot Sarah an uncomfortable look. 'We didn't see anyone leave. Who are we looking for exactly, sir?'

'Yes, Peter. What's happening?'

He was wondering how much to tell Sarah when his earpiece crackled into life. 'You were right. Someone has made a way through. The attic appears empty next door, but we need a team there now.'

'We're on it. You stay there; I'm sending Jack up.'

His head buzzing with Khenan's confirmation, Peter placed his hands on Sarah's shoulders. 'I've got to go, but I'll explain everything when I get back.'

# CHAPTER THIRTY-THREE

The fence came up to Louise's thigh, and seeing DCI Peter Graham straddle it easily she considered following him. Crap, who was she kidding? Before Khenan had called, she had been planning to accompany the prostitution liaison officer to speak to their local sex workers and was stupidly wearing a skirt rather than her usual black trouser suit. Landing on her backside in front of the DCI wouldn't be a great move.

Cursing, she took the safer route round. Luckily, she hadn't sacrificed her sensible shoes for anything more fashionable and was able to race up the old lady's path to catch Peter up before he knocked on the door.

Louise held her arm out to restrain him. 'I'm sorry, sir,' she said breathlessly, 'you have to leave this to me. You're too close to this.'

Peter glared at her defiantly. Was he going to argue? She tensed, ready for a confrontation. Was relieved when he looked away, saying nothing. Perhaps it was fortunate that two other members of her team showed up at that precise moment.

'What have we got then, sergeant?' asked DC Tony Brooks. It

was obvious to Louise that he had recognised the DCI and was staring at him with unabashed curiosity.

Not having the time to go into details she summarised the findings so far; eliciting a low whistle from Tony when he heard about the man-made opening connecting the two attic spaces.

'What we don't want to do is alarm this elderly woman unnecessarily. There's no evidence at this stage to suggest the suspect is still around. We need to go in quickly but softly.'

She reluctantly agreed when Peter suggested he should accompany the uniformed officer round the back, half wondering whether she should issue the PC with instructions to arrest him if he interfered with anything. It was a notion she rapidly dismissed. Peter was her boss in rankings, and it would be a huge paperwork headache she would rather avoid. Also, his wealth of experience could be invaluable.

Taking a deep breath, she knocked loudly on the door.

Louise flinched as the constable whispered in her ear. Her hand automatically flew up to cover her earpiece: a reaction she had tried to curb over the few times she had used one.

'We're at the back door, ma'am. I can hear loud voices coming from the other side: the old lady and an unknown male.'

'Stay there in case someone tries to leave. Use limited force – we have no evidence to suggest they are anything more than innocent members of the public.' She prayed Peter was listening.

A shadow fell against the glass panel in front of her, and Louise wished she were more prepared. The identity of the mystery man worried her. She was already winging it. They had no search warrant and couldn't legally enter the premises without one. Louise needed to obtain Mrs Wilson's permission quickly without scaring the eighty-nine-year-old. She would tell her the partial truth: that they were investigating a break-in next door and wanted to eliminate the possibility the intruder had access to her loft space.

The door slowly opened to reveal a short, white-haired figure hunched over a walking stick. The elderly woman took a measured step back before lifting her head up.

'Mrs Wilson? I'm DS Clark,' began Louise, lifting up her warrant card.

To her surprise, Mrs Wilson only gave a perfunctory glance at her ID before beckoning her into the house.

'That was quick. Well, come in, and I'll show you where I saw him last.' Without waiting for a reply the old woman turned away.

Louise shared a confused look with the detectives behind her. 'I'm sorry, saw who last?'

'Pardon, dear?' Mrs Wilson stopped and tilted her head to one side. 'You'll have to speak up. I'm not wearing my hearing aids.'

'Who are you looking for?' shouted Louise.

'Barrie, of course. He's been missing since last night. The poor wee thing has never spent all night outside before.'

Gesturing for one of the detectives to stay in the hall, Louise followed Sarah's neighbour. She was unsteady on her feet, and Louise was glad when she reached the relative safety of the doorway. Trying to be patient, she hung behind, waiting for Mrs Wilson to push off from the door jamb.

'Who's Barrie?' Louise received no answer from the old lady. What on earth was going on?

'You'll have to shout, she's deaf.'

Louise's heartbeat quickened at the male voice. Her view of the room was impeded, and she had to wait until she could squeeze past. Once in the kitchen she could finally see the figure on their right. Dressed in a pair of dark tracksuit trousers and a white T-shirt, he was resting back on the sink unit, legs crossed and both hands shoved deep in his pockets.

'It's her dog, a white West Highland terrier.' The man stood up straight. 'I don't think that's why they are here, Hilda,' he shouted across the room, his Irish accent unmistakable.

Keeping a smile fixed on her face, Louise said, 'Can I ask who you are?'

'My name's Bryan O'Neall. A friend of Hilda's neighbour, Sarah Knowles. I was passing and...' He tailed off and stared at Louise.

Shit, her expression must have given something away, and he insisted he was told what was going on. 'Has something happened next door?'

Louise waited until Mrs Wilson had sat at the kitchen table, and then explained the reason for their visit. She watched Bryan's face carefully as she did so.

The man raised his eyebrows. 'Oh my God, is Sarah okay? I was over there this morning. In fact, it's not long since I left. I saw no signs of any break-in,' he added slowly.

He was suspicious she wasn't telling them the truth. She was about to reply when a disembodied voice informed her the DCI was heading for the front door. And, as if on cue, she heard Peter demanding to be let in.

Realising it was pointless to stand in his way, Louise remained in the kitchen. Not taking her eyes off Bryan. 'Why did you come over here after leaving next door?'

'I was walking to my car and saw Sarah's neighbour in her garden: very upset about her dog. I did what any good citizen would do, I asked her if she needed my help.'

Peter entered the room, and Bryan's jaw clenched. He clearly recognised the detective and smirked. 'I didn't realise that was a crime around here.'

The smugness vanished from the Irishman's face as Peter strode towards him. 'If I find you have anything to do with this,' he snarled, 'I swear, I'll...'

'DCI Graham.' The authority in her loud voice pulled him into check. 'I need you to step down. Let me handle this.'

Peter moved away from a stunned Bryan and then abruptly propelled forward again and slammed his palm on the table.

Bryan, who had lowered himself into a chair, jolted upwards with a cry.

It was echoed by Mrs Wilson, her distress and confusion clear on her face.

Bryan stared dumbstruck at Peter, his previous cockiness gone. Shakily, he wiped beads of sweat from his forehead. 'Listen, I don't know what this is about, but please, you have to know I wouldn't do anything to hurt Sarah.' He swallowed hard before continuing, 'I came back today because I'd got the impression on Wednesday that something was wrong. In fact, we've been worried about Sarah for ages.'

'Who's we?' Peter asked quietly. He now appeared in complete control.

'Me and her friend Anne. Well, mainly Anne. She was convinced Sarah was in trouble.' Bryan grimaced miserably. 'To start with, I actually thought Anne was making it up, to convince me to make a move. Especially when she disappeared, leaving us to...' He choked suddenly, and threw a glance at Peter before looking at the floor. 'Shit, I've messed up. I should have realised Anne wouldn't have taken it that far.'

Now the tension was over, Louise crouched in front of Mrs Wilson, who was watching the two men in astonishment. 'Do we have your permission to look in your attic?'

After asking Louise to repeat it, Hilda agreed straight away. 'But I don't understand how anyone could get up there without me knowing about it, dear. You should ask my nephew, Philip. He uses the space for working on his studies. He's a good lad. He'll be here soon.'


The next hour was frustrating. Louise appreciated the importance of keeping the footfall upstairs to a minimum but would have given anything to be up there. Raised voices and the clinking of metal as CSI equipment was lugged around could be heard, and she was dying to know what they'd found.

There was a proper loft ladder and, after pulling on overshoes and protective gear, she'd gone as far as the top step. She had seen the jagged hole near the bottom of the far brickwork, and Khenan crouching on the other side. Not wanting to disturb any forensics, no one had pushed their way past, but an average-sized person would've been able to squeeze through quite easily. The plywood that had covered the gap was lying on top of a large suitcase.

The fact that the hole on Sarah's side had been hidden by the boxes put there by her friend Bryan hadn't escaped anyone. It was a pale, subdued Bryan who was escorted back to the station, although Louise was sure he'd be happy to be out of the DCI's reach.

And she couldn't blame him. Since her transfer she'd heard lots of praise for the popular chief inspector. However, after his behaviour this morning the jury was well and truly out in regard to him being on her list of good and stable detectives. He was too emotionally involved.

She was concerned Khenan was allowing his friendship with the DCI to cloud his judgement. He had let Peter go into the attics. Letting him stay next door with Sarah was one thing, but giving him opportunity to possibly compromise evidence was, in her opinion, dangerous.

Mrs Wilson grunted as her head jerked forward. She was perched on the edge of the hard kitchen chair, and Louise was worried that if she nodded off again she would be in danger of falling. Louise suggested that they move somewhere more comfortable and offered her a helping hand.

Hilda smiled. 'I do seem to be very groggy today. I don't know what's wrong with me.'

Even with her stick, the old woman leaned heavily on Louise. They made their way into the lounge, where Hilda shuffled towards an armchair. She accidently knocked against a small table, causing an empty cup and saucer to rattle.

Seeing a plate littered with biscuit crumbs also on the table, Louise wondered how well Hilda had eaten recently. She had a quick glance around the room – it was hovering between dusty and neglected, with a foot into the latter. Everything was neat and in its proper place, but Louise suspected not many of the ornaments had been appreciated or moved in a long time.

'I'm going to call a doctor, Hilda. Get someone from your local surgery to come to see you.'

'Oh, I wouldn't want to bother them. I usually manage fine on my own. Although Philip was wondering if I was coming down with the flu as I've been off my food.'

'Well, let's put his mind at rest by checking you over, okay?'

As Louise arranged a home visit, her mind was mulling over the mysterious nephew. He had turned up on Hilda's doorstep a few months ago, and his aunt seemed to know hardly anything about him. A search of the attic showed no way into the other neighbours' houses. So it was becoming increasingly important to track down Philip Durham.

Turning back to Hilda, she asked, 'Have you any other family nearby, Philip's family for instance?'

'No, he's on his own too, you see. His mum and I,' Hilda gave a big sigh, 'well, we hadn't spoken for a number of years after a stupid falling out over a man. It was my Joe actually. She said I had stolen him from her, which was rubbish of course.

'Don't tell Philip I've spoken badly about his mother, but my sister was always jealous of me. She was married to Philip's father and yet wanted what I had. The last I heard was she had moved to Australia with her family. I never received an address,' she added sadly. 'I had hoped we could mend bridges before our time ran out.' A faraway look passed over her face. 'Philip told me it was her dying wish that he came to find me. I knew who he was straight away, even before he'd said anything. He has her eyes. I was happy to help him. He said the attic was exactly the space he'd been looking for.'

Louise thought it was bloody suspicious how he'd squirmed his way into the old lady's affections. She said he was a mature student at York University, in his final year of a photography course. And even though Hilda insisted she had suggested to Philip to use her attic for a makeshift darkroom, how much had truly been her idea? Her doubt must have shown because the old lady rushed to her nephew's defence.

'He refused the first time, saying he didn't want to get in my way. But I could tell it appealed to him. I think he was having trouble at the place he was staying – too noisy, or something.' She frowned, trying to remember the details. 'The other students were quite a bit younger than him. Anyway, it suited us both: he has the extra space and I have the company.'

Apart from taking a reasonable picture by pointing her digital camera and pressing a button, Louise didn't know a lot about photography. But her younger brother had shown an interest once. He had tried to set up a temporary darkroom in their mum's kitchen, arguing he needed a running water supply and a sink, as well as his print trays and drying racks. The idea hadn't gone down well.

She hadn't seen evidence of any of those things in the attic, although she'd had only a superficial glance around. It was possible there was photographic equipment in the large suitcase.

'Has he shown you any of his work?' probed Louise gently, raising her voice. 'You may be harbouring a David Bailey and you don't know it.'

Hilda's face lit up at the mention of Philip's potential as a famous photographer, and Louise averted her eyes. If her suspicions were proved right then poor Hilda would soon be faced with a different reality regarding her nephew's pastimes.

'Not yet, but he takes his work seriously. Some days he disappears up there for hours.'

'Have you been in the attic recently?'

'Oh no. My legs aren't strong, dear, and I don't have any need to. Before Joe died, God bless him, we used the space to store a lot of clutter, but it was no use to me rotting away up there so I asked Philip to sort it all out for me. Any heirlooms he wanted I let him keep. There was one time I...' Hilda paused, and her mouth tensed as if unsure whether she should continue.

'Go on,' encouraged Louise.

'He always locks the hatch when he's working, says he needs to cut down the amount of light while he develops the film. Well, this one time he left the ladder out and I stood at the bottom and called up to him, asking him if he wanted a cuppa.'

Louise sat forward, ignoring Tony hovering in the doorway.

'He shouted at me to go away,' whispered Hilda. 'He was so angry I hardly recognised him. He apologised later, saying I had caught him at a delicate time. He laughed at what he called his typical artistic temperament.'

Hearing Tony clear his throat again, Louise reluctantly excused herself and joined him in the hallway. He was rubbing his hands. He'd got news. 'We've found her nephew.'

Louise digested this piece of information in surprise. She hadn't anticipated them finding him so easily. 'That's great.'

Tony gave her an amused smile and she realised she was shouting. Lowering her voice she asked, 'Where is he?'

'Turns out he's living in Australia. Hasn't had any contact with his aunt for nearly thirty years.'

'Shit, you're kidding.'

'I kid you not. He didn't even know she was still alive. So far his story pans out.'

Poor Hilda had been conned. She deserved to know the truth, but Louise's priority had to be getting the information they needed. Swallowing back the guilt, she returned to Hilda and asked her when she was expecting her nephew.

'Well, he should be here this afternoon to drop off my

prescription from the chemist and take Barrie out.' At the mention of her beloved pet Hilda's face clouded over. She glanced at the empty dog basket near the bay window. 'He'll be so upset about him going missing, they loved their walks. Barrie would get so excited.'

'Did he say what else he was planning to do today?'

Hilda shook her head sadly. 'I don't think he'll be coming back now, do you? It was so cold last night, and he can be poorly if he gets a chill.'

It took Louise a few seconds to realise she was talking about the dog.

'The thing is, I can't understand how he got out. Philip didn't leave the door open, I checked this morning. If only I'd realised he was missing sooner.'

'In my experience animals can be extremely resilient. Don't give up on Barrie yet.' Louise had the feeling the hope of being reunited with him was keeping Hilda going. 'Listen, it's important we eliminate Philip from our enquiries. Does he keep any other belongings here?'

'He sleeps in my spare bedroom sometimes. There could be some of his things in there.'

Louise barked instructions into her radio, then waited, unsure if Hilda was going to say anything else. 'Hilda?' Louise squatted by the chair, concerned for its frail occupant. The bowed head looked so small, the scalp barely covered by thinning white hair, and she was reassured to see it was gently bobbing in time with the old woman's breathing.

How could that bastard take advantage of such a vulnerable person? There were so many unanswered questions: if this man wasn't who he had told Hilda he was, then who was he?

Thinking she was asleep, Louise jumped when Hilda spoke. 'Philip's a good boy, you know.' Hilda searched her face and then quickly turned her gaze away, but not before Louise saw the desperate look in her watery eyes. 'When he came to my door, I knew who he was straight away. He asked me if I recognised him, and I just knew.'

Louise laid her hand upon Hilda's. Her tissue-paper skin was cold to touch, and both women were silent as Louise gently caressed the swollen knuckles.

Hilda gave a sigh and withdrew her hand. 'Go and do your job. I'll be fine, dear.'

A soft knock at the door prevented Louise from answering. A woman with cropped brown hair entered. 'Good afternoon. I'm one of the doctors from Mrs Wilson's surgery.'

The slight shake in her voice reminded Louise how formidable it can be walking through police activity, especially if you've no idea what's going on.

'Thanks for coming.' Louise flashed her best disarming smile at the nervous GP. 'Hilda isn't having the best of days with us poking around, but I'm worried about her general health. She's feeling dizzy and more unsteady on her feet.'

Louise requested that the doctor seek her out once she had finished, and then left her to examine Hilda. She went upstairs, and Tony came out to meet her on the landing. 'You need to see this, sarge.'

On first glance the room was immaculate. Damn. Clean, dust-free surfaces. They were back to square one. But Tony was quick to hustle her forward.

'It appears our mysterious guest either has an obsessive compulsion to clean or wants to remain anonymous,' he growled. 'However, we've found this under the bed. I guess he thought there was no danger the old girl would find it.'

Louise's annoyance at being ferried across the room by Tony evaporated instantly. Careful not to touch anything she studied the contents of the shoebox in front of her. Two hearing aids were on top of a collection of foil blister packs and loose tablets.

'Photograph then bag everything,' she instructed. 'I'll go and ask Mrs Wilson if she knew these were here. We'd look pretty silly if we were to process her spare hearing aids and expired meds.'

There was an exclamation from behind her. She turned to see a male CSI squatting in front of an open wardrobe. He was trying to regain his balance. 'I'm sorry, ma'am. I thought it was nothing but an old blanket. Took me by surprise,' explained the red-faced technician.

Pulling on a pair of gloves, Louise walked towards the closet. It was empty apart from a pile of clean bedding on the left side of the bottom shelf and what did look like an old dirty blanket on the right. It reminded her of the long-haired white sheepskin rug she used to own and had to eventually throw away when it showed every spill and muddy footprint.

She wrinkled her nose in disgust. The light brown stains smelled of vomit and faeces. As she touched the coarse hair and felt the delicate bones underneath, the haunting image of an empty basket materialised in her mind.

Her mouth too dry to speak, Louise licked her lips and forced a small bit of saliva down. 'We've found her dog,' she rasped. 'Holy shit, Tony. The bastard put him in his wardrobe.'

Poor Hilda. If she'd found him the shock might have been too much. Blinking fast, she was about to move her hand away when there was a slight tremor underneath her palm.

# CHAPTER THIRTY-FOUR

The porter pushed the hospital trolley along the corridor. He kept his head down, not looking at the policeman. He'd seen it as a sign when the request had come up on their computer. Now he was cursing. Was he actually going to do this?

After accepting the job, he'd taken a detour to his locker and had arrived on the ward out of breath, convinced another porter would have already been assigned. At every hurdle he had expected fate to step in. To stop him from having to commit. But the collection went smoothly, and here he was, steering a sleeping Carl to his death. And very likely walking to his own.

Even if it went without a hitch and he left the hospital undetected, there'd be no hiding from this. His life would be effectively over.

Well, he was buggered anyway, what with the breathlessness and crippling chest pains. Last month, when his cardiologist had listed all the things wrong with his failing heart – he'd stopped listening after four blockages and two faulty valves – the news hadn't come as any big surprise. He'd refused surgery in the past and, although she didn't confirm this, he suspected it was already too late.

No, it wasn't the prospect of dying that bothered him, it was the way he was going towards it. He'd scuppered all hope of reaching the pearly gates a long time ago, but in these latter years, booze free, he'd began to wish for redemption. No such luck. After today he would be freewheeling it all the way to the bottom.

There was no choice. He couldn't risk Carl pointing the finger. At least, the killings would stop. Surely he couldn't carry on after today.

His grip on the trolley slipped, and the nurse escort looked across as the IV fluid bag wobbled against the drip stand. He muttered an apology. The porter hadn't met the nurse before and he could tell by the colour of her uniform she was agency staff, hired to fill in the shortfall in numbers. When he had arrived to pick up Carl she'd appeared stressed, and he felt bad that, thanks to him, her busy day was soon going to get a hell of a lot worse.

He stopped in front of the lifts and wiped his sweaty palms on his uniform trousers whilst stealing a glance at the young officer. Would he have to kill him? From the scenarios he had thought up, many had involved incapacitating the guards, killing them if necessary. Could he do that? He'd agonised over Carl but had come to the conclusion that he had to die. The officer hadn't done anything to deserve the same.

Would this mean he was just as bad as…? No. The difference was he had a conscience.

At least there was only one policeman to deal with. He had Carl's current sedation to thank for that. Apart from grunting and flickering eyelids when they had rolled him over, there were no further signs of life as they slid him across to the trolley. The nurse said she had given her patient something to calm him down, and that suited him fine. He had worried about coming face to face with a lucid, chatty Carl who could recognise him, even with a mask on.

He was certain he had guilt written all over him. But the

policeman's gaze was fixed, boredom etched onto his face. Probably wishing he were anywhere but babysitting a suspected serial killer, who looked like death warmed up.

As a ping announced the arrival of the staff lift, he stared at the prone figure swaddled in hospital blankets. He did look like he was dying. Maybe his prayers had been answered after all, and fate didn't need a helping hand.

'Is he okay?' he asked the nurse.

'Believe me, in a few days I bet he's stronger than any of us. If you'd seen him a few hours ago, shouting about his dead sister again, you wouldn't worry. It's the magic of sedation. It's just a shame it doesn't last very long.'

This was it then. He swallowed bile that was burning his throat.

The lift was empty. The anticipation boiled up inside him, and the porter felt a tightening in his chest as he turned the trolley around and backed in. Standing at the head end, he was pleased to see the other two stay near the doors.

He glanced at the intravenous lines snaking from Carl's neck. The relief when he had seen them was huge. From his reading he knew that 100ml of air injected very quickly through one of those lines would cause a large bubble to travel through the circulation with, hopefully, fatal consequences.

Heart beating fast, he took out of his pocket the 20ml syringe he had taken from stores and slid it under the pillow. He looked up to see the policeman staring at him expectantly.

'Which floor?'

'Umm, B.' The button was pressed, and the doors began to close.

No longer of interest to the cop, he exhaled; his wet breath moistening his mask. He didn't dare draw attention to what his hands were doing, so looking ahead he fumbled around blindly as the lift shuddered to life. With its plunger already pulled back he brought the hypodermic up towards Carl's neck. Not used to the fiddly ports on the end of the lines, his fingers slipped, and the syringe fell from his grasp.

As the nurse turned her head towards him, he panicked. Whatever he was going to do he had to do it fast.

He reached under the trolley, feeling the metalwork frame. Where the fuck was it? His breathing was coming too quick. The nurse frowned as his fingertips brushed against the tape. He ripped his improvised harness, and her puzzlement became horror as she saw what was in his hand.

She froze, and he swung the gun towards the policeman. He had the element of surprise and snatched at the trigger before there was time for even a flicker of concern on the officer's face.

Sound reverberated around the confined space. The recoil smashed through his upper body and the Glock jumped out of his hands, landing on the bed. Against a barrage of noise he picked the weapon up and pointed it at Carl's head.

He sobbed as he saw the boy's eyes were open: fixed on his, bulging and terrified. The nurse grabbed his arm, her scream deadened by the loud ringing in his ears. He wrenched free and jabbed his elbow hard in her face. As she fell, he fired the gun, looking away at the last second so he couldn't see the bullet rip though Carl's flesh. The force pushed him off balance and, tripping over the writhing nurse, he staggered into the closed door.

Shit! Why wasn't it opening? It should be opening. Dizzy and disorientated, he pressed his damp forehead against the cold steel. He was trapped.

# CHAPTER THIRTY-FIVE

Unbelievable. Sarah was sitting in the back of her car, smiling.

Louise stared at her through the driver's mirror. She didn't understand it. If someone had been stalking her in her own home (police training or no police training) she'd be petrified. With her head back and eyes closed, Sarah looked like she hadn't a care in the world. And she had seemed very composed whilst making her statement at the station. At their request, she had listed all the times she had found items moved in her house.

The DCI was right about how the loft hatch had been used to get in and out of Sarah's house. The rope, that he'd ignored a few days earlier, was actually tied around a thick piece of timber, and it looked likely that this wood had been placed across a pair of support beams and the rope thrown down. They'd also discovered Sarah's missing photo pieces in the large suitcase in Hilda's attic. It was bloody spooky, but if anything Sarah had acted relieved. If she was the innocent party in all this, then shouldn't she be more scared?

When she glanced in the mirror again Sarah was watching her. Louise forced her mouth into a smile. 'Are you okay?'

'Yeah, fine, you know, considering. I don't think it's all sunk in yet.' Sarah sat forward, maybe expecting Louise to engage further.

She didn't, deliberately kept her eyes on the road. Sarah's attitude bothered her. She needed time to think.

The rest of the journey back was in silence; neither woman speaking until they had pulled up in front of Sarah's house.

'You don't like me, do you?'

Louise turned in her seat. There was no sign of animosity on Sarah's face. Only a mixture of sadness and curiosity.

She decided to be honest. 'It doesn't matter if I like you or not, that's irrelevant. There's a lot happening around you and I don't understand that, and I don't entirely trust you.'

'Fair enough. Recently there have been times I haven't trusted myself,' Sarah admitted. 'I hope I can prove you wrong.'

'So do I.' Peter was jogging towards her car, and Louise continued hurriedly, 'Other people have put a lot on the line for you. I think you should know DCI Graham was taken off his case.' She watched Sarah's reaction. 'His involvement with you and your link to our investigation was seen as too much of a distraction.'

Seeing how miserable Sarah was as she clambered out, Louise grimaced. Maybe she had been a bit harsh. Sarah had seemed genuinely upset about the news.

But as Peter gave Sarah a hug and whispered, what was no doubt, comforting words into her ear, Louise wondered who would take the time to console poor Hilda. The moment that two paramedics carried Hilda into the ambulance, her pale face adrift with the shock of betrayal, was one Louise would struggle to forget.

They were trying to fit all the pieces together, although it was clear that the man Hilda had thought of as her nephew had been messing with her prescription drugs. No wonder she was ill. She'd had a lucky escape. And so had Barrie, who, according to the vet, was sleeping off an incredibly nasty drug hangover.

Someone cleared their throat, and she was surprised to see DCI Peter Graham standing in front of her. 'Sorry, sir. I was miles away.'

'It's allowed.' He smiled awkwardly. 'I apologise for the whole improvised bad cop – good cop bit earlier. I wanted to put the frighteners on Bryan, to cut through his veneer, so, thanks for not chucking me out. At one point I thought maybe you were going to.'

'At one point I nearly did.'

At least he had the grace to appear sheepish. But, while there was no hint of the aggression she had witnessed in Hilda's kitchen, how much had been staged? His tall muscular frame had made him an imposing spectacle, and she had certainly been convinced he was going to hit Bryan.

'If I want any acting lessons in the future I'll know where to come,' she said diplomatically, searching the chief's face for any sign of hostility.

It looked like Peter was about to reply, but a car door slamming shifted his focus and Louise saw a wave of recognition soften his smile.

'Doug, thanks for coming.'

Before the inevitable meeting with the superintendent, Peter had brought his friend up to speed on what was happening with Sarah and the bizarre turn of events embroiling her in Khenan's investigation.

'I wouldn't miss it for the world,' he assured Peter, placing a hand on his shoulder, 'although I'm afraid it can't be a long play date. I can feel the reins tightening as I speak.'

'Please tell me you're still assistant senior investigating officer?'

Doug sighed theatrically. 'After a lot of arse-licking, and based on my previous behaviour, I'm the super's right-hand man.' He grinned. 'The team are covering our backs. He thinks I'm sat in your office trudging through all the information we've gathered on Carl. He's pushing for us to find him guilty.'

'Crap.' Peter had put on a brave face when talking to Sarah, reassuring her his replacement was temporary while they worked out what was going on here. The truth was he was gutted. He saw his removal as a personal failure and felt like he'd let down both his team and the women they were trying to find justice for.

'I know, buddy. But Carl's all we've got at the moment. On a brighter note, if I'm to call your office mine for the foreseeable future then redecorating may be in order.'

'Don't you dare. I know exactly what accessories are buried in those drawers of yours, and no swimsuit calendars. I mean it,' hissed Peter, as he followed a chuckling Doug up the outside steps. Thank goodness Louise had already entered the house. He didn't want her opinion of him to sink any lower. His involvement in someone else's case was untrodden territory for him but having Doug on his side meant a lot, and his presence was quickly lifting his spirits.

It was, however, with trepidation that he introduced Doug to Sarah. The hope they would like each other had become very important to him.

'So, this is the woman who has pushed the great Peter Graham – lover of justice but lover of none – off his pedestal and sent him reeling head over heels straight into Alice's wonderland.'

Peter groaned. It had probably taken the whole journey from the station for Doug to come up with that opener. Anxious how Sarah would react to his brash colleague, he found he needn't have worried when after a moment of silence she quipped back.

'From what I've heard he's got into many scrapes with Tweedledum long before I met him.'

Doug blinked in surprise before bursting into laughter. 'Oh, I like this girl, Peter. She's good.

'You've got it wrong, of course,' Doug explained to Sarah as he took her arm, 'I'm Tweedledee; muggins behind us is Tweedledum. Once we've sorted this mess out I'll tell you all the times I've had to save his butt.'

Absurdly pleased that Sarah had passed the Doug test, Peter followed them into the sitting room where the others were waiting.

---

Frustration clawed at Louise. Resisting the temptation to stomp down the stone steps like a child gripped in a giant temper tantrum, she combed her fingers hard through her short hair. Damn it. Why wouldn't he listen?

A few minutes earlier she had talked to Khenan, sure he would agree with her misgivings about Sarah. Instead he'd tried to placate her and had the nerve to tell her to give Sarah a break. 'She's going through a lot. I value your instincts, but I think she's on the level.'

Seriously? Give her a break? Clenching her fists, Louise kicked out at a stubborn clump of snow at the side of the road. He'd better be right. The shit would hit the fan if he weren't. She slowed as she approached her car, needing to calm herself before tackling the Friday afternoon rush hour.

'Excuse me?'

Louise, unaware anyone was behind her, twisted round. She didn't recognise the man with the messy blond hair and moustache, but her mind sagged wearily as she spied the card grasped in his hand.

'It's DS Clark, and I'll save you the trouble, Mr...' she looked at the business card he was holding out to her, 'Armstrong. I have nothing to say to the press.'

How had they got wind of the story already?

'I'm not here in a professional capacity,' he assured her, pushing his dark-rimmed glasses back up his nose.

Oh great, another follower. 'You're a friend of Sarah's,' Louise stated flatly.

'No. In fact, the opposite.' He checked over his shoulder and stepped close. 'My mother worked at the same law firm as Molly Campbell. She's always believed Molly's daughter, Sarah, was somehow involved in her death.'

Louise stared with renewed interest at the reporter. 'Did she have any proof of this?'

'No, but there were whispers at the time. My mother and Molly Campbell were good friends, and I know it tormented her not knowing what really happened. When I was tipped off there had been fresh inquiries... I had to come. Until I saw you, I wasn't sure what to do. I guess I was curious enough to want to see her.'

He waited a moment, but when he saw she was hesitant he backed away a little, a finger hovering close to his spectacles in case they slid down his nose again.

'Look, I can see you're busy with something, so I'll leave. But here's my number if you want to discuss her at all.' He nodded towards Sarah's house. 'I'll be in the area for a few days.'

Too engaged in her own thoughts to say goodbye, she stood undecided. Car keys in one hand, his card in the other. Glancing at her watch she sighed; she should get straight back to the station. But she was smarting from having her doubts dismissed so readily by the DI; and where was the harm? She could hear Armstrong out, decide how much weight to put on what he had to say, and Khenan need never know. Unless, of course, she learnt something useful.

'Wait!' she called after him. 'There's a Costa round the corner. Fancy a coffee?'

# CHAPTER THIRTY-SIX

The porter swore as his hand slipped on the gear stick. Not wanting to draw attention, he now had no choice but to stop at the lights. As he wiped his clammy hands on his trousers, he glanced through the window at the hospital.

How the fuck had he got this far? Carl's terrified face flashed before him. He shouldn't have got this far. He'd ran from the lift and careered straight into a steel trolley piled high with notes. As patients' paperwork littered the floor, he had yelled at the shocked secretary and those nearby to get down, shouting that someone in the lift had a gun. In the ensuing chaos he had somehow managed to escape out the fire doors and down the steps to a side exit.

He had been hysterical when he'd reached his car without being stopped, expecting shouts, or worse. He'd dropped his keys and had to fumble on the ground to find them; staying on his knees whilst he'd used his angina spray under his tongue.

One hand on the steering wheel, the other now rubbed his chest. Sweat had soaked his shirt, but the pain had dimmed to a two out of ten. Maybe he was already on borrowed time, but he had to sort things out with his son. Then he couldn't care less what happened to him.

As he reached across for the spray again, his fingers brushed against the gun. He'd left it on the passenger seat, and he hastily chucked it in the glove compartment. A horn pushed through the loud ringing in his ears.

*Shit.* The car juddered as he almost stalled. *Focus.*

He would drive straight to his son's house. No. Wait. That wasn't a good idea. Couldn't risk being followed. He would dump the car and walk.

What about the gun? He should get rid of the bloody thing. But he had a feeling he might have to use it. He'd bought it in Ireland over twenty years ago, when buying handguns illegally was more of a walk in the park, or rather if he were being literal, a few drinks in the pub. He had convinced himself he had bought the gun just in case the police caught up with them, and not because he was scared of his own flesh and blood. The truth had been too painful.

After Debs' murder, he'd faced up to him. Accusing. But his son had cried, swearing he'd nothing to do with it. And he'd buckled. In the end, it needed a stronger man to face up to the truth that his boy was capable of killing his own mother.

When his son had suggested that they both make a fresh start and move up to Ledforth, he'd been happy, thinking that they could finally put all the bad stuff behind them. He'd helped him buy a house. Took a job at the hospital so he could continue to help with the mortgage payments, whilst he rented a bedsit for himself. He didn't mind. He owed his son. Everything looked okay, until he saw Sarah. And he then knew that their move hadn't been as random as he'd first thought. It had all been part of his son's plan. Even then, he'd had no idea how lost his son really was.

It wasn't the boy's fault. They'd been crap parents. Another time and place maybe they would have made a decent go of it, but they were young and selfish. He'd had his whole career ahead of him, people from the art world were beginning to stand up and take notice. He was finally being asked to the right parties when Debs had announced she was pregnant.

His life crashed. She didn't care. Had it all worked out: she'd continue working as a model for easy cash, and he would stay with the baby. She had argued that there was no reason why he couldn't paint his pictures while looking after their son. And because she had been dead against having a stranger looking after her little precious one, he'd given in. Where had that left him? Kicking his heels at home holding a screaming child he had never wanted, addicted to his dad's generosity and his wife's second-hand narcotics.

Of course he'd been bloody resentful.

Okay, he shouldn't have taken it out on his family, but he'd suffered too. He had tried after Debs had left, once he'd begun to get his shit together, but his son had rejected any attempt he'd made to play happy families.

He drove into Tesco's car park. As he opened his door, ready to abandon the vehicle, he caught his own reflection in his side mirror. Guilt and self-loathing stared back, and he glanced away quickly. But not before a vision of Carl's terrified eyes replaced his own.

———

Sarah and Carolyn had gone upstairs, and their movements and muffled voices could be heard by the four men in the lounge.

Peter sat forward. 'There is one explanation we haven't discussed yet.' He waited until all eyes were on him. 'Your prostitute killer and whoever killed Sarah's mother almost three decades ago, are one and the same person.'

'How is that even... shit. Okay, so I was having the same crazy notion,' Khenan admitted reluctantly.

Doug's mobile rang. Pulling his phone out of his pocket, he said, 'I'll have to get this, but you can definitely put me down for a membership into the wild deductions club too.'

As Doug left the room, Geoffrey remained quiet. Peter paused in case he wanted to contribute, but when the ex-detective didn't speak, he took the floor.

'Okay, let's ignore the problems with the time period. What do we know? Sarah's mum was found with multiple stab wounds, and Ben, her son, was battered about the head.' He glanced surreptitiously at Geoffrey before adding, 'It suggests an angry impulsive killer, and not a professional hit as previously thought.'

This time, Geoffrey was the first to respond. 'We had considered that, of course, and then, in the light of the confession, came to the conclusion the killer had staged the crimes to appear like a burglary gone wrong.'

The exuberance he had shown yesterday had vanished, and as he exchanged a look with Peter, the truth was visible in his mortified face. He nodded sadly, as if acknowledging the real reason the initial investigation was flawed.

'Excuse me,' Khenan interrupted, 'I'm not quite up to speed yet. Who provided the original confession?'

'It came from a crime syndicate boss, whom Oliver and his team had put away in the early nineties. A nasty scumbag, well known to have the influence and connections to orchestrate the whole thing,' snarled Geoffrey, curling his fist into a ball. 'The sick bastard retracted his statement when his parole date was approaching.'

Peter could tell Khenan still had plenty of questions about the first inquiry, but he leaned back in his chair and gestured for Peter to carry on.

'Another link to the original crime is the appearance of the locket that both Sarah and her aunt identified as her mother's. If it is Molly's, then why was it left in Anne's car?' He sighed. He was struggling to make much sense of it all.

'Could Anne have left it there as a message to Sarah? How much do we know about her?'

Peter thought about the messy but colourful flat, and the beaming face peeking out from the overlarge sun hat. 'They've been friends for over ten years. Nothing in her past has flagged up any alerts.'

'But the police wouldn't have known what to look for,' stated Khenan. 'Louise will be back at the station by now, I'll ask her to liaise with the missing person team.

'From our street contacts we had a vague description of a man in his late thirties to mid-forties, and that ties in with the sketch of Mrs Wilson's phoney nephew. If he's at the latter end, then that would make him around fifteen years old at the time of the Campbell murder.'

Geoffrey grunted as he eased up from the sofa and wandered over to the fireplace. Peter stared at him. 'Remember anything?'

'I'm not sure.' In spite of the chill outside, the air in the sitting room had become hot and stale, and Geoffrey wiped the beads of sweat from his forehead. 'There was a friend of Ben's… he wasn't a suspect but…' He faltered and swore under his breath. 'I need to see the old reports. There could have been something off with him, I'm not sure. Sorry.'

'Copies are being faxed over to the station this afternoon,' Khenan informed them. 'We'll head over there when I get confirmation of their arrival.'

Trying not to get distracted by Doug's continuing absence, Peter continued, 'If we're right, then where has he been all this time, and why now?' He recalled what Matt had said about repressed memories being triggered. 'It could explain why Sarah is beginning to remember what happened.'

'According to the information Louise gleaned from the neighbour, the man posing as her nephew first appeared four months ago and he's had the run of her house pretty much since then,' said Khenan. 'He hid her hearing aids, and Hilda had no clue he was spying on Sarah and accessing next door via the attic.'

'Jesus,' muttered Geoffrey, horrified.

They all fell silent as there were footfalls on the stairs.

'What are we going to do with Sarah?' whispered Peter. 'She can't stay here.'

'If we place twenty-four-hour surveillance…' began Khenan.

'No. I know why you're saying that, but no,' declared Peter firmly. 'She doesn't deserve to be bait.'

Khenan sighed. 'No one ever does. Okay, a stand-in can stay here; we'll move Sarah to a safe house.'

It was what Peter wanted to hear, but he knew persuading Sarah wasn't going to be easy. She wasn't going to like any suggestion that kept her hidden away. When she'd arrived back from the station, she had wanted to go to the hospital to see Hilda, only finally agreeing not to after she was reassured by staff over the phone that her neighbour was going to be okay.

He was right. The decision wasn't popular with Sarah, especially when she heard where they were planning to place her. 'I need to be close to Ben. He was upset yesterday. I can't move out of town. And anyway, if I go into hiding then I am admitting I'm a victim. I need to get back some control.'

'You can't stay here,' argued Peter, exasperated. He was worried she might welcome Khenan's suggestion for her to stay in an attempt to lure her stalker back.

'Okay, we'll book into a hotel then. There's two or three near Ben's home.'

He was about to protest further when Doug re-entered the room. Something was obviously wrong. And he confirmed Peter's suspicions as he hurriedly said his excuses. 'I'm sorry, whatever you decide will have to be without me. That was the station; I've got to go.'

'What's happened?' asked Peter, moving forward to grab his arm.

Rather than shaking him off, Doug returned the grip and steered him into the hall, the conflict clear on his face. 'I shouldn't tell you but, well I guess you'll see it on the news. There was a shooting at the hospital. Someone tried to kill Carl.'

'Shit.' The expletive exploded from him before he was able to rein it in. It was his turn to manoeuvre Doug further away from the living-room door, and with a tremendous effort lowered his voice to ask, 'You said "tried" – so he's alive?'

'Only just. They've taken him straight into surgery. A bullet penetrated his skull, but the shooter was a lousy shot. They think he's got a chance to pull through.'

'Christ. Was anyone else hurt?'

'Not seriously. Thanks to his body armour, the officer escaped with bruising and possible cracked ribs, and a nurse might have a busted nose.' Doug growled, 'They let him go off the ward to have a scan; we screwed up big time. The shooter got away – a porter by the name of Robbie Clifton. Our researcher is cross-checking everything but so far she's drawn a blank.'

Reeling from the news, Peter followed Doug outside. He was further taken aback when his friend turned and placed a determined hand on his chest. 'What?... Oh, come on, you can't stop me from coming. Not now, Doug, this is my case.'

'I'm sorry, mate. The super would have my guts. And you're needed here. I'll keep in touch. I promise.'

He was right, but it didn't make it any easier to swallow. And as Doug drove off, Peter wondered whether his situation could possibly get any worse.

---

Louise was fidgeting. It was a habit she had tried to curtail in the past, but as she twirled her phone on the table, she reflected that she hadn't been very successful.

The problem was she should be back at the station,

coordinating their inquiries from there, rather than listening to gossip. And what Ian Armstrong was relating to her was all hearsay – about Sarah being a difficult child and how she was always telling lies and getting into trouble – but she couldn't help hanging onto the journalist's every word.

Her instinct was not to trust Sarah, and maybe he could help to prove her right. Louise leaned forward. 'Why did your mother think Sarah was involved in Molly's death when the police didn't?'

'Her dad was their chief; it doesn't take a genius to work out he would have done anything to protect her. The way she was whisked off so quickly; they didn't even bring her back for the funeral. My mum thought it was very suspicious. All their friends did.'

Louise pinched the top of her nose and closed her eyes for a moment. This was beginning to feel like a huge waste of time. If that was all he had, then Louise sided with the Campbells. If their only crime was to shield the young Sarah from the horror of what had happened to their family, then the attitude of so-called friends bugged her.

'Was there anything specific–' Her phone vibrated on the table, and she broke off. 'I'm sorry,' she said, as she saw the DI's number. 'I've got to take this.'

She hurried outside the café before accepting his call. As she listened to Khenan, she watched Ian through the window as he pushed up his oversized glasses. He grimaced slightly and massaged his left hand. He'd done that a few times whilst they had talked, rubbing a scar at the base of his thumb. He looked towards her, and she turned away, hoping he hadn't seen her staring at him.

What had Khenan said? 'Wait. Why there?'

'Sarah wanted to be near her brother, and don't forget this is purely for her protection. She's not under suspicion.' Louise could tell from his voice that Khenan wasn't happy about the decision.

'So, Sarah gets to stay at the Ledforth Hotel whilst we twiddle our thumbs and have got nothing. That's great, sir.'

Louise finished the call, trying not to care that she'd cut off her DI. She could always blame a dodgy signal once she'd calmed down.

'Unbelievable. The bloody Ledforth,' she muttered, throwing the phone straight into her bag. She turned round and bumped into Ian.

'Oh!' *Shit.* How long had he been standing there?

'Sorry, Louise.' He put his hands out to stop her from stumbling. 'My wife has just phoned. There's a bit of a crisis at home. I've got to go.'

'Erm, okay. Well, I hope everything is all right,' she said, awkwardly. *Thank God for that.* She wasn't in the habit of talking to complete strangers about a case and was already kicking herself.

He left with the promise to contact her if he, or his mum, thought of anything concrete to share, but from his expression she wondered if he'd somehow gained more from the conversation than she had.

# CHAPTER THIRTY-SEVEN

The door crashed open. Anne shied away from the torchlight but had no strength to move from his touch. She whimpered as his cold fingers caressed her burning skin.

He lifted up her chin and, cupping her face, brushed aside her matted hair. 'It's all right, I'm not him,' he whispered. 'Oh, what the hell has he done?'

He cursed, loud enough to create a small echo in the underground room. 'Why you? How can I save him if he does something stupid like this?'

His voice. Did she know it? It sounded so familiar. She tried to focus. Everything was so hazy.

'Anne, can you hear me? I need you to get up. You have to get out of this cellar.'

His tone was impatient, and the unfairness of it all hit her. A little help would be better than getting cross at her. She was trying for fuck's sake. Wait, he was moving. 'No. Don't leave me,' she rasped.

He was gone. How could he abandon her? She sobbed in disbelief and tried to drag her useless body towards the open door.

A shadow fell over her. 'Here,' he growled. A damp cloth was held to her swollen lips. She had no saliva to swallow but the wetness pooled in her mouth, and she retched as the liquid hit the back of her throat.

'I'm sorry. This is going to hurt.'

Anne groaned as the cloth was removed. She reached for it, but he easily batted her hands away. And ignoring her protests he bundled her up in his arms. She yelped in pain.

'Shhhh,' he pleaded, 'Please, you have to be quiet.'

*Why?* Helpless, Anne felt no relief at being out of the darkness. Only exposed and vulnerable. Her head banged against his shoulder as he carried her up a flight of stairs. Every movement piled on another layer of agony. Where was he taking her? Blinking against the brightness that burned her light-starved eyes, she peered through her tears but couldn't see anything beyond her rescuer's face. A blurry portrait, whose unclear features gave her no clue to who he was.

A giant to her fragility: he looked straight ahead – his breath unsteady with the exertion of carrying her. Downstairs she had recognised his voice and now she struggled to dredge up his identity from her muddled brain.

His grip loosened and she scrabbled to keep hold of him. What was he doing? It wasn't safe. 'No. We have to get out of here.'

'Don't worry, Anne. I'm going to take care of this.' He gave a big sigh as, peeling away her feeble embrace, he laid her down. 'I shouldn't have let it go on so long. It's all my fault.'

Confused, she watched him close the door and then walk back to the bed. It creaked and shifted underneath her as he sat. Anne peered through the gloom of the bedroom, and his hunched outline kick-started a memory. The giant diminished with the sudden realisation of who had found her.

'It's you.' Her voice barely a whisper. She inhaled unsteadily. 'I know you.' Desperately, she fumbled for a name as he brought his face close to hers. The grey pallor sleek with sweat.

Oh my God, it was Robbie. The porter. What was he doing here? And why wasn't he calling for help? His image rippled. She moaned as the room and her rescuer rose and fell in an invisible current.

Her body felt too heavy to move. Maybe she was safe. Would it be so bad if she let go? She was tired of fighting when all her body wanted to do was rest. She had to sleep. For a few minutes. Only.

Wait. She had to wake up. Had to warn Sarah. Didn't she? Of what?

Anne opened her eyes and saw Robbie hadn't moved. He was talking to her, but she couldn't hear him. It was hard to concentrate. Confusion bombarded her. What was he doing in her bedroom? Should ask him but so bloody tired.

---

Robbie wasn't sure Anne could hear him anymore, but he carried on regardless. 'I thought if I helped him, let him play it out, I could stop him. I would tell my son what I'd done, and he would finish it.

'God help me, I even planned to help him snatch Sarah, if that was what it was going to take to bring an end to his obsession.'

Two days ago, he'd been following his son but had lost him in Hillside Park. He knew it was no coincidence that Sarah was there too. And when he had approached her, he'd struggled with the desire to warn her, to tell her to run before it was too late. Misplaced love had prevented him.

'But, you… I never saw that coming.' He'd almost missed the key left in the cellar door but, once seen, he simply couldn't have ignored it. 'He won't stop. I know that now.' He looked over at the motionless body, glad there was no understanding in those sightless eyes that stared back at him.

'I'm sorry, Anne, I really am.'

He massaged his chest. His pain was seven out of ten.

Someone was climbing the stairs.

'If I'd been a better father maybe he wouldn't have done the things he's done.'

Robbie held the gun, the metal slipping with his perspiration. The bands in his chest gripped harder and the air was thicker. Indigestible. He gasped a breath. The steps outside ceased.

'Dad?' Silence…

Robbie grimaced. 'Come in. We need to talk.'

'Have you taken her, Dad? Is she in there with you?'

He couldn't match the composure in his son's voice, so didn't answer. Each breath was more difficult than the preceding one.

His son opened the door and calmly took in the scene before him. A slight widening of his eyes: the only indication he had seen the gun. 'You look awful. Are you having a heart attack?' he asked dispassionately. 'Where's your spray?'

How could his boy act so relaxed whilst he was finding it a struggle simply to talk? 'Downstairs… but I don't want it. This has to stop.'

Eight out of ten. He used both hands to steady the barrel.

'Dad, what are you doing?'

As Robbie wiped his clammy forehead on his sleeve, the gun wavered.

His son took a step closer. 'You're not well. Let me help you, Dad.'

He was helpless as his fingers were prised away from the trigger. His own ineffective body had eliminated any form of resistance.

Nine out of ten. The heaviness had spread from his chest to his arms, and with a sense of relief he allowed his hands to be guided downwards.

'That's better. I'll go and get your medication. But, first…' His son placed the gun on the bed and crouched down. 'I need to know what you've been up to. Have you spoken to anyone about… her? Because I didn't mean to do it, Dad.'

Robbie laughed weakly in his face. 'And the others? Did you think I wouldn't realise it was you? The likeness between those women and Sarah.' He finally saw a reaction. 'It was always about her, wasn't it? I wanted to understand so I followed you. Saw you with the whores. That's when I realised you needed help to stop. The Sarah copies were never enough; you had to have more.'

He avoided looking back at the steely blue eyes glaring at him. At one time his would have matched them for aggression. How much of his rage, fuelled by alcohol and drugs, was responsible for creating this monster?

'You had no idea I was there.' Robbie panted between words. 'And I wasn't the only one. A man came… said he'd seen me watching you. Told him I was a private detective… investigating fraud. He asked if I thought you were capable of killing.'

Ten out of ten. He gulped down the vomit in his mouth. Had to finish. 'Carl had no evidence… no reason… other than recognising you from one of his sister's parties. Said he was desperate. Looking at all her friends. But if he had investigated your past… I couldn't let him find out.' Feeling a strong pair of hands on his shoulders, he continued, not sure how long he could keep talking. 'I killed him. For you. I thought we could leave here together.'

Robbie's voice was quiet, and his son had to lean closer to hear him. 'I've tried to understand your compulsion – but her,' he gestured towards Anne, 'It's never going to end, is it? The police are on their way.'

For the first time Robbie saw real fear as his son looked at the discarded mobile phone. 'They know I'm here,' he finished triumphant, before bending over and puking violently.

'Oh, fucking hell! That almost hit my shoes.'

He stared with revulsion at his father. Judging by his grey complexion, and the blue around his lips, he was going into cardiac shock. It was tempting to let nature do the dirty work, but he didn't have time to wait. If he were telling the truth the police would be there soon.

'Come on, Dad.' He pulled his dad to his feet. 'You better not be sick on me,' he said, coiling his free hand round his thin waist. He hadn't realised how much weight he had lost. His old man must have been ill for a while.

His father whispered into his ear, 'Was it my fault? Did I do this to you?'

He was contemplating the answer when he pushed the blade upwards into the soft flesh. There was barely any fat to resist and perhaps it was his imagination, but he thought the knife scraped against bony ribs before settling in the chest.

If there really was a heart, he was sure he had struck it hard. He kept hold of the hilt as the body jerked in his arms. On the other side of the room, the reflection in the cracked bedroom mirror showed a father and son embracing; as he stared at the back of his dad's head, he planted a soft kiss on his hair. 'It wasn't you. You were never that important.'

When the body was motionless, he laid him gently down. 'You're correct about one thing though – it is time to finish this.'

He strode over to his chest of drawers and retrieved Anne's phone and battery. 'If she won't come to me, I'll go and get her,' he said, not caring his words were not being heard.

His image in the mirror smiled as he tugged off the wig and moustache. They were beginning to itch, and he was happy to be getting rid of them, although he'd thought he was rather dashing as a blond.

'I know where she is, Dad. And it's what she wants too.'

At the door, he hesitated and glanced back at Anne. She wasn't moving. If not already dead, then she soon would be. He didn't care either way. Couldn't remember why he had taken her in the first place. She'd been close to Sarah, but none of that mattered anymore. It was now just him and Sarah. As it should be.

# CHAPTER THIRTY-EIGHT

M cDonald's drive-through hadn't improved the mood within the car. Small talk had died; everyone occupied with their own thoughts. The heavens had opened, and as large drops pelted the windscreen, Peter was glad Geoffrey had offered to drive them to the hotel.

Rather than dragging Sarah, kicking and screaming, to a designated safe house, they had reached a compromise. They had used the Ledforth Hotel in the past when babysitting a dignitary, so although not perfect, at least they knew all the entrances and exits.

In the back seat Sarah was gazing out of her window, with a half-eaten cheeseburger in her hand. Her earlier optimism seemed to have deserted her, and despite Carolyn trying to engage her in conversation, she'd been quiet since they'd left the house.

Peter reached over and touched her knee. 'Are you okay?'

'Oh, I'm... I'm fine.' She glanced at her burger and smiled ruefully. 'Just not hungry. What about you?'

He hadn't told her about Carl, not wanting to add to her

misery, but she had obviously picked up that something had happened. 'I'm all right.'

'Well, I'm bloody not,' complained Geoffrey, peering over the steering wheel. 'If we don't get clear of this traffic soon we'll all be needing life jackets.'

The rain was relentless, and by the time they reached the hotel foyer they were all soaked.

'Well, I don't know about you three,' declared Geoffrey, using his wool hat to dry his face, 'but I intend to inspect their hospitality services for a while.' And with a decisive nod, and a cheerful wave, he headed towards the bar.

'Do you think he's safe to be left on his own?' joked Sarah, as he strode away swinging his backpack over his shoulder.

'Knowing Geoffrey, probably not. I think I'll go and join him. Keep him out of mischief,' said Carolyn. 'Then I'm going straight to my bed. You know where I am if you need anything.' And with a meaningful look at them both, she too strode across the foyer pulling her red suitcase on wheels behind her.

Seeing Sarah blush, Peter knew she hadn't missed Carolyn's unsubtle hint that they wouldn't be disturbed, allowing them privacy for a proper goodbye.

They rode the lift in silence, the easiness of previous conversations deserting them. Peter mumbled an apology as he accidently brushed against her. Sarah struggled with the door card before letting them into the room.

Whilst Peter put her case on the double bed, she headed straight for the bathroom and grabbed a couple of towels.

Trying not to stare as Sarah released her bedraggled hair from her ponytail, Peter towelled dry his own messy locks quickly. He glanced towards Sarah, and she was looking across at him shyly.

'Thank you for everything, Peter. I know the last few days have been crazy, and I'm sure there were times you wanted to run away from it all.'

'And leave a fair maiden in distress? Never.' He became

serious. 'I was glad to help, and I'll be here for you for as long as you need me. Okay?'

Sarah nodded.

The ensuing silence weighed heavy. 'I had better go,' Peter said reluctantly. 'Let you get some rest.'

'Yes, of course. You'll have to leave this here though,' she added with a smile, removing the damp towel from around his neck.

Feeling stupid, he grinned as she put her arms around him. 'The Rocky look suited you,' she told him, giving him a hug.

'If you need anything there's two police detectives sitting downstairs in the lobby. Call the front desk and they'll come up.'

'I'll be okay. And Geoffrey's threatened to camp outside in the corridor rather than in his room,' she muttered into his shirt.

Neither moved to end the embrace. Sarah's head was resting on his chest, but she'd tensed up against him. Daring to break the spell, Peter lifted a hand from her shoulder and slowly pushed her wet hair back from her face. As she looked up, he read the longing in her eyes and with a shaking hand softly traced the outline of her cheekbone.

'Sarah, I…'

'Shhhh.' She placed a cold finger on his lips. And pulling his head towards her, replaced her finger with her warm mouth. The kiss was soft and hesitant then, as the need overtook, it deepened, becoming hard and wanting.

Desire flooded through him. Near to losing control, Peter steered Sarah backwards until she was up against the hotel's dressing table. Her lips were laughing underneath his, and as she hit the furniture the cups on a tea tray clattered. Lifting her up, he was rewarded by her legs wrapping around his, drawing him in. They hadn't broken their first kiss yet, and his hands were getting braver with each caress. Wet cloth slid over wet skin. He pushed her skirt up, his fingertips brushing the top of her thigh.

His lips left hers, and Sarah moaned as he nibbled her neck.

He wanted her so much and when he pulled away the physical disappointment was painful.

'I'm sorry. I can't do this,' he gasped. 'I want to.' God, he really did. 'But not here. I can't… sorry.'

Sarah's shoulders heaved as she struggled to catch her breath. 'It's okay.' She exhaled loudly. 'You're right. I don't want you getting into any more trouble because of me.'

Peter rested his forehead against hers. Her soft breath tickled his upper lip, and their breathlessness synchronised as the closeness of their lips tempted.

'I'd better go,' he groaned.


Damn his inner DCI. Peter leaned back on the cool wall of the lift. He was mourning his thwarted passion when the lift reached the ground floor and the doors opened. Peter hurriedly straightened as Geoffrey bustled in, but he was too busy struggling with Carolyn's luggage and swearing when the wheels caught on the metal plate to notice anything amiss.

'Blasted woman. Wouldn't settle until I'd brought her case up to her room. I've got a good mind not to go back. She'll only nag me.' He sighed loudly. 'How's Sarah?'

'Erm, okay. Putting on a brave face.' Peter stuck his hand up to stop the lift closing. 'I'm going to have a word with the detective constables in the foyer. Ask if one of them would watch the corridor upstairs. There are too many ways in and out of this place, and not enough manpower to cover them all.'

'You're worried he'll find her?'

'I can't see how, but I'd have been happier if she'd agreed to using a safe house.'

'She's stubborn, like her old man was,' said Geoffrey, with a sad smile. 'My body has got used to surviving on little sleep, I'll do a few patrols myself overnight.'

Sarah eased off the table. She caught a glimpse of her flushed reflection in the mirror, and shuddered as she recalled the strength of Peter's desire. To distract herself she picked up her bag and tipped its contents onto the bed. She reached for her mobile, planning to leave it next to her pillow. Sarah lit up the display and saw that someone had sent her a message. When the sender's identity appeared, she almost dropped her phone. Anne!

> I need your help. Sorry I disappeared but in trouble. Please meet me tonight at 6pm outside Bailey's. No police. Come alone. I'll explain then. Love you, A x

Oh no. Her stomach flipped as she stared at the time. It was nearly seven. Would Anne still be at the restaurant? Panicked, she dialled Anne's mobile, but it was switched off.

The place Anne had chosen was round the corner from the hotel. Sarah quickly changed out of her wet clothes. She would have to sneak out, so the detectives didn't see and stop her. There was a good chance the message hadn't come from Anne, but no way was she going to give up on her friend.

After the police station, she'd felt relief. Rather than being scared, she'd wanted to laugh. Celebrate. She wasn't mad. It was terrifying when she thought she was losing her mind. Having an actual person to blame, and to direct her anger on, had been liberating.

She'd wanted to hold onto the jubilant feeling, share it with Peter. Now there was only guilt. Guilt she'd pushed Anne to the back of her mind. Her friend was in danger, and she'd been thinking about herself.

Sarah was wondering about leaving a note when there was a knock at the door. What if it was Peter coming back? She bit her lip anxiously; there was no way she would be able to lie to his face. Well, she wouldn't let him stop her from going. If there was any chance she could help Anne, then she had to try.

Taking a deep breath, she opened the door, and stared in shock at the figure standing in front of her. 'What are you doing here? Is it...?' Her words died as she saw the weapon in his hand.

She screamed and turned to run into the bathroom, but he was too quick for her. A heavy push in the middle of her back catapulted her forward, and in the few seconds before she cracked her head on the corner of the table, she had time to wonder why he was doing this.

---

Peter loitered, unsure what to do now he'd spoken to the waiting detectives. He was toying with the idea of joining them for the night. Of course, he wasn't officially part of Khenan's team, but it beat twiddling his thumbs back at his flat. He could take his turn in wandering the corridor outside Sarah's room.

He was about to sit in one of the green velvet armchairs dotted around the foyer when Carolyn appeared. She looked worried; her hand playing furiously with her bangles. She was striding towards the lifts but changed her direction as soon as she noticed him approach. The corner of her mouth twitched. 'Peter, thank goodness. I need to tell you something,' Carolyn began. 'I might be wrong, but I think I saw someone when we arrived. Back there,' she added, gesturing towards the bar. 'I should have said, but I couldn't remember where I knew him from. And I'm not sure. I only saw his face briefly as he walked past me – he had a hood up. If it was him then it's weird he'd be here.' She worried at her nail. 'I was waiting for Geoffrey so I could talk it through with him, but he hasn't come back yet. I guess he's–'

'Carolyn!' he interrupted. 'Who are you talking about? Who did you see?'

'Well, as I said, I'm not one hundred per cent sure it was him but–'

'Sir.' One of the detectives was jogging towards them, his radio held out in front of him. 'Excuse me. I'm sorry to interrupt, but he's adamant he needs to speak to you immediately.'

If the gravity in the constable's voice wasn't enough to panic Peter, then seeing the other detective making his way to the stairs was. *Shit, what is going on?*

'Sorry, Carolyn, sounds like I need to take this.' He grabbed the radio. 'DCI Graham.'

'Sir, it's DC Adams. Me and DS Marsden are on our way to the hotel.'

Doug was shouting in the background. 'Tell him we're bringing Sarah in now.'

'What the hell has happened?' Peter's pulse quickened.

'It was the son, sir.' In his excitement the DC was forgetting Peter was in the dark about recent events. 'He's behind everything.'

'Calm down and tell me who you are on about.'

'Sorry, sir.' He took a jagged breath in. 'We found Robbie Clifton, er, the porter, at his son's address. It turns out that Robbie's proper name is Sean Robert Clifton – that's why it was harder to find him in the system.'

'Get to the point,' Peter growled.

'He called the police at the end, but they arrived there too late. He was already dead: killed by his own son.'

'What?' Trying to make sense of what he was being told, Peter didn't immediately zone in on the movement on the other side of the foyer. Then as the other detective set off at speed, he swore loudly and raced to catch up.

'What has this got to do with Sarah?' he shouted into the radio. The panicked eyes of the housekeeper stared at him as he ran past her and up the stairs.

'Robbie wasn't alone. We've found Anne Baxter – she's in a bad way.'

The DC reached the open hotel room before him and skidded to a stop next to his colleague who was crouched over a body. Peter dodged round a red-wheeled suitcase that had been left in the middle of the corridor.

'We've found evidence linking the son to The Beautician and the prostitute killings.' The constable carried on, oblivious that his narrative was now secondary compared to the scene of violence that Peter was staggering towards. 'And it looks like he killed Sarah's mum, sir, and has been obsessed with her daughter ever since.'

With the DC's words echoing in his head, Peter's first thought was to locate Sarah. He groaned as he saw the overturned chair, and spots of blood on the carpet.

*No, no, no.* How could he let this happen?

He turned his attention to the prone figure near the doorway. Peter pressed his face close to the damaged features of his friend. 'Geoffrey? What happened to Sarah? Where is she?'

The battered ex-cop slowly raised his head and focused his one open eye on Peter. 'I erd 'er screamin' from the 'orridor,' he mumbled through thick lips. 'Ee was too strong... I'm sorry...' his voice started to fade, 'Ee took her.'

'The back stairs,' Peter barked at the detectives. 'He must have taken her down the back stairs. Go!'

'I 'ouldn't 'op him.'

His effort exhausted, Geoffrey fainted. Peter placed a hand on his shoulder. 'It wasn't your fault. We'll get her back.'

It wasn't Geoffrey's fault. It was his. And they would find her. He would never forgive himself if they didn't.

# CHAPTER THIRTY-NINE

'It's okay, Sarah. You're safe now.'

The soothing voice caressed the edges of her sleep. Reluctant to wake, Sarah nestled her head further into the soft pillows. With a nagging pain in her left temple, her drowsy sixth sense told her that when a migraine started this early it's worse when eyes are open. So she screwed hers shut, trying to prolong the dreamy state between slumber and full consciousness.

She was so uncomfortable and must have slept with her arms flung above her head. Her right arm stiff and cold. Why couldn't she lower it? The tight bonds around her wrist shocked her into waking fully. The indecision of flight or fight rattled her synapses: whether to be paralysed by the overwhelming fear or to be kick-started into an adrenaline-induced struggle for survival. She chose the latter.

Her feet pushed against the mattress until her back was pressed hard against the wooden slats of the headboard. She cried out as the rope dug deep into her skin.

'You're home, where you belong.'

Her vision blurred, she peered towards where the voice was coming from. Home? Her heart was racing, and it was difficult to breathe. She didn't know where she was, but it definitely wasn't her home. A light shining near the floor barely touched the unfamiliar shadows gathered around the large bedroom.

Pain exploded in her head and its violence brought to her the moment she had cracked her skull on the table. Oh God. He'd attacked her. Questions dying on her lips as he had lunged.

She gulped back a sob. Her left wrist wasn't tied up and curling into a ball she hugged her legs close.

'Please, don't hurt me.' She hated how feeble she sounded, but she was begging for her life. 'Please, Will. You don't have to do this.'

There was no point in pretending she didn't know who he was. He had given her that knowledge back at the hotel and it was too late for both of them to pretend otherwise.

He didn't answer her immediately, and the silence was so thick Sarah felt like she was choking. When he did finally speak, she welcomed his voice.

'Sorry if I've tied the rope too taut. Once you've shown me you can be trusted I'll loosen it a little. The truth is, Sarah, I've lost my faith in you.'

'Why?'

His chair creaked as he sat forward. His face was caught in the star-filled glow of the night-light, and the memory he triggered popped into her head with no resistance. There were no fireworks or any feelings of revelation. It was as if she had always had the memory: the one of him standing in front of her with the bloody knife in his hand.

The young Will she now remembered had the softness of youth and none of the confidence and arrogance of the man. He smiled, and her heart thumped painfully.

'Why?' he repeated. His smile disappeared. 'Do you remember me, Sarah? Do you know who I am?'

She nodded, and when he stared at her expectantly, she whispered, 'You killed my mother. And poor Ben...' Tears spilled down her cheeks. Tormented by the image of her brother being comforted by the person who was responsible for ruining his life, she shouted, 'It's because of you he's like he is.'

Will shrugged indifferently. 'You heard him – he likes me, I give him chocolate. The idiot has no idea who I am.'

Sarah screamed. Her rage and anguish unleashed as she struggled to reach him. The bastard. She wanted to hurt him. To smash the amusement off his face. Unable to break her right wrist free she wrenched her shoes off and threw them. The last one hit him on his chest as he rushed towards her.

He slapped her hard. She wailed as her head slammed into the headboard. Grabbing her left arm, he secured it to a wooden slat.

'It'll be your feet next. It makes no odds to me whether I let you sit up or have you spreadeagled on the bed. Although I would prefer our first proper meeting to be a more civilised one.'

Lifting up the child's pink chair, he swivelled it round before sitting on it again. He rested his chin on its hard back. 'Please believe me, Sarah, it gives me no pleasure to hurt you like this. All I want is the truth.'

His stare became thoughtful. 'When we first met at the care home I couldn't decide if you were toying with me, pretending you didn't recognise me.'

When she didn't respond, he shrugged. 'Well, I guess I've changed quite a bit from the lanky Goth kid your mother felt sorry for. For a time I was scared you had forgotten me altogether. You see, Sarah, you were the one who cared.

'I'd done the unthinkable, and you held me in your arms and told me everything was going to be okay. Yes, I hated you before I realised it was love I was feeling, but I never ever forgot you. It was always your face I saw when I was with the others.'

Sarah whimpered when he stood up from the chair. Dizzy from the second blow to her head, she strained against the rope as he crouched close to her.

'If I thought you didn't...' He closed his eyes and pressed his fist to his mouth as if he would find the words too painful to say. 'I need to know it was because you were giving me the gift of love, and that you meant what you said. Sarah, I…'

He stopped and tilted his head, listening.

'Hello up there. Anyone in?'

Will swore. 'It's always the fucking daddy who pisses on my parade.'

As he stood up and caressed the large knife strapped to his leg, Sarah opened her mouth to shout. He was a step ahead and pounced on her, forcing his hand over her face.

He hissed at her, 'I'm sorry but I can't have you scaring him off.'

Sarah tried to twist her head away to gain enough space to bite him, but he was too strong. She squirmed as he pinned her down. With his weight on her legs, she could do nothing but watch terrified when he reached towards the bedside table. She saw a flash of white and then he was forcing something past her lips. As the cloth was pushed further back it made her retch and she flung her head side to side in a desperate attempt to dislodge the suffocating gag.

'As soon as I've finished out there I'll come back and take this off,' he whispered to her as he tied a second piece of material between her teeth, jamming the first in tight. 'It's best not to fight it. I wouldn't want you to choke while you're waiting for me.'

After he climbed off her, he paused to adjust the gag and kiss her forehead.

Sarah pulled against her restraints; her head full of her panicked screams when in reality all she could produce was muffled grunts.

'Shush. I promise I won't be long.' He scowled as the male voice shouted again. 'Okay, I'm coming. He's so impatient,' he complained, before slipping out of the room, grasping his knife.

Left alone, Sarah wept hysterically. The more she cried, the harder it was to breathe. She was going to die here. Alone and helpless.

Fuck that. She had to calm down. Think of Peter. Concentrate on his face. Back in the hotel room when they had held each other close, she had felt a new strength. It was this she drew on now.

On the brink of a crashing wave of dizziness, Sarah forced snot and mucus out of her nose before noisily sucking it back in. The air was still too little but trying not to panic she cleared her nasal passages again and breathed in. Her chest hurt with the exertion but slowly the wooziness receded. And by pushing her tongue against the stifling material she was able to inhale and exhale small amounts of air through her mouth. She was damned if she was going to give up the chance of happiness without a fight. Peter would find her. All she had to do was to hold on.

She hadn't immediately recognised where she was and when she had, she'd wrestled against the knowledge. Not wanting to see the familiar bay window where she used to sit reading her books, and the memorable way the chimney breast cast its shadow.

As a lack of feeling slowly crept up both her arms, the same painful numbness left her subconscious. She wasn't ready to accept where he had brought her but if she were to survive this she had to face her nightmare.

He hadn't lied to her. She was home; tied to a single bed in her childhood bedroom. Little Pony paraphernalia and Disney Princess dolls stared out from the inky darkness. Still a little girl's bedroom. Where was the owner now?

*Please don't let her be here. If Will has harmed her...?* She couldn't bear to think about it. Tears threatened again as she recalled Will's chilling words: 'It's always the fucking daddy who pisses on my parade'.

But why had he brought her here? He didn't act like he wanted to kill her. He'd said about needing the truth. What truth?

*Think, Sarah. Think.* She had to remember what had happened between them. Even if it broke her.

Tentative, she probed her mind. The hairs on the back of her neck rose as a picture of young Will at her birthday came to her. Chilled, her body shook as her defences unravelled.

---

She had stormed upstairs to confront Ben. She couldn't believe he had trampled all over their snowman. He was probably showing off in front of his weird mate; unless it was what's-his-name who had done it.

Sarah slowed. It was one thing to be angry at her brother, but something told her the younger boy may not take it too well. As she hesitated in front of his door, the loudness of the drums and guitars hurt her ears. She was surprised the wood wasn't vibrating to the same boring beat. It wasn't fair. If she'd had friends round and they had played their music to the max, she'd have got into so much trouble.

*Why hasn't Mummy told Ben to turn the noise down?* On edge, Sarah passed Ben's bedroom and continued to her parents' room. She grasped the doorknob. The music matched the beat of her heart. She was staring at her red, sticky hand as the knob started to turn.

The boy's mouth fell open. He obviously hadn't expected to see her standing there. Taking a few steps backwards, he dropped the knife and slowly wiped his gloves on his shirt.

As the music reached its peak, she looked at the bed. There was blood everywhere: on the sheets, on her mum's body, darkening her long hair. The sightless eyes stared up at the ceiling, as if in silent protest at what had happened to her. Her silver locket was pulled to one side – the chain broken.

He had touched Sarah's face and his hot caress scorched her icy skin. She didn't flinch. His heat absorbed into her as his fingers stroked her cheek. She couldn't move. His fiery breath surrounded her: suffocating her. Struggling to comprehend what she was seeing, yet unable to look away from the bed, Sarah had ceased to function.

---

Sarah, bound and gagged in the present, helplessly watched as her past unfolded. She understood, as a sobbing Will clung onto the catatonic shell of a girl who had already run far away. She wished she could intervene, as the girl stirred. And then wished she could look away and not see their embrace.

---

Life began again. Minutes that had stood still now hurried by.

Sarah looked down, puzzled. Kneeling on the floor, he was hugging her close; great sobs shook his body. She shifted uncomfortably, her coat dragged downwards by his persistent pull. Unsure what to do, she laid her hands gently on his shoulders.

'There, there,' she whispered. When she was younger she remembered her mummy would say those words to her if she was upset. Sarah didn't know if they would help now.

'It'll be okay.' Her voice trembled. This was wrong... very wrong. She wrinkled her nose in disgust. Yuk, he smelt awful. Sweat, and something worse.

'Please, let me go. I'm sorry if... if I upset you.' She hadn't a clue what she had done, but it must have been bad.

*DON'T LOOK UP. DON'T LOOK AT THE BED.*

Sarah jumped at the loud voice in her head. She was confused, and frightened.

*YOU HAVE TO GET OUT OF HERE.*

'Why?' she whimpered.

His grasp around her waist loosened and he lifted his head to look at her.

*RUN, SARAH. GO NOW.*

She pushed him hard, causing him to fall backwards. He grunted in surprise.

*RUN.*

Sarah hesitated, choosing to ignore the urgency in the voice. Their eyes met.

'Sarah?' Pulling off his remaining glove, he reached towards her. 'What shall I do?'

She covered both her ears with her hands to blot out the cry of pain that followed her. Her tights slipped on the tiled floor in the hallway. Crashing down, she landed heavily on her front. Sarah scrambled up, terrified the boy was chasing her. She screamed as she saw blood on her coat and struggled to get it off as she fled towards the front door, her feet still sliding in every direction.

---

Feeling all the little girl's fear, Sarah couldn't stop the tears any longer. They ran freely as she saw her in the old summerhouse, huddled in the corner. Desperate to step back in time and help the shivering girl, whose dishevelled hair hid a ghostly, vacant face, adult Sarah didn't care that she was dying. She barely registered her erratic breathing as a build-up of mucus in her nose blocked off her air.

Sarah settled next to the trembling girl and held her close, mentally keeping her safe; while, in the present, she was suffocating.

# CHAPTER FORTY

Faint and overloaded with adrenaline, Will collapsed on the stairs. Dealing with the father had taken a lot out of him. He clasped his trembling hands. Everything was moving so fast. He hadn't slept in the last few days, and his head was all over the place.

It didn't help that his dad had interfered, so he'd had to rush his carefully orchestrated plans. What had he been thinking going after Carl? Why hadn't he come to him in the first place? It was due to this stupidity he was dead.

He should be sad. Despite their complicated relationship, the old man had been his dad, after all. Surely that meant he was expected to mourn his passing. But he felt nothing.

Actually, that wasn't true. He was scared. Underneath all his bravado, a small seed of self-doubt was growing. Why hadn't he known about Carl? He hadn't even been aware the police had found a suspect. Was he so fixated on Sarah that his command of events around him had slipped away?

Well, he was in control now. Okay, grabbing Sarah from her hotel room wasn't planned and the execution was clumsy. Nevertheless, how they had arrived at this point no longer mattered – his initial anger when Sarah didn't leave the hotel to meet Anne had gone. She was here. That's all that mattered.

If the police did work out where he had taken her, and goody-two-shoes Peter 'dickhead' Graham tried to come to her rescue, he would be ready for them.

Will took the gun out from under his belt. Unlike his trusty knife, which fitted snugly in its holster around his thigh, it was cumbersome and dug into him. Although he'd had shooting experience on the farm, he wasn't a big fan of firearms, preferring the more personal touch of a blade. But it would have been wasteful to leave the gun with his dad's body. At the moment though he'd left the ammunition in his bag; it wouldn't be at all useful if he accidently fired into his foot.

The truth was he didn't visualise himself fighting his way out of this. If necessary he was quite prepared for this to be his last stand. Of course, he hoped it wouldn't come to that. If he were right about Sarah, they could get away together before the police stormed in. Even if the rain destroyed his artwork, hopefully he'd done enough to delay anyone planning to get inside.

He wasn't too worried about her reaction to him so far; he didn't blame her for being scared. After all his preparations, having to tie her to the bed was crude and not at all how he had fantasised their first date.

Never mind. At least it can only get better. He grinned and, with renewed energy, bounded up the rest of the stairs.

As he visualised what was waiting beyond the bedroom door, the images of his elite group of ladies slid into his mind: how they were lying on their beds when he had crept into their rooms. Maybe he should finish this now. Give in to his impulses and go in and place his hands around her neck.

No. This was his Sarah. Not a cheap imitation.

Will shook his head and squared up to the door, grimacing as he saw his bloody handprint on the white frame. He was about to wipe his dirty hands on his jeans when he thought better of it and rushed to the bathroom. It wouldn't give a good impression.

He saw his glistening face in the mirror and wondered about having a swift shower. Better not. The longer he left her gagged the more pissed off she'd be.

Using water he slicked back his hair, and then scowled at his dark armpits. He wished he had worn something other than a tight grey T-shirt – great for showing his muscles but not so great for hiding large sweat stains.

It was a shame the head of the household was an unfit guy with a large paunch, otherwise he could have raided his wardrobe. Well, he'd have to do. Will grabbed a bottle of aftershave and sprayed himself liberally before leaving the bathroom.

Nervous, he combed his hand through his wet hair then flattened it down. Exhaling loudly he pushed the door open, ready for Sarah's wrath at being abandoned. His eyes not accustomed to the dim light, Will was halfway to the bed before he sensed something was wrong. Sarah was sitting against the headboard, like he had left her, with her head lolled to one side. The silence of absent breathing stabbed at his heart. Stumbling backwards he scrambled for the light switch; his soul dreading what the brightness would unveil. He moaned as his shaking fingers turned the dimmer control on.

Around the garish gag, the dusky blue of her lips and skin was visible. He shouted in horror at the unblinking white of her eyes.

'Sarah!' He tripped over the small pink chair as he ran over to her. Frantically yanking off her gag, he shook her lifeless body. 'Shit.'

Panicked, he pressed his fingers against the side of her neck. 'Shit.' Moving them slightly he gasped as he felt a weak pulse. He pinched her nose and placed his mouth over hers, breathing into her. She couldn't die. Not like this.

'Come on, Sarah.' He blew into her mouth again. This time as he withdrew, her body shuddered. He held her head up, as she coughed and spluttered into life.

Not trusting himself to speak he rested his forehead on hers, feeling her clamminess cling to him. Her lungs wheezed as she inhaled big mouthfuls of air greedily.

'You're okay,' he told her finally.

She flinched as if she was only now aware of his presence.

'If you had relaxed and not fought against it, this wouldn't have happened. You were lucky I came back when I did.'

---

Sarah thought her body was never going to recover. The effort to slow her breathing had exhausted her. He'd put a pillow behind her back, and the blood pulsating in her neck rocked her head side to side.

How near had she been to not coming back? At the end it'd felt so easy to give in. Not wanting to dwell on that, she forced her eyes open and turned her head towards Will. He looked as bad as she felt, if not worse. Drained of colour, he was staring at a spot between his feet. Rocking gently.

Her death had obviously not been part of his grand scheme, and, for a second, she rejoiced that she had come close to messing up his plans.

When her first attempt at speech ended in a fit of coughing, he didn't respond. Sarah tried again. 'Can I have a drink of water, please?' she croaked.

'Of course.' He rushed over to a green canvas bag and grabbed a plastic bottle.

His eagerness to please sickened her, though she could use it to her advantage. If her head would stop throbbing, she'd be able to think.

With her wrists tied to the slatted headboard, she had no choice but to let him guide the drink to her lips. The first mouthful caught the back of her throat, caused a fresh bout of coughing. Blinking through the tears, she pursed her lips and sipped the stale water. She didn't want to keep him waiting in case he took it away, but he kept the bottle close, tipping it up when she was ready.

After she'd finished, he reached for the garish silk scarf. No! Not the gag. She'd be unable to breathe. Had almost died... 'No, please.'

He shushed her, and dabbed her mouth, wiping the water running down her chin, taking his time. Feeling his breath on her face, Sarah tried not to flinch. When he glanced up, she didn't look away. His eyes widened in astonishment. He blushed, his breathing quickened – but he was the first to break eye contact.

This was her chance. If she could get him to talk. Gain his trust.

'Why have you brought me here, Will?' Sarah forced her voice to sound friendly; intimate.

He shifted on the bed, his thigh in contact with hers. 'It's where we first met. When you saw who I was. You were kind, and you didn't tell.'

Licking his thumb, he avoided looking at her and concentrated on cleaning a dark stain on his jeans. She followed his gaze. What was that? Blood? Oh shit, whose blood? Sarah bit down on her lower lip hard. She had to know. 'What happened to the family who lives here? The little girl...?'

'Would you mind if I had killed them?'

*God, why would he ask that?* Sarah nodded slowly, not trusting herself to speak.

'Well, they're okay.' He sounded disappointed in her. 'I thought they might come in useful later if we needed hostages.'

He was hiding something. The blood on his jeans. It was better if she didn't find out who it belonged to. That knowledge would overshadow everything, and she had to get out of this nightmare. Grieve for others later.

His hip was pressing harder against hers, and his hand caressed her skirt, ruffling the material. His touch made her skin crawl, but she forced herself to stay still.

'It doesn't have to be like this, Will. Let me go, and you can get help.'

'It's too late.' His eyes were wet, and he wiped them on the bottom of his T-shirt. As he lifted his top up he uncovered the lower half of a woman's face. The hair was inked so it flowed across his abdomen: a few strands disappearing under his waistband.

When he saw she was looking at the large tattoo he raised his top further. Sarah gasped. It couldn't be.

'What do you think? The tattooist only had your Facebook profile picture, which was my favourite at the time, to copy, but I thought the likeness was pretty good. 'Do you want to know something funny?' he continued. 'The other women I had chosen to be with, because they reminded me of you, must have thought I had their face inked onto my body. Did it make them feel loved? If I'd realised sooner I'd have asked them before they died.'

'What women? I don't understand…'

'Oh but I think you do. Although you'd be forgiven if you were put off by the ridiculous name they gave me. The Beautician. Really? Was that the best they could come up with?' He chuckled. 'Good job I couldn't give a shit what they called me, I might have been pissed off otherwise. I rather fancied The Ledforth Strangler. What do you reckon?'

He scowled as she jerked her legs away. She couldn't pretend. Not anymore. 'It's you… all of it is you. All those women…' Sarah broke off, horrified.

'And I'm tired. So tired of being alone. What they give me is over so quickly; the images fade, and then I need more. I thought you would understand, Sarah. Like you understood that night.'

The significance of what he was saying sunk in. *He thinks we're the same. That I'm a monster.*

'I know what I'm asking is huge and I don't expect an answer yet. All I ask is you keep an open mind. Okay?'

Speechless, she stared at him. His madness was unfathomable. Maybe his insanity was contagious as she was feeling unhinged. Crazy. Did he think she'd feel anything but hate for him? She began to laugh uncontrollably. His shocked expression made her laugh louder. She didn't care if this angered him, instead she revelled in the release it gave her.

Will joined in, misreading her laughter and giggling long after she'd stopped.

Sarah jumped as he stood abruptly. 'Where are my manners? You must be starving, Sarah. I'll go and fix us something for supper.'

'Can I come too?' Careful now, she mustn't appear too keen. 'It's a long time since I've seen the place, I'd love to see what has happened to it. And it would give us more time to talk,' she added. This got the reaction she'd been looking for.

'Are you going to behave if I release you?' he asked, indicating her restraints.

'I'll be good, Will. I promise.'

'If you're not, I will have to hurt you. And I don't want to do that, Sarah.'

Too scared to reply, she nodded. Her jaw clenched as he pressed up close, their cheeks nearly touching as he untied her wrists. His aftershave was overpowering. She prayed she wouldn't be sick as she took shallow breaths.

Once she was free Sarah flexed her arms, trying not to show how much pain she was in. But as circulation was restored to her numb hands it was impossible not to cry out.

'I'm sorry I had to tie you up,' he told her, sounding genuinely remorseful. 'Once I can trust you completely then we can dispense with all this unpleasantness.'

Sarah moaned as he came towards her holding the rope out in

front of him. She showed him the angry red welts that criss-crossed her wrists. 'Not again, Will. Please.'

He rocked back on his feet, glaring at her. 'Can I rely on you to do the right thing? I don't know whether I can, Sarah.' He sighed. 'But I'm not a cruel person.'

Will crossed over to where his bag was sitting innocently on a small dressing table. 'I didn't know whether to show you this or not.' And delving into the canvas sack he pulled out a long red-and-pink scarf. 'I doubt you'll remember this. Not sure why I've kept it. Maybe you could wear it round your neck later,' he added. 'Don't you think the colours are lovely?'

Without waiting for a reply, he wrapped the soft wool over her wrists. 'See, I'll put this on first and it will stop the rope digging in.'

'Was this my mum's scarf?' Sarah asked quietly.

'Yes. Although technically I took it from the snowman, and he didn't complain,' he said, laughing.

# CHAPTER FORTY-ONE

*C ome on.* This was getting them nowhere and they were running out of time. The bastard could be doing anything to her. Peter was close to reaching over and shaking Ben, desperate to learn something to help them find Sarah before it was too late.

He took a deep breath and tried again. 'Is there anywhere you think Will might have taken her? A place he talked about – somewhere that was special?'

Ben shook his head vigorously. 'N-n-no, I've told you. He wouldn't hurt her. He said he loved her.' He bounced on his bed, distressed. 'Where's Sarah? He was g-going to take her home. She should be home.'

Struggling to keep his anger in check, Peter stood up and paced around Ben's room. It was nearly three hours since Sarah was taken, God knows where, and they were no nearer in tracking her down. He combed his fingers though his hair and looked around the tidy bedroom, at a loss at what to do.

Although Ben didn't realise it, he was a part of William's past, like Sarah was. And Peter was sure their quarry had the sort of personality that wouldn't be able to resist teasing Ben; telling him about his plans for Sarah, knowing he wouldn't understand.

Carolyn was doing her best to calm Ben, and it reminded Peter of his agitation yesterday, and how he had quietened when Will was by his side. The poor man had trusted him. The betrayal made Peter sick.

So far they hadn't found any evidence to suggest that Will had abused Ben. He had used his position to get closer to Sarah and had left her brother unharmed. But what would have happened if Ben had recognised him?

Peter clasped his closed fist. Will had fooled everyone. Including him. And his colleagues at the residential home and the gym, where he worked a few hours a week, were shocked at the depth of police interest. They described Will as a dedicated worker.

The only interesting interview so far was with the younger man Peter remembered from the corridor the previous day. Apparently over the last few weeks, boxes of Diazepam had gone missing from the medicine cupboard. Bumping into Will coming out of the supplies room after his shift had finished, he had become suspicious. But, as he liked his co-worker, it was reluctantly he had approached him with a vague accusation. Even when confronted with the knowledge Will was wanted for questioning about a serious matter, his colleague was apologetic when accusing him in his absence.

Of course, Will had stolen the sedatives. But was it for his own use or was he planning to give them to someone else? Either way, what did it mean for Sarah? And, how had Will found her so quickly?

They had been careful not to be followed to the hotel. Beefed up security. But evidently not enough. Will had caught them napping. No one had thought she'd be in danger so soon after they'd arrived. *Damn. Why the hell didn't I insist on her going to a safe house? I fucked up big time.*

Not wanting to linger on the last time he had seen her, Peter picked up one of the family pictures standing on a nearby shelf. 'Where are you?' he asked the photograph. Sweat prickled the back of his neck.

Apart from insisting his sister had gone home, Ben had said little else. If he knew anything he either didn't realise the significance or he deliberately wasn't saying.

Peter sighed. Home was the one place they were certain Sarah hadn't been taken. Her house was under constant surveillance. If he'd gone within ten metres of the place they would know. Unless... He examined the photo he was clutching. It showed a young Sarah and Ben standing in the garden of a large house. Dressed in shorts and T-shirts, they were striking different dramatic poses. Sarah, one hand on her hip, the other flung up in the air, was nine or ten years old.

How long after the photograph was taken did William come into their lives? What if they were approaching this all wrong? Peter's heart was racing. 'Tell me exactly what he said, Ben.'

'He was going to take her home. If I was g-g-good, he was taking me too. We were going to be a family.'

His shock must have been clear to see as Doug was quick to ask, 'What are you thinking, Peter?'

'Everything hinges around Sarah's past. What if he's taken her "home" home?' He showed Doug the picture, pointing at the detached house in the background. 'Where it all started.'

'Bloody hell,' began Doug, but Peter was already rushing out the door with Ben's cries of 'he loves her' ringing in his ears.

---

Louise collapsed back in her chair. Jesus Christ, what had she done? She stared, unseeing, at the phone in her hand.

'Hello, are you there?' The tinny voice sounded annoyed. 'Hello? I'm going to hang up.'

'No, please, don't.' She raised her mobile back up to her ear. 'I'm sorry, the reception is not very good at this end.'

'Well, okay, detective sergeant.' His scepticism was evident, probably doubting she was from CID at all. 'Is there anything else I can do for you? It's getting late.'

His brusque manner irritated her, and she sat forward. 'I'm sorry,' Louise repeated, but this time with an edge to her voice. 'This is very important. Are you sure you don't recognise the man I've described to you?'

'Aye, as I've said already.' The Scottish accent belonging to the real Ian Armstrong, who she figured was nearing retirement age, felt like a final nail in her coffin.

How could she have been so stupid? Grasping at straws, she asked, 'And you're positive you haven't got another Mr Armstrong working for you. Maybe he's new?'

As she rattled off the description again, Louise reluctantly looked at her desk where the facial composite they had obtained from Hilda lay mocking her. She had penned in a moustache and glasses whilst waiting for her call to be picked up.

Okay, it was time to move on. The journalist had nothing to offer. She thanked him and cut him off mid-sentence as he was explaining how anyone could have picked up one of his business cards from a number of places.

Shit. Louise screwed her eyes shut, as she remembered how the bastard had been behind her whilst she'd been on the phone to Khenan. He must have heard what she'd said about Sarah being at the Ledforth Hotel. How on earth was she going to admit to the team that it was her fault Will had found Sarah?

The door to the incident room burst open and Khenan entered. 'We're on the move! Peter thinks he's worked out where Will's taken her.'

'Wait, sir.' She lowered her eyes, not able to meet his. Mouth dry, her confession died. What she had done could destroy her career. Even if her boss and colleagues believed that it was an accident, the damage would creep in later. No one would fully trust her again.

'Yes, what is it?' Khenan asked sharply, poised to leave. He tapped his fingers on the edge of the door and scowled. 'We have to go, Lou.'

Cheeks flaming hot, she cleared her throat. Then smiled. 'Yeah, sorry, it's nothing. It can wait.'

# CHAPTER FORTY-TWO

It was hard to coordinate her limbs and Sarah had to rely on Will to help her down the wide staircase. She stumbled as he hurried her along. The blow on her head had affected her more than she had realised, and she shuffled across the hallway like an automaton. The wooden floor wavered in front of her if she turned her head too fast, so she stared straight ahead, not able to take in her surroundings fully.

There was no sign of the family, but Sarah suppressed a sob as they walked over splashes of blood on the kitchen tiles. *Please let them be okay.*

Lowered onto a dining chair, she didn't protest when Will dropped a lasso of rope over her head and tightened it around her waist. She waited silently, her heart thumping hard against her chest, as he opened all the cupboards and called out their contents.

A lamp on a side table provided the only light, and her eyes were already accustomed to their shadowy existence. Around the kitchen there was evidence of a happier, brighter time: a pink Barbie lunchbox discarded by the sink; a scattered group of coloured fridge magnets spelling out the names 'Chloe', 'Emma' and 'Finn'.

'I'll be honest, I'm too excited to be very hungry,' Will declared, after finishing his quick inventory of what was on offer. 'Soup would normally be enough for me at this time.' He picked up a tin of chicken soup. 'We can have bread rolls with it. It might be a while till we eat again.'

Sarah didn't think she would be able to stomach anything he was going to make her, but she nodded. She had to maintain what little strength she had left. Ever since she had felt how easy it would have been to give up when gagged with no air, she'd vowed to fight. She couldn't let the bastard get the upper hand. He couldn't win.

Will grinned. He whistled as he prepared their supper and laid the table. Picking up a bunch of keys, he threw them into the air and caught them, before putting them into his pocket.

He placed her soup in front of her and pulled up a chair. Surely he must untie her now. Sarah raised her hands, forced together as if she were praying, and pleaded with Will to release them so she could feed herself.

The new restraints around her body restricted her movements further, and as she struggled to lift her arms up she accidently knocked against the table, causing soup to spill out the bowl. Will tutted and pushed her hands roughly onto her lap. He leaned on the back of her chair, shoving her closer to the table's edge. The dish rattled and more soup slopped onto the mat.

'Look what you've made me do.' He picked up the tea-towel and tucked the corner in her top. 'Come on, Sarah. It'll be quicker if I do it, won't it?'

She instinctively yanked her head back, then seeing his disapproving scowl sat submissively, opening her mouth like a good girl so he could spoon the soup in.

'That's better. I added cold water so it wouldn't be too hot.' After each spoonful he wiped her face with the tea-towel. He didn't stop until she had eaten every last morsel of bread and soup.

'There you are. I guess I should eat mine now.' He paused on his way back to the microwave and swivelled round to face her. 'I never know whether you should say you are eating soup or drinking it, as it's mainly liquid.'

When she didn't reply, he stared thoughtfully at her. 'I'm sorry it wasn't up to Bailey's standards of cuisine. Their soups are probably like a five-course dinner.'

*Shit. Anne's text.* Seeing the look on his face, Sarah knew her friend hadn't sent her the message.

'Where is she?' she whispered hoarsely.

Sorrow overwhelmed her as Will confirmed her worst fear. Anne was dead. Poor Anne, she must have been so scared. Sarah couldn't stop the tears. 'Why? Why did you kill her? She had nothing to do with this.'

His eyes narrowed. 'She was a distraction. But you're not on your own now.' Will stepped towards her. His fingers touched the hilt of his knife. 'Don't cry, Sarah. I didn't think you'd be so upset.'

Between gulps she battled to hide her grief. Will glowered at her. 'It's my head,' she cried. 'It hurts.'

'Oh, my poor Sarah.' The idea that she would feel pain from a head injury seemed as unexpected to Will as the inconceivable notion that she would grieve for a friend. 'Of course, silly me. You're hurt.'

He peered at her forehead, perhaps seeing the wound there for the first time. 'You need paracetamol. That'll help.'

Will rooted around in the drawers and then gave a big sigh. 'It'll be quicker if I ask.' He strode across the kitchen and flung open a door on the far side of the room. Muffled cries rang out as he disappeared inside.

Left alone, Sarah wrestled her restraints but to no avail: the climbing rope he had used was strong. She tried gnawing with her teeth on the binds around her wrists. They wouldn't give at all. It was hopeless. Desperate, she surveyed the kitchen; she had a few minutes at the most before he would be back. *Come on, Sarah, think.*

This part of the house bore little resemblance to the home she remembered, but despite the modern restructuring the door Will had gone through sparked a faint memory. She was sure it used to lead to a utility room that linked the garage to the house. And if that was still the case then it might be a way out.

How? Will was so unpredictable. He'd eagerly spoon-fed her the soup and showed pleasure after every thank you and smile but had reacted badly to her remorse over Anne. It was clear it wouldn't take much to anger him. She had to persuade him she could be trusted. And quick. He was going to want to talk about her mum, and even if her life depended on it she wouldn't be able to mask her true feelings.

When Will returned, Sarah smiled. 'Any luck?'

'No problem. She was more worried about her daughter: she thought I'd tied her ankles too tightly. I had to put more tape over her mouth to shut her up,' he said, grinning.

Sarah was glad when he turned towards the cupboards. Her cheeks as well as her heart ached with the effort of smiling. What could she do? He had been careful not to leave anything near her to grab hold off. If she tried to move her chair, the noise would alert Will. And anyway what would the point be of scraping its legs a few inches to the left or right? She had to get him to untie her.

'Will?' She didn't look up, making her voice as meek as possible. 'I… I need to go to the bathroom. I'm sorry.'

'Can't you wait?' he whined. 'There's so much we have to discuss.'

Sarah shook her head. 'I'm getting desperate,' she added, with what she hoped was the right amount of panic. 'I can be quick.'

There was agonising silence. Shit, he was going to tell her to go where she sat.

'Well, I've got this fucking paracetamol for you now,' he said, disgruntled, banging the glass down in front of her. 'Take this first, then.'

Sarah's legs shook as she sat on the toilet seat. Will could look into the open door at any time, and she didn't dare wander from the expected script.

He had stayed close to her all the way to the downstairs bathroom, his gun stuck painfully into her back. No chance to get away, she had to play along.

Sarah was pulling up her knickers when he poked his head in. 'Have you finished yet?' As she straightened her skirt, he caressed the edge of the door with the tip of his gun.

Making a show of her unsteadiness, she shuffled to the sink. She had to do something now. If she let him tie her up again, it would be over; the possibility of escape gone.

What to do? She exchanged a desperate look with her reflection in the mirror, and her hope withered. She barely recognised the woman who stared back: her eyes were sunken and her face shiny with sweat.

If it was only fear that haunted the stranger, then she might have a chance. What scared her was the laceration trailing through her hairline and snaking its way onto her pale forehead. Clotted blood masked the growing purple bruise, but how long before her body couldn't mask the symptoms of concussion?

Okay, so she was exaggerating her weakness to fool Will, nevertheless her strength was dwindling fast.

Automatically reaching with the bar of soap, Sarah stopped as she focused on the soap dish. It was marble. She looked in the mirror, checking that he hadn't moved from the doorway. Hardly daring to breathe, Sarah dropped the soap and grabbed hold of the rectangular block. Her hand shook and the resulting ring as the surfaces collided brought Will fully into the bathroom.

'What are you doing?'

Thinking quickly, Sarah slumped her shoulders. 'I feel sick.'

'You'd better stay there for a bit,' he answered irritably.

'No, Will, I think I'm going to faint.' She threw her left hand back as if desperate to cling onto him so she wouldn't fall.

He moved to her side and took her outstretched arm, maybe eager to play the role of nurse. She didn't give him a chance.

Twisting round she swung her improvised weapon towards him. *Take this, you bastard.* The trajectory of her strike was wild, and the dish glanced off his left temple. Sarah cried out as it slipped in her soapy fingers.

Will staggered back, looking more shocked than badly hurt. Feeling where she had hit him, he cursed as he saw blood on his fingers. 'You bitch,' he spat at her.

He was advancing unsteadily when the second blow impacted solidly. This time he fell backwards, hitting his head on the side of the bath with a sickening thud. All the atmosphere was sucked into that dull-sounding blow; time only kick-started when the soap dish fell from her fingers and crashed onto the floor.

Apart from the rise and fall of his chest, Will was motionless. Laid crumpled in a heap, his front was facing her, and she could see the large lump on his forehead where she had hit him again.

'Will?' Not sure why, she had a sudden need to move closer to him. 'Will? Can you hear me?'

Falling onto her knees Sarah reached out to touch him. She was a nurse after all, shouldn't she be helping him? The possibility of him faking it and lunging to grab her flashed into her mind, and she withdrew. *Shit, what am I thinking? I must be in shock. I have to get out of here.*

Not wanting to turn her back on Will she scrambled in crab-like movements towards the open door. The further away she retreated the more convinced she became she was still a pawn in his sick fantasy, and he was letting her get so far before grabbing her. Sarah didn't tear her eyes away from his prone body until she had crossed through into the hall and clambered to her feet.

The prospect of his hot breath on the back of her neck fuelled her flight to the front door and she hit the wood hard. She pumped the handle. Locked. No, no.

She had to find another way out before it was too late. But wait, hadn't she seen Will with keys? Yes, the bastard had put a set of keys in his jeans pocket.

Taking three excruciating steps towards the bathroom, her legs wobbled as she saw him sprawled on the floor. The idea of having to go inside filled her with terror but knowing he would have made doubly sure all windows and exits were locked there was no other option. And no time to consider alternatives.

Will's gun was lying in the open doorway, after slipping from his grasp when she'd hit him. A picture of Anne flashed in her mind and remembering all she had lost Sarah picked the weapon up. Holding it out in front of her she walked into the bathroom.

It didn't look like Will had moved. She had never hit anyone before and was clueless as to the force needed to render someone unconscious. How long before he would begin to wake up? If, in fact, he did at all.

Approaching slowly, Sarah prodded him with her foot. Getting no response she kicked more forcefully, aiming at his hips. She was rewarded with Will flopping onto his back. As well as helping her search, the movement had exposed the hilt of his blade, and she took his knife out of its sheath and slid it out of his reach.

Keeping the gun barrel pointed towards him, Sarah gingerly felt the front pockets in his jeans. *Oh, thank Christ.* The fingers of her left hand found the tell-tale bulge. She slid out the bunch of keys and resisting the temptation to flee, continued to search. A mobile was too much to hope for, but she looked anyway. A folded photograph was in his back pocket: a Frankenstein mismatch – Sarah on one side holding a wedding bouquet and smiling coyly into the camera, and next to her was Will, his face stuck over Mike's, deposing his rightful place at her side.

She stood up and kicked him again. 'You bastard,' she hissed venomously.

Sarah turned the key in the lock. And stopped. If she opened the door, she'd run and not think twice. It would be impossible to turn back. The colourful fridge magnets tugged at her conscience. Chloe, Emma and Finn – the names of the people she was leaving behind. If Will regained consciousness then God knows what he would do upon finding her gone.

Breathing deeply she tried to clear her head. The throbbing had spread to her neck, and it was getting difficult to think around the pain. She couldn't leave without them; it was her fault they were in danger.

Not quite believing she had the strength to stay, Sarah lunged from the door. She cursed as she lost her grip on the gun and knife, wobbling precariously when she stooped to pick them up. Scared she was pushing her luck, Sarah hurried past the bathroom.

# CHAPTER FORTY-THREE

The orders given to PC David Kingsley had been simple: establish if anyone is inside, but don't engage with any of the occupants. Keep your distance until back-up arrives.

The word *simple* hadn't applied as soon as they had heard the address. As he approached the front of the house, he prayed it was nothing but a sick joke. Startled, he jumped back as the driveway flooded with light.

Shit. The bloody security lamps. He gasped, trying to get his breathing under control. So much for stealth mode. Maybe he should wait until the immediate area was dark again. Then, with a shock, he realised he wasn't alone. Someone was slumped on the nearby garden bench.

Oh thank God, he'd recognise that stocky profile anywhere. He hadn't been consciously holding his breath, but now he let it out in an audible whoosh. 'Jesus, Finn, what are you doing there? You had me going.'

Not getting an answer, David walked out on the immaculate lawn. 'We've had a weird communiqué about your place. Why are you...' He stopped mid-sentence.

His senses tunnelled. At first he couldn't comprehend what he was seeing. The large dark stain on the grass, one he had taken to be a shadow cast by the angled lights, was alive: a growing, pulsing mass that had already darkened Finn's lap and the lower half of his shirt.

It couldn't be. Not his blood. There was so much. In the second it took for David to finally register the truth, he saw Finn's wrist was tied to the bench.

*Fuck.* Fumbling with his radio, his first instinct was to retreat; to run far away and take cover. Images of his young family waiting at home elbowed into the front of his mind, and as he radioed for back-up and an ambulance, he was torn between self-survival and his duty to his friend.

Finn moaned. Indecision over, David crouched and saw a flicker of recognition in the otherwise vacant eyes. 'Hold on, Finn, it's going to be okay.'

In Finn's free hand there was a bloodied cloth, and David grabbed it and pressed where he thought the blood was coming from. But he couldn't be sure he was stemming the flow at all. Pulling the shirt up, he glimpsed a long gaping wound running across Finn's abdomen before he rammed down hard.

His hands, now committed to applying pressure, shook as he imagined an unknown assailant watching him. The hairs on the back of his neck stood up as he visualised himself in someone's crosshairs. He scanned the large, detached house but struggled to see beyond the pool of light.

Sensing movement at his side, he jumped instinctively before seeing his partner's shocked face. 'Holy shit, David. What the fuck...?' Staring at Finn, the policeman tailed off.

David hissed, 'Kill the lights.' He kept repeating this until he saw understanding seep through the horror. Their scared eyes met before his partner turned away, his quick footfalls too loud on the gravel path.

Pale and clammy, Finn groaned incoherently. David bent closer to the blue lips of the waxy replica of the man he knew. He was running out of time. 'Where are they, Finn? Where's your family?'

More incoherent sounds. Nothing he could make sense of. Fearing the worst, tears pricked David's eyes. Where were Emma and Chloe? What was he going to tell his daughter about the fate of her best friend?

Pressing on the wound was futile: he'd already lost so much blood. He ripped Finn's shirt and tied a strip round his middle as tight as possible. His hands were then free to tug at the rope, and he was trying to release Finn's wrist when everything went black.

Although he knew it was coming, he couldn't help but yell. Stupidly, he'd dropped his torch on the grass and so was relieved to see the frantic bobbing of his partner's light approaching. He hoped whoever had attacked Finn wasn't equipped with night-vision goggles or any shit like that.

'Help me. I can't untie him,' David cried. 'It's too slippery. My hands are covered in blood.' He didn't think they should be moving Finn, but every nerve ending was screaming at him to get further away from the house. In the open, they were sitting ducks.

With his colleague's help, he loosened the rope enough to yank Finn's hand free. David retrieved his torch, and together they dragged his lifeless body across the lawn. Rain had started to fall a few moments before and now it intensified, masking their heavy breathing.

They reached a low wall and cowered next to it. 'I need to find his family,' panted David.

'You can't,' the young PC hissed, 'we don't know who's in there. Back-up is on its way. We have to wait.'

'I'll have a look outside. Won't go in.' He avoided looking at Finn so his courage wouldn't fail him. 'I owe it to him to try.'

He left his partner cursing; not giving him the opportunity to talk him out of it. The last thing he wanted to do was to run back towards the house, but he had to try. He steered clear of the noisy path but ended up slipping on the wet grass and tumbling into a border. He rolled onto his feet quickly and tried to get his bearings.

The beam from his torch glanced off tarmac and bounced on white metal. It was the integral garage, to the left of the main house. Before he could steady the light, disconnected images gave the impression of abstract art. Red on white canvas.

Dread crushed his breath, suffocating him. Paralysing him. He couldn't breathe. Couldn't move. The red letters morphed in every passing flash, and it took a massive effort to still his hand.

The paint was bleeding in the rain, but the message scrawled on the garage door would haunt David's nightmares for a very long time.

# CHAPTER FORTY-FOUR

The utility room remained dark as the light switch clicked ineffectively under Sarah's fingers. There was enough illumination snaking in from behind her, however, to see the two hostages. The cowering pair struggled to move away, eyes wide with fear. Their arms were twisted cruelly behind their backs, and their legs were bound with thick, black tape. A strip of the same duct tape covered their mouths, and when Sarah fell to her knees next to the mother, the terrified woman wailed loudly.

Putting the weapons on the floor, Sarah hurried to reassure them. 'It's all right, I'm not with him. I'm going to take your gags off, and I need you to be quiet, okay?'

She waited for a nod of agreement before ripping off the mother's tape, wincing in sympathy as the stubborn adhesive pulled at her skin.

Tears streaming, the woman gulped a few times before she was able to speak. 'Where is he?' she rasped, looking over Sarah's shoulder.

'In the bathroom. I knocked him out, but he might wake up any minute. I've taken the keys and unlocked the front door.'

Sarah turned towards the girl. Hair plastered to her wet face, and in her school uniform, she looked so vulnerable. The poor child.

'Now it's your turn, sweetheart.' The girl whimpered as Sarah took hold of the large piece of tape. 'I'll take it off quickly, like your mummy does with a plaster, okay?' But she shook her head violently and Sarah was unable to maintain a grip on the gag.

Her mother tried to help. 'It's all right, Chloe. You need to be brave, my darling. I know you can do this, Clo.'

But not even someone who she loved could convince her to keep her head still. Not wanting to cause her any more distress, Sarah turned her attention to freeing her limbs. She had to use the knife to cut through the tape and the exertion left her sweating. As she struggled to free the woman next, she kept stopping to wipe the perspiration out of her eyes.

Chloe's mum stared. 'You look dreadful. Are you all right?'

'My head hurts, that's all.' Sarah remembered the blood she had seen. 'Are you both okay? Did he hurt you?'

'No. He grabbed us when we came home from school, but… but my husband was late. He comes in the front and must have surprised him.' She hesitated and looked at Chloe, who was carefully peeling the tape off her mouth. 'He dragged him into the garage,' she finished, nodding towards the closed door on the other side of the utility room.

'Where's Daddy?' The child's quivering voice was almost too much for her mother to bear, and Sarah saw she was fighting not to break down completely.

'I don't know, darling,' she managed. And the instant Sarah cut through the tape holding her wrists together the mum pulled her daughter into her arms.

'Why is this happening? What does he want with us?' she asked Sarah fearfully. 'When he tied us up he said it wasn't anything personal, and we didn't matter to him.'

Sarah helped them both to their feet. 'It's because of me. I used to live in this house years ago. I didn't know who he was or what he was planning, I swear.'

'You're Sarah.'

She looked at the girl in amazement.

'He kept saying he was bringing Sarah home. Didn't he, Mummy?'

Glaring at Sarah, her mum nodded slowly. Her face was inscrutable, but Sarah didn't need to be a mind reader. She blamed her.

'Sorry,' she began, but was then left speechless when the other woman hugged her.

'I'm Emma. You could have run but you came to help us. Thank you,' she whispered into Sarah's ear, before pulling back. 'If he's only interested in you, then Finn may still be alive.'

She took her suit jacket off and put it over her daughter's shoulders. 'I want you to go with Sarah.'

'No, Mummy,' she cried.

Sarah also disagreed. 'I don't think we should split up.' It had probably taken only a few minutes to untie them but to Sarah it was far too long. 'We have to hurry.'

'Chloe, listen to me.' Emma caressed the little girl's face and wiped away her tears. 'You have to be brave. I'm going to get your daddy.'

'I want to come too.'

'No. But I promise I'll follow you as soon as I've found Daddy.'

She pushed Chloe into Sarah's arms. 'Please, take her out of here. I have to try to find him.' She hurried over to a drawer and searched frantically, pushing through piles of paper and pens. She brought out keys attached to a smiley emoji keyring.

Emma's jaw was set, and Sarah didn't have time to argue. 'Okay.' She handed over Will's knife. 'Take this in case you have to cut him free. I'll get Chloe out, then come back for you.'

Sarah peered into the kitchen. Everything was quiet. The hallway beyond was in darkness. Had the hall light been on? She hesitated and glanced back at Emma, who was unlocking the door into the garage. Sarah understood why the mum didn't want Chloe to see what had happened to Finn, but her gut told her that splitting up was a bad idea.

Chloe tugged the bottom of her blouse. 'What's wrong?'

'Nothing,' she whispered back, 'follow me.' Clasping the gun to her chest, she pulled Chloe with her, moving around the central island towards the hall.

The bathroom door was open as she had left it. A few steps to the right and she should be able to see Will.

He was gone. Shit. No, she hadn't moved far enough. That was all. A bit further and she'd see him. One step. Her legs were shaking. Two…

Her heart slammed in her chest. The floor was empty.

Sarah staggered backwards, knocking into Chloe. The shadows stirred by the front door, and Will stepped out of the darkness. Grinning. Blood was trickling past his left eye and, as it continued unabated, he shook his finger at her, tutting.

She raised the gun.

He continued to smile. 'You're not going to use it on me. We both know…'

There was a snap as the hammer hit the firing pin.

Sarah was processing that she had actually pulled the trigger, and the gun was empty, when Will's shocked expression dissolved into anger.

'Oh Sarah, you shouldn't have done that.'


Chloe was propelled into the room by Sarah, who flung herself against the door. 'Help me!' Sarah shrieked, as she fought to keep Will out. He was a lot stronger than she was and she screamed as his hand thrust through the growing gap.

Emma had been feeling for the garage light, and now pushed past a crying Chloe. She raised the knife and lunged. The point embedded itself deep in Will's forearm. He yelled and withdrew his arm, dragging the blade with him. The door slammed shut underneath their combined weight.

'Run, Chloe,' Emma shouted.

The little girl hesitated and reached out. 'Come with me, Mummy. Please!'

'Just go. I'll be right behind you.' Emma sobbed as Chloe fled into the garage.

The door shuddered, and Emma looked at Sarah as another roar of anger and pain emanated from the other side. If they let go, Will would be on top of them in seconds. They had to find a way to slow him down.

Sarah searched for something heavy to pull against the door. The washing machine was within reach. At first it refused to budge, but by lifting it up by the drum she was able to tug it backwards.

It was overlapping the door a few centimetres, not enough to keep him out for long, when it stopped – halted by its cable and hoses. Emma moved to pull the cable out of its socket when a bang made both of them jump back in fright.

Where Emma had been leaning against the door there was a jagged crack and splintered wood. More bits fractured as the knife twisted violently.

'Sarah!' Will's cry sounded as contorted as the shattered wood, as he launched blow after blow. 'You fucking bitches! You'll pay for this.'

The washing machine juddered with each impact. Sarah gave one last desperate shove and this time it broke free, and she was able to push it firmly against the door. Emma grabbed two large towels from the utility shelves and jammed them under the handle.

The room lurched and Sarah sank to her knees.

'Sarah?' Emma pulled at her shoulder, trying to yank her back up, 'We have to go… now.'

Her head hurt so much. She peered at Emma, and her stomach flipped as her face swam in and out of focus.

'Come on, Sarah. He's going to break through.'

Sarah staggered to her feet and allowed herself to be ushered towards the garage. Will's fist smashed through the wood, demolishing the upper panel. His features were unrecognisable as he thrust his head and naked torso through the battered door. He had wrapped his T-shirt around his forearm, the material dark with his blood. It didn't slow his progress. Neither did the splintered pieces of wood that dug into his bare chest. He glared at her a split second before the second door closed.

His eyes were full of rage. And hate. She prayed this door would hold. It felt stronger than the other one, but as the key engaged in the lock Sarah knew it wouldn't keep Will out for long. Nothing would.

She could hear Emma's heavy breathing and sensed she hadn't moved away from the door. There was no time. They weren't safe here, not even in the dark. Will would find them.

'We have to get out of here,' she urged, moving to her left. Emma flung out an arm to hold her back. 'Wait. We need light.'

As she waited for Emma to find the switch, Sarah tried to fight her rising panic. A nearby thump startled her, and her body started shaking. What would Will do?

Click. Nothing.

'Fuck,' exclaimed Emma breathlessly. 'He must have flipped the switch for all the bloody lights. Stay here. I picked up the spare car keys, I'll turn its lights on.' Chloe was crying somewhere, and Emma called out reassurances to her daughter as she moved away from Sarah.

Not wanting to stay near the door, Sarah was feeling her way along the wall when the car's lights came on. The interior lights barely touched the edges of the darkness but when Emma turned on the headlights the front of the garage was lit up.

After untangling herself from Chloe, Emma frantically

searched their car and the rectangular space around it. Finn was nowhere to be found.

Sarah staggered towards the roller door and cried out at the sight of the smashed control panel on the wall. They wouldn't be able to raise it electronically. She looked for an emergency release cord, as Will's ranting resonated throughout the garage.

'Sarah. You can't escape me, Sarah.'

Unable to lift the door manually, she shouted for Emma. She didn't know whether Will had jammed the mechanism, but it refused to move upwards, even when Emma ran to help.

'I'm going to have to kill the little girl and her mummy – that's your fault, Sarah. Are you listening?' Will yelled from the utility room. There was a fraction of a pause before he launched something heavy at the door. 'It's... all... your... fault.' Each word was followed by a thunderous bang.

As the women stared in horror, the panels began to buckle under the onslaught.

# CHAPTER FORTY-FIVE

The second Doug brought the car to a halt, Peter was out and running towards the barrier. They had been speeding along the motorway when the report was broadcast over their radio. When he had heard about the message 'DO NOT ENTER OR THEY WILL DIE' painted on the garage door, he had felt physically sick.

He flashed his badge at the policeman on his way past; his insides in chaos, he didn't wait for the nod but impatiently ducked underneath the tape. And ignoring the young guard's protests he made a beeline for the small group gathered near a police van.

Despite the cold wet conditions, a few neighbours had begun to mill around the far side of the cordoned area, watching the armed response vehicles, fire engines and ambulances arrive.

'Get those people out of here,' Peter growled, pointing at the civilian onlookers. 'We need this whole street evacuated. Who is in charge here?'

'That'll be me,' answered a tall, black woman, thrusting her hand out. 'I'm DI Jewell, and this is our hostage negotiator,' she added, indicating the man next to her. 'You must be the DI from Ledforth; I understand this is your perp in there.'

'DI Bacchas is on his way; he'll be here in a few minutes,' answered Doug, appearing next to Peter and seizing the outstretched hand of the female DI. 'I'm DS Marsden, assistant SIO. If you could bring me up to date about what you know?'

As the group huddled round the van, using the bonnet as a makeshift desk, Peter reluctantly backed away. He understood why Doug was steering the attention away from him, but there was no way he was going to kick his heels idly. Fuck that.

He grabbed a passing policeman. 'Who was first on the scene?'

Without giving him a second glance, the officer pointed to one of the ambulances. Muttering his thanks, Peter headed over to where a man was receiving first aid in the back of the emergency vehicle.

'I fell on my fucking hand,' the young man was growling, pushing away the paramedic. 'I'm fine.'

His protective vest was covered in blood, and Peter suspected it wasn't the first time he'd tried to convince the medic to leave him alone.

The PC breathed out explosively. 'Look, I'm sorry, but I need to speak to someone. I think I know where the hostages are.'

Hearing this, Peter stepped forward and flashed his badge. 'DCI Graham. What do you know?'

Throwing a blanket off his shoulders, and nodding apologetically at the paramedic, the officer clambered from the ambulance. 'PC Kingsley, sir. When I found Finn... sorry, the owner of the house, he was barely conscious. Mumbling nonsense. Repeating letters U and T,' he explained, his words stumbling nervously. 'I thought he was delirious. But what if he was trying to say utility? I've visited the house thousands of times, and I know the layout well. There's a utility room that runs from their kitchen into the integral garage. Maybe that's where his family is.'

302

The wind was getting stronger, and as it blew around them Peter raised his voice to be heard. 'Is there any other access?'

'No, only through the kitchen or the garage.'

Glancing over at the van, he saw that Khenan and Louise had joined the team and were talking to Doug. Peter took the PC by the arm. 'Show me. Take me to the garage.

'Now. C'mon,' he declared, as uncertainty passed over the other man's face. 'We've got to find them.'

Not daring to take another quick scan behind, he was relieved when the officer set off in the direction of the house. The truth was he didn't have a clue what he was planning but he needed to do something. He couldn't wait for the negotiators to realise their input was superfluous. Will wouldn't be negotiating.

Peter was convinced Khenan would come to the same conclusion and taking a closer scout around couldn't hurt. They passed the discarded empty paint pot and approached the garage door. Some of the message had washed away, but... oh God. His heart hammered in his chest as he read 'THEY WILL DIE'.

*Don't think... don't imagine what is going on in there.* If he thought about Sarah he'd lose it. Had to keep control.

He was following PC Kingsley when he heard a car engine start up.

---

'If this works, get ready to run with Chloe.'

Emma chewed her lip. 'What about you?'

'I'll be right behind you.' Sitting in the driver's seat, Sarah could hardly hear herself above the rhythmic crashes. 'Just get yourself and Chloe out of here,' she shouted.

An extra loud crash startled her, and she dropped the keys in the footwell. She cursed and fumbled by her feet. Sweat stung her eyes and she struggled back a sob as she imagined Will's hand squeezing her shoulder. Her fingers brushed against the keyring. *Oh, thank God.*

Sarah grasped the smiley emoji, one hand keeping the other still as she aimed the key towards the ignition. She glanced at Emma and her daughter cowering in the corner all set to sprint outside if she succeeded. The noise would galvanise Will's attempts to reach them, and she winced as she started the car. Not daring to look behind her, she flattened the clutch, found first and slammed her foot on the accelerator. Her sock slipped on the pedal: the engine howled, juddered then died.

Shit. Come on. She tried again. The tyres screeched in a wheelspin, but this time the Audi shot forward. She was flung against the steering wheel as the bonnet crashed into the garage door. Pain in her head and neck exploded, and she cried out as she rebounded into the hard leather upholstery. In agony, she didn't immediately focus on the door.

No. It can't be. She'd failed. The metal slats had held firm: there was no buckling, no aluminium ripped from the vertical tracks.

She was so sure it was going to work. It must work. She'd insisted it should be her in the car as the other two would be able to run faster to get help. She couldn't give up. Emma and Chloe were depending on her.

The Audi had stalled on impact, and she was turning the key when the window shattered. She flung her arms over her head, trying to shield from the flying glass. Sarah struggled as she was yanked out of the car; her scream ending abruptly as hands squeezed her neck.

She kicked her legs. Clawed at his grip. *Please God. Can't end like this. Can't breathe.*

Through tunnelled vision she saw Chloe forcing her way past a ruptured section of garage door.

*Yes. It worked. It's only me, you bastard.*

*What the hell... no, Emma... run. Leave me and run.*

Realising Emma hadn't followed Chloe, but had turned to face Will, Sarah thrashed against him.

No one else should die for her.

Desperate, Sarah rammed her fingers into the blood-soaked tourniquet round his arm. Will howled and his grip loosened.

Armed with a spanner, Emma rushed to help, flinging the improvised weapon and hitting Will's shoulder. He roared and pushed Sarah away. She fell heavily onto the concrete floor. The impact reverberated through her entire body, and she lay there stunned, not able to focus on anything except her own gasping.

She didn't know how much time elapsed before she became aware of what was going on. Seconds, minutes perhaps? Over the ringing in her ears, the male voices began to separate and solidify. One voice, calm and authoritative, sent a shockwave to her heart. It couldn't be.

She had landed close to the Audi, and she used its body as leverage to help her clamber unsteadily to her knees. The first people she saw were Will and Emma: highlighted in a beam of light. Will was brandishing his terrified captive in front of him, his knife held against her neck, while Emma's stricken face was pleading for help from someone out of Sarah's line of sight.

'Put the knife down, William.' The command was spoken from the other side of the car. 'It's all over. Give yourself up. No one else has to get hurt.'

Sarah almost collapsed with relief. It was Peter. He had found her. She kept her eyes fixed on Will and inched her way to the back of the vehicle, planning to run round to reach Peter. The unnerving sound of Will laughing stopped her. He was insane. She could see his arm muscles tense as he pressed the blade further into Emma's neck. He was going to kill her.

Sarah dragged herself up. 'Will,' she rasped, trying to force as much power as she could into her broken voice, 'don't do this.' Her heart was racing as all eyes were now staring at her. 'Take me instead. It's me you want.'

'Sarah. No!' cried Peter.

The torchlight wavered. She held her hand up, hoping to quieten him and edged closer to Will. 'Let her go, and I'll come with you.'

He tilted his head in her direction. Listening.

'You were right, Will, I could have told them about you, but I didn't. Let her go, and we can go back into the house. We can talk.'

'Do you think I'm stupid?' he sneered. 'You want me to let her live. You'll say anything.'

Emma gasped as he jabbed the point further into her skin.

'Kill her and you'll never know if you were right about me. You're not going to get another chance, Will.'

Sarah's stare didn't waver from Will's face. She couldn't look at Peter. If she did then her resolve would vanish.

'I shouldn't have run.' Her throat felt swollen and bruised: speaking was hard.

Will relaxed his tight hold around Emma and, for a moment, Sarah thought it was going to be okay. But he moved so fast, she could do nothing to prevent him slashing downwards. His knife entered Emma's body and then he dropped her, discarding her like she didn't matter.

Well, she did matter. Sarah couldn't take her eyes off the growing pool of blood. This was all her fault. She was barely aware of Will grabbing hold of her and she didn't resist as he flung her round.

Peter had leapt over the car's bonnet when Emma was stabbed in the stomach. Now Sarah was forced between them, he skidded to a halt and stood helpless, his hands splayed out in submission.

Their eyes met, and Sarah called out his name.

'Quiet!' The steel of Will's blade pressed against her neck, and a warm wetness trickled down her chest. Shit, it was Emma's blood. Sarah struggled but was powerless to stop him dragging her backwards.

'If anyone comes in after us, I'll kill her.' The debris from the smashed door didn't slow him and, although Sarah's feet were flailing wildly, Will lifted her easily over the wrecked wood. The cast-iron umbrella stand he had used to break open the door was lying where he had dropped it, and he stumbled slightly as he stepped over it.

His grip loosened, and Sarah pushed against him. She had to get away. Her heartbeat thudded in her ears as she tried to escape, but Will recovered quickly and yanked her close. She cried out as she was hauled through the house.

# CHAPTER FORTY-SIX

Will's rage had transformed him into a beast with herculean strength. Sarah clung on as he despatched the washing machine with one heave and pulled her effortlessly towards the stairs.

His harsh breathing dominated her, but as she craned her neck backwards trying to glimpse Peter in the dark house behind them, another sound reached her. A loud voice was shouting – someone from outside was trying to negotiate her safety.

*I'm here. Please, you have to come in and get me. He's not going to let me go.*

Will carried on dragging her up to the first floor. Although the upstairs landing was dark, Sarah knew where he was taking her, and she dug her heels into the carpet. She fought hard, but barely slowed their progress towards the last door on the right.

Her mind cascaded back almost thirty years, to the place of her nightmares: outside the closed door, the doorknob starting to turn.

Sarah screamed as she was pushed into the master bedroom.

Peter crouched outside the utility room, listening intently. His first impulse was to run after them, not stopping until he had wrenched Sarah away from Will and she was safe in his arms.

However, he had seen the look on Will's face before – on desperate people who had nothing to lose. Cornered, Will was extremely dangerous and unpredictable. If Peter were to blunder through the house without knowing the exact whereabouts of Sarah he could endanger her life more.

Peter also had a hunch that now she had offered to talk, Will would want answers. But if he was wrong, the longer he waited before acting, the more time Will had to hurt her.

A scream simultaneously broke his heart and his indecision, sending him flying across the kitchen. It sounded like the cry had come from upstairs, but it had cut off so abruptly he couldn't be sure. He ran into the hallway, and then hesitated. His torchlight wasn't enough to penetrate the dense shadows and there were plenty of places where Will could have laid a trap or be lying in wait.

Peter was sidestepping to the relative safety of the wall when he sensed movement behind him. He spun round to see a firearm officer crouching low in the doorway he had vacated. Not wanting to get shot by mistake, Peter raised his hands slowly. He was aware he wasn't officially supposed to be there.

He tensed his body, ready to be challenged, as another dark figure appeared. Frustration clawed at him: he was desperate to continue searching for Sarah. A muffled conversation took place between the officers clad in Kevlar tactical gear, and Peter's exasperation mounted as precious seconds ticked by. For fuck's sake. There was no time to lose.

The newest arrival beckoned him over. He was up close before he recognised Khenan's eyes behind the protective goggles. Peter gave the tiniest sigh of relief. 'He's taken Sarah. He had a knife to her throat.'

Khenan raised his hand for silence and passed him a radio

and earpiece. 'They're upstairs. Stay behind us at all times,' he commanded, in a whisper. 'I mean it, Peter. Don't get in our way.'

Knowing his friend was laying his career on the line simply by allowing him to stay on the premises, Peter swallowed any objections and nodded.

'We've all put in a hell of a lot of hours to catch this guy, so let's go and get him. Besides, Doug is bringing up the rear; I don't want him to grab a gun and shoot me if I throw you out.' He patted Peter's arm, before falling into place behind the armed lead.

---

The bright light shining through the window disorientated Sarah, burning her eyes. Strange shadows were playing on the windowpane, blown different directions by the helicopter overhead. She shrank away and squinted tearfully through parted fingers until Will closed the blinds: casting their small world back into darkness.

Staying low, Will pulled a bedside lamp onto the floor before clicking it on. He was caught in its glow, and his dishevelled appearance bore no comparison to the immaculate care worker Sarah had known. His hair, normally styled, was plastered across his forehead. Underneath the blood and perspiration, he twitched uncontrollably: his facial muscles fired up with his madness.

Sarah's legs collapsed and she slid down the wall, depleted of energy.

Will paced round her parents' old room, where it had all started. And perhaps, where it was destined to end. He was agitated, his bare torso glistening with sweat. 'They're not going to give us time. You shouldn't have tried to escape. I should cut you, like you bitches cut me.'

The knife in his hand shook as he waved his wounded arm in front of her.

She stared defiantly up at his crazed face. 'Is this why you brought me here? To kill me, like you did my mother?'

'No,' he hissed at her. 'I brought you here so we could be together.' He retreated and banged his knife on the nearby dressing table. 'This isn't how it was supposed to be.' Leaning on the furniture, palms outstretched and head down, he gave a shuddering sigh.

Sarah squinted at the door, judging her chances of making it across the room. While he was distracted she could make a run for it. Easing her body forwards slightly, she glanced in his direction.

He was staring at her. 'It's not going to finish well for us, is it?' There was a level of lucidity in his voice, not present previously. 'It's my fault. I tried to take things slowly, I really did, but seeing you at the care home was so hard.' As he talked, he reached for the knife. He didn't pick it up but slowly caressed the blade. 'Even my special ladies – did I tell you that's what I called them? – were no substitute. They'd look in my eyes and I'm the most important person in their world. And then they'd leave me.

'I can't stop... I don't think I want to,' he added, almost reluctantly, before finishing in a rush, 'but I want to feel peace afterwards. You can give me that.' He walked over to her. 'I need you to hold me, to tell me everything will be okay, like you did all those years ago.'

Heart thumping, Sarah nodded. She choked back her revulsion as his clammy hand clutched hers. As he helped her to the bed, dizziness separated her from reality, and she shook her head. She had to concentrate.

'Before I do, I want to know why you did it.' The words struggled to get out and stuck to the roof of her mouth. Swallowing hard, she whispered, 'Why you attacked my family.'

She sat on the edge and squeezed the duvet with her fingers, as he responded zealously, 'I heard them talking about me, and it was obvious they didn't like me. Your brother didn't want me there. Your mum was pretending...' He stopped, as if only now aware of the look on Sarah's face.

'I didn't mean to do it,' he whined. 'She came in his room and saw what I'd done. She stood there and screamed. The knife was in my hand... I had to shut her up.'

She gaped at him. His sulky expression was bursting with self-pity. The final pictures slotted into place: Will standing solitary, with his hands shoved deep into his pockets, refusing to join in at her party; a girl, happy at turning eleven, but sad that not everyone was enjoying themselves, telling her mum about the lone boy at the edge of the dance floor.

The senselessness of it all stung. Her mum had died because he'd had a fucking tantrum. He had been invited to tea, and he'd repaid their kindness by...

Oh God.

Maybe encouraged by her silence, Will sat next to her and carried on. 'If you'd told me to give myself up, I would have. But it was as if you were thanking me by keeping silent. Did you hate her?' he asked, eagerly, his acrid breath on her cheek. 'I used to fantasise about something happening to my dad, and I wondered whether I had fulfilled your fantasy.'

'Oh, Will.' Turning her body towards him, she reached up and caressed his damp hair. She met his gaze: one full of hope and desire. Licking her cracked lips, she said, 'You're wrong, I wasn't like you.'

With satisfaction, she saw confusion cloud his eyes.

'You want to know the truth?' Sarah continued, relishing the effect of her words. 'I loved my mummy, and you took her from me. I was a little girl, scared of what I saw. My mind let me forget. I forgot you.'

She stood up. Her voice grew stronger. 'And I'm glad I did. You would've controlled my life, and you don't deserve that.' Her unbridled anger gave her strength, and she lashed out. 'You mean nothing to me. Do you understand? Nothing.'

The ferocity of her attack seemed to catch him off guard, and he curled into a ball as she hit him again and again. He shielded his face from her; his shoulders shaking as he sobbed into his hands. Seeing his torment, Sarah hesitated. Too late, she realised her mistake: his arm shot upwards. He gripped her wrist hard, twisted it and pushed her against the window.

Before she could shout, his fingers closed around her neck. Her legs and arms flailed about in a desperate attempt to throw him off, but her movements already felt distant. The increasing pressure dominated her: squeezed her final moments into a silent battle as she pleaded to his dry, emotionless eyes.

Knowing this time he wouldn't let go, and he would keep pressing until she died, Sarah tried to galvanise her limbs into one last coordinated attack. He pinned her legs tight, with her spine bent backwards over the sill, so she launched her fingers at his chest and face, scratching and gouging with her nails.

Will swore and adjusted his grip, freeing one hand to wrestle hers away. With both arms forced above her head, she grasped at the blind and pulled it on top of them. The weight on her larynx eased as Will grappled with the encircling fabric, but her breath was cut off too soon.

'I didn't want it this way, Sarah. You have to believe me.'

His voice started to float away.

'I did everything so we could be together. I loved you.'

I did everything... the possible significance of what he said bombarded her as she clung onto the last fragments of life. She yelled at him to say what he had done, who he had hurt to get to her, but her pleas were trapped inside her head. As his face loomed large in her decreasing vision, another face replaced his: it was Mike, gazing into her eyes on the happiest day of their lives.

She blinked him away. Her final message was for Will. And him alone.

'I would never love you. I hate you,' she mouthed, not knowing if Will could understand her. 'You're a monster.'

Sarah closed her eyes. Time to let go. She was ready to embrace unconsciousness. Ready for the pain to disappear.

She'd gasped her first agonising breath and was on her second before she realised he'd removed his hand from her neck. Will was still holding her, and through her coughing and tears she peered up at him. He was staring through the window, lights flickering across his face. Looking down, he smiled sadly.

He lowered her to the floor. And stood up as the door burst open and a multitude of voices yelled intent. He stepped away from her, his wet eyes not leaving hers as he put his hands behind his back. He kept smiling as he walked towards the armed officers, his hands not reaching his sides before they fired.

Sarah blacked out to a chorus of gunshots and shouting.

# CHAPTER FORTY-SEVEN

The ill-fitting plastic lid on the jug rattled as fresh water was placed on the bedside table. And as the door closed with a thud, Sarah was brutally jolted into the land of the living. She lay there until her pulse slowed. Unlike the last few times she had woken up, there was no disorientation, no dying flashes of a dream. She knew where she was. Sarah found the remote control with a practised sweep of her arm and raised the head end of her bed.

If the visit from the hospital housekeeper was a reliable indication, then her breakfast should be arriving soon. Her stomach rumbled. She was hungry. Analgesia, to keep on top of her pain, and lukewarm water was all she had managed up until now, so thinking about solid food without being sick was a good sign.

Sarah took a deep breath and sat forward. Yesterday, she had walked a few tentative steps unaided before stumbling, and she waited uneasily in case a wave of dizziness descended.

She was suffering from concussion and an array of sore bruises, but she had escaped any major injuries from her ordeal and was desperate for the medical staff to follow through with their promise to discharge her. So Sarah was relieved when, although her joints creaked and her bones complained, she wasn't light-headed.

The fogginess in her mind had also cleared. She had spent the last seventy-two hours either asleep or in a state of bewilderment, listening to the hushed conversations around her bed. Trying to join in but always feeling unconnected. When Peter had pushed her in a wheelchair to visit the neighbouring ward, it was like it was all happening to someone else.

Thinking of Peter, she looked across at the empty chair. He had barely left her side for two days, initially only agreeing to leave when Carolyn had taken over. Sarah had managed to reassure them both that she was okay. It was what they needed to hear, if not what they actually believed.

The truth was, every time her thoughts drifted back to Will, she was far from okay. She'd played a big part in Will's delusions, however unwillingly, and the guilt was weighing heavily on her mind. People had suffered because of her amnesia.

So many secrets had resulted in death. Secrets her family had tried to keep hidden. What if her dad had pushed harder to reach the information in her head, then over two decades later, another desperate father may not have had to follow the awful decisions he had made to protect his son.

Her dad was nothing like Robbie, and she felt bad as soon as the thought had occurred to her. It was hard to feel sorry for the man who, from what Peter had told her, had been fully aware of his son's grisly activities. He had kept records of all his trips to the city, even documenting his observations of his son stalking his Beautician victims. Seemingly hardened to the women's plights, he had written about his hope that Will would eventually come to him to confess and ask for his help to stop.

She remembered the day they had met in the park and was certain Robbie had been close to telling her something. Perhaps, if she hadn't run off, then…?

Sarah sighed. Eventually she was going to have to let it all go. She couldn't allow Will's madness to ruin her life. A vision of Will came to her: a sad smile on his lips as he'd hid his empty hands behind him. Sarah touched her neck, where the pain whisked her back to their last moments together. She'd been close to death. Had tasted it. And yet he'd let her go.

Why? Why had he done that? At the end, had he seen the truth? Seen her hate. Was that why he'd goaded the police into shooting knowing they would shoot to kill? With Will dead, she was resigned to never getting the answers to these questions, but there was one that would keep her awake at night.

*I did everything...* He was begging her to understand, and all she could see when the world was going black was Mike's face on their wedding day.

The arsonist responsible for the fire that had killed her husband had never been found, but suspicion had fallen heavily on the owner of the building. It hadn't occurred to her it was anything more than bad luck that Mike was on duty. Now, if her gut feeling was right, and Will had done more than obliterate Mike from her photographs, then she possibly had the weight of his death on her conscience too.

If Robbie's diaries didn't reveal an answer, she'd have to accept she may never know the whole truth. And, although she had told Peter she was okay, it would take her a long time to get over that.

Desperate to steer her thoughts to a happier place, Sarah reflected on what they had tentatively discussed yesterday morning: a plan encouraged by both Matt and Geoffrey when she had put the idea to them later that day.

'The Yorkshire Dales, eh? A great idea. If anyone deserves R & R, it's you two,' Geoffrey had said, thickly. The swelling on his face had reduced, but his speech was stilted.

Even as Peter had explained the necessity to keep Sarah out of reach from the press, her cheeks burned as she'd caught the glint in Geoffrey's good eye. She had managed to remain straight-faced; however, she'd been unable to suppress the small knot of pleasure inside.

When Peter had asked her to go with him he had been careful not to pressure her, making it clear it was on her terms. The hotel room was a lifetime ago, and they were both wary of expecting or promising too much.

Anyway, she hadn't definitely said yes. There was someone else she needed to get approval from.

———

Tears were in her eyes as Sarah heard a sound she thought she would never hear again. She entered the ward bay and smiled as the raucous laugh exploded once more. A lady in one of the other beds grimaced and burrowed under her sheet.

Approaching the far corner, Sarah slowed when a deep male voice spoke from behind the hospital curtains. She hesitated for a second, her hand hovering, and then, steeling herself, pulled back the curtain.

'Oh, thank God you're here, Sarah. You can tell Bryan it really does hurt when I laugh – any more of his crappy jokes and I don't think I'll make it.'

Bryan stood up with horror on his face. 'Well, I know when I'm not wanted.'

Her joy at seeing Anne awake was marred by the embarrassment when she glanced at Bryan. 'Please don't go because of me.' Sarah struggled to meet his eyes. 'I…'

'Don't worry, I was going anyway,' he interrupted. 'Anne's right, she's in no condition to appreciate my witty banter.'

He winked and turned to say goodbye to Anne. As they embraced, Anne reached for Sarah's hand, and pulled her into a hug after Bryan had straightened up.

Sarah had been shocked how fragile Anne had looked

yesterday so was careful not to squeeze too hard. She buried her face into her hair. It smelt musty and Anne's curls were hidden under a coating of grease and dirt. But she held her close. They had almost lost her. Sarah sniffed.

Anne pulled back to look at her face. 'Hey, I'm all right. Please, don't go all gooey on me, you'll set me off. Honestly, I'm going to be fine. Although, no one has passed me a mirror yet, and seeing how awful you look – no offence – I hope I look a lot better than you do.'

'Careful.' Sarah grinned. She wiped her nose on a crumpled tissue she found in her pocket. 'I'm off duty, remember, so punching a patient isn't out of the question.'

They contemplated each other for a long moment before reaching out again.

'We're both okay,' Anne whispered in her ear, perhaps sensing Sarah's need to hear this. 'It'll take more than a madman to keep us down.'

Behind Sarah, Bryan coughed. 'I hope I'm not number one bad guy now. I know I acted like an idiot, and worse,' he carried on awkwardly as Sarah turned to face him, 'but I would without doubt draw the line at stalking. Oh!' he exclaimed as Sarah flung her arms around him.

'I'm so sorry. Can you forgive me?' she said.

'There's nothing to forgive. After speaking to Peter yesterday, I'm amazed how you kept everything together so long. If it'd been me I'm sure I would have suspected everyone, even the milkman.' He smiled at her. 'Come to think of it, mine is a bit suspicious. Anyway, I wish you had confided in me when it all started.'

'Ditto,' called out Anne. 'Don't think I'm letting her off that one either.'

Bryan stepped away, as if suddenly aware of their proximity. 'I'll be off now, but you better call me when you return. Fancy some more torture tomorrow?' he asked Anne, grinning.

'As if I need any more pain,' she groaned, her head flopping back on her pillow. 'Bring chocolate, and it's a date.'

Bryan disappeared through the curtains, his hand raised in a goodbye. Sarah sat on his vacated chair. 'Does everyone know I'm going away?'

Anne laughed. 'Never tell an unconscious girl about plans for a dirty weekend with a detective chief inspector if you don't want everyone to know.'

'I didn't say anything about a dirty weekend, and anyway, I've not agreed yet. Ben needs me, especially since Aunt Carolyn is going home. And there's you. I shouldn't be disappearing–'

'Don't you dare say no. Look at all the trouble I've gone through to hook you up with someone,' she said, with a wry smile. 'You have to go. I'm all right – really I am.'

It was true Anne did seem better. She was having intravenous fluids pumped into her to correct an acute kidney injury from being severely dehydrated and septic, and her broken ankle would take time to mend, but she would recover.

If only everyone had been so lucky. Emma had survived, but she and Chloe had to face a future without Finn. And Carl's parents, so soon after losing their daughter, now didn't know if their son was going to fully recover after his brain injury. Not to mention all the women… She sighed. It was obvious that Louise blamed her for everything. The detective had barely looked her in the eyes when she'd visited with Khenan earlier.

Seemingly reading her mind, Anne's protest cut through Sarah's thoughts. 'It wasn't your fault.'

'So many people have suffered because of me,' began Sarah, gravely.

'No, you mustn't blame yourself; no one else does. You didn't force me to talk to Will at the gym.' Anne averted her gaze as her voice dropped to a whisper. 'I didn't stop to think it was strange he was asking about my friends too. I enjoyed his extra attention, I…' she looked at Sarah miserably, 'I thought he liked me.'

'He was able to fool a lot of people.' Like poor Hilda. Sighing angrily, she grasped Anne's hand. 'You have nothing to feel ashamed about.'

'Then please let something good happen out of all this,' begged Anne. 'You deserve happiness.

'Richard has hardly left here since I woke up. Let him do the brotherly thing. And Bryan keeps popping in. I think he feels guilty for not taking my disappearance seriously at the beginning. What I'm trying to say is we can all cope without you.'

'It's not a dirty weekend,' Sarah objected weakly.

'Yeah, like I'm going to believe that. The lady doth protest too much.'

They both grinned.

Sarah remained with Anne until she fell asleep. The warmth of the ward was threatening to lull her to sleep too, and it was with great effort she prised herself from the chair.

She slowly walked along the corridors of the hospital and, with a ghost of a smile touching her lips, out to where Peter was patiently waiting for her.

## THE END

# ACKNOWLEDGEMENTS

It's no exaggeration to say that Out of Her Mind has taken years to write, so I firstly have to say thank you to my family and friends who resisted the temptation to ask, 'Haven't you finished it yet?' and 'When is it going to be published then?' The fact I now have an answer to both of those questions is thanks to everyone at Bloodhound Books who have helped to make my dream a reality. A special thank you to Betsy Reavley, Fred Freeman, Abbie Rutherford and Bloodhound's marketing team, Vicky Joss and Katia Allen. Thank you to my editor, Clare Law – I'm so glad you enjoyed the journey with Sarah. It was indeed my aim to have a heroine with a good support network and one who almost never acted in a way that exasperated. And thank you to Bloodhound's proofreader.

A big shout out to the Farsley Happy Scribblers – Jaye Sarasin and Roger Webster. Thank you for your support and critiques. I really value our monthly get togethers – and I'm not just saying that because of the tasty food! Also, thank you to Jericho Writers for helping the Happy Scribblers to meet in the first place. I have learnt so much from your online webinars, and I know that the online Summer Festival of Writing was a lifeline to many writers during the lockdown year. A huge thank you to the tutors of the Jericho Writers Self-Edit course, Debi Alper and Emma Darwin, for teaching me the magic of psychic distancing and what editing truly is. Hello to my fellow class of January 2021, with a special thank you to Stephen Beatty for beta reading after school was out.

Thank you to my friends and work colleagues who braved the

early drafts – Laura McVeigh, Vicki Bentley, Sheena and Graham Bennett, Aparna Vinayan, Helen Sharp, Fiona and James Richardson. And thank you to the beta readers who read the almost final (but not quite final) draft – Mary McShane Vaughn, Marysa Vanpatten-Dermond, and J O'Neil.

Thanks, Mum, for patiently working your way through the drafts, and sorry for all printer ink you had to use to do that. Lastly, a massive family hug to my husband and children. Your love and support is everything.

# A NOTE FROM THE PUBLISHER

**Thank you for reading this book**. If you enjoyed it please do consider leaving a review on Amazon to help others find it too.

**We hate typos.** All of our books have been rigorously edited and proofread, but sometimes mistakes do slip through. If you have spotted a typo, please do let us know and we can get it amended within hours.

**info@bloodhoundbooks.com**

Printed in Great Britain
by Amazon